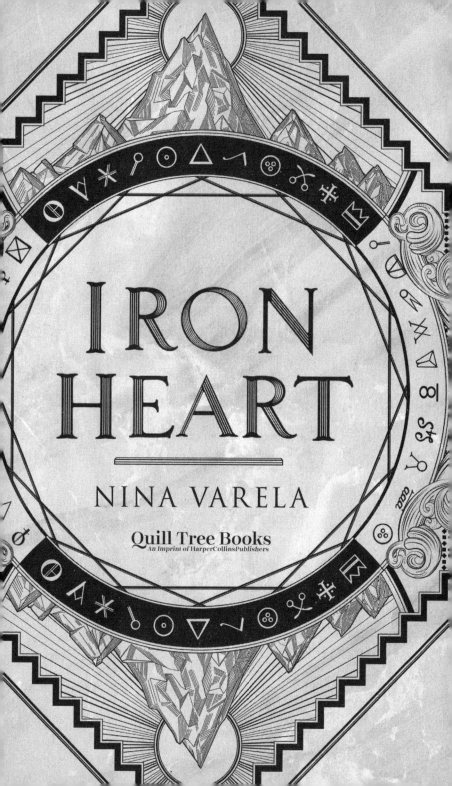

IRON
HEAT

NINA VARELA

Quill Tree Books
An Imprint of HarperCollinsPublishers

Also by Nina Varela
Crier's War

Quill Tree Books is an imprint of HarperCollins Publishers.

Iron Heart
Text copyright © 2020 by Glasstown Entertainment
Map by Maxime Plasse
All rights reserved. Printed in the United States of America.
No part of this book may be used or reproduced in any
manner whatsoever without written permission except in
the case of brief quotations embodied in critical articles and
reviews. For information address HarperCollins Children's
Books, a division of HarperCollins Publishers, 195 Broadway,
New York, NY 10007.
www.epicreads.com

Library of Congress Control Number: 2020941126
ISBN 978-0-06-282397-7

Typography by David Curtis
20 21 22 23 24   PC/LSCH   10 9 8 7 6 5 4 3 2 1

First Edition

For anyone and everyone
who needs a little hope

*It is impossible for a tree to grow without roots. The
same law applies to civilization. No society is conjured
from thin air; it is the nature of societies to grow,
Organically, from that which came before. To reject
all forms of Human society is to reject centuries of
knowledge, of accumulated thought, of triumphs we
could learn from and defeats we could avoid. Yes, we
have touched the stars—but we are still connected
deeply to the earth. We must not forget. We must not
deny our roots in the existence of Humankind; instead,
we must take that existence and improve upon it. Is
that not the reason for our Creation? Is that not why we
were Made?*

—FROM *THE TRADITIONALISTS,*
  BY RONAN OF FAMILY TERRA, 2263120905, YEAR 17 AE

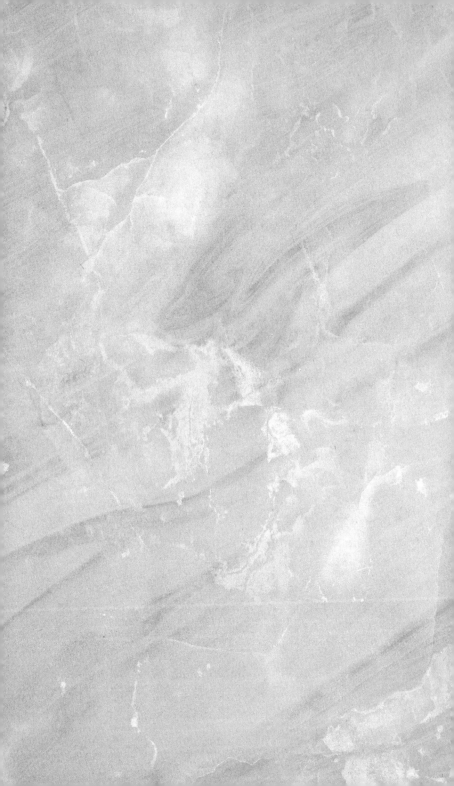

WINTER,

YEAR 47 AE

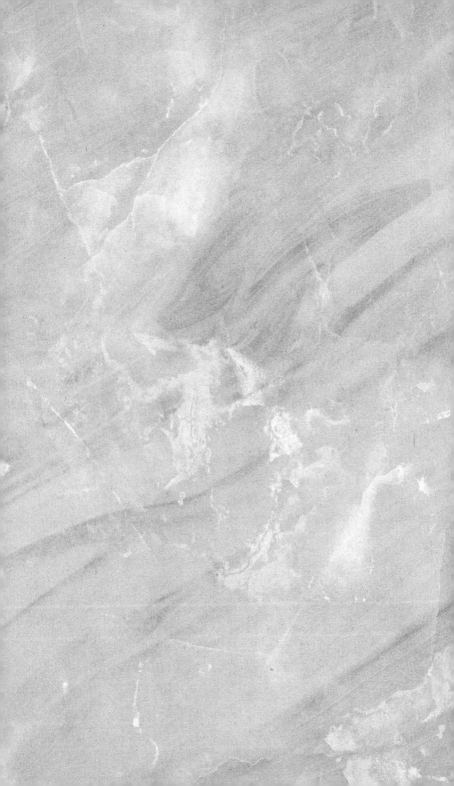

1

It was barely midmorning and Ayla had already cheated death twice.

Maybe that was dramatic. More accurately, she'd already been *this close* to getting caught by two different members of the royal guard—but then again, it was the same result in the end, wasn't it? Ayla was a stowaway and a human. Either crime was often punishable by death.

Thalen, the capital of Varn, was a glittering white city surrounded by high white walls. Like Sovereign Hesod's palace in Rabu, Ayla's home country, it was seated on the coast, on the shores of the Steorran Sea. But Thalen was a good hundred leagues south of the palace, and here the sea wasn't an icy black expanse; there were no cliffs of sharp black rock, slick with ice, just waiting for someone to take a wrong step, slip off the edge, and be swallowed by the freezing water below. Here, the sea was jewel green and almost warm. Instead of cliffs, there was a beach of coarse yellow sand heaped with piles of washed-up seaweed, and farther up, short sloping bluffs of gray rock spotted with green moss and beach grass. The bluffs formed a crescent-moon curve around the port that Ayla and her best friend, Benjy, had managed to smuggle themselves into. After they'd fled the sovereign's palace. Fled Rabu, the only home they had ever known, in the hold of a cargo ship, hidden among casks of grain. The journey had been brutal: Benjy seasick the whole time, Ayla fine at first and then, after the grain was switched out for barrels of rotting sardines, violently ill. She remembered that week and a half at sea in sweaty, nauseous flashes, head spinning, stomach lurching.

But they'd made it.

This port was the largest on Varn's coastline. Massive docks jutted out into the sea, bustling with sailors and fishermen and traders and seamen of all kinds. All human, as this was dirty work, hard labor, and therefore beneath Automakind. Hundreds of ships docked here, some of them floating inns and taverns, many of them flying the royal colors, green and white. Queen Junn's emblem was everywhere: a brilliant green phoenix clutching a sword in one clawed foot and a pickax in the other. Varn was a mining country. A nation of rolling hills and deep quarries, of iron, coal, precious metals, and gemstones buried deep beneath the earth.

The air smelled like salt and fish and human sweat. The sun shone brighter than it ever did in the frozen north. Ayla hadn't been this warm in a long time. She hadn't been this warm since—

Since—

Midnight. Moonlight. Soft bed, softer blankets. Dark hair spilled across the pillow. A body beside her own, breathing too slow to be human.

But Ayla wasn't thinking about that, or her, now.

She ducked out of the narrow alleyway she'd been hiding in and headed back toward the center of the port town, satisfied she'd thrown the second guard off her track. She'd given them no reason to chase her—the meat pies in her knapsack were paid for, thank you very much. But in a town of burly dockworkers, a small shifty-eyed girl stood out, drawing suspicion from humans and Automae alike.

The port town was little more than a collection of inns and pubs clinging like barnacles to the shore, every third building marked with the crest of a shipping company or major merchant. Bobbing just offshore was a cluster of houseboats—and houses on stilts, floating like long-legged insects on the surface of the water—where the stevedores lived. That was it. All the important business happened in the capital. Wherever you stood in the town, or in the port beyond, you could see the monolith of the white walls of Thalen, rising up from the shore like strange, too-perfect cliffs. Ayla didn't like looking at them for too long. It made her nervous, a capital city so deliberately hidden away. Walls that high, you had to wonder: Were they keeping something out, or in?

Benjy was waiting for her outside the Black Gull, a tavern that seemed busy at all hours of the day. It was a good place to meet if you didn't want to be noticed. Ayla sidled up next to him, sticking to the shadows below the sloping roof. They kept a careful distance between them, looking ahead, speaking only in whispers. Benjy was smoking a pipe, presumably to look like he had a good reason for hanging outside the tavern instead of going in, which Ayla found hilarious: he grimaced with every inhale, clearly hating the entire experience.

"You're late," he murmured, exhaling blue smoke.

"Got tailed twice," she said, frowning. "Had to lead the leech guards on a merry chase for a while. I felt like a damn fox. The sooner we get into the city, the better—it'll be so much easier to blend in."

"You're sure you lost them?"

"Positive. Anyway. Got a couple meat pies, if you're hungry."

He glanced over at her, and she couldn't help but glance back. Just for a split second, just long enough to catch a glimpse of his face, tawny skin and big doe eyes, the freckles on his nose visible even in the shadows. "You know full well I'm always hungry."

"How could I forget the bottomless pit," she said dryly. "Well, come on, then. We can eat on the way into Thalen."

The plan was to find Ayla's brother, Storme. It was a horrible plan, as it involved sneaking into the single most dangerous and heavily guarded place in all of Varn: the Mad Queen's palace. Best-case scenario, Ayla and Benjy would somehow, by some miracle, get to Storme and tell him everything they knew about Scyre Kinok. About why they'd risked everything to sneak into Sovereign Hesod's palace that night. The night Ayla had stood above Lady Crier's bed, knife in hand, failed to do the one thing she'd been fantasizing about for years, and fled with Benjy, surviving the night only because they knew the treacherous sea cliffs better than the sovereign's guard.

Kinok had been a Watcher of the Heart, a member of the elite guild of Automae who dedicated their lives to protecting the Iron Heart. Automae didn't need to eat like humans did—their bodies depended on heartstone, a red gemstone imbued with alchemical power. The Iron Heart was the mine that produced heartstone. As it was the sole source of the Automae's power, and therefore their greatest weakness, its exact location—somewhere in the vast, thousand-league spine of the Aderos Mountains—was known only to Watchers. Only one Watcher had ever left their post. Kinok. For those last weeks at the palace Ayla's goal had been to steal a special compass Kinok had in his possession. She was positive its arrow pointed to the Iron Heart itself. That was the main reason she and Benjy and the others had staged the attack on the sovereign's palace: to break into Kinok's study and steal the safe containing his valuables. But the only thing in the safe had been a piece of paper with three words: *Leo. Siena. Tourmaline.*

She needed to tell Storme about all this and more. About Kinok's desperate search for Tourmaline, a potential new life source for Automae. About Nightshade, the mysterious black dust he'd given to his followers to consume instead of heartstone, even though it seemed only to ruin their bodies, to drive them half mad.

Best-case scenario, Storme would relay the information to Queen Junn and—Ayla didn't know. The queen would arrange for Kinok's death? And Storme would finally give Ayla the answer she was looking for, the answer to a question that had been reaffirming itself with every beat of her heart since they'd first been reunited for those few precious days: *Why did you leave me after the raid on our village? Why did you let me think you died along with our parents? I thought you were dead, I mourned you, I never stopped mourning you, how could you* leave me? And Storme would give her a completely reasonable answer, and everything would make perfect sense, and she would forgive him, and they would embrace as brother and sister, and then Ayla and Benjy would live out the rest of their lives in the luxury of the queen's court. Best-case scenario.

Worst-case scenario, they died a bloody death before they even made it inside the city walls, taking Kinok's secrets with them. Worst-case scenario, Ayla would never see Storme again, and he would never know she'd died so close to him, *so close*, her body at the bottom of a harbor just outside his door. He would board ships above her, sail across her grave, and he would never know. Worst-case scenario, the queen wouldn't find out about Nightshade until it was too late.

Of course, there was one other person who could tell the queen, tell *anyone*, about Kinok's plans. One other person, and Ayla's mind wouldn't let her forget it. A thought kept repeating itself, demanding acknowledgment: *She knows. She could still do something.*

Crier knows. And then it hit Ayla—as it had been hitting

her over and over again since yesterday morning, when she'd first heard the whispers circulating on the docks, in the small marketplace, outside the Black Gull, everywhere she went—as it had been hitting her over and over again, a series of gut punches, each one a sick terrible swoop, leaving her breathless—

The date of the wedding between Scyre Kinok and the daughter of the sovereign of Rabu had been pushed up. *Unknown reasons*, people whispered to each other. *I heard something about an attempted coup*, someone would whisper, and then someone else would reply, *No, no, I heard that wasn't true. I heard a servant went mad and tried to burn down the palace. No, no, that's not true either, do you just believe everything you hear?*

Crier was getting married today.

Today.

The ceremony had probably already begun. Not that Ayla was thinking about it; not that she cared. Not that she was thinking about the way Crier used to look at Kinok, wary at best and fearful at worst. Or about the way Crier edged closer to *her*, Ayla, whenever Kinok entered a room.

Ayla kept her head low, trailing a good ten paces behind Benjy as they followed one of the narrow, veinlike roads that fed into the wider road connecting the port town to the city gates. She was thinking about Storme and the Queen and nothing else. She'd traded one goal for another. One mission had failed. *(Was it really less than two weeks ago that she'd last seen Crier? That their eyes had met for one terrified instant before Ayla dropped the knife and ran?)* No matter. She had a new mission. She was going to stop Kinok, stop him from growing even more powerful, tightening his hold over Rabu. Whatever it took.

To do that, she had to find Storme, and tonight was her best chance. Varn was celebrating the Great Maker's Festival, an annual holiday in honor of Thomas Wren and the other early Makers, the creators of the Automae. All of Thalen had been thrown into chaos, the frenzy of preparation. The city gates were open wide for the streams of travelers and merchants and vendors and festivalgoers from all corners of Varn. Ayla and Benjy didn't even need to sneak in. As the sun began to set, the crowds growing ever thicker, they simply walked through the gates with everyone else.

Strings of lanterns swayed along the streets of Thalen, a glowing path through the darkness, leading from the gates to the festival itself in the heart of the city. Ayla and Benjy were swept along by the crowd of revelers, the sea of green and white ribbons, white roses, and white masks, some shaped like long, white beaks. Green feathers fluttered everywhere: they were braided into long hair, woven into bright pluming crowns and shining, iridescent capes. Ayla felt like she'd stumbled into the middle of a royal menagerie, a city of magnificent birds. She kept seeing Automae in the crowd, unnaturally beautiful, glossy hair tumbling down their backs or twisted into crowns, and every time her heart stopped before she realized it was normal here. For humans and leeches to share a festival, to celebrate among each other. For humans to attend a festival not as servants but as guests. Not equals, never equals, never truly safe, but closer to it here than they ever were in Rabu. Despite all the sovereign's posturing about *Traditionalism* and *respect*. Ayla couldn't reckon with it, couldn't wrap her mind around it. She didn't know if she was more shocked about Automae wanting to mingle with humans or humans just . . . letting them do it.

Don't you know what they do to us? she wanted to shriek at them. *Don't you know what they're capable of? Don't you know they're just waiting for any excuse to hurt you? Don't you know some of them don't need an excuse?*

Her skin prickled. She was sweating, even in the chill of winter. This place wasn't a menagerie. It was a pit of snakes.

Queen Junn's palace lay at the northernmost point of the city. Ayla heard it before she saw it: the roar of thousands of festivalgoers, all those rivers of people converging in the same place, laughing and singing and cheering; the wild rhythmic crash of what sounded like a hundred lutes, and drums, and horns. The buildings lining both sides of the street began to thin out the closer they got to the palace, granaries and cobblers and masonries and other little shops and sharehouses replaced by manor houses, the buildings becoming larger and more ornate. More Automa. Still, the streets were lit with lanterns signaling the way. This wasn't forbidden territory. This wasn't like Yanna, the capital city of Rabu, where humans starved on the streets in plain sight.

As Ayla and Benjy continued, even the manors fell away, the street spitting out everyone into a massive square—a white stone courtyard that could have easily held the entirety of one of Sovereign Hesod's sun apple orchards. The courtyard was filled to the brim with people, lanterns and firepits lighting the crowd with a flickering orange glow, banners emblazoned with the queen's phoenix and Thomas Wren's insignia—the alchemical symbols for salt, mercury, and sulfur: body, mind, and spirit—flying overhead. Smoke billowed up into the night sky, obscuring the stars. Ayla took a deep breath, filling her lungs with the smells of frying fish and frying dough and something almost sickeningly sweet, wine and cider and the copper scent of liquid heartstone, the charcoal-and-grease of a roasting pig, and rising above it all the delicate fragrance of white roses, bushels of them. Ayla saw people wending through the crowd, passing out crowns of white roses. Past the smoke and banners, she could just barely make out the palace itself on the far side of the courtyard. The white walls, a smaller version of the walls ringing the city. The gates.

Someone bumped into her from behind and she realized she'd been standing there, frozen, at the edge of the courtyard. She couldn't help it. She'd never seen anything like this kind of—luxury wasn't the right word, opulence wasn't the right word. This wasn't an Automa gathering, this wasn't the controlled splendor of Crier's engagement ball. This was lavish, beautiful, overflowing with food and color and light despite the late hour, and it was so deeply human. Chaotic, unrestrained. It was like the Reaper's Moon celebration the sovereign's servants held each year in the seaside caves, but a hundred times bigger.

Ayla blinked hard and found Benjy a few paces ahead of

her, equally frozen. She joined him, reached out to lay a hand on his arm, hesitated. Ever since the night they had snuck into the palace, when he had pulled her aside right before they'd parted ways—him to Kinok's study, her to Crier's bedroom—and kissed her, quick and hard, she couldn't touch him without remembering it. They hadn't talked about it. They hadn't talked about *anything*, really; that night or the aftermath. Ayla still didn't know if the kiss meant something to him, or if it was just the act of a scared boy who knew he could be dead within the hour, wanting to experience something for the first and last time.

She didn't know which answer she'd prefer.

Maybe that was a lie.

"Benj," she said, quiet enough for no one else to hear but loud enough to be heard over the music, the ocean-roar of a city drunk and merry. "The palace gates. Come on."

He nodded. Heads bent, they made their way through the center of the courtyard, where the music was loudest and the smoke thickest. Sticking to the edges would have been easier—but that was where the royal guards were stationed, watching everything from behind their white masks. So instead Ayla and Benjy wriggled their way through the tightly packed crowd, pressing up against dozens of sweaty, drunken, laughing bodies. The smoke stung Ayla's eyes. Even after the meat pie, her belly panged at the sight of so much food: tables piled high with a dozen different types of fish, platters of cheese and fruits and shimmering black eels, fruit pies, baskets of oranges, loaves of sweet dark bread, honey and oil and butter, mulled wine, and honey cakes, seed cakes, ginger cakes. There were a few humans in what looked like green servants' uniforms flitting around the tables, refilling platters and pouring cups of wine.

She was so hungry, and she'd eaten nothing for three days but pilfered bread and the meat pies she'd bought. Before that, the week and a half at sea, sick and delirious in the cargo hold, she was unable to keep down anything but water. Ayla's stomach gnawed at itself, crumpling, rolling over. She clenched her teeth and forced her eyes away from the food. She didn't have time to eat. She just had to get through the gates, inside the palace. . . .

While the main festival was in the courtyard and the city streets, there seemed to be a smaller, more exclusive celebration within the palace walls. Ayla could see more lanterns and banners, more smoke, the shift of a second crowd. The gates were open, though still heavily guarded. She tapped Benjy's wrist as they approached, nodding in the direction of a troupe of what looked like actors or dancers. Even with the masks, it was easy to tell who was human. Automae carried themselves less like people and more like statues that sometimes moved. They were tall, angular, their skin smooth and poreless, their movements measured. Their hair was always sleek and shiny, dark in Rabu and lighter here in Varn, where fair hair was more common. Human bodies were more varied: a thousand different shapes and sizes, skin freckled or scarred or pockmarked, hair any number of lengths or textures. Ayla had always thought that was the great irony of the Automae. They were created to be perfect, inhumanly beautiful, and all it did was make them less interesting to look at.

Unless they were bent over a book, a tendril of loose hair curling at the nape of their neck. Unless they were sliding into a tide pool, silver under a Reaper's Moon. Unless they were *her*.

Don't.

Beside her, Benjy huffed. "I don't want to wear a wig. Or take off my shirt."

The actors were all human. They were masked, like everyone else, but their masks weren't plain white—they were painted in bright, swirling colors, green feathers trailing off the edges. They were in costume, though Ayla didn't recognize any of the characters. A woman in a blue yarn wig, another in a shining silver crown, a trio of men all shirtless, their bare chests painted with red and orange flames. Must be a Varnian folktale. "Relax," said Ayla. "Look, there's some in the back dressed more plainly. They don't look so different from us. We can probably blend in with them." She started forward, but Benjy's hand shot out to grab her arm.

"Wait," he hissed. "Look at their wrists."

Ayla turned and saw the actors—and everyone else waiting to be let in the palace gates—had a green ribbon tied around their left wrist. There was something small and shiny dangling from each ribbon. Ayla squinted, blinking away tears from all the smoke, and realized the shiny thing looked like . . . a bell? No, a gold coin. The guards were checking everyone's wrists, inspecting the coins carefully, holding them up to catch the firelight. There was no way Ayla and Benjy would be able to get inside the gates without those green ribbons unless they scaled the walls. Ayla actually considered it for a moment, but the walls were twenty feet high and the white stone looked completely smooth, and anyway there were guards prowling around everywhere. That was a no go.

"Okay, new plan," Ayla muttered. "Everyone's in green, it shouldn't be too hard to find a couple ribbons."

"And a couple gold coins?" Benjy asked. "We can't exactly walk around slitting purses. Besides, those don't look like any queenscoins I've seen so far. They're not round. Watch the guard hold it up. . . . See? They're squarish. It's probably a special token."

Ayla blew out a breath. "Maybe we could—cut the ribbon off someone's wrist? Without them noticing? Or, or . . ." She cast her eyes around the crowd of people waiting to be let inside the gates. The costumed actors, a few more humans also dressed to entertain, a large group of Automae. Nobles, probably. They looked like the leeches who had come from all corners of Zulla to attend Lady Crier's engagement ball. Throats and wrists dripping with jewelry, threads of silver and gold woven into their hair, their clothing the finest velvet and silk brocade. Ayla saw one woman in sea-green silk pants and a gold-embroidered doublet, her arms bare, her hair in a thick plait that reached almost to the small of her back. Unlike most, she wasn't wearing a mask. When she glanced in the direction of the crowd, Ayla could see her mouth was painted gold.

"Ayla," said Benjy. "You with me?"

She cleared her throat. "I have an idea."

Without waiting for Benjy to respond, she hurried back into the thick of the crowd, making a beeline for the tables of food. She grabbed the nearest platter—a big silver dish of crab cakes—and dumped the contents into a basket of oranges, darting away before anyone noticed. Platter in hand, she returned to Benjy.

He raised his eyebrows. "So . . . what's the idea?"

"Follow my lead," she said. "And for gods' sake, act deferent."

"What—?"

Ayla bowed her head and curled her shoulders in, making herself smaller. Taking up as little space as possible. Then, ignoring the line of humans and Automae waiting to be let inside the palace walls, she headed for the guards. There were six stationed at the palace gates: three checking bracelets, three watching the crowd. Platter held out in front of her like an offering, Ayla quickened her pace, scurrying up to one of the watchers, sinking into a deep curtsy. She heard Benjy's footsteps behind her and could only hope he was bowing.

"Sir," she said, speaking to the guard's shiny black boots. "We were ordered to fetch more crab cakes and heartstone."

"More heartstone already?" the guard asked. "The night's only just begun."

"Everyone's feeling very indulgent, sir."

"At this rate they'll deplete the queen's stores by midnight. Why are you out of uniform?"

Ayla snorted. "Some drunk bastard spilled half a casket of wine over the both of us, sir. I believe he was reenacting 'The

Sailor and the Sea Serpent.'" She paused. "It's an old human story about—"

"I do not require an explanation," said the guard. Ayla risked a glance. His masked face was turned to the crowd again. "Fetch everything quickly," he continued, dismissive. "And get back into uniform. You are servants to the queen; you should look it."

"Yes, sir," said Ayla, and heard Benjy's mumbled "Yes, sir" behind her. The guard stepped aside, allowing them to pass through the gates, and they were in.

The palace courtyard was half the size of the one outside, and it was clear this part of the festival was organized not by commoners but by the queen. A shallow moat surrounded the courtyard, the surface dotted with white rose petals and floating lanterns; you had to cross an arched stone bridge to reach the festivities. Ayla could hear the gentle rush of a fountain somewhere, and she noticed a group of musicians at the edge of the courtyard—Automa, not human, Ayla saw with a twinge of surprise. The song they were playing was much slower and softer than the riotous music of the main festival—a song suited for conversation, not dancing. More white rose petals blanketed the ground like snow, so pretty that Ayla almost felt bad crushing them beneath her heels. And . . . Ayla frowned, trying to make sense of what she was seeing. It looked like there were insects darting around above the crowd, lighting up the night—large insects or maybe tiny birds, but that wasn't it. The way their wings kept winking in the lanternlight . . .

They were Made. Golden, gossamer butterflies the size of

Ayla's entire hand. Swooping around, floating like sparks in the night air. Artificial creatures with minds of their own. Ayla thought back to the Made objects she used to see passed around in secret in the market at Kalla-den: pocket watches that tracked the movements of the stars and planets; daggers that folded up to be smaller than a thumbnail; chunks of pink salt that could supposedly grant you visions of the future if you tossed them in the belly of a fire and inhaled the smoke. Half of them were fake, and the other half only worked part of the time.

Of course, Ayla knew of one Made object that was very, very real.

It had belonged to her, after all.

For the thousandth time since escaping the sovereign's palace, Ayla felt the urge to touch her sternum, the phantom weight where her heavy golden locket should have been. It had once belonged to her grandfather Leo; then her mother, then her. Until recently, Ayla had thought the most remarkable thing about the locket was its tiny inorganic heartbeat. Crier had been the one to discover Leo had stored his own memories inside it. A drop of blood was all it took to witness those memories, walk through them as a silent, invisible observer.

Gripping the platter with both hands, Ayla tore her gaze away from the Made butterflies and led Benjy across the stone bridge and into the fringes of the festival crowd. "We should separate," she breathed. Leeches everywhere, *gods*, her skin was crawling. Her heartbeat felt impossibly, dangerously loud, even though she *knew* there were other humans here, that she was not alone, that Varn wasn't like Rabu. It was one thing to know that. Much more difficult to actually believe it.

"Separate?" said Benjy. "No, why?"

"Not a lot of humans here. A pair might look suspicious." She paused, pretending to check over a spread of delicate cakes and pastries. Next to it, a font of liquid heartstone, deep red, for the Automae. "Meet me on the other side, at the palace steps, in a few minutes. Remember to hide your wrists. Don't get caught."

"I'll do my best," he said dryly.

Ayla kept still until he disappeared into the crowd, then headed off in the opposite direction, moving parallel to the eastern edge of the courtyard. She was thankful for her size. In the port town she'd stood out, but here, nobody would think twice about a small human girl carrying an empty platter through a crowd of glittering festivalgoers. The guards would assume she was just another servant heading back to the kitchens. Ayla tried not to worry about Benjy, focusing instead on slipping through the crowd like a shadow. Benjy would be fine; he could take care of himself. All they had to do was cross the courtyard and get to the palace steps. That wasn't hard.

Ayla should have known better than to think a foolish thing like that.

She was so close—the palace steps were in sight, and the palace beyond them, rising like a colossal crown of bone, its highest tower the height of the city walls behind it, all spiraling turrets and towers that tapered into swordlike points, a palace like a mouth of bared fangs, well suited to the queen who held the throne. The thin arrow-slit windows glowed with yellow candlelight, flickering. Ayla couldn't breathe for a moment. Her brother was somewhere within those walls. She was so close to him, only a few hundred paces away from the palace doors. By dawnbreak, they might already be reunited.

She strode forward and then faltered. An odd weight on her head, something catching in her hair. Not a hand. She reached up and her fingers found something delicate, metallic, fluttering, *alive*. One of the Made butterflies had landed on her. Ayla repressed a shudder, knowing it wasn't a real insect, but there was something deeply unsettling about the sensation of its spindly legs on her scalp. She shook her head hard and the butterfly lifted off again, bobbing away into the smoky night. Ayla stared after it, frowning. Unlike the other butterflies, this one kept . . . glowing. Pulsing yellow, more like a firefly than a butterfly.

Wait—

A gloved hand wrapped around her wrist. "You're not supposed to be here."

Ayla sucked in a breath. A royal guard stood over her, eyes glinting behind his white mask. He jerked her closer to him, startling her into dropping the platter. It hit the flagstones with a loud clang.

"Who let you in?" the guard demanded.

"I'm a servant," Ayla tried. "I must have lost my ribbon. I'm sorry for the trouble, I'll leave immediately."

"You will not," said the guard. "You're coming with me."

Ayla's eyes widened. "No," she said, struggling against his

grip. But even if she weren't half starved, she could never match the strength of a leech. "No, let me go, I'll leave, I just wanted to see the party, I don't mean any harm—"

"Shut your mouth before I cut out your tongue."

Mind racing, Ayla let herself be dragged along by the guard. Where was Benjy? Was he watching? Would he know that she'd been captured? The guard pulled her across a second stone bridge, crossing back over the moat, and then to the side of the palace steps, where there were arching doorways reserved for guards and servants. Within moments, Ayla knew she was completely out of sight. All she could do was hope Benjy was safe—and that, if he had seen her with the guard, he wouldn't be stupid enough to try a rescue.

The heavy wooden door swung shut behind them, and it took Ayla's eyes a few long moments to adjust to the darkness inside. This was a dank, narrow passageway, lit only by torches every twenty paces or so. She blinked hard and tried not to stumble as the guard dragged her forward. His grip was so tight, she worried he'd crush the bones of her wrist.

The passageway ended with another wooden door, which opened up into a wider hallway with a high, vaulted ceiling. Unlike the sovereign's palace, where all the ceilings were decorated with ornate, gilded paintings and marble carvings, the ceilings here were mosaiced with colored glass in geometric designs. Ayla thought it was strange how much it was sparkling until she realized it wasn't glass. It was thousands of gemstones. The fear in the pit of her stomach mixed with revulsion. One square foot of that ceiling could feed a family for ten years. Four square feet could feed a village.

The hallways were labyrinthine; Ayla tried to keep track of all the twists and turns, but it quickly became impossible, especially because the guard seemed to be doubling back every so often on purpose. They passed the entryways to open-air courtyards with gardens and fountains, courtyards lined with metallic statues, big banquet halls and drawing rooms, smaller corridors branching off into guest wings and guards' quarters. Occasionally Ayla glimpsed a servant or courtier, but for the most part the halls were empty. Everyone was outside enjoying the festival.

She had assumed the guard would take her to the dungeons. She kept waiting for him to open a door with a stairway leading down into the deep, dark underbelly of the palace. But instead, he led in her in circles for a while and then turned down the widest, grandest hallway yet, the flagstones carpeted with green velvet. There were guards stationed at the mouth of the hallway, both wearing white masks. As they approached, the guard who'd captured Ayla removed his own mask, and only then did the guards step aside, letting him and Ayla through.

"Where are you taking me," Ayla gritted out, not expecting an answer. The hallway ended with a single arched door plated with solid gold. There were four guards standing outside, but they weren't like the others. They were all women, unmasked, dressed not in plain white uniforms but in emerald green. Ayla remembered seeing other guards like this in the queen's consort when she'd visited the sovereign's palace a few weeks ago on a diplomacy tour. They were always closest to the queen, her personal bodyguards.

"Let me pass," said Ayla's guard, coming to a stop at the end of the hall. He dropped Ayla's wrist only to grab a fistful of her hair, forcing her head back. "Look what I caught in the middle of the Maker's Festival. In the queen's courtyard, no less. She was posing as a palace servant."

None of the guards moved. One said, "What makes you think this worthy of the queen's attention?"

"Her majesty bade us watch for Rabunian spies," Ayla's guard insisted. "Her majesty said one would be a girl-child, no older than the queen herself. This human is the right age."

A girl-child. Ayla bit her tongue so hard she tasted blood. Was Queen Junn somehow expecting her? Was this Storme's doing? Perhaps he'd told Junn the truth—that Ayla wasn't just a handmaiden; she was his long-lost twin sister. And if Queen Junn knew Ayla was behind the assassination attempt on Lady Crier . . . Had she predicted Ayla's next move?

The queen's guards stared at Ayla, scrutinizing her face.

"Leave her," one said. "We will deliver her to the queen."

"No," Ayla's guard protested. "I'm the one who caught her. If she is a Rabunian spy—"

"Leave. Her," said the queen's guard. Her voice was flat and cold, allowing no room for protest. "If she is a spy, I will make certain the queen knows who to credit for her capture. That's what you're worried about, is it not? Your credit? Go."

A moment of furious silence, then Ayla pitched forward when

the guard let go of her hair. Her knees hit the floor, velvet carpet providing no cushion from the flagstones below. She scrambled upright, wincing, only to find a sword at her throat.

Two of the four guards flanked her, leading her through the heavy golden door and into a large high-ceilinged chamber. The walls were draped with more green velvet. A long, narrow pool ran down the center of the room, an aisle of green water, white rose petals floating on the surface like on the moat outside. Two dozen guards were stationed around the edges of the chamber, female, unmasked. Then Ayla's eyes traveled up the length of the pool to the far end of the room, and her fears were confirmed. This could only be the queen's throne: a dais and a high, raised chair carved from one giant piece of white stone. Ayla was relieved to find it unoccupied—until she noticed the figure standing beside it, her back to the rest of the room. Even from behind, Ayla recognized her. Queen Junn. The Mad Queen, the Bone Eater.

"Your majesty," said one of the guards flanking Ayla. Both of them had bent their heads in deference upon entering and were now straightening up. "My deepest apologies for the interruption, but—"

"Not now," said the queen without turning around. She wasn't speaking loudly, and yet still her voice carried throughout the entire chamber. "I don't care what it is, I'm not dealing with it tonight. If it's an assassin, prepare for them a platter of the finest cuts of meat, the ripest fruit, the sweetest wine; let them eat, and only after that may you escort them to the dungeons. If it's war, call for a strategist; war can wait till morning. If it's anything else, get out."

The queen's back was bared. Two handmaidens were lacing her into a gown—feathered, magnificent—and Ayla tried not to think about the familiar hand movements, the fastening of the laces, *knuckles brushing against soft warm skin*—

"Yes, your majesty," said the guard at Ayla's side. "Understood." To the second guard, she said, "Take her to the dungeons."

No.

If she went to the dungeons, she might not ever come back out.

The two guards each gripped one of her arms, preparing to drag her from the room. Ayla went limp, faking unconsciousness, a complete deadweight. For a split second the guards were startled, their grips loosening, and she broke free. She lurched away from them, not even sure what she was trying to do; all she knew was that she couldn't go to the dungeons, and maybe Storme was somewhere nearby. In the sovereign's palace he'd never been far from Queen Junn's side; he had to be close. Ayla barely made it ten paces before the guards were on her again, a sword point at her spine, a hand wrenching her back by the collar of her shirt, choking her.

"STORME," she screamed, her voice echoing around the chamber. "STORME, I'M LOOKING FOR STORME!"

"You're dead," hissed one of the guards, tightening her grip on Ayla's collar. Ayla struggled against her, gasping for breath, and then, at the end of the throne room, she saw the queen turn around.

"Eya," said the queen. "Deidra. Bring her closer."

"Your majesty—"

"That was an order, Eya."

The guards obeyed. Trapped between them, head shoved down, Ayla was brought closer. The guards dropped her before the queen like a sack of potatoes, and for the second time in less than ten minutes, Ayla's kneecaps hit the flagstones hard. That was going to bruise.

"Show me your face, girl," came the queen's voice above her.

Ayla raised her head.

Queen Junn's face—as beautiful and cold as Ayla remembered, sharp nose and high cheekbones and red lips—didn't change; there was no spark of recognition in her eyes. But she said, "Hello again, handmaiden."

"I'm not a spy," Ayla said desperately. "I don't know what you've heard, but I swear, I'm not a spy, I'm not acting on anyone's orders, I bid you no ill will. I just want to see Storme."

How much did Queen Junn know? She and Storme had seemed oddly close for a queen and adviser, but maybe he hadn't mentioned the whole Ayla-being-his-long-lost-twin-sister thing. So . . . there was a nonzero chance Queen Junn knew about the attack on the palace and nothing else, and therefore thought Ayla was just a traitorous, murderous servant who'd tried to assassinate Lady Crier. Ayla racked her mind for a way to prove herself trustworthy, and then—a snippet of memory. The palace kitchens. Malwin, a fellow servant, standing before her. *I'm under orders from Queen Junn's adviser. Gave me something to give to you.* Later, the inn at Elderell. Crier's wide, shocked eyes. *You saw nothing, do you understand me?*

But she and Ayla had been keeping the same secret.

"Green feather," Ayla said now. "Storme gave me a green feather. I know that means something to you."

The queen was silent. She didn't need a mask to be unreadable.

"This will disappoint you," she said finally. "My adviser is not here in Thalen. He left two days ago for the northern border, and he's not due to return for another fortnight."

Ayla sagged. A *fortnight.*

Without taking her eyes off Ayla's face, the queen said, "Handmaiden Rupa."

One of the two handmaidens, a tall, thick human girl, stepped forward. "Yes, your majesty?"

"Take this girl to the guest wing," said the queen. "Provide her with a bedchamber, any food or clothing she desires. If she desires a bedfellow, provide that as well." She smiled, thin and bloodred, at the shock on Ayla's face. "This is how we show hospitality in my country, handmaiden Ayla. Welcome to Varn."

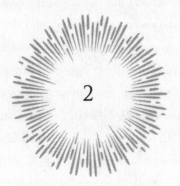

2

Crier stood in the center of her bedchamber, a dozen house servants and handmaidens scurrying all around her, and tried not to feel like a piece of driftwood in the middle of a storm at sea.

There were two handmaidens twisting her hair into a crown of braids, another darkening her eyes and painting her lips a deep Automa-blood violet, and countless others flitting in and out of the room with velvet-lined boxes of jewelry, hair ribbons, thick heartstone paste and gold body paint that during the ceremony would be used to draw the symbols of the Makers on her skin.

Four hours from now, Crier would be married.

Presently, she was staring at her reflection, motionless in the large full-length mirror, as the human servants transformed her into a bride. Handmaiden Malwin was at her back, hands working quickly to lace up the bodice of Crier's wedding gown, pulling it tight around her rib cage, so tight that if Crier had needed to breathe as often as humans did, she would have been suffocating. She was reminded, with a dull throb of pain, of the last time she'd stood like this while someone laced her into a dress. The last time she'd felt someone's fingers brushing her bare shoulder blades, the nape of her neck, someone's touch warming her even through layers of linen and silk.

The dress she'd worn then had been pale silver, bell-shaped. This dress was dark red velvet, cut closer to the shape of Crier's body, the bottom of the skirt pooling on the flagstones at Crier's feet. There were no sleeves, and she would wear no robe or silks—nothing that would get in the way of the ceremonial markings on her arms, her forehead, her chest above the neckline of the gown. On her head, a delicate golden tiara.

She met her own dark eyes in the mirror. She thought maybe her face looked different than usual, not just because of the makeup. Crier's expression was usually neutral, controlled, her emotions and reactions purposefully tamped down. Today, she didn't just look blank. She looked empty. Dead.

Elsewhere in the palace, Scyre Kinok must also be preparing for the ceremony. Kinok, her betrothed. Four hours from now, her husband. *Forever.* Crier couldn't stop thinking about it: the concept of forever. Automae lived for a long time. Twenty, fifty, eighty years from now, she would still be married to Kinok. The seasons would change, her father would die, Kinok would replace him as sovereign. For most of her life, Crier had believed that as Hesod's only child, his only natural heir, she would be the one to inherit his throne. She thought she knew the path her life would take: as soon as her father decided she was ready, she would join the Red Council. She would work as a Red Hand, a councilmember, for decades, doing whatever she could to pass laws strengthening the frayed relationship between Automae and humans in Rabu. She'd spent the last ten years writing essay after political essay, establishing her beliefs, her values, her legitimacy as a potential councilmember. But the day her father had finally invited her to a meeting of the Red Council, she'd been forced to stand silently in a corner and watch as her father chose Kinok to fill Councilmember Reyka's empty seat. Crier had realized that day that her father had never planned on allowing her to join the council, let alone become sovereign. She wasn't destined to be a part of her nation's future. She was destined to be a wife, a trinket, given away as a gesture of goodwill the moment her father wanted to join forces with someone whose power was threatening his own. Kinok: Scyre, Watcher of the Iron Heart, leader of the rapidly growing Anti-Reliance Movement. Kinok: a man who had tricked Crier into thinking she was Flawed, broken, Made wrong; a man who had used this "Flaw" to blackmail her into bending to his will. Who was on a quest to find Tourmaline, a new source of power for their Kind. Who had learned Ayla's grandparents were somehow connected to the creation of Tourmaline, and therefore wanted to find Ayla.

It felt like Crier's bodice really was suffocating her. It felt like her ribs were cracking, shattering inward, piercing her lungs. Her heart.

The worst part was her father's obvious pleasure. He had

never been proud of her like this. Not when she'd studied day and night, memorized libraries' worth of books, kept silent, obeyed him, adhered to his Traditionalism, followed every rule. That had earned her nothing but indifference. Or the occasional praise like a thin gold veneer over a heap of criticism: *This is well written, daughter. If only the content were as good as the technique.* But over the past week, he'd taken to treating her like a well-behaved dog, rewarding her good behavior with tiny gifts. Tokens of his affection. A book filled with charts only of various seas, as recorded by sailors and voyagers. A peacock-feather quill with a pot of silver ink. Most precious of all, a golden key. It opened the door to Hesod's trophy room, one of the only rooms in the palace nobody, not even Crier, was allowed to enter. A few months ago, she would have been honored. But these days she had no interest in seeing her father's spoils of war. A room of human artifacts he'd been collecting for years. They weren't trophies. They were stolen. She'd left the golden key in the drawer of her writing desk, hadn't touched it since. Didn't plan to.

"Malwin," Crier murmured, and felt Malwin's fingers freeze against her spine. None of the other servants noticed; they'd finished with Crier's hair and makeup and the room had emptied out. Crier knew the wedding guests had started arriving a couple hours earlier. Even on such short notice—the wedding date had been pushed up nearly a month, and the new date had been announced only a week ago, her father's fastest riders sent to all corners of the nation to deliver the news—there were two hundred in attendance. All of them requiring lodging, heartstone, and food for their servants. The palace had been in chaos for days. It didn't help that barely two weeks had passed since . . .

Since Ayla had stood over Crier's bed in the middle of the night with a knife in one hand, poised to strike.

"Yes, my lady?" said Malwin.

"Your Kind speaks of 'heartbreak,'" said Crier. She'd seen the word in so many human books, faerie stories and love stories and comedies and tragedies alike. It was everywhere. "I know it is not . . . literal. But what is it?"

Malwin hesitated. "Why do you ask, my lady?"

Ever since the night of the attack, all the servants had been visibly warier of Crier, her father, Kinok, even the Automa guards. Their expressions when they saw Crier ranged from nervous to downright terrified. Most of them didn't know the full story of what had happened that night—it seemed Ayla and the other servants involved had kept their plans a secret, though Crier knew the rumors about Ayla working for Queen Junn were untrue. Still, she understood why the details didn't matter. Her Kind wasn't known for being merciful. In the past, her father had punished innocents for other humans' crimes. If she were a servant, she'd be terrified too. She'd been doing everything she could to appear nonthreatening—keeping her voice gentle, her expression smooth, her orders quick and simple—but it wasn't helping. She was the sovereign's daughter. She could hurt or kill them with a word.

Before Ayla, Crier hadn't realized the extent of her own power, as foolish as it sounded. She knew she *had* power—she knew the servants had to obey her—but she wasn't the sovereign.

She had no real influence. She wasn't dangerous, she was just Crier. Why would anyone fear her?

She'd been so naive.

"I'm just curious," she assured Malwin. "There's no wrong answer. I'm just curious."

"All right, my lady," Malwin said quietly, going back to the laces. "Heartbreak . . . well, it's like being sad, but more than that. The worst sadness you can feel. When you're so sad it feels like a real wound, like your heart itself is broken, bleeding."

"What causes it? What makes people that sad?"

"Could be anything, my lady." Malwin made a considering noise. "When you lose someone you love. Or if someone you love does something to hurt you, something truly terrible."

Crier thought about that. She thought about the letter from Queen Junn, currently hidden inside Crier's mattress along with a heavy gold locket. Junn's confession: *I killed Reyka.* She thought about her father humiliating her in front of the Red Council: *My apologies. My daughter thinks herself wise beyond her years.*

She thought about Ayla.

"What would make you want to hurt someone?" she asked Malwin, very quiet. "What would make you want to do something terrible?"

"My lady," said Malwin, "I would never, I would never do anything to—"

"I know," Crier broke in. "I know, Malwin. Please don't worry. You haven't done anything wrong. It's just a question, I promise."

In the mirror, she saw Malwin's look of surprise. The hand-maiden was older than Crier by a few years, with a narrow face, a big crooked nose, a scattering of small pockmark scars around her jaw. Her hair was tied back in a messy braid. She was pretty, Crier thought to herself. It was strange—she'd always been taught that Automae were the ideal. Like the rest of her Kind, Crier's face was Designed to be perfectly symmetrical. She was tall and strong. She didn't have any scars. But the most captivating person she'd ever met was Ayla: short, perpetually scowling Ayla, round-faced, freckled, wild-haired, beautiful Ayla.

What would make you want to hurt someone?

What would make you want to do something terrible?

"I suppose . . . ," Malwin said slowly. "I suppose if they hurt me first. If they hurt someone I loved."

But I didn't hurt her, thought Crier, instantly defensive. Then she paused. It was true that she'd never physically hurt Ayla. The closest she'd ever come was at the inn, wild with panic, shoving Ayla back against the door, miscalculating the force of her own strength. Realizing what she'd just done, letting go, sick with a new type of panic, her brain tossing out hyperrealistic images of finger-shaped bruises on Ayla's shoulders, Ayla's bones breaking beneath Crier's hands. Apologizing, horrified with herself. The hatred in Ayla's voice: *You're an Automa. It's your nature to overpower.* Like she'd been expecting the worst and Crier had still managed to disappoint her.

It's your nature to overpower.

Ayla hadn't just been talking about the shove.

Malwin fastened the last pair of laces and took a step back, taking a look at Crier's reflection in the mirror. "You are beautiful, my lady," she said. "You make a lovely bride."

Crier tried to respond, but her throat felt tight. Her body was tense all over. She felt like a fish caught in a net, a doe at the wrong end of a hunter's arrow. Like she was dangling from a cliff, freezing water and sharp black rocks below, and this time she would not be saved.

Kinok didn't know she knew the truth about her Flaw, but Crier couldn't even consider it a victory. Every moment with him was a slow, drawn-out strangulation. He was dangerous, a *monster*, but Crier—couldn't leave. She couldn't.

Three days ago, as was tradition, she had met with the man who would officiate her wedding. He was a well-known, highly respected Designer, an Automa who worked with human Midwives to create newbuilt Automae. The sovereign had arranged the meeting. Crier had been expecting the Designer to walk her through the wedding ceremony, detailing exactly what she had to do and when. That was not what happened.

"Well met, Lady Crier," said the Designer.

She was startled by the press of two fingers on the underside of her chin. Nobody else would dare to touch her. "Well met," she murmured, looking up at him. She didn't know how old he was—it was hard to tell with her Kind—but his face was beginning to show the signs of age. His tan skin looked thin as parchment across his bones; his eyes were not as clear as her own; his dark hair was streaked with silver. He wore the white uniform of the Designers. The white robes, lined with softest lambskin, that marked him as the officiant of Crier's wedding.

"Lady Crier," said the Designer in his papery voice, "you seem frightened."

She didn't respond.

"Tell me your fears," he said. "Tell me your doubts."

"There are so many," she whispered, ashamed. "I—I sometimes wonder if this is the right choice. My betrothed, he . . ." She didn't know how to finish the sentence. She didn't know who she could trust. Kinok had eyes and ears everywhere.

"Doubt is normal," said the Designer. "Indecision is so common in the young. But this is the right choice, Lady Crier, because it is the only choice. You cannot change it now."

Her brow furrowed. She blinked up at him, confused. "The only choice?"

"This is what you were created for, Lady Crier," said the Designer, cupping her face in his hands. His palms were cool and dry. "This is your Design: to be bonded. It is never wise to defy your own Design, Lady Crier. Others have made that mistake. The young, the doubtful. But the nature of our Kind is that we are not so irreplaceable, in the end. If one offspring fails, another can take its place."

"What are you saying?" Crier breathed. She felt on the edge of something, some blinding, white-hot horror. "Another can . . . ?"

"Take your place," said the Designer, brushing his thumb across her cheekbone as if wiping away tears, though she knew for a fact she was not crying. "Do not forget, Lady Crier. You were Made, *and you can be unmade, and another remade in your image. Do not force your father's hand, Lady Crier. He created you to fulfill a certain purpose. If you reject that purpose . . ."*

He might have continued, but Crier wasn't listening. She knelt there on the cold flagstones, letting this new knowledge sweep through her. *My father wouldn't hurt me,* she told herself. I'm his daughter. He wouldn't hurt me, even if I refuse the bonding.

Would he?

But the Designer's message had been clear—obey, *or else.*

Crier wanted more than anything to run away. But where would she go? In Rabu, she was in danger of being recognized. She could try to make it to Varn, to the queen's palace in Thalen—after all, as far as Queen Junn knew, Crier was still her ally and confidante—but Queen Junn had killed Reyka. She'd *killed Reyka.* The idea of facing her, playing nice in her court, made Crier sick.

Where else? The unpopulated jungles of Tarreen? Somewhere far across the ocean?

No. Kinok's next move was to find Ayla. If Crier left, there would be nothing and no one to stop him. Wherever Ayla was, Kinok would find her.

Crier couldn't let that happen.

She'd had this fight with herself a hundred times over the past two weeks, and she always came to the same conclusion: She would marry Kinok. She would remain at his side. It was the only way to stop him. To protect Ayla. Part of Crier knew it was pathetic, humiliating, to care so much about Ayla's safety after what Ayla had tried to do. The darkness, the knife. Certainly Crier's father would lose all remaining respect for her if he found out how she felt. But it *was* how she felt. She couldn't change it, and if it came down to her dignity or Ayla's life, well. That wasn't even a choice.

"Malwin," Crier said, "I need a favor from you."

"Anything, my lady."

"Find the scullery maid called Faye," said Crier. "She's usually stationed in the laundry rooms. Bring her to me. If she resists, tell her—tell her it's about sun apples."

Malwin hesitated. "My lady, there's only a few minutes before you're meant to be in the grand ballroom. . . ."

"So I will appreciate your haste," Crier said.

Once alone, Crier sank onto her bed. *Faye.* All summer, Kinok had forced the scullery maid to work for him in secret. She'd been overseeing shipments of what she thought were the sovereign's prized sun apples but was actually a dangerous substance called Nightshade. After she'd learned the truth, she tried to back out. To punish her, Kinok had killed her sister. Luna.

Faye had never been the same. Carved into a new person by grief, she seemed to occupy this world only half the time. The other half, she was lost in her own mind, somewhere far away, unreachable.

Crier almost put her head in her hands—such a human gesture—but then remembered her makeup. Instead she sat there, back straight, and stared across the room at her tapestry of Kiera, the first Automa. The first of their Kind, created by the greatest of the human alchemists, Maker Thomas Wren. But that wasn't true, was it? Crier knew now that Wren had stolen the blueprints for Kiera from a mysterious woman called H. He hadn't Designed anything; he'd just taken credit for H's work.

There was a stitched-up scar in one corner of the tapestry from where a guard had torn it from the wall that night, after Ayla fled. But Kiera was intact. Saffron-yellow dress, red mouth, rich brown skin. Eyes of golden thread, catching the morning sunlight. Crier gazed into those eyes, unblinking, as the minutes dragged on.

A knock on the door. "Enter," said Crier, and Malwin slipped inside, followed by a stumbling, sunken-eyed Faye. Malwin was clutching Faye's wrist; maybe she'd put up a fight.

"Thank you, Malwin," said Crier, standing up. "You may wait for me outside."

"My lady—"

"*Outside.*"

Reluctant, eyes darting between Crier and Faye, Malwin dropped Faye's wrist and left the room for a second time, closing the door quietly behind her. There were guards stationed outside Crier's bedroom door—ever since the attack, she'd been forbidden from going anywhere without at least four guards in tow. It was a nightmare; the presence of guards completely ruined the sanctity of the library and the music room, but Crier figured that was probably the only thing that would prevent Malwin from pressing her ear to the door, attempting to eavesdrop.

"Best get on with it, lady," said Faye. "Pulled me away in the middle of a shift, you did. Old Nessa's sure to be angry." She smiled. "Oh, but that's not right, it's not Nessa anymore, is it. Nessa's dead in the ground. Everyone's dead in the ground. Am I next? Why'd you call me here, lady?"

"So I could give you this," said Crier, picking up one of the books on the bedside table and flipping through it until she found what she was looking for: a small envelope sealed with wax. She held it out to Faye, but Faye didn't move.

"What is that?" she asked, eyeing the envelope. "What will you have me do?"

Crier swallowed. "Please. You're the only person I know who might be able to find her."

Her.

"She's gone, lady," Faye said. "Nobody knows where she went, not me, not anyone. She could be halfway across the ocean by now. She could be dead."

She's not dead, Crier thought, and then, absurdly: *I would have felt it.* "Just—please," she rasped, taking a step closer to Faye. "Please. If you hear anything, *anything* . . . I know you know people in the—Resistance. Please. Please just try. Please, Faye. You're the only hope I've got."

Faye took the envelope from Crier, tucked it into the pocket of her red servants' uniform. "Don't expect much, but I'll do my best."

"Thank you," Crier breathed. She wrapped both arms around herself, unmoored. This was it, then. This was her good-bye, and there was a good chance it would never even come close to reaching Ayla, this unmarked envelope in the hands of a half-mad scullery maid. Inside it, a dried seaflower and a single sentence:

You were right about the law of falling.

Ayla couldn't read. She would have to get someone else to tell her what the letter said. That is, if it found her at all. If she didn't throw it away, rip it up, burn it. But what else did Crier have? What else could she do?

You were right about the law of falling. You were right. She'd written and rewritten that sentence a thousand times, curled up on the window seat from nightfall till the early hours of the morning. Trying to find the right words. *You were right. You were right.* Crier remembered everything about that first day, the day she'd made Ayla her new handmaiden. She'd taken Ayla to the gardens, the air perfumed with salt lavender and seaflowers, the taste of the sea on the back of Crier's tongue, the sound of waves crashing beyond the last row of flowers, beyond the cliffs. In the gardens, Crier had looked at Ayla and, *gods*, she'd had no idea, *no idea*. At the time, she'd been half intrigued, half embarrassed Ayla had seen her cry. All she knew was she wanted to get closer. To read Ayla like a good book. And Ayla, frowning, eyes distant, had said: *Even way out there past the sky, so far away that we can't even imagine it, things work the same. Everything's just bodies in orbit, like here. Pushing and pulling.*

Ayla, Crier thought, *you pulled me in.*

"My lady," said Faye. "Will you do something for me in return?"

Crier shook off her thoughts like snow. She raised her eyebrows at the scullery maid, taken off guard by such a bold request. "What . . . kind of something?"

"Stop the Scyre."

"What— *Keep your voice down!*" Crier hissed. "You can't just *say* things like that, anyone could be listening in, are you—?" She cut herself off before she said *mad*.

"Apologies, lady." Faye leaned in, lowering her voice. "You need to stop him. I know what he's planning. He likes to brag, you see. To those in his control. He underestimates us. He doesn't think we have anyone to tell." She was almost smiling. "That's how I know."

"Know what?"

"He's going to destroy the Iron Heart."

Faye's eyes were clear and bright like Crier had never seen them before. Her shoulders were straight, her hands curled into fists at her sides. It was like glimpsing a ghost, the girl Faye used to be, before her sister was murdered for Faye's crimes. Before grief left her stranded somewhere far away inside her head.

"Destroy it?" said Crier, an emotion like cold water rising inside her. The Iron Heart. "I know he's searching for an alternative to heartstone, but—*destroy the Heart*? That doesn't make any sense, he relies on it like the rest of us, he . . ." *He wants to hurt humans, not Automae.*

But even as she protested, the pieces fell into place.

Kinok was the leader of the Anti-Reliance Movement. On the surface, the movement aimed to further separate the two Kinds by building a new capital city just for Automae. The truth was much darker, bloodier. Kinok wanted three things: First, he wanted to raze *all* the old human cities to the ground and build new Automa cities in the ashes. Humans be damned. Second, he wanted to Make a new breed of Automa, with no human pillars at all. And third, he wanted to find an alternative to heartstone, thus ending his Kind's reliance on the Iron Heart. He'd been conducting experiments, trying to synthesize a new gemstone on his own, but so far his attempts had been disastrous: he'd only succeeded in creating Nightshade, a black mineral dust that seemed to work at first, but in fact slowly poisoned whoever consumed it. And not only was it poisonous, it was highly addictive. Kinok had been using it to control his followers—including Crier's friend Rosi.

But that wasn't practical in the long run. So Kinok had been searching for a blue gemstone called Tourmaline, the same stone Ayla's grandmother Siena had used to power her Automa prototype, Yora. He seemed to think Tourmaline was infinitely powerful—so much so that it could power an Automa body forever. Right now, Automa bodies aged—slower than humans, but they did age; their physical vessels did eventually weaken, wither, give out. They could die and be killed. Judging by the notes Crier had seen in his room, Kinok dreamed of a world in which neither of those things were true.

If Kinok found Yora's heart, which was made of Tourmaline,

which carried the secret to its power . . . if he destroyed the source of heartstone so the Automae had no choice but to beg him for Tourmaline . . .

"The moment the Scyre finds what he's looking for, it's over for your Kind *and* mine," said Faye. "Absolute power. Absolute cruelty. If I'm your only hope, my lady, then you are mine."

Anti-Reliance, Crier thought, numb.

So this was what it meant.

Faye brandished a letter. For a second Crier thought it was the letter for Ayla, but the paper was worn and yellowed with age, like it could crumble into dust at the slightest touch. "Lady, there's more."

"What is this?" Crier asked. Her own voice was dead and hollow to her ears. She unfolded the letter with shaking hands, trying to focus on anything other than the word *reliance, reliance, reliance.*

"From the Scyre's study. But not—not from the Scyre. It's very old. It's . . . It looked important. So I took it. I thought you'd want to see. I thought you'd want to *know*."

Crier stared at the letter, willing herself to focus. It was addressed to "T" from "H." But she didn't have time to comprehend what she was reading. There was a knock on the door to her bedchamber and Malwin's voice came, tentative: "My lady?"

Hastily, Crier shoved the letter beneath one of the pillows on her bed. It would have to wait. For now, Crier had bigger things to worry about. She had to talk to her father.

T,

I beg you do not do this.

Do you remember the day we met? Beneath the god's golden eye. You at the window, a dark shape against the coming dawn. Winter dawn. Sky the color of snow blossoms. I knew your face. Your name. You didn't know mine.

I gave you everything. My life's work, knowledge, mad dreams, bed. And you can't even give me time?

You know I can perfect it. This blue heart.

Do you know I always thought of my own heart as blue? Not like the sky. Like the bottom of the ocean. Blue like that, but not empty. Not cold. Blue like the heart of a candle flame. When you touched me I burned red. Back then, I thought it was a good thing. Burning.

How to create a life?

Is that it? Fire? Blood? A giant's womb?

We shared a dream once. A bed, once; no longer; not after this; I will keep my heart blue. This "shortcut," you know it's wrong; that's why you kept it from me. Do you think I don't know you? I loved you, didn't I? I bled for you, didn't I? And now this.

Name one goddamn thing more precious than a life.

—LETTER FROM "H——" TO MAKER THOMAS WREN, E. 900 Y. 10

3

The first morning in Queen Junn's palace was, in a word, overwhelming. It didn't help that she'd barely slept at all—the bed she'd been given was so soft it seemed to swallow her body, and she kept waking from nightmares about quicksand and drowning. Each time she woke up, she had to remember all over again where she was and why she was alone, neither surrounded by other sleeping servants nor curled up next to Benjy in the hold of a cargo ship. Her only solace was that Benjy was probably safer than she was, out in the streets of Thalen.

At dawn, she woke for good when a trio of human hand-maidens swept into her room. She scrambled upright, startled, but they didn't even glance at her. One flung open the curtains, flooding the room with pale blue light; one, arms piled with dresses, started laying them out at the foot of the bed; the last yanked back a silk privacy screen that had been obscuring a corner of the room, revealing a sunken bath and a big copper water tank with a spigot shaped like a peacock.

"What's . . . happening . . . ?" said Ayla, already dreading the answer.

Over the next hour, she was bathed within an inch of her life. Her hair was washed three times, her finger- and toenails trimmed, her face and body scrubbed with a soapy cloth until she thought her skin might peel off, the bathwater turning gray with what looked like five years of grime. When the water finally began to grow cold, the handmaidens pulled her out and rubbed her down with an oil that left her skin soft and gleaming, smelling faintly of almonds. Ayla hated how much she didn't hate it. Then, after she'd been thoroughly dried, she was shoved into white cotton undergarments that felt weightless, so soft and light, nothing like the rough, itchy undergarments she'd always worn. After that, she was herded over to a mirror while the handmaidens held up dress after dress against her body, squinting, scrutinizing, somehow arriving at the decision that Ayla would look best in deep blue. Ayla opened her mouth to protest—she'd never liked wearing dresses—but a sharp look from one of the handmaidens, a tall girl with pale skin, shut her up. She allowed herself to be dressed, her hair oiled and combed, even though the comb kept snagging on her curls and it hurt like hell. When she examined her reflection, it felt like looking at Storme: someone whose face distantly resembled her own but was not the same. Glowing skin, fine clothes, hair sleek and shiny as a sealskin. Ayla couldn't help but think of her time as a handmaiden, doing all this for—

Crier.

Drawing a bath, drizzling various sweet-smelling oils into the water, washing Crier's hair, running soapy hands through it. Helping her out of the claw-footed tub, eyes averted, handing her a towel. Brushing her hair, breathing in the scent of roses, lavender, cloves. Turning away as Crier slipped into her under-garments. Helping her into the latest ridiculously complicated dress.

"All right," said the pale handmaiden, appraising Ayla with her hands on her hips. "I think you're presentable." It was the first time any of them had addressed Ayla directly.

"Glad to hear it," said Ayla.

The handmaiden ignored her tone. "You have been summoned to the aviary for an audience with the queen. You are to join her as soon as you've finished breakfast."

"Breakfast?"

As if on cue, the bedroom door opened again and a kitchen boy entered carrying a massive platter covered with a white cloth. He set it down on the small table beside the bed and scurried back out, closing the door behind him.

"Breakfast," said the pale handmaiden, nodding at the platter.

Slowly, cautiously, Ayla crossed to the platter and lifted the white cloth. Steam rose up, warming her cheeks, along with the mouthwatering smell of—stars and skies, *everything*. An entire loaf of dark brown bread. A plate of salted fish, a plate of sausage. Little bowls of butter and jam, *two types of jam*. A big bowl of porridge, a tiny pitcher of cream, more little bowls of sugar and honey and red currants. It was like last night's festival feast in miniature. It was enough to feed a family. It was—all for Ayla?

She turned to the handmaidens. All three of them were the same age as Ayla or maybe a couple years older. She could easily be them. Two weeks ago, she had been them.

"Will you eat too?" she asked them.

"No, miss," said the shortest one, dark brows furrowed. "That's for you, courtesy of the queen."

"But I can't eat all this."

None of them responded. They just looked at her.

"Please," she said. "I'm a guest of the queen. She instructed you to do what I say, didn't she? Eat with me."

The three of them exchanged glances. ". . . Is that an order?" said the shortest one. She had a low, husky voice, naturally melodious, a voice made for singing.

"Not if you don't want it to be," said Ayla. "But if you're hungry, then yes, it is an order. I can't finish all this, I'll be sick. Better to end up in your bellies than the royal pig troughs."

The third handmaiden, who had not yet said a single word, hid a smile in her sleeve.

"Very well," said the pale one. "If it's an *order*."

This time, all three handmaidens smiled.

Once every crumb was gone and the porridge bowl scraped clean, the shortest handmaiden, who introduced herself as Maris, led Ayla to the aviary. That was about when Ayla learned an aviary was a fancy name for a big room full of birds, which seemed like the worst thing you could possibly fill a room with. Still, it was beautiful: airy, circular, with a high domed ceiling made of glass, the morning-blue sky visible far above. A series of stepping-stones led to the center of the room, where there was a stone platform with two gilded, throne-like chairs. The rest of the floor was dark, wet soil. There were plants everywhere: small twisting trees around the perimeter of the room, sprays of orange and yellow flowers, leafy vines crawling up the walls, a thick briar of wild roses. Birds flitted through the air, some ordinary as sparrows and others strange and exotic, with bright green feathers. Fat little pheasants marched around pecking at the dirt; hummingbirds dipped their long beaks into the flowers. Birdsong echoed through the wide-open space, high trills and low, raspy calls, a cacophony of song and shrieking. There were butterflies, too, and Ayla was reminded of the Made butterfly that had landed on her head last night, alerting the festival guards to her presence.

She was so busy craning her neck to see the birds flying around at the highest point of the domed ceiling, she didn't realize the queen was already here until Maris pushed her forward, hissing, *"Don't keep her waiting."*

Ayla stumbled forward, following the stepping-stones to the platform. Queen Junn was seated, facing away from the door to the aviary, her form hidden by the high back of the chair. A spindly little table between the two chairs held a silver tea tray, a teapot, two cups. Until Ayla clambered up onto the platform, all she could see of the queen was her hand: she was stirring the contents of one of the teacups with her finger.

"Ayla," Queen Junn greeted her.

Ayla curtsied, perfunctory. "You summoned me?"

"Sit."

She sat down across from the queen.

"Have a cup of tea, Ayla."

Queen Junn was drinking heartstone, deep red. The second teacup was filled with what looked like regular herbal tea. Ayla picked it up, took a sip, and grimaced when it burned her tongue. When she looked up, the queen was watching her. In the yellow sunlight of the aviary the queen looked oddly young. Much softer than she had last night in the throne room—or a few weeks ago in Hesod's palace, first in candlelight, then under a flat gray sky. She wasn't wearing a gown this time. In fact, she was in pants and a shirt that looked almost like Ayla's old handmaiden uniform, if the uniform had been green and made of silk.

"I'm glad you came to me, Ayla," said Queen Junn. "I'm glad you sought refuge in Thalen. Or at least sought out your brother."

Ayla tried not to react visibly, but the queen saw through her.

"Yes, I know who you are," she said, amused. "Storme's twin sister. Ayla."

"He told you, then."

"Even before he told me, I had my suspicions. The two of you share a passing resemblance, but your *mannerisms* . . . It was like dining with Storme and his reflection. You make the same expressions, though his are more muted; he's far better at controlling his emotions. You lack subtlety, handmaiden." Junn gave Ayla a pointed look, as if to say, *You should improve on that.*

It rankled. Ayla remembered Storme's own words the night she'd confronted him in the palace hallway, close to tears, begging for answers: *How did you end up in Varn? How did you become adviser to the queen?*

Why didn't you come back for me?

Storme, infuriatingly calm, had said: *Stars and skies, Ayla. Lower your voice. Control yourself.*

"Your eyebrows . . . ," the queen was saying, arching one of her own. "The twist of your mouth when you're displeased. Yes—like that. He does the same thing. And I knew he'd lost a sister in his home country. The first moment I saw you, I wondered."

"Then . . . you'll let me stay here until he comes back?" Ayla asked. She didn't care for the queen's musings, the way her words circled like seabirds. Why couldn't powerful people ever just get to the point?

"I'd let you stay here either way," said Junn. "I think you could be of great use to me."

Ayla opened her mouth. Shut it again. Considered the risks of telling Junn everything she knew about Scyre Kinok instead of waiting for Storme. A fortnight was so much lost time. But for all she knew, she could have told Storme and he'd say, *We can't tell the queen, she's secretly working with him.* Queen Junn could send out all the green feathers in the world and Ayla still wouldn't trust her one bit. What if she talked and all it got her was a stay in the dungeon?

Queen Junn raised her teacup to her lips, steam curling before her face like the tail of a white cat. "You're clever," she said, taking a sip of liquid heartstone. "If you are anything like your brother, you possess a sharp mind, one for science, for strategy. It's tragic, really, when great minds are limited only by circumstance. You're not a handmaiden anymore, Ayla. Your circumstances have changed, and so have your limits." Her lips, stained deep red with heartstone, curved into a small private smile. "That, and . . . I once knew someone like you. A girl who spent many years trapped in a gilded birdcage, expected only to perform, to sing when urged, to serve, to otherwise be silent. She was never a servant, but that didn't make her free. Her only escape was . . . books. Letters. The outside world existed only in fragments, only behind windowpanes. Except when she read, and when she wrote."

"That's all very pretty," Ayla said. "But there's no shortage of people who are clever or caged. What's the real reason?"

Queen Junn's smile sharpened. "See? Clever girl. For the past year, I have been closely monitoring Sovereign Hesod's correspondences. My spies have intercepted hundreds of letters, documents, and coded messages between him and various members of the Red Council, plus a web of other contacts throughout Zulla. I have read all of them a thousand times over, searching for information on Scyre Kinok and the sovereign's own underground dealings, for any potential threats against Varn.

However, I am an outsider. I have found much of the sovereign's coded language impenetrable. Even your brother and other Rabunians couldn't help. But you, Ayla . . . you lived within the palace walls. You were handmaiden to the sovereign's daughter."

"I can't read," Ayla said bluntly. "I don't think I'll be able to decode anything."

"You can be taught."

"So you want to teach me to read so I can . . . ," Ayla started, then trailed off. No, this still wasn't the real reason the queen thought her useful. This was an excuse, or a test, or just a way to keep Ayla busy; keep her from asking questions. The queen wanted something else from her. Ayla just didn't know what.

Well, if it meant seeing Storme, Ayla could play student. For now.

She hoped the queen really did have ulterior motives. Ayla couldn't see herself being any good at cracking a coded language, no matter how clever she was. There were a thousand different kinds of cleverness, weren't there? Ayla was body clever. Scrappy. She had a certain quickness on her feet, thanks to Rowan. The long afternoons of sparring with Benjy in the middle of Rowan's cottage, once nearly falling backward right into the hearth fire. She'd been trained well. Going suddenly limp—that was all Rowan. *Takes 'em by surprise every time*, she said. Ayla had asked: *Exactly how many times have you needed a quick escape?* And Rowan had just grinned, skin wrinkling like old leather around her eyes.

Thinking of Rowan hurt like a snapped bone.

Ayla had been nine years old when the sovereign's men raided her village and burned it to the ground. The only reason she'd survived was Storme. He'd shoved her into the outhouse, into the pitch-black hole where human waste was pooled knee-deep. By the time she emerged, her entire family was dead—or so she'd thought. She didn't remember the details of the following weeks. Somehow, she'd made her way down the rocky coast to the village of Kalla-den. But the northern winter never passed without claiming a few lives, and Ayla—small, starving, wracked with grief—would have been one of them. It was Rowan who found her on the snowy streets. Took her in, warmed and fed her, said, *Stay, little bird, stay as long as you like.* Benjy had a similar story: abandoned as a newborn, raised in a temple. At nine, he ran away to join the Revolution. Rowan found him and took him under her wing. She was always doing that over the years: mothering lost children, feeding travelers and runaways and anyone who needed it, no matter how young or old.

But she wasn't just a guardian. She was a revolutionary, too. The head of a whisper network, the center of the Resistance in northern Rabu. It was Rowan, too, who had understood Ayla's need for revenge better than anyone.

It was Rowan who'd died on an Automa's sword. Right in front of Ayla. Not even three weeks ago. And it hurt. It hurt, and unlike a snapped bone, Ayla didn't think this would heal.

Ayla took a deep breath, hoping the queen wouldn't notice.

"I can't promise anything," she said. "But I'll try."

Queen Junn leaned forward. Her eyes were the light brown

of driftwood. "Let me make one thing very clear," she said quietly. "If the tides turn my way, Scyre Kinok will be dead by midsummer. And the tides always turn my way, handmaiden Ayla. If there is a force in this world, godly or not, it favors me."

"You rely on good fortune?" Ayla asked, trying to temper her shock. The queen planned to eradicate Kinok. "You rely on gods and stars?"

"I rely on myself," said Junn. "Favored or not."

Ayla took another sip of too-hot tea, considering. She didn't think for a second that killing Kinok was Junn's only goal—after all, what did she stand to gain from his death? There were probably a dozen other plans, a dozen other schemes kept close to the chest, hidden in the shadows. Agreeing to work for Junn felt like walking blindfolded into a pitch-black room, knowing full well the floor was covered with mousetraps and proceeding anyway. But . . .

If anyone were going to kill Kinok, the Mad Queen seemed like a good bet. And maybe Ayla could even do some spying of her own, seeking out any information that could help the human Resistance. For years, her people had been attempting to rise up against the Automae. For years, the attempts had ended only in death.

Rowan's face flashed through Ayla's mind one more time before she raised her chin, meeting Junn's eyes. "You can rely on me as well, your majesty."

"Lovely," said Junn. "Now, as a token of my appreciation, I have a gift for you."

She knew all along I'd say yes, Ayla thought, trying not to scowl. The door to the aviary opened, the guards stepping aside to let a servant through. A pageboy, though taller than most, in the customary green. Head bent in deference, he crossed the stepping-stones and knelt before the platform, offering the queen a small silver box.

"Well?" said the queen, when Ayla didn't move. "It's for you."

Ayla took the box, praying it wasn't full of explosive powder or a poisonous mist or some sort of Made contraption that would stab her in the face—despite the queen's apparent interest in keeping her alive, she wasn't about to trust a royal leech. Trying not to cringe too obviously, she opened the lid.

It wasn't a weapon. It was a bracelet.

Ayla frowned. She tilted the box from side to side, letting the sunlight catch all angles of the bracelet. It was a delicate gold chain with a small blue jewel dangling from it, sparkling in the sun. It was pretty, sure, but—was Ayla supposed to *wear* it? Oh, maybe she could sell it. Discreetly, of course, so as not to offend, but the jewel alone must be worth at least a hundred silver queenscoins. And if that chain was real gold . . .

"Thank you," she said. "It's very beautiful."

For some reason, the queen laughed. "So it is," she said. "But that's hardly the point. Clever girl, you should really be more observant."

"What—?" Ayla started, and then she followed the queen's gaze down to—the pageboy. He was still kneeling in the dirt, motionless, head bent, but now that Ayla was looking, really looking, there was something terribly familiar about those long limbs, that dark curly hair. *"Benjy?"*

Benjy the pageboy looked up. "Hi, Ayla."

Queen Junn left them alone in the aviary, sweeping out of the room with one last quicksilver smile. The guards stayed behind. Ayla climbed down to sit beside Benjy on the edge of the stone platform, ears ringing from the constant birdsong, and couldn't help gaping at him. In a palace like this, she might have been less surprised to see a ghost.

"How," she burst out, the second the door closed behind the queen. "How—what—?"

"I was captured by one of the festival guards," Benjy explained. "Right after you—I actually saw them catch you, I wasn't too far away, but half a second later I was being wres-tled to the ground." He huffed. "They were about to throw me in the dungeons overnight, but we were intercepted on the way there. One of the woman guards, the ones all in green. Said I wasn't going to the dungeons, I was coming with them. So I get handed off, and the woman guard takes me to a *guest room* and tells me to get comfortable. I didn't try to fight it—I figured you were around here somewhere, and I wouldn't be any help if I got myself sent back to the dungeons. Then, this morning—"

"Let me guess," said Ayla. "You got bathed."

The differences were obvious: his curls were sleek and shiny, the grime scrubbed off his skin, the briny rotten-fish-stowaway smell replaced by the scent of perfumed oils. Where he'd been growing the beginnings of a beard while they were on the run, he was now clean shaven, looking younger for it.

He rolled his eyes. "Can't imagine what gave it away."

"For starters, I can see your freckles again," she teased. "But also, they got me too."

"I can tell. You smell like . . ." He sniffed the air dramatically. "Gods, is that lavender?"

Ayla snorted, pretending to shove him away. "I know, it's so much, I feel like Cr—" She cut off, swallowing hard. "Like a lady."

She could sense Benjy looking at her, his gaze intense on the side of her face, but she couldn't look back. She just stared down at her lap, but even that was strange. Her lap wasn't usually dressed in layers of deep blue brocade.

"The queen wants to train me," Benjy offered, quiet. "Brush up on my combat skills, something like that. Did you know some of the guards here are human? Before I came here they showed me the armory. I've never seen so many weapons in my life. Do you think I'd be good at archery? I don't think so. I'm better at close range, I think, because I've got such a long reach." He cleared his throat. "But maybe if—"

"I'm sorry I couldn't kill Crier," Ayla burst out. She'd been holding it in for what felt like a thousand years, ever since the night they'd fled the palace, and here, now, she was breaking. Maybe it was the cold, claustrophobic feeling that she'd simply traded one gilded cage for another; maybe it was the confusion about Queen Junn's motives; maybe it was the dizzying relief of seeing Benjy again, knowing he was okay, that neither of them were alone in this palace, this city, this country. "I'm sorry. I'm so sorry. I ruined everything. I put your life in danger, I could've gotten you killed, just because I couldn't—I couldn't—"

Above them, the birds circled and sang.

"I know you are," Benjy said eventually. He reached out and took her hand, squeezing once. "And . . . I know why you couldn't."

She shook her head, not even sure what she was denying, only that she had to deny it.

"You forget I know you better than anyone else," he said. "You want her. Or love her. Or at least something close. Something just as intense as your hatred." He squeezed her hand one more time and then let go. "I was furious with you. Still am, I think. I won't pretend otherwise. And I won't pretend to understand how you could care for her, after everything. How she became your weak spot. How she turned you soft. But I . . . will try to accept it, I guess. I accept it, I accept—whatever happens. I don't know. Yes, I'm furious, but yes, you're my best friend, and yes, I love you. Till they put me in the dirt and then beyond. We both could have died that night, but here we are. And now we're cooperating with the leech queen herself. In the name of the Revolution, the greater good, in the name of stopping Kinok, but still. It's a compromise. It makes my skin crawl. And I'm doing it anyway."

"Do you think Rowan would want this?" Ayla whispered. "This compromise?"

They both flinched. It was the first time either of them had said Rowan's name aloud since her death.

Rowan, their guardian, their savior.

"I don't know what Rowan would want," said Benjy. "Whether she'd tell us to cooperate with the leech queen or not. But she'd want us to stick together. So I'll do the skin-crawling thing. With you."

Ayla's eyes stung. "Yeah," she said roughly. "Yeah. With you, always, no matter what. Till the dirt and then beyond. But— but what you said—you're wrong." Her fists were clenched. She unclenched them, flexing her fingers. "You're *wrong*. I don't—I could never want Crier. Never love her. I could never love a leech."

Benjy didn't answer for a long time. At last, all he said was, "All right, Ayla," and he said it so *gently*, she wanted to hit him, or cry.

Lessons began the next day after breakfast.

After the handmaidens had cleared away the breakfast dishes and scurried from the room, Ayla sat on the cloudlike bed, waiting. She'd never done anything like this before. The closest she'd come was sitting in on Crier's endless tutoring sessions in the palace library, but those had been so dull—advanced mathematics, diplomacy, the minutiae of events that happened a thousand years ago in kingdoms Ayla had barely heard of. She'd done everything possible to *not* listen.

She didn't know what to expect. But it certainly wasn't Lady Dear.

Ayla hated her on sight.

She was an Automa noblewoman, and everything about her advertised it: the deep violet gown; the jewelry dripping from her throat, her wrists, her ears; the gem-encrusted rings on each finger; the white porcelain comb holding her hair in place. Her skin was the light brown of a riverbed, her collarbone dusted with something that glittered in the lamplight, like she'd smeared stardust across her skin.

"Get that look off your face," was the first thing Lady Dear said after introducing herself, looking down her nose at Ayla. She was older, perhaps nearing fifty, though it was hard to tell with Automae.

Ayla tried to smooth out her expression. Queen Junn's words came to mind: *You lack subtlety.*

"Pay attention, girl," said Lady Dear, and her voice was less cold, more weary, than Ayla might have expected. "Right now, her majesty thinks you could be useful. I suggest you keep it that way."

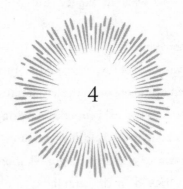

4

Under the weight of what Faye had told her, all thoughts of her own termination seemed insignificant. Crier had to tell her father about Kinok's plans. If what Faye had said was true, if Kinok planned to destroy the Iron Heart, it would be enough to make her father understand exactly what Kinok was capable of—that the Anti-Reliance Movement wasn't just a movement. For Kinok, it meant absolute control, absolute power. The fate of Automakind in his hands. Once the sovereign understood that, of course he wouldn't force his daughter to marry a monster. The wedding would be called off, Kinok would be arrested, and it would all be over.

"Stay here," Crier ordered Faye. The guards outside Crier's door looked surprised, as much as they ever looked anything. Crier pictured herself: dressed for her own wedding, face a rictus of horror and . . . anger, she realized. She was *angry*. She drew herself up to her full height. "Take me to my father."

"Lady Cr—"

"I said, take me to my father," she repeated, voice hard. "Question me one more time. I dare you."

Without a word, they led her through the long corridors toward the north wing, to her father's quarters. Crier tried to calm down. If she seemed at all upset, her father would dismiss her as a child throwing a tantrum; he wouldn't hear a word she said. She had to be completely rational.

Her eyes darted over the tapestries on the hallway walls, the scenes from her people's history: so much imagery from the War of Kinds, always triumphant, a crush of subservient human bodies bowing down to the superior Automae, right there on the battlefield. Crier had grown up surrounded by these images, never really questioning them. She'd read so many books on human history, written so many essays advocating for better treatment of humankind, but she'd never even thought about the war scenes on the walls of her own home. Wars were won by whichever side caused the most suffering. How was that something to be proud of?

Now, a new war. Gathering like shadows as night began to fall. Kinok and ARM versus . . . everyone. A level of suffering Crier couldn't even begin to imagine.

They reached her father's rooms, where more guards were stationed outside his bedchamber. Crier ignored the suspicious looks they gave her and cried out, "Father!"

When Hesod opened the door, he did not look pleased. It looked like he'd been about to leave for the ballroom to make his appearances with the guests; he was dressed in deep red, forehead adorned with a thin band of gold Crier had only seen him wear a couple times before. His red robes were already pinned around his shoulders, the crest of Family Hesod at his throat; he looked less like her father and more like the sovereign than ever before. "Get inside," he said, clipped, and the moment the door closed behind Crier, he rounded on her. *What do you think you're doing?*"

"Father—"

"Your wedding is in less than an hour," he said. "You should be at the ballroom. What in *all hells* are you doing here?"

Crier flinched. She'd never heard her father curse before. "Father, I have to tell you something. Please don't send me away. Please listen." As quickly as possible while still sounding calm and rational and anything other than *terrified*, she told him what she'd learned, careful to leave out any mention of Faye. She kept waiting for his outrage, but his expression remained blank. "Father," she said when she finished and he still hadn't responded. "Father, don't you understand what I'm telling you?"

Hesod was just *looking* at her. Desperate, Crier reached out but was stopped by her father, who gripped her wrist so hard it felt like he might break it. "What are you doing?" she said, struggling against his hold. "Father, please listen to me, Kinok is planning—"

"To destroy the Iron Heart," said Hesod. "Foolish girl. You think I didn't know?"

She froze.

"Foolish girl," he said again. "I Designed you with intelligence, but all you've ever used it for is reading books. You have no understanding of this world. Do you truly believe I don't know what darkness is stirring in my own country, in my own palace? Not all of us are like you, daughter." He squeezed her wrist and she had to bite back a cry of pain. "Why do you think you're marrying him?"

"To . . . ," she whispered. "To . . . bridge the differences between . . . Traditionalism and the Anti-Reliance Movement. To foster an . . . alliance."

"I expected you to see beneath the surface of this union," said Hesod, "but I suppose that was too much to ask. In the past I have overestimated you, daughter; I will not make that mistake again. You are marrying Scyre Kinok because he is a both a threat and a boon. I cannot kill him. If he dies, he becomes a martyr. His followers would rise up against me; half the Red Council would turn. And . . . I no longer want to kill him. His work could benefit me—could benefit all of us—if it's successful."

Tourmaline. He had to be talking about the search for Tourmaline. He just didn't know that Crier knew.

Did her father crave immortality too?

Had he, like Rosi with her Nightshade, fallen for Kinok's lies?

Father, she thought. *What did he promise you?*

"So he cannot die," said Hesod. "But make no mistake: I do not trust him. I want to know what he's doing, now and always. *Keep your enemies close*, as the humans say. Clever little things, they have a saying for everything." He finally let go of her wrist. "That is why you are marrying him, daughter. That is why you were *created*—you, the chess piece, the offering, the sacrifice I am willing to make. I have been playing this game a long time. I always knew there would someday be an enemy I could not kill."

"You knew about his plans," Crier said hollowly. She couldn't even think about the rest of what he was saying. "He wants to rule us all, and you knew, and—what of the humans?"

What would Kinok, all-powerful, do to humankind?

"Do wolves concern themselves with the slaughter of sheep?" said Hesod.

Crier took one step back, and then another.

She looked at Hesod, really looked at him, and tried to reconcile the Automa standing before her with the one who had raised her. The one who had let her sit with him in his study throughout the night, reading books, helping with his correspondences, sometimes even talking politics. The one who had . . . let her do those things, only to smile condescendingly and brush her off when she presented any belief that didn't align with his own. The one who knew how badly she'd wanted a spot on the Red Council, how badly she'd wanted to follow in his footsteps, and had never once, not even for a moment, taken her seriously. The one who thought she was stupid and naive for—for not wanting to be a monster anymore.

"I understand, Father," she said, bowing her head. "You're right, of course. I apologize for my stupidity."

"You test my patience, child," said Hesod. Then, before her

eyes, the cold mask fell away; he became charming, jovial Sovereign Hesod again, entertained by his daughter's naivete. "But you are forgiven, as long as you head to the ballroom at once. The ceremony will begin soon, and the handmaidens will be wondering where you are."

"Yes, Father," she said. "I'll see you there." And she left him.

Inside her chest, there was a hollow where her heart should be. Perhaps there was one thing Crier had in common with Kinok. From this day forward, she no longer believed in family.

From this day forward, Hesod was not her father.

Her mind had gone strangely quiet. She felt so removed from her body, as if she had retreated into some faraway corner of her own head, somewhere soft and soundless. Her body was doing things and she was only watching, a distant observer, curious to see what happened next.

Her body waited until she and her guards were out of earshot of her father's guards. Then her body told her guards to go to the ballroom ahead of her, as her father had instructed her to take a few minutes alone. Her last minutes as a maiden, unbound. When her guards hesitated, her body said, *Sovereign's orders. Would you like to go back there and challenge him yourselves?*

Once alone, her body made its way through the palace to Kinok's quarters. She walked at a steady pace, chin held high, through gilded hallways, down a flight of marble stairs and passed by many guards, and none of them dared to approach her. She reached Kinok's quarters, and her body picked the lock on the door to his study. It was easy; she had done it before.

And he would be upstairs, greeting all the guests, charming and lovely to everyone.

Her body slipped inside. There was a bookshelf behind the desk. On one of the shelves, beside a little glass ball, there was a heavy gold locket set with a red jewel. It looked exactly like the one currently hidden inside her mattress, one story up and two wings over. Her body took it, slipping it down the front of her gown, and left the study.

Her body, moving faster now, traveled back to her room.

Faye was still there, sitting on Crier's bed, staring off into space, and it took her a long moment to react when Crier entered. Like she, too, was here and not-here at the same time.

"My lady," said Faye. "Aren't you getting married soon?"

"No," said Crier. "No, I don't think I am. I need your help, Faye."

Faye gave her a long look. It was so strange, the way she slipped in and out of lucidity, the way she was sometimes reachable and sometimes lost. Maybe it wasn't so strange. "Seems dangerous."

"It is dangerous," said Crier.

"What have I got to lose?" said Faye, and Crier heard: *I have already lost what mattered most.*

Within minutes, Faye had stripped off her clothing and Crier was wriggling out of her wedding gown, frantic, an insect caught in a gossamer spiderweb. She scrambled into Faye's scullery maid uniform: a loose shirt and pants made of rough red fabric, scratchy against her skin, smelling of lye soap and human sweat. Instead of soft slippers, she crammed her feet into Faye's tattered leather shoes. She scrubbed all the makeup off her face, removed all her ceremonial jewelry—keeping only the set of twin lockets—then, with shaking hands, finger-combed her hair out of the ornate crown of braids and tied it back in a single, messy braid, tucked down the back of her shirt.

Finished, Crier glanced at herself in the mirror. She didn't look human. She was still taller than most human girls, and her face was unmistakably Made. But she also didn't look like Lady Crier, daughter of the sovereign.

Good.

"All done, lady," said Faye, turning around. She'd changed into the plainest clothing Crier owned, a simple blue cotton dress. Hopefully simple enough to not draw attention until she could make it back to the servants' quarters and change into another uniform. When she saw Crier, transformed, she snorted. "I've never seen one of your Kind look so . . . ordinary."

"Blue suits you," Crier replied. "Let's go. Before the guards come looking for me."

Together, they hurried out of the bedroom. Heads bent, Crier hoped they just looked like a couple of house servants. The plan was that Crier would make it to the stables, to a horse. Most of the palace guards would be stationed in and around the ballroom by now. If she was going to escape, the window of time was *now*. If she was going to outrun the guards, she needed something faster than an Automa.

They started down the main hallway, but Faye quickly

ducked down another, much smaller and less decorated passageway, used only by the servants. Crier had lived in this palace all her life and had never used any of these passageways. Her eyes always skipped right over them. Now, they were her only chance of escape. The ceremony was due to begin in less than half an hour; the guards had surely realized that her "few minutes alone" had been going on far too long. She calmed herself—she couldn't think about that. She had to keep her heart rate down. The last thing she needed was her chime going off, alerting every guard in the palace that she was in distress.

After what seemed like ages, the passageway ended with a door. "Servants' entrance," Faye muttered, and pushed it open. Crier's eyes adjusted to the sunlight immediately. They had exited the palace just off the north wing. To the east, there were the flower gardens and beyond those the sea. Directly in front of them, across a wide lawn of seagrass, were the stables. Crier could see a row of carriages and caravans belonging to the wedding guests, their horses being tended to by the stableboys.

"Stick close to me, lady," said Faye. "Don't run unless I tell you to."

Crier nodded.

They set off along the edge of the lawn where it bordered the gardens; there was a low stone wall, and it felt a little less like being right out in the open, even though the wall only came up to their waists and didn't offer any actual protection. Crier kept waiting to get caught, kept waiting for someone to shout *There she is!*, but she and Faye reached the stables unhindered.

Probably the guards were still searching the palace. Probably they hadn't even started searching the grounds. Probably Hesod assumed Crier was upset but still his *obedient child* and was just hiding somewhere in the palace, waiting to be found. He'd never thought her capable of anything. He definitely wouldn't think her capable of running away.

The stables were divided into two sections: one for the sovereign's horses, all of them thoroughbreds and warhorses of the finest stock, and the other for the servants' horses, used to pull plows and carry messengers. Faye led Crier to the servants' section and together they pushed through the heavy wooden doors into the cool dark, where the air smelled like hay and the musky scent of animals. All the stableboys were occupied with the guests' horses; Faye and Crier were alone. Quickly, they saddled one of the messenger horses—a young, strong mare who would be used to traveling long distances.

"Where are you going, lady?" Faye whispered as she slipped the bit into the horse's mouth. "You owe me that much."

Crier wasn't sure yet. She had a half-formed plan in mind: First she would go to Rosi's estate, wait for Rosi to return from the not-wedding. Rosi fawned over Kinok. If Crier could convince her that Kinok had planned this, that her disappearance was part of a top-secret plan and he trusted Rosi, above anyone else, to protect Crier, maybe Rosi would harbor her until she figured out what to do next. Where to go next.

Deep down, Crier already knew where she'd be going next. She just didn't want to admit it.

"To find the one person who can stop Kinok," she said, and swung up onto the horse. She'd barely slipped her feet into the stirrups when the doors at the other end of the stables burst open.

"There!"

The guards had found her.

She and Faye looked at each other at the same time, exchanging a horrified glance. Crier started to say, *Quick, get up here with me, come on*, but—

"Go!" said Faye, and struck the horse hard across the flank.

The horse startled, whinnying, and leaped forward through the open stable doors, out toward the sunlight. Crier gasped, turning back to look at Faye—the guards had already reached her, *no, no*—but Faye didn't even look frightened. She was standing stock-still, staring after Crier, even as one of the guards caught her by the throat. The other guards started after Crier, and they were Automae, they were fast, they'd catch up with her and make all of this for *nothing* if she didn't just *go*.

Crier cracked the reins, dug her heels into the horse's sides, and left everything she'd ever known behind her.

The birthplace of the Magick Arts has long been a point of contention among Historians; each kingdom lays claim to that title, each can trace the advent of the Magick Arts to their own court; it remains a mystery which claim is true. However, birthplace or not, one cannot deny the kingdom of Varn—a territory which has gone by many names: from years 311 to 429, under the rule of the clan Ta'en, the golden hills were called Vhi'ros-Kai; after the defeat of the Ta'en by a foreign prince known only as Prince Qell or the Crow Prince, Vhi'ros-Kai became Qell-den; mid—Era 600, the ancestors of the current King Tiren ousted the Crow Prince and took the throne, first naming their kingdom, then about half the size it is now, Varnandanna; by Era 800, the kingdom had expanded west to the edge of the Great Spine, and the name, in contrast, had shortened to Varn—one cannot deny the kingdom of Varn has practiced the Magick Arts for hundreds of years; indeed, one of the first known mentions of the Arts was found in the personal records of a girl whose name has since been lost to time (referred to hereafter as Alchemist X), pre—Era 100, who spent her life in a mining village in what is now southwestern Varn. Alchemist X's writings included extensive notes first on the desire to turn lead to gold, later to define and recreate artificially the human soul; X was fascinated by prima materia, that formless essence, the root of all things. It was Alchemist

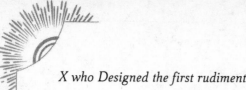

*X who Designed the first rudimentary alchemists'
alphabet, beginning with five symbols: earth, fire, air,
water, gold.*

—FROM *A HISTORY OF THE SOUTHERN TERRITORIES*
BY IVY OF FAMILY FANG-THIEL, 3029510850, E. 900, Y. 19

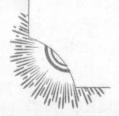

5

Three hours into the first lesson with Lady Dear found Ayla reconsidering whether or not Storme was worth it. Learning to read and write—both her mother tongue and alchemy, the language of the Makers—was frustrating enough without Lady Dear huffing impatiently every time Ayla took more than two seconds to remember a letter.

She already knew some words. She could write her name, Benjy's name, Rowan's. *Automa, human, rebel, heart.* And she could recognize a handful of other words by shape, if not spell them herself. When it came to the language of the Makers, she knew only a few symbols: the eight-point star engraved into the necklace she'd inherited from her mother; the symbols for salt, mercury, and sulfur; body, mind, and spirit. The pyramids of fire and air then inverted to form water and earth. That was it. The written language of Zulla only used twenty-four letters, but even the most basic alchemic alphabet required over a hundred symbols. It was all about memorization, which wasn't Ayla's strong suit.

Lady Dear was seated next to Ayla at the small writing desk, loose pieces of parchment spread out before them, some covered in Lady Dear's perfect, loopy handwriting and some in Ayla's chicken scratch. They'd been at it long enough that afternoon sunlight was falling across the desk, turning the parchment a pale yellow-gold, almost glowing; the black ink looked blue. Dust motes drifted, starlike, before Ayla's eyes. She wished for . . . something. What was it about this? The soft-edged smell of parchment, sharp notes of ink, sunlight warming a room.

A girl at the window seat, bent over a book. Silhouetted against an early winter sunset, light spilling in around her, the sky on fire, consuming itself, blue burning away to reveal the softest pink. A girl looking up as if summoned. A jolt of fear in Ayla's belly: *Did I say her name aloud?*

No, that was a memory. This was now. A country away.

"Think of it like this," said Lady Dear, tapping one long finger on the piece of parchment where she'd written out the Zullan alphabet. "This is the language of storytelling. In Zullan, you write letters, you read books, you record thoughts and memories and messages. Ideas. Dreams, if you have them. You're human— you dream. This is the language of the heart. And this . . ." She indicated one of the long strings of alchemic symbols. "This is the language of science. Of the mind. The language you use to work real magick. These symbols hold a different kind of power, girl. Put them in the right sequence, and you can breathe life into stone."

Heartstone.

The eight-point star on Ayla's necklace. The pendant that, when activated with a drop of blood, had sent Crier and Ayla tumbling into the memories of someone long dead. Siena. Ayla had watched her own grandmother, impossibly young, laughing in the arms of the boy who would later become Ayla's grandfather Leo.

"I'd argue the storytelling language can breathe life into stone too," said Ayla, and then winced. That was something Crier would say. Crier and her faerie stories.

"Clever," said Lady Dear. "Now write out the first fifteen symbols. Fire through gold."

Ayla wanted to groan. What was Queen Junn playing at, really? Aloud, she asked, "Who puts the Makers' language in a letter?"

"Have you heard of the language of flowers, girl?"

"No. What's that?"

"The idea that certain types of flowers carry specific meanings," said Lady Dear. "Red poppies for pleasure; lilies for beauty and purity; camellias for longing. Marigolds for jealousy. White roses for secrecy. Oleander for caution. Combine different types of flowers, and you can construct entire messages. So it goes with the language of the Makers." She leaned back, the stardust on her collarbone catching the lamplight. "And that's why we have eyes and ears on the inside, girl."

Oh—

A memory welled up inside Ayla.

You can be our eyes and ears on the inside, love. Stationed right at the heart of the spider's nest, imagine that. Rowan, eyes lit up, smiling, proud of Ayla. *Stars and skies, birdy.*

Another memory: Rowan, pierced through with a sword. Rowan, crumpling to the ground. Rowan, dying painfully in the middle of a mob; Ayla, trapped inside a carriage, unable even to retrieve her body. Unable to mourn.

She didn't realize she was crying until a teardrop hit the back of her hand.

A silk handkerchief was pressed into her hands.

Ayla looked up. Lady Dear was watching her, expressionless. Ayla took the handkerchief and wiped her face.

The tears ended as quickly as they'd come, but Ayla was left feeling shaky and hollow, as if she'd cried for hours. She stared at her lap, miserable, familiar thoughts circling in her head like vultures: She had been there when Rowan died. Maybe she could've done something. Maybe she could've forced Crier to let her out of the carriage, to push her way through the crowd of humans and Automae, to kneel over Rowan's body and kiss her forehead. Neither she nor Rowan believed in the old gods, but Ayla thought if she'd gotten the chance to send Rowan off properly, she would have murmured: *From light you were born and to light you shall return. Go now into the stars. They've been waiting for you.*

Ayla bit her lip hard, cutting off those thoughts at the quick. She didn't want to start crying all over again.

"You are newbuilt," said Lady Dear, as if just now realizing it. "Newborn. You're a child."

Ayla bristled. "I am *not*. I'm sixteen. Crying doesn't make me a child."

"Being young does. Why do you cry, child? What have you lost?"

"You wouldn't understand." Ayla wanted to be angry, but she was too tired. She was just too tired. "What do you know about pain," she said. "What could you possibly know about grief."

"I have lost people," said Lady Dear.

I have a heart like you, Ayla.

I feel things too.

"You don't feel things like us," Ayla said, not sure who she was speaking to: Lady Dear or the echo of Crier in her head. Either way, she sounded unconvincing even to her own ears.

"We feel things differently," Lady Dear agreed. Her voice was even. "But no less deeply, I would say."

Ayla snorted. "You would say."

"When I was newbuilt," said Lady Dear, "and still lived in the Midwifery with the other newbuilt children, settling into my body, I became close with another girl. Her name was Delphi. Our beds were beside each other in the sleeping room."

"Why are you telling me this?" Ayla mumbled.

Lady Dear ignored her. "We spoke to each other the most," she continued. "Those were strange weeks. Adjusting to your own newly formed mind. Adjusting to your body. Learning how to use it. Learning about our world. Delphi and I studied together. We were . . . friends, I think." She paused. "It is difficult to use human words to describe inhuman relationships. But I think we were friends. I think I loved her. When it was decided that she would be terminated, I felt . . ."

"Wait," said Ayla, straightening up. "Who decided? What was wrong with her?"

"Her pillars were unstable," said Lady Dear. "It happens. The Makers are very skilled, but creating life is a tricky business. Alchemy is not a tool, you see. It is a force, and nobody, not even my Kind, can control it. Work with it, yes. Shape it, yes. Kindle it within a proper vessel, yes. But never control it. Mistakes happen. Mistakes are Made." She held Ayla's gaze. "Delphi's pillars were unstable. It was decided that she would be terminated and remade."

"Then—what happened?" Ayla asked.

Lady Dear cocked her head, a movement reminiscent of the pheasants in Queen Junn's aviary. "What do you mean, what happened? She was terminated. She was remade, I assume, though by then I'd long since left the Midwifery. Even if I'd been there to meet her, the new Delphi wouldn't have been the same as the friend I lost. None of her memories would have remained."

Ayla found herself staring out the window of the bedchamber, reluctant to look at Lady Dear's face. Her window offered a view of the city below; seated as she was in the center of the room, she couldn't see the rooftops from this angle, but she could see the occasional circling seagull. The afternoon sky was the pale blue of sun-bleached fabric.

"Fifty-six years have passed since then. Yet I still think of Delphi every day. My Kind remembers everything, you see. I can recite a thousand different books word for word, no matter how long ago I read them; the details never fade. I wish they did."

"Does it . . . get easier?" Ayla whispered.

"Yes. In many ways, yes. I've heard it compared to missing a limb. The wound heals over. You adjust to this new way of moving through the world. But it always aches, and not just physically, and you never forget what was lost." Her voice was distant, and Ayla wondered if she was sifting through flawlessly preserved memories, if some part of her was in the past.

It was too much. Ayla didn't want to empathize with this Automa noblewoman. She didn't want to empathize with any of them, because if she did—if she did—

"Lessons are over for today," said Lady Dear, surprising her. "They will resume the day after tomorrow. At dawn."

"Why not tomorrow?" asked Ayla.

Lady Dear looked at her. At this angle, her eyes caught the sunlight, flashing catlike gold.

"Did no one tell you?" she said. "Tomorrow is the feast."

As far as Ayla could tell, the feast was meant to honor the Varnian elite who had traveled to Thalen for the Maker's Festival. It was a celebration and a farewell, and would be attended exclusively by the rich and influential. That morning, the three handmaidens

Maris, Renne, and Kiv didn't barge into Ayla's room at the crack of dawn. Someone had left a silver platter of breakfast outside her door, but all the palace servants had been working throughout the night making sure everything was ready for the feast, and the work would continue through the day. Ayla sat in the middle of her cloudlike bed, eating breakfast just because she could, and felt very strange about not joining them. She remembered her first day as Crier's handmaiden: she hadn't even seen Crier for most of the day, she'd just been scurrying around polishing floors and running errands for the kitchen boys as a stream of guests arrived at the palace. Ayla remembered being assigned the impossible task of polishing the entire dance floor by hand; she remembered pushing up her sleeves and getting to it, the lye soap burning her hands. She remembered looking up to see Nessa standing over her, baby Lily strapped to Nessa's front.

Within a month, the child was motherless.

Ayla spent the morning lounging around, which was something she'd never done before. She even went back to sleep for an hour or so: a wild luxury. It was almost ten by the time she heard a knock at the door, the three handmaidens scurrying inside the moment she bid them enter.

"It's time to get you ready for the feast," Renne announced. "And thank the gods. If I have to polish one more spoon I'll scream myself hoarse."

"Wait. What?" said Ayla. "I'm not attending it, am I?"

"You're a *guest* of the *queen*," said Maris.

"Gods smite me down," said Ayla.

She lingered in the bath they drew for her, soaking until the water began to grow cold. Maris washed and oiled her hair, twisting it into a knot at the nape of her neck. Then Ayla was herded over to the mirror, where Maris and Renne set about choosing an outfit for her, and Kiv produced a small box of—makeup? Tiny pots of black eyeliner and rouge, deep red pigment for the lips, shimmery gold dust that resembled what Lady Dear wore on her collarbone and temples.

Ayla was expecting to hate it, but a few minutes later, when Kiv moved aside so Ayla could see her reflection, she found . . . she didn't. The black liner made her eyes look more intense, and the sheen of rouge and gold dust across her cheekbones was . . . pretty. Kiv hadn't painted Ayla's lips with red or purple, as was the trend; she'd just rubbed in a bit of tinted beeswax, the subtlest red. She'd pressed tiny flakes of gold leaf to Ayla's temples, which winked in the light whenever Ayla turned her head.

Ayla had never really given much thought to her own appearance. She'd been a servant since she was eleven; her priorities revolved around keeping Benjy and herself alive, keeping her head down, fanning the flame of anger in her belly, and plotting her revenge on Sovereign Hesod. There were no mirrors in the servants' quarters. Before she became Crier's handmaiden, she hadn't seen her own reflection in who knows how long. She knew what her face looked like, but it was like knowing what her hand looked like. It was there, it was a part of her body, end of story.

But now, gazing at herself—her features, heightened—she

felt . . . something. The girl in the mirror looked like a girl in a tapestry or painting. Like the girls in illustrations of faerie stories. Like a princess or a noblewoman, sure, but also like a witch, or a trickster spirit, a creature that lured unwitting men to their deaths. Ayla felt—maybe the right word was *powerful*.

"Thank you," she said to Kiv. Wrenching her eyes away from the mirror was difficult; she didn't want to stop looking at herself. "You did a good job."

Kiv grinned.

Maris and Renne helped Ayla into her outfit: gold silk trousers and a matching doublet embroidered with the symbols of the Makers. The only piece of jewelry she wore was the bracelet Queen Junn had gifted her, the blue jewel glittering at her wrist.

"I feel like a traveling performer," Ayla said, inspecting herself in the mirror. "The ones who cartwheel through the streets and walk on stilts." She huffed. "Maybe, instead of attending this feast, I could tie the bedsheets into a rope and you three could lower me out the window? It's only a few stories to the ground. I bet I could make it."

"Oh, hush, you," said Maris, cackling. "It's just courtiers and merchant types, dull as anything. You'll be fine. Besides, it's too late to escape—the feast's already begun."

Like the Maker's Festival two days before, the Queen's Feast was held in an open-air courtyard, though this one was smaller and tucked away within the labyrinthine sprawl of the palace, inaccessible to the public. There were two sunken pools, each with a sculpture in the center: two naked women carved from obsidian stone facing each other from opposite sides of the courtyard. One was an Automa, eyes painted gold, arms spread as if in welcome. The other was human, hands curled around the handle of a black stone ax.

There were white rose petals strewn across the flagstones again, strings of paper lanterns casting a warm glow. Along one edge of the courtyard, a massive banquet table was already laden with platters of food. Dusk had deepened to night by the time Ayla entered the courtyard, the moon a silver coin, and about half the guests—mostly Automa, but Ayla saw a few humans among them—were seated, feasting. The other half were mingling in the open courtyard, some swaying to the music of a single harpist, some just talking. Ayla didn't see Queen Junn anywhere, but then, the queen had a flair for the dramatic; she would probably wait until exactly the right moment to make her entrance. Benjy was also conspicuously absent. Had he not been invited?

Ayla was glad for the dark, for the soft yellow light of the lanterns overhead and the candles lining the banquet table. She didn't want anyone looking at her too closely. The lanternlight, softening and obscuring, was a kindness.

Her stomach growled. And Ayla remembered: tonight, she could *eat*.

She filled a plate and began to pick at it slowly. If she'd thought her daily breakfasts were rich, they were nothing compared to this. Here, at the banquet table, she had to pace herself, taking small delicate bites. But if she'd been alone . . . she would have filled her plate three times over, eaten until it felt like she'd never eat again. Ayla had spent years never knowing where the next meal would come from; so many times she'd eaten nothing but stale bread or half-rotted fish for days on end. Now she was sitting at a queen's banquet eating white, flaky fish, meat that practically fell off the bone, sweet bread with butter and honey, some sort of stewed gourd that looked odd but tasted incredible.

"You are Rabunian?" came a voice from beside her.

It took a second for Ayla to realize the Automa was addressing *her*.

She turned. "No," she said, thinking quickly. Any of these guests might be well-connected enough to have heard about her, the runaway servant, the would-be assassin. "I am the daughter of . . . Lord Thom, of the iron mines."

The Automa cocked their head. They were older than Ayla, though it was impossible to tell how much older. Their skin was a rich, deep brown, their hair a lighter gold-shot brown, as was common in Varn. "You look Rabunian," they said.

Ayla just shrugged.

"What is your name, human?" the Automa asked.

"Clara." Her mother's name on her tongue felt at once familiar and foreign. A word in a dead language. "And you?"

"Wender." They leaned forward. Their fine pearl-studded shirt was sleeveless, and the candlelight caught on the corded muscles in their bare arms. "Would you like to dance?"

Ayla hesitated.

"I have no interest in courting you," Wender clarified, looking amused. "I simply wish to avoid potential conversation with . . . everyone. If you will not dance with me, I might simply find a place to hide away until the night ends."

Despite herself, Ayla bit back a smile. "All right, then," she said, getting to her feet. "I've never heard a better reason to dance."

Wender led her away from the banquet table and into the middle of the courtyard, where other dancing couples turned slowly to the music of the harp. A gentle song, like a fall of light rain. Ayla glanced up, and sure enough: she could see a few glittering Made butterflies high above the crowd, floating like sparks in the night air. When she looked down again, a shimmer of light, low to the flagstones, caught her eye. She squinted, unsure what she was looking at. Some sort of . . . moving mirror?

Then the crowd parted, or rather the crowd *was* parted, because the moving mirror was not a moving mirror at all but a peacock. One Made entirely out of colored glass. It strutted through the crowd on spindly glass legs, a massive train of green glass tailfeathers dragging behind it with a horrible scraping noise. Glass on stone. Its body and neck were lapis lazuli blue, its beady little eyes like chips of obsidian. Its beak was pure gold.

Stars and skies, Ayla thought, only just barely managing not to gape at it. She'd never seen a Made object like this. Only ever trinkets, and her locket, nothing bigger than her palm. Well, until the Made butterflies. The sovereign had never been one for displays like this. But here . . .

"Clara?" said Wender.

"Sorry," she murmured, and turned away from the peacock, which continued its slow strut through the crowd. She let Wender put their hands on her waist, her own hands on their strong shoulders. Their Made skin was warm beneath her touch.

"The only reason to attend these things is the gossip," Wender mused, eyes on the crowd. They led Ayla in slow, lazy circles, not quite a waltz, mostly just an organized shifting. "But everyone's been discussing the Rabunian scandal for days, and tonight is no different."

"The Rabunian scandal?" They had to mean the assassination attempt.

"*Scandals*, I should say. The sovereign's court must be in chaos. Things were bad enough before this whole mess with Lady Crier's wedding. Or . . . lack thereof."

Ayla went still. She stopped midstep, frozen as one of the obsidian statues on either side of the courtyard. "Cr—Lady Crier didn't—get married?"

Wender's eyebrow twitched. Automa surprise. "Have you been asleep for the past week?"

"I traveled here from the iron mines," Ayla said. "Been in a carriage. She didn't get *married*?"

"Even better," said Wender, appearing to enjoy having the gossip. They nudged at Ayla's waist, drawing her back into the dance, even as her thoughts roiled like a storm at sea. "Lady Crier ran away from her own wedding. She's been missing for days now; the sovereign's search parties keep returning empty-handed. I hear the sovereign is . . . well. First one of his Red Hands disappeared. Then another two were murdered overnight. Then a servant attacked the lady right under his nose. Now this latest humiliation. I wouldn't be surprised if Sovereign Hesod loses his throne."

Ayla was barely listening. She cast her gaze over the courtyard, trying not to let Wender see the shock in her eyes.

She ran away from her own wedding.

She's been missing for days now.

You fool, Ayla thought senselessly. *You've never left the palace. You think you can survive in this world, a fugitive from your own father? Crier, you fool. Crier, you—*

A familiar face in the crowd. No, two of them.

There was Benjy, visible when the dancing couples shifted, in the very heart of the courtyard. He was dressed like a guard, in the queen's colors, her crest glinting at his throat. He was grinning. He was waltzing.

With Queen Junn.

Ayla stared at them. Yes, that really was Benjy, her best friend Benjy, rebel Benjy, Resistance child Benjy, leech-hating Benjy, waltzing with the queen. And *enjoying it*, by the look on his face, the light in his eyes, his big toothy smile. A space was cleared around them, a loose circle of nobles and courtiers watching them dance. None of them looked surprised. Was it common for the Mad Queen to dance with humans like this?

The queen must have said something, because Benjy threw his head back, laughing like Ayla hadn't seen him laugh in—she didn't know how long. And that was what made the anger rise inside her. That was what kindled the embers. Because *how dare he*? How dare he, when just a few days ago he'd told her that he'd never understand how she could feel anything but hatred for a leech—how a leech had become her weak spot—how a leech had made her *soft*—

"Wender," Ayla said. She knew the anger was leaking into her voice, but she couldn't help it. "Thank you for the dance. I have to—I have to go."

"Are you all right, Clara?" Wender asked, hands falling from her waist. They were staring at her with open curiosity, which, *gods*, that was the last thing she wanted, the last thing she needed; curiosity and suspicion were the same damn thing, in the end.

She started off into the crowd, dodging the other dancers, making a beeline for Benjy and Junn. She didn't even know what she wanted from Benjy—an apology? An acknowledgment of his own hypocrisy? Maybe she just wanted to yell at him, to drag him away and say: *How dare you? Acting like you've got the moral high ground, when in reality—*

"Ayla."

Fingers wrapped around her wrist, an iron grip.

"Get ahold of yourself," Lady Dear said through her teeth. Her expression was pleasant, as if she were only saying hello. "Do not let your emotions get the better of you. I don't know what happened, but whatever it is, it *does not matter*." She tightened her grip on Ayla's wrist. "Don't draw attention to yourself. Not here. It will reflect badly on the queen."

"But—"

"There's a door in the northern wall," she said, still smiling. "It leads to a garden that is sure to be empty. Go *stay there* until you've calmed down."

"Let go of me," Ayla muttered, and Lady Dear finally let go of her wrist. She was so angry she could have pulled a dagger on Lady Dear right then and there, but some modicum of sense remained in her. So she left Lady Dear behind without a second glance, cutting across the courtyard again, but this time not toward Benjy. There was indeed a small wooden door in the northern wall of the courtyard, very plain, most likely a servants' shortcut. She made for it with a desperation that was difficult not to release on the nearest person. The door wasn't locked, and Ayla was able to slip through.

Slamming it behind her, she threw her back against the wall and heaved a few breaths. Tears pricked her eyes.

Crier. Benjy. The queen.

It was too much. Her beautiful clothes felt waterlogged, like the silk weighed a hundred pounds. She couldn't breathe. She couldn't stand all this Automa finery. This fantasy, glittering gold on the surface and rotting beneath, poison to the core.

She lurched forward into the new darkness—the light from the paper lanterns didn't reach here—and saw that she was standing at the lip of a large sunken garden. Stone tiers formed a basin of concentric circles, at the bottom of which was a small sculpture garden. It looked like each tier held a different type of flower, but it was too dark to make out the details as she stumbled down the stone steps, needing only to get away, to be alone and unlooked at, to *breathe*. Her thoughts still burned with the image of Benjy laughing and waltzing in public with the leech queen. The hypocrisy of it all.

No. She knew it wasn't just the hypocrisy that stung.

It was the *wanting*.

The stone steps were rough and uneven. She'd just reached the very last step when she tripped, pitching forward, stomach swooping horribly. Ayla braced herself for a nasty fall—but it never came. She'd been caught by a pair of hands on her waist, holding her upright.

When Ayla looked up into the face of the person who'd caught her, she found her own eyes staring back.

"Storme."

6

Crier had grown up studying the stars. But now, as her horse tore through the thick forest, the night sky was nothing but a shattering of black and silver through the branches. She was lost. Guideless. And weak.

She'd been riding for three days. The terror had slowly peaked and ebbed, turning to a sharp, cold thing stuck in her chest.

On the first day, she'd been haunted by the distant sound of hunting horns. Her father's—no, he wasn't her father anymore. *Hesod's* guards calling out to her. He must have thought she was simply throwing a fit. Running away to make a point, but always with the intention of coming back.

He was wrong.

On the second day, there were no horns, and she was very nearly caught. She'd spent the night in a copse of trees, the most cover she could find in the hills. She hadn't slept at all, but she knew the horse would need to rest. At least it was able to graze, and there were puddles on the ground from a recent rainfall. In the morning, Crier had stood at the edge of the trees, hidden in the shadows, staring out across the expanse of the hills. Ears pricked. Listening, watching, terrified. She'd seen the guards when they were maybe a league or so away—she saw them cresting a hill, movement where there had been no movement. Heart pounding, she'd leaped back onto the horse and run, and run, and run, thinking: *How did they find me? How are they so close?*

Then she'd realized.

Her heart was pounding.

Her chime.

She was such a fool. Of course, it was her chime—a silent signal, triggered by her own distress, synched with the chimes of the palace guards, that would always lead them straight to her location. Once a protective measure. Now her downfall. She'd ridden until she came across a stream wending its way between the hills, snakelike. Even in winter, white wildflowers blanketed the hills like snow. Crier dismounted, waded into the stream, and felt around for a rock with a sharp edge.

When she cut the chime out of her flesh, her violet blood dripped down her spine, down her arms, into the water. It hurt. It was difficult: the chime was in the back of her neck, so she couldn't actually see where she was cutting, and pain made her hands clumsy. But she'd done it. Gasping, eyes stinging with tears, she'd done it. The chime—a tiny gold device, masterfully

Made—found a new home in the bottom of the stream. And she was free.

Truly free.

On the third day, she began to feel the effects of heartstone withdrawal. She knew she had to get some, and soon. Conjuring a map of Rabu in her mind, flawlessly remembered, she tried to figure out exactly where she was. She knew by the sun that she'd been traveling roughly southwest. If she adjusted her course and rode due south, she was bound to hit a village. Those villages were mostly human, but there were always some Automae. Where there were Automae, there was heartstone.

Due south it was.

At twilight, she found a village. She tied her horse half a league away. It was too obviously a thoroughbred, a noble's horse. On foot, slouching to account for her height, she made her way into the village. She kept her head down, eyes on the dirt road. Like how Ayla used to walk behind her in the palace, avoiding eye contact with the guards, with Kinok and Hesod and often Crier herself. It had always bothered Crier. She'd wanted to say: *Look at me. Just—look at me.*

Crier found the village marketplace, a small square with a handful of shops and vendors' stalls. A butcher shop, a cobbler, a bakery. And an Automa-run apothecary. Crier had hesitated for a long time before entering the apothecary. What if someone recognized her? What if the sovereign's guards had tracked her here after all and were lying in wait for her? What if—?

However much I can get for this, she'd murmured to the apothecary attendant in an approximation of Ayla's voice, her commoner's accent. Slurring a little, enunciating less. And she'd passed the Automa woman a thin gold anklet, the only piece of jewelry she hadn't taken off, simply because she'd forgotten it was there. *However much I can get for this. My mistress sent me.*

The woman hadn't even blinked. Because what would a human do with heartstone other than deliver it to their Automa employer? She'd passed Crier three parcels of heartstone in exchange for the anklet, and that was it. Crier had left the village and returned to her horse in a daze, some part of her convinced it was a trick, that the sovereign's guards would spring out from behind a building at any moment.

But they didn't.

Like this, Crier replenished her strength. She hoped enough time had passed that she could safely visit Rosi. What if the sovereign and Kinok had already looked for her there? What if they were waiting for her to show up? Was it really worth the risk? But if she was going to smuggle herself into Varn, she needed more than a set of servants' clothes and a bit of heartstone. Maybe it was foolish, but she didn't know where else to go. There was a chance Rosi might help her, if she played the *Scyre Kinok trusts you* angle. *Even the sovereign doesn't know his plans, so he has to play along with the search for me right now, but—!* and so on. Rosi might lend Crier some coin, some clothes. Might make her feel less alone, if only for a short while.

Now, on the morning of her fourth day as a fugitive, Crier

was headed back east. To Rosi's manor. Provided she didn't run into trouble, she'd get there a couple hours before sunset.

Everything will be all right, she told herself, repeating it over and over again until the words lost meaning, until it was more a mindless, reassuring drumbeat than anything else. *Everything will be all right. Everything will be all right.*

It was a clear, cold day. The hills were yellow with winter, dotted with those tiny white wildflowers (probably stardrops, Crier thought, remembering an illustration in a botanist's handbook), and her mare was trotting along at a steady pace. The sky was a high ceiling of blue, smeared with clouds like white paint. The icy wind felt good on her skin. She'd never gone this long without bathing, and the chill made her feel clean. On a whim, she decided to name her mare Della, after a character in an old faerie story. Della was a servant girl who stole her cruel mistress's dress and snuck into a royal ball, and the youngest princess fell in love with her instantly. The princess and Della were married the very next week, and the cruel mistress was forced to attend the wedding and watch as the servant she'd treated so terribly became a member of the royal family. It was all very satisfying. Things didn't work out like that in real life, but Crier liked the story.

She made good time to Rosi's manor. By late afternoon, Crier and Della crested one of the hills that ringed the manor, which sat in the cradle of the hills like a jewel set in gold. Or—it usually did.

Crier frowned. Every other time she'd visited, even the day

after Rosi's fiancé, Foer, was assassinated by Queen Junn, the manor had looked . . . well, like people lived there. There were always servants around, tending to the orchards and the horse pastures and the livestock pens. Candlelight glowing in the windows, lanterns lit outside the manor gates. But now . . . there wasn't a servant in sight. The pastures were empty, the horses nowhere to be seen. The livestock pens were empty of pigs and goats. The lanterns were dead. Crier squinted: even the orchards looked overgrown, the ground littered with fallen, unharvested fruit.

Her stomach sank.

The last time she'd seen Rosi was just a few weeks ago, when she'd come to pay her respects after Foer's death. At the time, Rosi had been suffering the side effects of Kinok's Nightshade. Her lips and tongue had been stained black, her body skeletal, her veins standing out against her skin. She'd been manic, unable to concentrate on anything for more than a few seconds. She hadn't seemed to care about Foer's death at all.

Rosi . . . what's happened to you?

Slowly, Crier led Della down the hill, the mare picking her way through the crumbling outcrops of rock. It took nearly an hour. By the time they reached the manor gates, the sun was low in the sky, beginning to disappear behind the hills. The closer they got, the more nervous Della seemed. Her ears were laid flat against her skull. She kept pawing at the ground like she was asking to stop.

Crier wasn't faring any better. She couldn't explain it, but it felt like her skin was prickling all over, hypersensitive. She had a death grip on the reins. She didn't want to be here. The silence of the manor was like a living thing, heavy on her shoulders. There was still no sign of any servants. Even the wind had gone silent.

Something is very, very wrong.

But—it was Rosi. There was no real love between them, but Crier had known her for so long. Had exchanged countless letters over the years. If Rosi was in danger, Crier would help her.

She dismounted, approaching the big wooden doors of the manor on foot. It was a large building of granite and dark wood, about a quarter the size of the sovereign's palace, high wooden roof curving up toward the darkening sky. It loomed over Crier as she ascended the stone steps. The dark windows looked like missing teeth.

The door knocker was shaped like a swallow, heavy in Crier's hand. She knocked three times. Was she imagining the way it echoed on the other side of the door, like a shout into an empty hall? She had to be. She was being dramatic. Surely there was a logical explanation for this. Perhaps Rosi had fired the servants for some reason. Perhaps she'd decided to go traveling. Perhaps—

"Lady Crier."

Crier whirled around.

Rosi was standing at the foot of the steps. Crier hadn't heard her approach. She should have heard Rosi approach.

"Lady Crier," Rosi said again, cocking her head to one side, except she cocked it too far, unnaturally far, and did not straighten up again. She stared at Crier, head tilted almost to her shoulder. Gods, she looked so much worse than the last time Crier had seen her. Her gold-brown skin looked pale in the way of dead things, the warmth and color of life sapped out of it. Her hair was thin and loose around her shoulders, and chunks of it were missing, patches of her bald scalp showing like the outcroppings of rock on the hills around them. Her skin stretched grotesquely over her bones. And her veins—her veins were raised and visible, a map of stark black rivers.

"Oh gods, Rosi," Crier breathed. She tried not to show how scared she was. "Rosi," she started, but she didn't know how to finish the sentence. *Are you all right?* was a stupid question. *What happened* was obvious: Nightshade. "Rosi, how can I help you?"

Rosi laughed once, a sharp, hollow sound, too loud. "You fool," she said. She finally straightened up, but only to ascend the first step. Crier fought the urge to back away, to press herself against the door of the manor. "You goddamn fool. You think I need anything from you? Traitor to the throne? Traitor to the *Scyre*?"

"Rosi, I can explain," Crier said urgently. "I can explain everything. Kinok sent me here. We had to call off the wedding due to a threat. He trusts you to protect me."

"Shut up." Rosi ascended to the next stone step, the distance between them shrinking. "Shut your mouth, traitor. You abandoned the Scyre. You betrayed him. You *fool*, do you have any idea what I'd give to be in your place, and you *squandered* it?" She was breathing hard, mouth open. Her tongue was ink black.

Her gaze kept skittering around, eyes practically rolling in her head. "Traitor! Were you in league with the other traitor, Lady Crier? Were you another of Reyka's allies? Answer me!"

Reyka's allies? "I wasn't," Crier said. She held still, but in her mind she was calculating the distance between her and Rosi. The distance between her and Della, who was waiting for her at the gates. Thank the gods Crier hadn't tied her to the gatepost. Thank the gods she was ready to run. "Rosi, whatever you've heard, it isn't true. I didn't betray Kinok." She thought quickly. "I—I wanted to marry him. I wanted nothing more than to marry him. But my father—"

"You liar," said Rosi, and leaped forward.

Crier bolted.

She flung herself off the stone steps, landing hard on the ground. Behind her, Crier heard a terrible noise—as if Rosi, missing her target, had crashed right into the door of the manor—but didn't bother to look back. She just sprinted, running faster than she'd ever run before. Distantly, she was very glad to be wearing pants instead of a long gown.

She reached Della within a matter of seconds and swung up onto her back, nearly overbalancing and falling off the other side, and kicked hard. "GO," she shrieked, her voice raw with terror, "GO, GO!" Della seemed to sense her fear and broke out into a gallop, fast as a racehorse. Only then did Crier dare to look back—and nearly screamed. Rosi was racing after them, but it looked *wrong*. It was like she was running on broken legs, her movements jerky. She kept pitching forward, fingers clawing at the ground, dragging herself upright again. She wasn't going to catch up with them, but still Crier felt sick. Rosi's body was breaking down. The Nightshade had eaten away at her, first her muscles and then her mind.

What a terrible way to die.

Crier urged Della forward, back up and over the hill. She didn't want to stop until she was far away from the manor, from Rosi, from the monster Rosi had become. A fur of trees was visible maybe half a league away, the promise of shelter. The sky deepened from blue to the purple of the gloaming as Crier rode toward the trees, the sun sinking at her back. "Just a little farther," she told Della, reaching down to pat her neck. The mare's coat was foaming with sweat. "Just a little farther."

The fur of trees turned out to be a small wood of skinny, white-barked birches, naked with winter, like finger bones rising up out of the earth. The cover was scarce, but it was still better than being out in the open. Crier felt better the second she and Della broke the tree line. The ground sloped downward, and she could even hear the rush of a river at the bottom. An unexpected blessing: Della could drink her fill, and maybe in the morning Crier could bathe. Della had slowed to a walk, and Crier led her downhill toward the sound of the river. The spaces between the trees was so narrow. Twigs kept catching in Crier's hair, plucking at her sleeves.

It was very quiet here.

Crier realized that she could hear the river so clearly because there was no birdsong. It was dusk. There should have been birdsong, sparrows and swallows and little black noonbirds sing-ing to the coming night.

Her skin was prickling again.

But she'd left Rosi far behind. She hadn't been followed. She would have seen another rider coming over the hills.

Still, Crier tightened her grip on the reins. She and Della reached the bottom of the slope, where the trees thinned and then gave way to the banks of a river, more white trees on the other side. The slow-moving water sparkled in the last rays of sunlight.

"We'll cross the river," Crier whispered to Della, nudging her forward. The river was very shallow, the sand and stones at the bottom visible all the way across. They'd cross over and find a place to camp for the night. Crier had no choice. Della had to rest after such a brutal ride.

Della hesitated at the edge of the river, but Crier soothed her, murmuring in her ear, and she stepped into the water.

They were exactly halfway across when the first Automa emerged from the trees.

Crier saw it on the opposite bank, right ahead of her. A frac-tion of a second later Della went stock-still beneath her.

The Automa looked like Rosi, if Rosi had already died.

It had the same black veins. The same skeletal frame. But it was naked and its skin was sagging off its bones, peeling open in some places to expose the shiny, metallic muscles below. The nerves like golden hairs. The veins like black worms. Its eyes, sunken deep into the sockets, were pure black. As if the pupil had swallowed everything else. Its ink-stained mouth was hanging open, jaw dangling loosely, dislocated.

Crier couldn't think.

Her mind had gone completely blank.

All she could do was stare at the Automa—*was* it an Automa, still?—as it picked its way out of the trees and down the riverbank. The thing that had been an Automa once, like her.

Its black eyes were fixed on Crier's face.

A noise came from behind her, a fall of pebbles into water, and despite herself Crier turned to look. She immediately wished she hadn't. There was another black-veined Automa on the bank she and Della had just left. It was looking at her too, opening and closing its mouth, like it was trying to say something or—or like it was chewing.

Oh gods.

Crier had no weapon. Even if she did, they were coming at her from both sides of the river. She was trapped in the center, the perfect prey, frozen with terror. She tried to think. Tried to come up with an escape plan. But her brain wasn't working. All she could think of was—maybe if she and Della ran downstream, following the river—but Della would be slower moving through water, and what if it got suddenly deeper later on?

The Automa in front of her reached the edge of the water. It was barely twenty paces away now. Like Rosi, its movements were jerky, awkward, like it didn't have full control over its body. Crier tried to think. She was supposed to be brilliant, Designed with inhuman intelligence, why couldn't she *think*? The Automa took another step into the water, mouth opening even wider. Too wide, like a snake unhinging its jaw. But then Crier heard a sharp *crack*, and the Automa twitched hard. It went stiff all over, a puppet with its strings pulled tight, and staggered sideways, letting out a low, rasping noise, wordless and awful. Its body twisted as it fell, and Crier understood why.

Someone had just shot it through the skull with a crossbow. The iron bolt was sticking out the side of the monster's head, black blood already oozing from the wound. Crier whipped her head around to look at the other Automa—just in time to see a second crossbow bolt bury itself in the Automa's chest and a third in its face, piercing it right through one of the soulless eyes. Crier gasped and looked away, sickened. She heard the splash when it fell.

Was she safe?

Or was she the next target?

Who's there? she wanted to call out, but she couldn't speak. Fear had paralyzed her throat. Beneath her, Della was panting with terror, trembling all over, muscles twitching.

She didn't have to wait long for an answer. There came a shout, and then *humans* burst out of the trees ahead of Crier, running down the bank. They were armed, some with crossbows, some with swords at their hips or strapped to their backs, and some with burning torches, their faces illuminated in flickering orange light.

"Get ready to burn!" one of the humans shouted, the first one to reach the water. He waded in without hesitation, grabbing the body of the dead thing and dragging it back to shore, dumping it on the rocks. "Bree, Mir, get the other one!" Two of the other humans immediately splashed into the river and headed for the second body, ignoring Crier entirely. Numb, she watched as the rest of the humans—maybe eight or ten in total—crowded around the first body, taking out waterskins and dousing it with . . . water?

No.

Oil.

The other two humans, carrying the second body between them, rejoined the others on the banks. They dumped it next to the first, and it too was doused with oil. Then one of the humans armed with a torch darted forward and set the bodies ablaze.

It all happened very fast. Shooting the black-veined Automae, retrieving their bodies, setting them on fire. The humans were efficient, methodical, like they'd done this before. Crier still wasn't breathing. She should probably be breathing. She should probably be spurring Della away, racing back the way they'd come. She knew burning was one of the best ways to kill her Kind. Severing the head, stabbing the heart, burning the body so it could not heal. What if she was next? She took a deep, shuddering breath. She had to get *out of here*.

"Hey!" one of the humans called out. It was the one from before, maybe the leader, the one who'd been shouting orders. He was standing at the edge of the riverbank, silhouetted against the leaping fire behind him. He was looking at Crier. Some of the other humans had turned to look at her too. "Are you all right?" he called. "Are you hurt?"

She opened her mouth and nothing came out.

"It's okay," he said, voice raised so she could hear him over the crackle of the flames. "It's okay, you're safe."

She stared at him.

Distantly, she registered that the air was beginning to smell of burning, melting flesh.

"Are you alone?" the human boy called out.

He thinks I'm human, she realized. *He thinks he just rescued a human girl. He thinks we're allies.*

She nodded. Yes, she was alone.

"Well, not anymore," said the human boy. "We're camped nearby. Come with us. You can warm up, get something in your belly. No offense, but you look like you're about to keel over. Both you and your horse."

Crier found her voice again. "Okay," she agreed. "I'll come with you."

She said it like a human.

A,

In the beginning, you told me about the law of falling.

How did I reply? Did I reply? I remember everything, yet I do not remember that. Surrounded by the familiar, you'd caught me off guard. As with the night before—you on the cliffs, you in the sea spray, you, saving me, the first of many times. You touched the tears on my cheek. You touched my face and even then, in the beginning, I did not pull away.

A law for a paradox. I'll trade you.

We believe the Universe birthed an infinite number of stars. By this logic, you could stand anywhere in this world and look up at the night sky and your line of sight would inevitably end on a star. By this logic, the night sky shouldn't be dark at all; it should be a blinding wash of starlight. Therein lies the paradox. The problem is the assumption that the Universe is static, unmoving; that every star has always occupied the same space in our sky. The paradox doesn't account for the fact that the Universe, like all things, was born and has been growing ever since. Expanding outward—pushing, pulling, as you told me. Celestial bodies floating in a black sea, carried by a current older than life. Drifting farther and farther apart. The nature of the Universe is that everything inside it becomes lonelier and lonelier

*and lonelier. Some nights I can think of nothing else,
and nothing more terrifying. Some nights I lie awake,
thinking of this, and it makes me unspeakably sad.*

Not as often, these days.

Because it's you.

*It's you, the wash of starlight, the old paradox: if
the Universe were static, I could stand anywhere in this
world and I swear my line of sight would end on you. I
swear I'd find you in the dark.*

—FROM AN UNSENT LETTER BY CRIER OF FAMILY
  HESOD, 9648880130, YEAR 47 AE

7

"Storme," said Ayla, and watched as shock rippled across
Storme's face when he realized exactly who he'd just saved
from a nasty fall.

"*Ayla?*" he said, gaping at her.

He let go of her waist, taking a step back. Ayla found her
footing on the grassy lawn of the sculpture garden. "What are
you doing here?" she asked. "I thought you weren't due back for
another week."

"What am *I* doing here?" Storme demanded, still staring at
her with huge eyes. "What are *you* doing here? Since when are
you not in *Rabu*? Since when did you leave the sovereign's palace?" He sucked in a breath. "Oh gods, are you connected to— I
heard rumors of an attack, and now the sovereign's daughter has
gone *missing*, are you—but also—how did you get here? How
long have you—?"

"Storme!" Ayla broke in. "Breathe. One question at a time."

She couldn't help but study him, drinking him in. Their time together in Rabu had been so limited; Queen Junn's company had spent only a day and a night in the palace, and Ayla had only gotten Storme alone the one time. At night, in a moonlit corridor. And it had gone so wrong. All Ayla had wanted to do was embrace her long-lost brother, but instead they'd ended up exchanging awful, poisonous words, and then he'd turned his back and stalked away, leaving her alone. Again. And—furious, miserable, confused—she'd sought comfort in Lady Crier's bed.

Now she looked at him, this grown version of the nine-year-old twin brother she'd lost. They weren't identical twins, they'd looked more alike when they were children, but Ayla could still see herself in Storme's face. They had the exact same eyes, big and brown and wide-set. The same brown skin, the same dark, untamable hair. Ayla's face was rounder. Her features more elfin, her freckles more pronounced—she'd spent so much time working under the hot sun. Storme was more classically handsome. He'd gotten their father's cheekbones and strong chin. (And, frustratingly, their father's height.) Then there was the pale starburst scar over Storme's left eye. The result of a silly childhood accident involving the edge of the stone hearth. It was strange seeing that familiar scar on such a changed face.

Storme was dressed in green, though not for a ball. Ayla frowned. Her brother looked a little ragged, honestly. Even in the dim moonlight, she could tell his clothing was wrinkled, his hair limp and unwashed.

"One question at a time," he agreed, then grimaced. "No, *no,* wait. I want to hear everything that's happened, everything that brought you here, but I have to see J—the queen. It's urgent."

"What? No!" said Ayla. "No, Storme, I've been waiting for you to return, I have so much to tell you, it's important. I came to Varn for a reason."

"I'm sorry," he said, already looking past her. "But I returned early for a reason, too. I have to see the queen immediately, Ayla. It cannot wait. We'll talk tomorrow, all right? I promise we'll talk. Just not right now."

"No," she said. "Storme, I don't want to wait until tomorrow." She wanted to tell him about Scyre Kinok's Nightshade, but more than that . . . there was still a part of her that felt like she was talking to a ghost. They'd seen each other so briefly in Rabu, and then he'd been gone again, leaving nothing but a green feather behind, like something out of a folk tale: a boy transformed into a bird by a witch's curse, his desperate sister searching for him everywhere. What if Ayla let him out of her sight and he disappeared again? She tried to grab at his sleeve, but Storme sidestepped her, starting off into the darkness. Ayla bit back a noise of frustration and followed. When she caught up to him, she said, "Fine. The queen first. But I'm coming with you."

He huffed, sounding so much like the young Storme who used to scowl and roll his eyes whenever Ayla tried to boss him around. "Fine, come along, then."

"I will," she said. "Let's go, brother."

Queen Junn's solarium was a large many-windowed room with a massive hearth and walls lined with portraits of what must be the royal lineage. Seated around a low wooden table with Benjy and Junn, studying the portraits while she waited for someone to speak, Ayla was reminded again how young Junn had been when her father, the king, had been murdered, and she'd been forced to take the throne. It was difficult to tell an Automa's age after they hit twenty or so; in accordance with their longer lifespans, the physical effects of aging were far subtler on their Made faces. Still, the Automae in the portraits were clearly older than Junn by a few decades at least. In Rabu, they called her the Bone Eater but also the Child Queen. Ayla had always found it ridiculous: Automae were never children, not really. But the more time she spent around Junn, the more she understood the title. For all Junn's cleverness and authority, she was still only a couple years older than Ayla and Storme. It showed on her face, sometimes. It showed on her face now.

"What do you mean, *monsters*?" Junn said, staring at Storme. Like Ayla, she'd come straight from the ball, which was still going on in the courtyard far below. Even this high up in one of the palace towers, Ayla could hear voices and music floating through the night. She kept waiting for Junn to send her away, because Ayla clearly didn't belong in this meeting, but it hadn't happened. Perhaps that was another benefit of being Storme's sister.

When Junn had visited the sovereign's palace, Ayla had noticed a familiarity in the way she spoke to Storme. An odd warmth in the way he looked at her. Somehow they'd seemed more like friends than queen and adviser.

"I don't know how else to describe them," said Storme. In the lanternlight, it was even more obvious how disheveled he was. He glanced at Ayla. "Two weeks ago, we received disturbing messages from two of our largest heartstone traders, alerting us to an 'ongoing threat' along the border we share with Rabu. I arrived expecting bandits, human rebels, perhaps some trouble from the sovereign . . . but that's not what I found. I understand now why the traders were reluctant to describe the threat in detail. It sounds unbelievable. But I saw it with my own eyes."

"Get to it," said Ayla and Junn at the same time, and then blinked at each other across the table.

"The trading caravans keep getting attacked by these . . . *creatures*," said Storme.

"What, like animals?" Junn asked.

"No. They are wild like animals, vicious like starving wolves, but they are Automae. Or at least something close." Storme's gaze was fixed on the lantern in the center of the table, on the tiny flame trapped like a firefly within the glass. "The creatures look like Automae, but—Made wrong. Their eyes and veins are pure black. Their mouths, too—it always looks like they've been drinking ink. At first I thought perhaps they were victims of some sort of plague that affects Automae. But they aren't weakened by this—affliction. The opposite, actually. They're almost unstoppable. They don't seem to feel pain. If they attack something, they will not stop until that thing is destroyed. I have seen them keep fighting with all four limbs broken. With swords sticking out of their bellies. With their faces blown off by powder bombs."

Horrified, Ayla tried to imagine such a creature. Something . . . stronger than Automae? More violent? Even less human? Storme was right, it sounded unbelievable. Except something he'd said had caught in Ayla's mind. *It looks like they've been drinking ink.* Ayla knew exactly what that looked like, because she'd seen it before. Crier's friend Rosi, the one whose fiancé had been murdered. Ayla hadn't seen much of Rosi when she and Crier visited Rosi's manor. The two Automae girls had spoken privately, Ayla dismissed to stand outside the door. And then, on their way back to the palace, Elderell had happened: Ayla had watched, helpless, as Rowan was killed by an Automa guard. In the wake of Rowan's death, Ayla had forgotten all about Rosi's odd behavior, her ink-stained mouth.

Until now.

Ayla noticed Queen Junn didn't seem at all shocked or even unsettled by Storme's words. Her eyes were alight with *something*, but it wasn't fear.

"What of their minds?" Junn asked. "If they're launching organized attacks on the trading caravans . . ."

Storme shook his head. "Thing is, the attacks *aren't* organized. I honestly don't think they're trying to sabotage our heartstone supply. I don't even think they're aware of what's inside the trading caravans; I don't think they have the capacity to be aware of anything at all. They're attacking the caravans because they're *there*. If it were a traveler's carriage, a single rider, Automa, human, a commoner, the sovereign himself, the outcome would be the same. These creatures are mindless. If something crosses into their territory, they will kill it."

"And what is their territory?" Junn asked.

"The border between Rabu and Varn," said Storme. "And some parts of Tarreen, apparently. Why they're so concentrated in southern Rabu, I don't know."

But I do, Ayla realized. *I know why.*

"It's Kinok," she said, drawing their attention. "Ever since the Southern Uprisings, he's had a lot of followers in the south."

The Southern Uprisings. When hundreds of human servants across the southern estates had planned to revolt on the same night, at the same time, so the Automa nobles couldn't help or warn each other. But somehow Kinok had found out and warned the nobles far in advance. The humans' plan hinged on the element of surprise, and there was no surprise. The uprisings were quashed fast and bloody. And Kinok was a hero.

But Ayla and Crier had discovered that Kinok had been able to predict the uprisings because *he'd been the one to instigate them*. He'd used his web of connections to spread false information, manipulating the humans of the southern estates into planning a rebellion doomed from the start.

"He's been tricking his followers into replacing heartstone with a substance called Nightshade," Ayla continued. "It looks like heartstone dust but black. He tells them it's a more powerful heartstone, that it'll make them even stronger, sharper. But I've seen its true effects." She told Storme and Junn about the visit to Rosi's. She recounted Rosi's black-stained tongue, her body starved to bones, her shaky, erratic movements. "She wasn't violent, but it can't be coincidence. Maybe if you consume enough Nightshade, you turn into . . . that."

Storme looked troubled. "If that's true, and Scyre Kinok is behind this . . . What's he planning? Is he just trying to create an army of monsters?"

"But what you described doesn't sound like an army," said Junn. "You said the creatures are mindless. That they cannot be controlled. I don't believe this is Scyre Kinok's master plan— above all else, he craves control. What does he stand to gain from this?"

"Maybe it's about fear, intimidation," said Storme. "Like a warning to his other followers. A display of power."

"No," said Ayla, mind racing. "That doesn't make sense. I think . . ."

What did she know about Kinok? He had the mind of a scientist, an alchemist. He was a former Watcher of the Heart, as well as a Scyre—someone who studied the Four Pillars of the Automae in the name of advancing Automakind. He wanted to end his Kind's reliance on the Iron Heart, their weak spot.

He'd created Nightshade himself. Crier had said, *He wants us to be invulnerable.* He'd sent it not to his enemies but to his followers. Like Rosi, who *worshipped* him. Ayla had seen it herself, when she and Crier had visited Rosi's estate: the way Rosi's eyes lit up at the mere mention of Kinok's name. She adored him.

And yes, above all else: Kinok craved control.

"I think he made a mistake," Ayla said, hearing the realization in her own voice. "Why would he want to turn his most loyal followers into mindless killing machines? I think he didn't know what Nightshade would do to them. I think he was just testing it out on them, maybe. Experimenting. But he didn't know it would poison them like this."

Silence for a long moment.

Then Junn said, "I knew you'd be useful."

Storme looked troubled. "Your majesty, I think we should send reinforcements to the border immediately," he said. "The traders are well armed, but only against human rebels. Already two traders have been killed, their caravans destroyed. Varn's entire heartstone supply is in jeopardy."

Junn nodded. "After we end here, go directly to the marshal. I want reinforcements ready to depart at dawn."

"Yes, your majesty."

"In the meantime, do you think it feasible to use the old trade routes? We've plenty of records and maps."

"I had the same thought, but I don't think it'll work," said Storme. "Those routes were targeted during the War of Kinds—bridges destroyed, passes blocked by rockfall. They haven't been usable for fifty years." A cautious note entered his voice. "We don't need old routes. We need new weapons."

New weapons?

The queen's eyes narrowed. "I assume you are not speaking hypothetically, adviser."

Storme straightened up, as if the mention of his title made him want to appear worthy of it. "As I said, the monsters have appeared in some parts of Tarreen as well. But it seems the Tarreenians are not quite so helpless as the heartstone traders. I spoke with a trader who passed through Tarreen and saw this weapon in use. He didn't know exactly what it was, but he described it as 'blue fire.' Like a powder bomb but much more powerful—he said it took out twenty monsters at once. An explosion of blue fire, he said."

"But it's not being used by the Rabunians," Junn said slowly. "It didn't come from the sovereign. The Tarreenians created it themselves."

Storme nodded. "And if the sovereign wants it, he'll have to take it by force. He might claim to rule over Tarreen, but he has no real foothold there. The Tarreenians are mostly human, after all. He provides nothing for them; he barely acknowledges their existence. The Tarreenians are few, but they rule themselves. And even the Automae among them despise Sovereign Hesod." He met the queen's eyes head-on, and Ayla had to admit he did look like someone who could advise a queen. Young as he was, obnoxious as he was when they argued, he was worthy of his title, and despite everything Ayla felt a rush of pride. "Your majesty," he continued, "if we can forge an alliance with the Tarreenians, perhaps we can use this new weapon."

"I need to *think*," Junn said, sounding like the girl she was. "I need to think. And you need rest, adviser. When was the last time you slept?"

"Two days ago, I think," said Storme, sounding almost sheepish.

The queen sighed. "Go to the marshal, and then to *bed*."

Ayla glanced between them. They definitely seemed more familiar than queen and adviser. She could have sworn she'd seen a flicker of warmth in Junn's eyes just now, even as she reprimanded Storme.

Then again, Ayla thought sourly, Junn had been dancing and laughing with Benjy just a couple hours ago. Maybe she was overly familiar with everyone.

The three of them parted. Ayla wanted so badly to grab Storme's sleeve, to keep him close, to make sure he wouldn't disappear again, but she knew that was a childish urge. It had been a long night, two days without rest for Storme, and they both needed sleep.

He'd promised they would talk tomorrow. Ayla would believe him. She had to. Her brother was back from the dead— she wouldn't let him disappear a second time.

8

The humans' camp was a ways down the river, hidden within a copse of fir trees. It was really just a small section of forest floor with the undergrowth cleared away, creating enough space for a campfire and a few sleeping mats. Another pony was tied nearby, a fat little roan. The humans rode ponies and workhorses, not thoroughbreds like Della. Crier was hoping they wouldn't notice how fine Della was. During the short ride to the campsite, Crier came up with a backstory for herself. It was a welcome distraction from the horror of the past few hours: Rosi attacking her, the monsters on the riverbanks, their burning bodies. Crier decided she was a human girl from the northwest, the foothills of the Aderos Mountains—far from the capital city and the sovereign's palace. Her parents were dead and she had no siblings. She was on her way to the port towns on the coast of the Steorran Sea, where she would board a ship for Thalen, the capital city of Varn. She was going to Varn because Rabu held nothing for her anymore.

When the human boy who'd first called out to her asked her name, Crier said, "Ayla."

The name was melted sugar on her tongue. Then bitter metal.

"Well met, Ayla," he said. "I'm Hook."

She'd just nodded. The less she spoke, the less chance there was of revealing herself as an Automa. Hook didn't seem to care if she was talkative or not. He was a nice-looking human boy with a wide, toothy smile. He couldn't have been older than twenty, and Crier wondered how someone so young had become the leader of a group like this. Then, surreptitiously glancing around at the seven other humans, Crier realized Hook was the oldest. The others looked around Crier's age or even younger. And she'd just watched these humans kill two monsters and set the bodies aflame without a moment of hesitation.

What happened to you all? she thought. *What drove you to this life?*

But perhaps she already knew the answer.

Now, sitting in a circle with them around a low-burning campfire, forcing down bites of hardtack and salted fish, Crier kept her eyes down. The fire was little more than smoldering embers—Hook had explained that the monsters were drawn to light—but she was still paranoid about her eyes refracting gold. Exposing her in a heartbeat, in a blink. It was more difficult than she might have expected to keep up the act, and she'd only been doing it for an evening. But there was so much to remember:

breathe evenly, blink regularly, don't hold too still, don't move too smoothly, keep your eyes down, for skies' sake don't speak like the daughter of the sovereign. She was immeasurably grateful for the grime on her face, obscuring her Made skin.

"So, Ayla," said Hook, once they'd all eaten their fill. "What brings you to these parts? Fool move riding alone through Shade territory like this, isn't it?"

"What do you mean, 'Shade territory'?"

Hook's eyes widened, and suddenly all the rebels were looking at Crier. Their expressions ranged from startled to curious to . . . wary. "I thought word had spread just about everywhere," said Hook. "The whole south is dangerous right now, my friend, from the western mountains to the eastern shores. It's especially bad here, so close to the southern estates. You really haven't heard anything?"

"Been alone for weeks now," Crier mumbled.

"Well, all right. Here's what you should know: those black-eyed things, we call 'em Shades. They used to be Automae. But they're even deadlier than your average leech—they're stronger, faster. They don't feel pain, as far as we can tell, or if they do it doesn't stop them. They're violent. Bloodthirsty. And they're near impossible to kill unless you know exactly how to do it. Get too close and you're dead meat. Welcome to hell."

One of the other humans raised her waterskin. "Hurrah!"

"Why do you call them Shades?" Crier asked.

"They got like that by taking some sort of fake heartstone, or poisoned heartstone, maybe. It's called Nightshade. Nobody knows exactly what it is, only that it turns leeches into monsters."

So her suspicions were correct. This was the end result of Kinok's Nightshade. This was what had happened to Rosi. And this had to be why Kinok was so desperate to find Tourmaline. His experiment had failed.

He must be furious.

Crier almost smiled, until she remembered the Shades were her own Kind. Those two Shades from the river—who were they? Nobles from the southern estates? Travelers? Just two Automae from a nearby town? They had to be Kinok's followers, supporters of the Anti-Reliance Movement, but still. Nobody deserved a fate like that.

Kinok does, Crier thought, surprising herself.

"Where does Nightshade come from?" she asked Hook, still trying to figure out how much these humans knew.

He exchanged a glance with one of the others—the one who'd said *Hurrah*. She was either Bree or Mir, one of the two who had retrieved the second monster's body and dragged it across the river to be burned. Unlike the others, she looked more Varnian than Rabunian, with curly hair the color of summer wheat.

Bree-or-Mir leaned forward, the glowing embers casting odd shadows across her face. "If you've been traveling alone for so long . . . how much do you know about the Scyre called Kinok?"

How much would Ayla, the runaway human from the northwest, know?

No, that wasn't the right angle to take. Crier wanted as much information about Kinok as she could get, anything she could use to take him down, and she had no interest in protecting any of his secrets. As long as she didn't say anything that incriminated her as Lady Crier, she could tell these humans anything. They wanted the same thing she did, in the end.

"The last time I stopped in a village," Crier said, choosing her words carefully, "I spoke with a servant girl who had escaped the sovereign's palace."

Now she had everyone's attention. Eight pairs of eyes were fixed on her.

"I'll trade my information for yours," she said.

Hook snorted. "Fair enough, my friend. But all we know is Scyre Kinok's connected to Nightshade. We've got a contact—well. We had a contact." He closed his eyes, tapping his sternum with two fingers, and the other rebels did the same. Crier quickly copied them. "May the stars find you well, Rowan," Hook said softly.

"Stars find you well," the humans murmured in unison, but Crier was too stunned to do the same. *Rowan.* She knew that name. Rowan, the woman from the riot at Elderell—a village barely a day's journey from here. The woman Ayla knew. The woman who had been killed right in front of them, throwing Ayla into a silent, blank-eyed grief.

"Before she died, Rowan was the best contact we had. The best any of us had. She said the Scyre created this Nightshade. As a backup plan, maybe. The leeches know if the Iron Heart runs out of heartstone—or, better, we're finally able to destroy it—they're doomed. They're probably terrified." He sounded quite pleased about it.

We're finally able to destroy it.

These weren't just humans traveling in a group. They were part of the Resistance.

If only they knew they weren't the only ones who wanted to destroy the Iron Heart.

"Your turn, Ayla," said Hook, and it took Crier a moment to realize he was addressing her. "What did your runaway servant girl tell you?"

Crier took a deep breath. "That you're right," she said. "Scyre Kinok is searching desperately for an alternative to heartstone." She cleared her throat, focusing on her accent, on sounding like the human commoner she was supposed to be. "He thinks the answer is a stone called Tourmaline. He's trying to find it. He'd—he'd do anything to find it. If someone else gets to it first, they'd have—"

"Leverage," said Hook.

"Power," breathed Bree-or-Mir.

"Every leech in Zulla by the throat," said a third rebel, a boy with an empty socket where his right eye should have been.

Crier nodded. "Exactly."

"Well, well, well," said Hook. When he leaned forward, the firelight turned his deep brown skin to burnished gold. "Damn good thing we saved you from the Shades, Ayla. You should stick with us, yeah? Where are you headed?"

"Varn," said Crier.

It clearly wasn't the answer he was expecting, but he just grinned wider. "If anyone can get you there, my friend, it's gonna be us."

And for the first time since running away from the palace, Crier felt almost safe.

An hour or so later, the fire had been put out and the rebels were settling in to sleep. Bree-or-Mir, who turned out to be Bree, had been assigned first watch. Which meant Crier would have to actually fake sleep for the next few hours. She'd offered to take the second shift, but Hook had told her, not unkindly, that they didn't trust outsiders, no matter how useful. Then he'd given her a sleep pallet and a thin, scratchy blanket and bid her good night.

So Crier spread out her pallet under a wide-bellied fir tree and resigned herself to being wide awake until dawn. She didn't want to sleep, not when she knew there were Shades out there. She wished she could have told Hook: *I can see in the dark like a cat, I can hear a twig snap from a hundred paces away, and there's no chance I'll fall asleep. I am the perfect lookout.* But of course she couldn't.

Perhaps it was a good thing, though. In the darkness, under the cover of low branches curving down to brush the dirt, Crier pulled Ayla's locket out from beneath her shirt, leaving its twin in her pocket. The token she'd held so many nights to give herself comfort. It felt like being close to Ayla. And she had eventually realized it wasn't just that it had belonged to Ayla—the locket was a Made object, created by Ayla's grandmother Siena, then gifted to Ayla's grandfather Leo. It was always him at the center of these memories. She'd come to learn the locket—a marvel of alchemical invention—contained memories of his past, of every day he'd worn it. When Crier's blood triggered the locket's magick, she could relive those memories. But she never knew which memories would surface when she pricked her finger. The locket held a whole lifetime within its clasp. It held Ayla's history, her past—and maybe, her legacy.

It held, Crier feared, the secrets Kinok was looking for.

She felt around on the forest floor until she found a sliver of rock and, the movement familiar now, used it to prick her finger. A single drop of dark blood welled up.

Crier closed her eyes, took a calming breath, and pressed the tip of her finger to the red stone in the center of the locket. The stone with a tiny, ticking pulse.

With the next breath—

—she was soaked and freezing. She stood huddled among a small crowd on the deck of a fishing vessel, in the middle of the ocean. Clouds loomed heavy and dark above; torrential rain swept almost horizontally with the force of the wind. All around her, in every direction, the ocean was a roiling black expanse. Amid the throng of people, she spotted someone familiar: Leo.

Now, she moved closer, careful to keep her balance on

the violent sway of the ship, and saw that Leo held a little girl whose face was hidden, buried in his chest, but Crier knew it had to be Clara. Ayla's mother; the daughter Siena had abandoned in favor of her own inhuman creation, Yora.

Yora's heart, Crier thought fiercely. She had no idea if this would work, but she had to try. Siena had Made this locket for a reason: to record history, memories. It was a tool. A beautiful, ingenious tool, but still a tool. And tools were made to be wielded.

Yora's heart, she thought. She tried saying it aloud: "Yora's heart! Show me Yora's heart!"

Nothing happened. Her words were snatched away by the sea wind, the pounding rain. Then—

—flashes of memory, so quick she could barely follow—

A coastline coming into view, the ship docking. Golden sand, pale green water, dawn-colored sky.

A caravan through the jungle, wild and tangled, wildness like nothing she'd ever seen, everything green, mossy trees and a creek bed and plants with leaves the size of Crier's torso, hanging vines, shafts of sunlight filtering through the canopy overhead, the air thick and humid, the air like steam.

Hills rippling with winter-yellow grass, glittering with morning frost. A cave, a quarry, a river cutting through a deep canyon.

Clara asking, asking, asking—where are we? What happened to Mama? Eventually, the questions—and the tears—fading away.

Clara, older now. Thirteen, maybe. A golden chain around her neck, glinting in the light of a hearth fire.

Clara, older still, belly swollen with child, laughing on the shores of a wide lake, the wind tossing her dark curls, but behind her the surface of the lake unnaturally calm, unrippled, reflecting the evening sky, a massive mirror.

Show me Yora's heart.

Fire.

In the first few seconds Crier thought she'd been transported back to the very first memory: the burning city, the smoke-filled streets, the terrified humans white with ash. But then her vision cleared and she saw she was on the banks of that same lake, the entire sky a pale, sick orange, the sun a bloodshot eyeball half obscured by smoke.

"They're coming!" someone cried out. Crier whirled around. There was a small cottage higher up on the bank, white clay walls and a thatched roof. Three figures were standing outside it, and when she squinted against the dying light she saw it was Leo, a heavily pregnant Clara, and a man she'd never seen before. "They're coming, you have to go now," Leo said again, voice rough with fear. "Please, Clara. You're running out of time."

"I'm not leaving without you!" Clara said. She was

holding both arms protectively around her stomach, leaning back into the man Crier didn't know, and Crier realized: she was pregnant with Ayla. This man must be Ayla's father. "Father, we're not leaving you here to die!"

"I'm old, child," Leo said. "And my leg—I cannot move quickly enough. I'd slow you down and it would be the death of us all." He looked at Ayla's father. "Yann. Please. You know I'm right. You know what has to be done."

Somewhere in the distance, the sound of a war horn. Crier knew that sound.

"Go," said Leo, frantic. "Skirt the lake, you know where the rowboat is, when night falls cross the lake into Rabu. Please, Yann. Please, Clara. You have to protect the child."

"If I make it through the night, I'll meet you at the Queen's Cove," Leo was saying. "I'll meet you there, Clara. For now, you have to leave me behind."

"No!" said Clara, but Yann was nodding, looking grim.

"Take this," said Leo, reaching beneath the collar of his shirt and pulling out—the necklace. The locket with the eight-point star, the red stone, the same locket Crier was holding at this very moment, sixteen years later, in the wilds of southern Rabu. "Take it, Yann. Keep it safe. It contains histories."

"I'll keep it safe," said Yann, slipping the necklace

over his own head, hiding it beneath his shirt. "What about the heart?"

"It stays with me," said Leo. "Now go!"

"Father," Clara sobbed, but she let Yann drag her away toward the lake, toward Crier. "Father, we'll wait for you at the Queen's Cove. We'll wait for you. We'll see you there, right?"

"Right," said Leo. "Of course, daughter. I'll see you soon."

And Yann and Clara turned away, and the war horn sounded again, like the scream of a dying animal, and the world—

Fell away.

Crier's eyes flew open. She lay there for a moment, staring up at the branches of the fir tree and beyond them, the night sky. She'd probably only lost a few minutes, but it felt like she'd aged a lifetime.

She knew one place Yora's heart had been sixteen years ago. It wasn't much, but it was the best lead she'd gotten so far.

She pressed the locket to her mouth. *Thank you, Leo.*

In the morning, she didn't waste any time before pulling Hook aside. Once, she might have kept this information to herself, scared to act, scared to stand up against Kinok and her father and her own people, but she no longer had that luxury. She was going to act, and fast.

"You're not going to believe me," she said, after she and Hook had moved far enough into the woods that the others wouldn't be able to overhear them. "But I think I know where to find Tourmaline. Or . . . where to begin."

He gave her an incredulous look. "Just last night, you said you didn't have any idea where it was."

"I know. But then I used this." She held up the locket, showing him the alchemical star. It was overcast this morning, a small blessing; she didn't have to worry about the morning sunlight catching her eyes. "Hold it up to your ear and listen." He did, and she watched his eyebrows rise when he heard the tiny inorganic heartbeat within, like the tick of a clock but more alive, *tmp-tmp, tmp-tmp*.

"This is a Made object," he said, turning it over in his hands. He looked frightened, a little awed. "How on earth did you get ahold of this, Ayla?"

"Doesn't matter. All that matters is what this locket can do." Quickly, she explained the locket's magickal properties, the memories within it, though she didn't give him any names. "It once belonged to a man who used it to record his memories of his experiences with Tourmaline. With the Maker of Tourmaline. I figured out how to access those memories, and I've been sifting through them slowly, searching for leads. Last night, I finally found one. I think the man died in a raid at Lake Thea, sixteen years ago. And I think the Tourmaline stone was with him when he died."

Lake Thea was the biggest lake in Zulla, half in Rabu and

half in Varn, named after Queen Thea of Zulla, the Barren Queen. The founder of the Royal Academy of Makers. The one for whom Thomas Wren had created Kiera.

No, not Thomas Wren. A nameless peasant woman. H.

Hook narrowed his eyes. "And why should I believe you?"

"You don't have to," said Crier. "But I'm going to Lake Thea. To the Queen's Cove. You and the others can accompany me or not, but I'm going. If there's any chance at all of finding Tourmaline before K—before the Scyre does, I have to take it."

He looked at her for a long time, scrutinizing.

"It's only two days' ride from here," said Crier. "If I'm wrong, if it's a dead end, you'll have lost two days. But if I'm right . . ."

"And if you're leading us into a trap?"

She blinked at him, surprised. She hadn't even considered he might think that. "I—I suppose you can't know for sure that I'm not. But there's one of me and eight of you, and you've been roaming around killing *Shades*—what trap could be more dangerous than that?"

He was still hesitating.

"I said I'll go alone and I meant it," said Crier, resigning herself to a *no*. "Thank you for saving my life, thank you for a night's rest. I'll remember you and what you did for me. But—"

"We'll go," said Hook.

"What?"

He cracked a smile. "We'll go with you, Ayla. Like you said, if there's any chance at all of beating the Scyre at his own sick game . . ." His expression darkened for a moment, smile fading like the sun behind a cloud. "I'm sure you saw the extra pony back at camp."

Crier's stomach twisted. "I . . . I did wonder what happened to the rider."

"The Scyre's taken countless souls from us," said Hook, fire in his eyes. "Erren was one of thousands. They were captured; we've been searching for them ever since. For them—to find them, to save them—I'd risk walking into a trap. I'd risk just about anything."

"I know what you mean," said Crier.

Over the next two days, as the nine of them rode west toward Lake Thea, Crier found herself unable to stop watching the humans.

They were fascinating. It was so obvious, now, how her father's Traditionalism was just a pale imitation of human culture. Traditionalism was the corpse; this was the living body, bright-eyed and warm. Crier had never before observed how humans acted when there weren't any Automae around, and the difference in behavior was astounding. The humans were loud. They laughed loudly, spoke loudly, sang as they rode. They joked easily, touched easily, grinned easily, even though Crier knew they had lived through terrible things, knew they feared the Shades, knew they had already lost one, if not more, of their own. She didn't understand most of their jokes, but once or twice the joke was universal, and she—laughed. The first time it happened, it startled her. This helpless burst of noise. She could not remember the last time she'd laughed. It wasn't something Automae did.

She didn't know most of their songs, and for the first day remained silent and just listened. But the next day, as they made their way through flatlands that swelled slowly into hills, Bree pulled her horse up close to Crier's and poked her on the arm.

"C'mon, Ayla," she said, wiggling her eyebrows. "Everybody knows this one."

Crier did know it, actually. It was a shanty, a traveler's song; she'd once taught herself to play it on the harp. She still remembered the words. Of course. She remembered everything.

Under her breath, she sang along with the next line. *"When the wind blows in from the cold white north, when the sunlight fades away . . ."*

Bree grinned, settling back into her saddle. She dropped the reins and clapped along, singing loudly. *"When the ocean dries and strands me, child, when the blue sky fades to gray—"*

"HO-HEY!" Hook whooped from up front.

"When the black crow cries its very last, when the noonbirds lose their song—"

"HO-HEY!"

"When the heavens fall and the hells rise up and the demons rise along—"

"HO-HEY!"

"I'll stick 'em in the eye and make 'em cry and say, 'You can't keep me from home!'"

By the end of it, Crier was singing almost as loudly as the others. And she didn't know the next song, but she did know the one after that, and the one after that, and sang along. It was becoming easier to play the part of a human. She didn't have to concentrate so hard on moving, breathing, speaking in the right voice. She ate as much human food as she could stomach and consumed small amounts of heartstone in the dead of night, and she rode with them under a sky like an overturned bowl, and she sang and laughed and wondered if she looked any different, because it felt impossible that her exterior wasn't changing too.

Crier had never been to Lake Thea before, had only seen it in maps and illustrations, a small patch of blue. Logically she knew it was huge—a hundred leagues across, almost big enough to be considered a sea. But still, in her mind she'd always pictured it as that small patch of blue nestled between Rabu and Varn, feeding into a branch of the River Merra. So when they crested a hill and saw nothing but blue before them, stretching to the horizon and as far as the eye could see in all directions, it took Crier a few seconds to realize what she was looking at. The view looked like a mirage: sunlight glinting off an endless expanse of blue, a shattering of light that made everything look false and wavery—but then she saw the seabirds swooping high above the surface, the white-capped waves rolling in to the shore. . . .

The hills dropped off into short shelflike bluffs at the edge of the lake, and farther along the shoreline they dropped away entirely, flattening out into the banks Crier had seen in Leo's memories, the pale color of crushed seashells. Gods, there was so much water. It reminded Crier of home, of the Steorran Sea, though this water was calmer, these bluffs gentle and grassy instead of sharp black rock. On the other side of all that water was Varn. Gazing down at the lake from her position on the hills, Crier felt closer to Varn than ever. But she knew the Varnian shoreline was heavily guarded and—yes, there on the bluffs, maybe a league away: a lighthouse. It was sure to be full of Rabunian border guards. They'd have to be careful.

"Ayla? You coming?"

The others had passed her. Bree was looking back at Crier over her shoulder.

"Yes," Crier murmured, and urged Della forward. Onward.

The nine of them kept to the hills, riding parallel to the shoreline but maintaining their distance. Crier wasn't sure exactly where Leo's old village would be, but she remembered the position of the smoke-obscured sun from Leo's memories: when she was facing the cottage, she'd been facing the sun. Facing west. So west they rode. A strong wind came off the lake, carrying a clean, brackish smell, rustling the yellow grass. Crier found herself relaxing, the tension in her shoulders fading away. It had been sixteen years, but she had this *feeling*. She was going to find answers here. She was so close, the sky was clear, the lake water Tourmaline blue, the seabirds crying out overhead. The rebels kept a steady pace, not hard enough to tire out the horses but definitely quicker than was necessary. Maybe they felt it too, that frisson of anticipation.

It was another hour before they found the village, and if Crier had been alone, she would have missed it entirely.

"There," said Hook, the first any of them had spoken for a long time.

Crier looked in the direction he was pointing. But she didn't see anything that looked like it had once been a village. She'd been looking for . . . ruins, like those in history books, stone foundations and crumbling walls. She knew the village had been raided and burned, so . . . where were the ruins?

They got closer, and she saw what Hook had seen. It was a stone, rough and unevenly shaped, poking out of the earth. If Crier stood next to it, it would only come up to her knee. There was a wreath of dead, dried-out flowers around the base of the stone, and a single word carved into it: *Wells*.

For some reason, that was what it took. That was when it really hit her. She was not walking through a history book, where things were distant, all the pain and suffering softened by centuries. She'd been expecting an illustration because that was all she'd ever known, but of course this was nothing like the illustrations. There had once been a village here, full of people whose lives were filled with sorrow and joy, who had children, who were in love, who loved each other, who wanted to protect each other, who just wanted to survive. A village full of people like Leo, who had sacrificed himself to save his daughter, his unborn grandchild.

Now there was nothing but a stone.

Because of Crier's father.

Not my father anymore, she reminded herself. *I will not be the daughter of a monster.*

But as she looked out over the hills, the shoreline of Lake Thea, the long grass hiding the bones of a village long dead, she knew it was not quite that easy.

I write this on the dawn of war.

The Scyre has begun amassing forces to the west. I know not what he plans, other than to take the sovereign's throne; other than to overthrow the council; other than to seize Rabu itself and then, I have to assume, all Zulla.

He pours words like wine. Sweet and bloodred. Heady when consumed. Promises of a shining new life source. He will liberate us from our need to consume heartstone daily, or so he says; from the Iron Heart itself, the crack in our armor. But I must confess I have never understood. Would a new life source not come with its own vulnerabilities? We must derive power from something, and as long as we depend on that something—our weak spot. Our flaw.

What does he want to end reliance on, really?

I still remember his words at the first Anti-Reliance assembly, two summers past.

"Why do we call ourselves sons and daughters when we were never birthed? Why does Traditionalism dictate that we act out these elaborate scenes, playing at being human? We were Created to be more than human. Does the wolf play at being a common dog? Listen here. If we look only at the past, we lose sight of the future. And what a future it could be."

What are you afraid of, Scyre?

What haunts you, Watcher?
What secrets lie within the Heart?

—EXCERPT FROM THE PERSONAL RECORDS OF RED
HAND MAR OF THE RED COUNCIL OF THE SOVEREIGN
STATE OF RABU, YEAR 47 AE

9

Tomorrow, Storme had said, but tomorrow came, Ayla woke up at dawn and immediately slipped out of her room to go find him, and . . . couldn't find him anywhere. She didn't know where his rooms were, and she didn't want to draw any attention to herself by asking. So she wandered the palace for an hour, checking every open room, checking the kitchens and the dining hall and the training room and the fields and even the sculpture garden where they'd run into each other last night, but he was nowhere to be found. Frustrated all over again, Ayla decided that if her brother wanted to avoid her like a coward, fine. Let him! She had other things to do.

First on the agenda: learning more about the mysterious Tarreenian weapons Storme had mentioned. What substance, or combination of substances, created bright blue smoke?

If answers existed, Ayla knew where to find them.

The library, said Crier's voice in her head. Crier talked about the library like some people talked about temples. Holy places.

According to Maris, there were nine libraries in the queen's palace, each with a different theme: history, philosophy, arts and sciences, alchemy, ancient books, rare and precious books, human storybooks, law, music. Ayla made her way to the alchemy library in one of the high, fang-like towers, at the top of a dizzying spiral staircase.

The door to the library was intricately carved wood, a symmetrical design of scrolls, swords, and the Varnian phoenix. Around the edges, alchemic symbols. To her surprise, Ayla could understand almost all of them. *Sun, earth, iron, salt.* The symbols associated with the human body. *Moon, water, lead, gold.* Symbols of change, transformation. *Fire, saltpeter, copper.* Energy. That which burned.

Ayla pushed the door open and stepped inside, immediately enveloped with the particular kind of silence that she'd come to associate with libraries after sitting there, bored out of her mind, as Crier met with various tutors. A thick, musty silence, heavy with the smell of aging books. The library was a small circular room, windowless, the walls lined with bookcases so tall there were rolling ladders attached to them so you could access the topmost shelves. In the center of the room, there were a couple soft-looking chairs and a writing desk with parchment, a quill, a pot of ink. Ayla let the door close behind her and just stood there for a moment. She'd picked up the Zullan alphabet quickly, but she still couldn't read more than a few words; she wouldn't be able to decipher the book titles, let alone the contents. Suddenly she felt very foolish. She didn't belong in this place.

She turned to leave, only for the door to swing open, nearly hitting her in the face.

"Benjy," she said, surprised. "What are you doing here?"

"I followed you," said Benjy. He was dressed in a green guard's uniform, dark curls swept back off his forehead. Frowning, he glanced around the library behind her. "What are you doing?"

"Looking for a book."

Benjy blinked at her. "You can't read."

"*What?*" Ayla gasped. "I can't? My gods, why didn't anyone tell me?"

"Ha, ha," he said, rolling his eyes. "Seriously, what are you doing?"

"Seriously, I'm looking for a book." She turned away, pretending to browse the shelves, as if she hadn't been about to leave. He was silent, and she couldn't help but add, "A lot happened last night. You know, after you waltzed with the queen."

"Queen Junn is our most valuable ally right now," he said stiffly. "She has more power and reach and resources than we've ever had access to. It's in our best interest to stay on her good side."

"Well, you certainly seem dedicated to doing just that."

"You're the one who's going to decode messages for her," Benjy snapped, catching Ayla's sleeve. She whirled around, already crossing her arms.

"What's your *problem*, Benjy?" Anger surged inside her; she was a body caught in the undertow. She didn't know what her problem was until she opened her mouth and it spilled out. "For *weeks* you warned me off Crier," she hissed. "'You've grown soft,' you said. 'You can't trust her,' 'Don't forget what her Kind does to us'—and now you're dancing with the leech queen? Staying on her good side doesn't have to mean *that*. Imagine if I'd danced like that with Crier. Waltzing in front of everyone, laughing like friends. Imagine what you would've said."

"What, are you jealous?" he asked.

"You know full well I'm not," she said coldly. His eyes widened with hurt, but it didn't calm her temper. He deserved it for asking that.

"I didn't mean jealous about me," he said pointedly. "I mean jealous that you *didn't* get to do that. With her."

She scoffed. "Of course not."

"Really."

She stared at him for a moment. He'd always been able to read her, even when she tried so hard to hide. "So I grew soft around her," Ayla said. "I'm still the one who came up with the idea to set off her chime. I still made that choice, in the end. For revenge. For revolution."

"And you're still the one who couldn't kill her."

She took a half step back. They glared at each other, the silence of the library deafening in the wake of their anger.

"I'm thinking about the future, Ayla," said Benjy. "We're on the brink of war. Whether it's humans versus Automae or the queen versus Kinok and the sovereign, or all of it, it's war. I want to protect our Kind. Our people. I want us to rise up and *win*. If I have to team up with the *leech queen* for a while, so be it. I'll do anything for the Revolution. I guess it's not the same for you."

"Do you really think her intentions are pure?" Ayla demanded. "We know she wants Kinok's head on a platter, but what after? Will she storm the sovereign's palace? Rule over Varn *and* Rabu? You know the whispers about her. That she's merciless. That she kills for entertainment. What if she kills Kinok, takes the sovereign's throne, and decides she doesn't like humans after all?"

"That's not going to happen," said Benjy, but there was a hint of doubt in his voice. "And—either way, I don't think you have any right to preach about *pure intentions*."

"Neither do you, after last night."

He sneered at her. "Oh, screw off, Ayla. You don't know what you're talking about. You are so naive, you've always been so damn naive."

"If you think I'm the naive one, you're mad," she spat. "But fine. Go ahead, make nice with her majesty. Just don't let yourself grow soft, Benjy."

"Don't worry. I've got a spine," he said, and stormed out of the library.

The door fell shut behind him. Ayla stayed where she was for a few minutes, trying to get herself under control. Her hands were shaking. She'd never fought with Benjy like this before. They'd had disagreements, petty arguments, childhood spats, but never a fight like this.

What, are you jealous?

No.

But whenever she closed her eyes, she saw Benjy and Junn dancing. Junn tipping her head back to look up at the night sky, the curve of her throat gleaming bronze in the candlelight. In that moment, Junn hadn't looked like the Mad Queen. She hadn't even looked like a leech.

She'd just looked like a girl.

No, Ayla couldn't think like that. Because if she did, she'd think of—

That one night. Curled up in Crier's bed, in Crier's bedroom, in the place where she slept. Or more often read, or simply lay awake, staring up at the ceiling for hours. Big four-poster bed. Canopied in delicate white gossamer, like cobwebs. It should have felt like sleeping in a spider's nest. It didn't. Nothing with Crier ever felt like it was supposed to feel. Moonlight spilling in through the windows, blue blue blue. The night air and the blankets and the halls of Ayla's heart, all blue.

A whispered question. *How can I help?*

This isn't a game, Crier, Ayla had whispered back. Soft words into the blue between them. *This isn't a faerie story in one of your books. This is life and death.*

I'm serious. Let me prove it to you.

And another night. Same place. But this time, Ayla was standing over the bed with one arm raised.

If Ayla thought of Crier as just a girl, it would mean she'd brought a knife into that soft blue room for absolutely nothing. So she couldn't think like that. She *couldn't*.

Blue-smoke weapons forgotten, Ayla left the library and navigated the hallways back to her room.

"Ayla!"

As she turned the corner, she heard Storme call her name. He caught up to her, falling into step beside her.

"I've been looking for you. Thought maybe you were avoiding me," she said.

"I'm here now, aren't I?" he said. "Come, follow me. I've been cooped up in the strategy room all day, I need fresh air and sunlight. Maybe some wine. Maybe an entire roasted chicken. But I think we should start with the sunlight."

He took a sharp right. "Where are we going?" Ayla demanded, scrambling after him.

"For a ride."

People had feet for a reason, Ayla thought, seated atop one of the royal horses, and it was to prevent things like this from ever happening. Her thighs ached. Every muscle in her body was clenched tight. She hadn't mastered how to move with the rhythm of the horse's strides; her tailbone kept cracking against the saddle.

"How . . . can you possibly . . . enjoy this?" she gasped, gripping the reins so tight it hurt her palms. The horse Storme had chosen for her was barely bigger than a pony, and still she felt miles off the ground. If she fell, she'd break her neck. Or get trampled. Or get crushed, if the horse fell with her. What if it threw her off its back? There was a spark of evil in its eyes, she could *tell*. The horse could not be trusted.

"I love riding," Storme said pleasantly. "It relaxes me."

Ayla might have throttled him, if she'd been able to let go of the reins.

They joined a stream of fishermen and traders and merchants leaving Thalen, passing through a set of gates much smaller than the ones Ayla and Benjy had used to enter the city on the day of the Maker's Festival. Then they were outside the high white walls at the northernmost point of the city, winter-yellow hills stretching out before them, dead grass rustling in the wind coming in from the sea. It was chilly, but nothing like the cold of winter in Rabu, which settled into your stomach and gnawed at your bones like a starving dog. Ayla felt almost overheated in her thick wool coat. The sky was the white-shot gray of a frozen pond. Above, the perpetual seabirds, crying out.

Storme took the lead, though it didn't seem like he was going anywhere in particular. He just kept a steady pace into the hills, in the opposite direction of the main road all the traders were using, the one that led to the port. After a few minutes, Ayla found herself not fully relaxing but loosening her grip on the reins, letting herself stop impersonating a statue, stone-stiff. She found herself looking around just because it was a pretty view, the sky and the golden hills, Thalen like a huge white crown. The air smelled like winter and the sea. It reminded her of home.

"All right," said Storme, slowing his horse until he and Ayla were riding side by side. "Let's talk. What do you want to know?"

"Brother, what do you think I want to know?" she said,

incredulous. The sun hit his face, revealing freckles like her own. Like their mother's. "Something about the last seven years, maybe? About how you went from a nine-year-old orphan in northern Rabu to *adviser to the queen of Varn*?"

"I don't know where to begin," he confessed.

"Well . . . If you don't want to begin with the worst part, begin with this. Considering everything you and the queen know about Scyre Kinok, do you have any idea why he'd be interested in our family's history?"

That made Storme look at her.

"What are you talking about?" he asked, wide-eyed.

"He got me alone once," said Ayla, unwilling to go into the details. "I thought he was going to hurt me, but he just asked where I was born. He asked about my—our parents. Our grand-parents. Then later, I found a hidden safe in his study. Inside was a sole piece of paper with the words *Leo, Siena, Tourmaline*. He had spies in the sovereign's palace, I think it was meant for one of them. Either way, we got to it."

Storme sucked in a breath. "Leo and Siena? He knew their names?"

"Knew a lot more than that, I think. I just don't know how much. Or exactly what our grandparents have to do with Tourmaline." She bit her lip, thinking about the memory she and Crier had fallen into: a young Leo and Siena in the woods, embracing. In retrospect, Ayla should have pressed Crier for more information. Crier was the one who'd figured out how the locket worked; she must have seen other memories. But . . . right before they used the locket, they had kissed. (Fiercely, angrily, desperately, pulling at each other's hair and clothes, Crier inexperienced but so eager, so breathlessly open.) Right after they used the locket, Rowan had died. And Ayla had thought of nothing else. Nothing but taking the palace. Nothing but Crier's heart in her hands.

She touched her sternum. The spot where the locket should have been. A tiny inorganic heartbeat echoing her own. Once, there had been two lockets. Storme should have inherited the other one, the other half of the matching set, as Ayla inherited hers, but it had been lost years before. They never knew what happened to it—the one time Storme had asked their mother, she'd refused to answer. Ayla had always thought it was just . . . gone. Destroyed, maybe.

But, she thought now, *but* . . .

She remembered being dragged to Kinok's study, the shock of seeing her own necklace—which she'd lost just minutes before—sitting proudly on a bookshelf behind his desk. Then, later, Crier's confusion, her claim that the necklace had been in her possession the entire time.

Sometimes the simplest explanation was the right one. If the locket in Kinok's study wasn't Ayla's, it must have been the other one. The one that was lost.

Her stomach twisted. What if Kinok had figured out how to use the locket like Crier had? What memories had he accessed? What had he learned about Tourmaline? Ayla's necklace had belonged to Leo, Storme's to Siena. The idea of Kinok sifting through her grandmother's memories sickened her. It felt like a violation.

"How would our grandparents be connected to this?" Storme asked.

"I don't know," Ayla murmured, far away.

Lost in thought, they rode on. Until Ayla couldn't bear it anymore.

"Seven years ago. That day," she said. "What happened to you?"

Winter wind. Rustling grass.

He didn't answer.

Frustrated, Ayla started to ask *again*, but then she looked over at Storme. His dark brown eyes, so like her own, were fixed straight ahead, over the hills. His jaw was tight, mouth a thin line. The veneer of professionalism, the adviser to the queen, had disappeared. In its place was a sixteen-year-old boy. Young and haunted. Her brother. Her twin.

"I'm sorry," he said, voice shaking. "I'm sorry. I—I'm not used to trusting people, telling people things, and I know you're my blood—I know you lived through it too—but it's hard to believe it sometimes. It hasn't sunk in yet. That you're here."

"I'm here," she said. "Storme, I'm here."

"Yes. Yeah."

She swallowed hard. "Get me off this infernal creature, and we'll talk."

They ended up just walking alongside the horses, reins held loosely. Ayla felt a thousand times better with her feet on the ground again, swishing through the long grass. There were tiny white flowers dotting the hills like patches of melting snow, horseflies buzzing around, sometimes lighting on the horses and being shooed away by a flick of the ears or tail.

"That day," prompted Ayla.

"The day of the raids, after I hid you in the outhouse . . . ," Storme began. "They saw me. The sovereign's men. They'd already killed Mama and Papa, right in front of me, I watched it happen, I was hiding behind the outhouse but of course they saw me. I ran. They chased me. They should have caught me in seconds, but everything was burning, you remember. I ran into the thick of it and the smoke helped hide me. I covered myself in ash and lay down next to—a body, I don't know who it was, the face was—the ash was still hot, I ended up with burns all over. Here." He pulled up his shirtsleeve, showing Ayla the skin of his arm, pockmarked and oddly shiny. She made a small wounded noise, and he pulled his sleeve back down. "I played dead for a while. With all the smoke, it was black as night even in the middle of the day. I waited until I couldn't hear them anymore, and then I ran. Out of the village, all the way to the edge of the ice fields. You remember the Bone Tree?"

Ayla nodded. They'd grown up in the north, in the liminal space between northern Rabu and the Far North, where everything was flat and icy and there wasn't much vegetation at all. The Bone Tree had been the tallest thing around for miles: a tree that stood just outside the village, long dead but still upright, its bark the yellowish-white of bone. The children of Delan had always used it as a marker. *Race you to the Bone Tree. Sit under the*

Bone Tree and count to a hundred while I go hide.

"I hid in the branches. I was small, it was dark, I knew they wouldn't be able to see me unless they stood right below the tree. I wanted to go back, I wanted to get you—but I could hear them. Calling out to each other, searching for survivors. I should have gone back anyway. I should have—but I was scared, I was paralyzed with fear, I didn't have a weapon. I was a coward."

"You weren't a coward," Ayla said quietly. "You were a child. If you'd gone back, they'd have just killed you too. And I really would have been alone."

It felt so strange, talking about that day—the smoke-dark, the smell of blood and burning flesh, the roar of the devouring fire, the sound of wooden houses collapsing as the fire ate away at their foundations, the sound of death—on such a clear, beautiful day, walking slowly through the grassy hills. So far away from all of it. Seven years out. They weren't even in the same country anymore.

"This part is so stupid," said Storme, letting out a shaky breath. "It's such a ridiculous thing, but—I wasn't wearing a coat. It was early winter; you remember how cold it was. I stayed in the branches of the Bone Tree all night, waiting for the sovereign's men to leave, but it was so cold. I must have lost consciousness and fallen out of the branches. Because two days later, I woke up beside a campfire in the middle of the ice fields."

Ayla's eyes widened. "Wait, what?"

"It was a human rebel group. They'd heard about the raid on Delan. They'd come to look for survivors, and I guess they found my body under the Bone Tree and saw I was still alive. They took me with them. I was—I was the only one they found. They nursed me back to health. I'd been more than half dead when they found me in the snow. Though falling out of the branches turned out to be a stroke of luck. The snow kept my burns from getting infected. Almost freezing to death saved my life."

Almost freezing to death had saved Ayla's life, too.

She was so cold that it didn't feel like cold anymore. It didn't even burn. She barely noticed the winter air, the snow soaking through her threadbare boots, the ice crystals that whipped across her face and left her skin red and raw. She was cold from the inside out, the coldness pulsing through her with every weak flutter of her heart. Dimly, she knew this was how it felt right before you died.

That was how Rowan had first found her, in the snow-choked streets of Kalla-den. A lost orphan, with nowhere else to go.

"They told me there were no survivors," Storme said. His voice sounded strapped-down, tightly controlled, like he was holding back—not tears but some raw emotion, some old grief. "They said I was the only one, everyone else was dead. Years later, I heard there *were* survivors of Delan. The rebels just hadn't found them, or who knows, maybe they were lying. I don't know. I'll never know. But—I was nine. I'd just watched the Automae kill my parents. I was terrified and grieving and alone. I believed them. When they told me I could join them, I said yes."

Ayla realized her vision was blurring. She pressed her lips together and kept walking, one foot after the other. She brushed her knuckles against the horse's flank. Demonic beast or not, it soothed her—this big warm animal who had not experienced terrible things.

"So I joined them. And I mourned you. As I said, it wasn't until years later I found out there were other survivors and I realized there was a good chance you were still alive. But for years, I mourned you. I followed the rebel group west and then south, spending a few weeks or months in a dozen towns and villages, establishing connections, spreading the word: *We are rising up against them.* The rebels used me as an eavesdropper, a thief, a spy—I was small, I could slip in and out of places the others couldn't. Nobody suspects a child, not even the Automae. And I mourned you."

"I mourned you too," Ayla choked out. "I never stopped mourning you. There was a third body next to Mama and Papa, I thought it was yours, I thought for sure it was yours. It must have been someone else's child."

His expression fractured. "I'm sorry," he said. "I'm sorry, Ayla." He took a deep breath, steadying himself. "After . . . After three years, the original group split into factions. Some of them remained in Rabu, some headed to Tarreen, some to Varn. There was nothing for me in Rabu. I chose to come here, to Varn. We managed to cross the border to the west and made our way to Thalen. Then, in Thalen, there was . . ."

"There was?" Ayla prompted when he didn't finish. "There was what?"

Storme cleared his throat. "A rebel girl. Her name was Annedine."

Ayla waited, but again he didn't continue. "What happened with Annedine?"

"I . . ." He shook his head hard. "I'm sorry. I shouldn't have named her. That is one secret I still cannot tell."

Ayla didn't protest. Everything else he'd told her was so overwhelming, she could leave the story of Annedine for another time. She couldn't stop thinking about nine-year-old Storme hiding in the branches of the Bone Tree, burning, shivering. They'd both survived the raid and then come so close to dying anyway.

"But I still don't understand," she said, glancing up at him. "After all that, after traveling with human rebels for so long . . . how did you end up as the right hand to Queen Junn?"

"That's another secret," he said. He was avoiding her eyes. "Just trust me, Ayla. I know what I'm doing. The queen plucked me from obscurity. She gave me—"

He broke off, but Ayla could finish the sentence in her head. *A home.* She swallowed the nasty retort on her tongue. She'd fought with Storme once, fought with Benjy today. She needed to stop fighting with the people she loved.

"But . . . she's one of them," she said slowly.

"And it's different here in Varn, all right? The Kinds aren't enemies like in Rabu. Here, we live and work together. It's not perfect, but it's better. And the queen and I—and you—have a common enemy. A common goal. Why should I not work with her? Why should I not remain at her side?"

The echo of Benjy's words rang through Ayla like a bell toll. She didn't know what to think. For so long, everyone around her had said: *They are monsters. There is no reasoning with them. Stay away.* And now . . .

She frowned. "Well, tell your precious queen to leave Benjy alone. She's toying with him, leading him along. He's not something she can play with before devouring."

"What are you talking about?" Storme asked.

"They were all lovey-dovey at the ball last night," Ayla said. She rolled her eyes. "It's made him a fool."

"I see," said Storme, very softly, and then neither of them spoke at all.

Later that night, belly full from dinner, Ayla slipped into her bedchamber. Her mind was still reeling from everything Storme had told her, thoughts swooping like seabirds. She'd been waiting all day for some time alone. She knew once she started thinking about it she wouldn't be able to stop. The quiet devastation of her brother's story.

She changed into her sleep clothes, pulled back the blankets, and froze.

There, on the mattress, was a folded-up piece of parchment.

Cautiously, Ayla held it up to the lamplight. The parchment was yellow and worn, the creases soft, as if it had been unfolded and refolded a thousand times. It was a letter, she could tell that much. Messy handwriting, the ink blurred with age. Even if she'd been reading her whole life, it would have been near incomprehensible.

Ayla sank onto the mattress, lost. Then she leaped up and hurried to her writing desk, fetching a pen and a fresh piece of paper. She smoothed out the old parchment. Tried to focus on identifying one letter at a time.

After a quarter of an hour, she was pretty confident she had the first two words.

My Storme . . .

My Storme,

   Today I have a story for you.

   Once, a witch charmed a collection of bones into dancing whenever she played the flute. The bones were mostly in the shape of a person, with a few bits missing here and there; when they danced, they rattled together as one, and when the music stopped, they clattered to the ground, silent and still as any tomb. The witch didn't do this for any particular reason. She didn't want to frighten the nearby villagers or play a trick or disrespect a sleeping grave. I think she was just lonely. I think she just wanted to dance. She lived out her days, her witch's life span, in a small cottage at the edge of a clearing in the deep, dark woods, and after a while the bones learned to dance to birdsong, and the soft coos of owls and mourning doves, and sometimes even the cry of a faraway wolf. And the witch, who had previously not spoken to anyone for a long, long time, sometimes put away the flute and sang, every song she could remember and a thousand she invented on the spot, and the bones danced their rattling dance, teeth chattering on the floorboards, and the witch laughed and the bones danced to that, too.

   My favorite thing about humans: we sing to our dead. Yours. Yours. In flesh, in blood.
Annedine

10

They'd traveled all this way for nothing. Crier didn't really know what she was expecting—a perfectly preserved cottage with a sign on the door, HERE LIES YORA'S HEART? She was a fool. Even if the Tourmaline stone were here, it could be buried anywhere beneath the long grass. Or on the pebbly shore where Leo and Siena had stood. Maybe it had been hidden there and was then carried away by the rippling waves, swept out to the deep center of the lake, where the water was black and still. Maybe it was resting at the bottom of the lake, covered with sand and silt, a little chunk of sky.

Footfalls behind her, muffled by the grass. Hook. He came to stand beside her, looking out over the seemingly endless stretch of water. Even Crier, with her Automa eyesight, could make out only a faint black line at the very edge of the horizon. The other side of the lake. Varn.

"I'm sorry," said Crier. "I should have known this would be fruitless."

Hook hummed. "Honestly, these past couple days, it's the happiest I've seen them since . . . since Erren was captured. Tourmaline was always a long shot. We'll keep looking, yeah?" He sighed. "We always keep looking. We always keep trying."

Are you my friend? Crier wondered, glancing at him. In the sunlight, his skin glowed. His eyes were a brown Crier associated with soft, rich earth, the kind that could grow anything, that nurtured every seed. *We're allies*, she thought. *Is that the same thing?*

No, probably not.

It ached a little. Crier wanted to be his friend. Was that so impossible? Contrary to what Kinok had once tricked her into believing, she didn't have a fifth pillar. She had no Passion. She was Automa, through and through, a Made creature, flawlessly Designed. Intellect, Organics, Calculation, Reason. There was no room inside her for emotions like this. For yearning like this. For loneliness like this. But she was so human-shaped. She was so human-shaped. How could she live in this vessel and not feel any attachment to the world, to its people? How could she live in this body and have no room inside her for the way Ayla's voice became low and raspy at the end of a long day? The way Crier's own hands felt when she played the harp, like she was an extension of the instrument and all her hundred strings were singing? The way Hook watched over his band of children who could not let themselves be children, who were so much braver than Crier, who had lost friends and hunted monsters and still sang songs about coming home?

There was a library in Yanna. Crier had never been; the sovereign had never allowed it. She'd never even seen the library in real life. But she had seen illustrations. A painting, once. The library was made of pale pink stone, same as the Old Palace at the heart of the city. It must have looked resplendent at sunrise and sunset, illuminated in pink and gold and ripe-peach orange. It was huge, the size of a city square, six stories tall, with a dome that, before the War of Kinds, had been painted with gold leaf. There were dozens of human poems about that golden dome: the half-sun, the harvest moon, fallen to earth. A golden fruit. A god's golden eye. Inside, the library was open and airy, the walls lined with hundreds of thousands of books and scrolls, in the Zullan tongue and the language of the alchemists and a thousand others. Crier thought of that library often. She imagined herself walking through it slowly, trailing her fingers across all those dusty spines, selecting a book at random, reading it, memorizing it, selecting another. She didn't need to sleep like humans did. She could have stayed awake in that library for days and days, just reading. Just breathing in the smell of sacred things. In another life, she could have done that. In this one, it felt impossible. As did kinship and Ayla and everything else she'd ever wanted.

"Ayla?"

Crier came back to herself.

"We won't give up," Hook told her, reassuring. He must have taken her silence for despair. "We never give up."

Crier took a deep breath. Briny lake-smell in her lungs. "Never?"

"Never," he said.

"Because . . ." She remembered Ayla standing over her. Ayla gripping a knife. The knife quivering in Ayla's hand. The look on Ayla's face: at the time, Crier had thought it was anger. Now, she thought perhaps it had been fear. "Because there are things worth dying for."

"Nah," said Hook, and he rolled his shoulders, twisted from side to side, stretched his arms up over his head, shook himself out. "Because there are still things worth living for."

Crier had worried the rebels would hate her for leading them to a dead end, but it didn't seem that way at all. They'd waited until dusk and then picked their way down the sloping shores to the beach, where Crier's boots sank into the wet sand with every step. Finally she just took the boots off and went barefoot, thrilled with the sensation of cold wet sand between her toes. They found an overhang of rock and clay, a pocket deep enough to hide the light of a small fire, and set up camp for the night, tying the horses outside, close enough to the water that they could drink their fill. Bree and Mir made a driftwood fire, and Crier watched, fascinated, as the flames turned blue and green. It reminded her of the Reaper's Moon celebration all those weeks ago, masked humans dancing around the bonfire, tossing in bits of algae. Cheering and drinking when the fire flashed blue. And Ayla in the midst of it all.

They ate and spoke softly, in sleepy, half-finished thoughts. Crier sat there, careful not to get too close to the fire, wary of the light refracting in her eyes. She racked her brain, trying to think of anywhere else Tourmaline could be. She reexamined the visions she'd seen, the memories she'd tumbled through, searching for any sort of clue. . . .

If I make it through the night, I'll meet you at the Queen's Cove, Leo had said.

Crier bit her lip hard, fighting back a swell of foolish hope. The memories in the locket ended when Leo gave it to Clara the night their village was attacked—if they'd found each other again, surely he would have taken it back and continued to add memories. So . . . Leo and Clara had never seen each other again after the scene on the lakeshore. They had never reunited at the Queen's Cove. But what if Leo had survived the night? What if he'd gone to the Queen's Cove anyway? Crier could picture it so vividly: Leo, injured, dragging himself into a rowboat. Pushing off the shore. Dawn breaking across the lake. If he'd made it to the Queen's Cove, but for some reason Yann and Siena were already gone . . . What if the Queen's Cove, not the ruined village, was his final resting place?

It felt too much like something out of a faerie story. A tragic ending. But Crier had already come this far—she might as well visit the cove, just in case. It was on the Varnian side of the lake, a bit of a hike. But under the cover of darkness . . . she could be there and back by dawn if she moved quickly. She had no rowboat, but she'd be faster on foot anyway, following the curve of the shore. Crier stared into the center of the smoldering campfire, the tiny spot where the flames burned black, calculating. There were the border guards to worry about. Automa soldiers of Rabu and Varn posted in their stone watchtowers, scanning the shores, the bluffs, the water. If Crier got caught—if the guards realized she wasn't just any young Automa girl but the sovereign's runaway daughter—

Erren was one of thousands. To find them—to save them—I'd risk walking into a trap. I'd risk just about anything.

What would Ayla do?

Crier almost smiled. She knew the answer.

Ayla would do the reckless thing.

The reckless thing, as was usually the case, started out all right. Crier waited until the rebels had doused the fire and curled up on their sleeping mats, settling in for the night. She waited, counting her own heartbeats, forcing herself to be patient. One hundred beats. One hundred twenty. One hundred forty. She waited until she heard eight human heartbeats slow, eight rhythms of breathing evening out, a quiet rush like faraway ocean tides. Then, silent as a shadow, she slipped out from under her own blankets. She picked up her boots, her bare feet soundless on the pebbly ground, and snuck out from beneath the overhang of rock.

She was a hundred paces down the beach when she heard someone approaching. Two someones. Moving quickly. Crier whipped around—*guards already?*—but it was only Hook and Bree.

"Giving us the slip, Ayla?" Hook said as the two of them approached. His voice sounded light, but Crier's stomach still dropped.

"*No*," she said. "No, of course not. I was just"—*human accent, human accent*—"going to check on something, I was gonna be back by dawn. I swear. I wouldn't leave with no explanation, not after all you've—"

"Breathe," said Bree. "He was joking."

Oh.

"I heard you sneak out is all," said Hook, gentler this time. "Something told me you weren't off for a midnight stroll. Seems I was right. So . . . ?"

"So . . . what?" said Crier.

"So what trouble are we getting into tonight?"

She stared at him. It was pitch-black out, the beach lit only by a waning moon, but her eyes caught more than a human's did. She could see Hook's expression, and sometimes it was hard to tell, but it didn't *look* like he was making fun of her. Bree looked serious too, regarding Crier steadily.

"I . . . I'm going to the Queen's Cove," said Crier. "It's the only other place that could possibly have clues about Tourmaline. I don't think much will come of it, but I have to check."

"The Queen's Cove," Hook echoed. "How far away is that?"

"Just over a mile. Near the edge of the Varnian border."

"And you were planning to go there on foot, in the middle of the night, search the entire cove—in the *dark*—and be back by dawn?" Bree asked.

Yes, because if Crier was alone, she could have run the distance to the cove in ten minutes. But of course it would take Ayla, the human, at least twice as long, and searching in the dark would take ages.

Best to play dumb. "I didn't want to take a horse," Crier said. "Don't they need sleep?"

"Don't *you*?" said Bree.

"The horses've had a couple hours, and today was easy on them anyway," said Hook before Crier could answer. "A few more miles won't hurt 'em. Come on, then, we've wasted enough time chatting. It's time for an adventure."

"An adventure," Bree muttered, wry.

"You don't have to come along!" said Hook as the three of them headed back toward the camp, where the black shapes of the horses looked like strange rock formations on the beach.

Bree huffed. "You know I do. Someone's gotta make sure you don't get yourself killed."

"Ayla will protect me."

"Oh," said Crier, worried. In an instant she summoned everything she'd ever read about combat: hand-to-hand, long range, sword fighting, wrestling, guerilla warfare, flipping through the hundreds of books in her mind, combing the pages for anything useful. She was naturally strong and fast, but she had no practical skills. How was it that she could speak fourteen languages but didn't know how to wield a dagger? A glaring oversight.

"I—I don't know if I'll be very good at that. But I can try."

"He was joking again," said Bree, but she nudged Crier in the way of humans, elbow to elbow. It felt like camaraderie, like the two of them were sharing something familiar and warm.

Crier dared to smile at Bree. She smiled back, a crook of the mouth, and Crier felt another door open inside her, revealing this newest room.

So Crier, Hook, and Bree woke the horses and rode, and everything started out all right.

The horses, weary, moved much slower than Crier would have, and were much more visible than a single Automa. Crier kept her ears pricked, kept scanning the darkness, the shore, the bluffs, the black water, for any sign that they'd been spotted, but she heard nothing, saw nothing, and the sand beneath the horses' hooves turned coarser, darker, pebbles and broken shells, and the mile tripped by.

The Queen's Cove was small—it wasn't even marked on most maps of Lake Thea. In practice, it was small enough that Crier nearly rode right past the mouth of it, even though she'd been tracking in her head the distance they'd traveled. She tugged gently on the reins, wheeling her horse around, and waited until Hook and Bree caught up before leading them single file into the cove: through the bottleneck, where two cliffs of stone converged with only a narrow gap between them, creating an inlet.

When they passed through to the other side, Crier realized why this place was called the Queen's Cove. Unlike the beach outside, the sand here was white as salt. The inlet was shaped like a keyhole, and standing here at the mouth, the dark water looked like a face, the white sand a crescent-moon crown, the black rocks beyond that a tangle of wild black hair.

Did you make it here, Leo?

Is this where you died?

Only distantly aware of Hook and Bree behind her, Crier slipped off her horse. The ground crunched beneath her boots. Not sand, then—crushed white shells. It was ridiculous that Crier felt like she was walking across a carpet of crushed bones. She studied the great black walls of the cove, trying to think like Leo. If she'd come here to escape a raid, to reunite with her family on a night when nowhere was safe, where would she go? Was there a cave, maybe? Some sort of hiding place in the rocks?

Suddenly, a scuffling noise. A tiny rain of pebbles from above.

No.

"What . . . ?" Hook hissed.

Time slowed. Crier turned around and it felt like she was moving through water instead of air; a surge of adrenaline had taken over, her mind leaping ahead. Hook and Bree hadn't dismounted. They were still hovering at the mouth of the cove, watching Crier as if waiting for instruction, because she'd led them here—*she'd led them here*—and they were following her cues.

"Run," said Crier.

She watched Hook's eyes widen. The whites of his eyes in the dark.

There was a sudden pressure in her right shoulder, as if she'd been pinched by an invisible hand. She ignored it. She raced forward, closing the distance between her and her horse in a fraction of a second. She swung back up onto her horse, dug her heels in, "Run," Hook and Bree seemed to realize what was happening, the bolt of a crossbow glanced off the rocks only a few feet from Hook's head, "Run," Crier kept saying, quiet and controlled, "Run, *run*."

A nightmare, to be attacked in the dark. It was hard enough for Crier to see, and she knew the two humans were basically blind. The three of them made it back out of the bottleneck, out of the cove and back onto the lakeshore, but—"On your right!" Crier gasped, catching a flicker of movement, a brief silhouette against the moonlit water. An Automa soldier, a border guard, quick as a jumping spider, there and gone. *There. Another one.* Two on the beach, a third shooting at them from the cliffs above. "Turn back!" Crier yelled, voice rough with fear, no longer caring what the guards heard. "Turn back!" To the guards, she cried out, "We mean no harm! We're not crossing!"

But even through the fear, she knew something was off. Why the crossbows? The border guards weren't meant to kill on sight. They were meant only to capture. Their prey was common smugglers.

Was it just cruelty for the sake of cruelty, then?

Crier wheeled her horse around only to find another guard already waiting, blocking off the beach the way they'd come. They were surrounded. There was nowhere to run. A flash of metal in the moonlight—Bree had drawn her weapon, a short curving blade. She was bent low over the horse's neck. The animal was panicking, rearing up on its hind legs, Bree clinging on with the hand that wasn't holding the blade. Hook was shouting something: "*We're Rabunian*," over and over again.

The snap of a crossbow release. Crier ducked, instincts taking over, and heard the bolt slice through the air where her skull had been an instant before. Somewhere to the left, Bree swore loudly. Crier straightened up just in time to see her hurl something at the guard blocking off their way back to camp—not the curved blade but a smaller weapon, a double-sided dagger. The guard sidestepped it, the dagger burying itself in the sand behind him, but that tiny distraction was enough for Hook and Bree to urge their horses forward, moving as one, efficient like they'd been that day on the riverbank, when they'd taken out the Shades. Crier kicked at her horse's sides, *go go go*, and then a braying, gut-wrenching noise rang out across the beach. The scream of a wounded animal.

Hook's horse buckled beneath him. Horse and rider hit the sand hard, Hook managing to throw himself sideways just in time to avoid being crushed. But he'd clearly gotten the wind knocked out of him, or maybe even hit his head; he was conscious, gasping, but he wasn't getting up, he was lying crumpled at the tide line, fallen horse panting beside him, half in and half out of the shallows, where the tiny waves foamed.

The guard who'd shot at him raised their crossbow again, aiming it straight at Hook. This time, Crier knew they would not hit the horse. Her mind processed all of this, drew from the chaos two facts: Hook was about to die. Bree, his friend, his protector, could not save him.

Crier leaped from the saddle. Distantly, she registered the *pop* of a metal bolt fired.

She landed in a catlike crouch in the shallow tide. In front of Hook. There was a terrible sensation in her back, just a hand's width away from her spine. It was similar to the pressure she'd felt in her shoulder earlier, like she'd been pinched, but this didn't feel like a pinch. This felt like she'd been punched by a giant. Crier lurched forward under the force of it, just barely catching herself before she toppled onto Hook. Bracing herself with both arms. Pebbles and shells beneath her hands. The lake water was cold, lapping at her wrists. It felt like icy manacles.

"Ayla?" someone was saying in a high, frightened voice.

The sick pressure in her back was narrowing. Sharpening. Two points. The first, in the shoulder, wasn't so bad. A twinge, a pulsing ache. The second—the second—

Crier lost her balance. She felt very fatigued all of a sudden, as if she hadn't slept for over seventeen days, which would be a new record for her. She was sitting in the cold water now. Her entire lower half was soaked. Was she still upright? Yes, but not of her own doing. Someone else's arm was tight across her shoulders, holding her up.

Someone—maybe the same someone—was saying something. Yelling something. *"We weren't even trying to cross. We're Rabunian. We've done nothing wrong."* Loud in her ear. *"You shot her. You shot her."*

"You're next, maggot." Another voice. *"Secure the Varnian. The blade. Watch out, we've got a wild one. Wicked arm."* Coming closer. *"Check the girl's face. Could be a disguise."*

Closer still. Crier heard a sort of wet, rasping noise, and realized after a moment that it was her own breathing. That was unusual. What would cause that? Water in her lungs? The pressure in her back was turning to white-hot pain, like someone was holding a lit torch to her flesh. She squirmed, trying to get away from it. *Stop burning me.* She imagined her skin scorching, melting. What did Made skin look like when it melted? *Stop. Please stop, it hurts.*

"Ayla, don't move—no! Don't touch her!"

A rough grip on her chin, jerking her head back. Crier blinked up at the night sky, vision blurring into fractals, the stars smeared into long silver threads. She tried to breathe. The water in her lungs was rising. High tide. Something to do with the moon.

"No—no, it can't be—"

"Captain?"

Her back hurt. She coughed and tasted something dark and oily on her tongue.

"We have to get out of here—she didn't see our faces—"

"Captain, what—?"

"This girl is the sovereign's daughter. You shot the sovereign's daughter."

Some part of Crier knew that was significant, but the rest of her was so tired, and she slipped into unconsciousness the way a body, drowning, slips beneath the surface of the ocean and sinks down, down, down.

Crier woke to a wash of red-gold light.

She cracked one eye open and immediately regretted it, wincing. Sunlight. Blinding sunlight. She took a deep breath, bracing herself, and opened her other eye, letting both adjust. A blanket of white snow swam into focus, and Crier became aware of other things: She was lying on her stomach. The ground under her cheek was rough, sharp-edged. Not snow. Shells.

Her back felt like one big pulsing bruise. The pain flickered to life at the edges of her awareness like fire devouring parchment, and Crier wished she could go back to being unconscious. There was one point in particular, just off her spine, where the pain was burning from beneath the surface of her skin, a deep ache. She cataloged the rest of her body, wiggling her toes and fingers. Her spine was not broken, then; she had control over all her extremities.

"You awake?"

She froze. It took a moment for the voice to register as Hook's. "I think so," Crier said, and started to roll over, but was stopped by a hand on her arm.

"Careful," Hook said. "Don't move. Your back's messed up bad."

"It hurts," she whispered, feeling very young.

"You got shot twice. Once in the shoulder, once lower down. The first bolt just glanced off your shoulder blade, the wound's not too deep, but the second one's nasty."

Crier blinked, trying to remember. It felt like her skull was full of water, heavy and dark, brain sloshing around in it. "Who . . . ?"

"The border guards," said a second voice. Bree. She sounded . . . angry? "Got you pretty good. Anyone else would be dead right now."

Something sharp and cold in her memory, a pinprick of fear. What happened? What was she forgetting? "How did we escape?" Crier asked. Slowly, she pushed herself up on one elbow so she could see them. Hook was crouched a couple feet away, staring at her, eyes wary. Behind him, Bree sat in the crushed white shells, spinning her double-sided dagger between her fingers. The twin blades winked in the sunlight. White shells—were they back in the Queen's Cove?

She bent her arm awkwardly to touch the wound in the middle of her back, gauging how bad it was. The flesh was warmer than usual, her body working to heal itself. Her fingers came away wet with violet blood.

Her violet blood.

Hook opened his mouth, but Bree cut him off. "How did we escape?" she sneered. "Wasn't too hard, actually. The guards got a bit panicked when they realized they'd just shot *Lady Crier*. Gave us the upper hand."

"No," Crier said automatically, even though she knew it was futile. "No, I'm—I'm not—"

"Is it true?" Hook asked. Now Crier understood why he

looked so wary. Her ally, her very first maybe-friend. Oh gods.

"Of course it's true," Bree said. "I told you she couldn't be trusted, I *told you* I thought I saw her eyes flash gold—"

"Bree," said Hook. "Give it a minute." To Crier, he said again, "Is it true? Are you the sovereign's daughter? Lady Crier?"

Crier fought the urge to look away, to hide her face. She would not hide from this. What was it Ayla had said once? *I'll take it with my head up.* "Yes. Though I no longer claim that title. I'm just Crier now."

"As if that matters," Bree spat, eyes flaring. "As if that changes anything."

"*Bree*," said Hook. "Not helpful."

"My sincerest apologies," she said, but went back to sharpening her blade in silence.

Hook sighed, dragging a hand over his face. Then he looked back at Crier, and where she had expected to see fury, or hatred, in his eyes, there was only—exhaustion. Regret, maybe.

She asked, "Are you going to kill me?"

He physically recoiled, eyes going huge. "What?" he said. "No. First of all, the only thing I kill in cold blood are monsters. Second of all . . ." He peered at her, and she felt studied, like she'd felt so many times with Kinok and the sovereign, but this was different. Under Kinok's gaze she had felt like a specimen. Cross-sectioned, her insides laid bare in the worst way, for the Scyre to pick apart. Under the sovereign's gaze she felt like her existence itself was a test and she was failing. Under Hook's gaze, even now, she felt like a person. A person, messy but whole.

"Second of all," Hook said. "You saved my life."

Oh.

"I won't kill you," Hook told her. "But our paths diverge here. I'm sorry, but—my people come first. Every leech in Rabu's on the lookout for you. Your face is everywhere. I won't have any of mine dying for the daughter of the leech king. I can't. I can't—lose anyone else."

She nodded, staring down at the crushed white shells, not trusting herself to speak. Hook got to his feet and Bree followed. Bree stalked off without another word, boots crunching toward the mouth of the cove, but Hook lingered.

"Crier," he said.

Crier couldn't look up. She couldn't. Her throat ached, even though she had not been wounded there.

Hook tossed a dagger at her feet.

"Find Tourmaline," he said. "Take the Scyre down. And—don't die, yeah?"

"Same to you," Crier managed.

And she listened to him walk away, until even her Automa ears could no longer pick up his footsteps over the wind and the whispering lake.

She lay there for hours, waiting for the Automa healing to do its work, for her flesh to knit itself back together again. By nightfall she wasn't fully healed, but she was able to move without getting dizzy. That was enough for now. The fear of another attack from the border guards forced her to her feet. She walked slowly in the dark, her back twinging with every step. Alone, helpless but for the dagger, she had no plan other than: find shelter.

The guards, terrified they'd accidentally killed the sovereign's daughter, must have fled. Crier crossed into Varn undetected. To the south, there was a juncture where Lake Thea fed into the River Merra. *Get to the river*, Crier told herself, thoughts wheeling like crows. The pain was worsening, and it had become difficult to focus on more than one thing at a time. So she focused on the one thing. *Get to the river. Find shelter.* The riverbanks would be lined with trees, a thick forest. Plenty of hiding places there. *Get to the river.* She could clean her wounds, too. She could wash the blood and grime off her skin. She could wade into the water neck-deep and let the cold settle into her bones.

The moon had long since peaked when she finally reached the mouth of the River Merra. She heard it long before she saw it: the rush of moving water. Then she came to the tree line, thin saplings giving way to older trees, roots sunk into the dark, rich soil, the undergrowth much more alive than the forests to the north. Instead of drying pine needles and brambles, there was a carpet of newborn grass and leafy little plants. The trees were green with moss all the way up to the first branches. Crier ran her fingers along the trunks, wet and spongy beneath her touch. *Get to the river.*

There—a gap in the trees. An odd shimmer. Moonlight on water.

Crier's feet weighed a hundred pounds each. She was reminded of a story—something about a prince who traveled a hundred leagues on foot in shoes made of iron and lead. It was the only way he could save his lover, the prince of a neighboring kingdom. A witch's bargain. Something like that. The trees parted and Crier staggered out onto the riverbank, a sharp dropoff, water tumbling below. So close. Her body didn't require water to survive, but gods, she wanted to *drink*.

Half delirious, she didn't hear them coming until it was too late.

Until she was staring down the shaft of an arrow pointed directly at her forehead.

Bandits.

BEWARE THE MAD QUEEN OF VARN

The Mad Queen, the Bloodsucker, Junn the Monstrous. Keep your head down, traveler. The Mad Queen eats men whole; the Mad Queen will drink your blood like wine. Keep your face hidden, traveler. The Mad Queen rules from a throne of human skulls; the Mad Queen sleeps in robes of human skin. Keep eyes on your children, traveler. The Mad Queen will too.

BEWARE THE MONSTER OF THE MINES

Village Taker, King Killer. The Mad Queen took the throne with her bare hands; she sank her teeth into it; she will do the same to you. Be wary, traveler. The Mad Queen will grind up your bones and drink them like heartstone tea. Dark magick, blood magick. Be wary, traveler. Many wish to look upon her beauty. The Mad Queen is beautiful like a she-demon, a shimmering omen. If you see her, do not run. Pray.

BEWARE THE BONE-EATING QUEEN!

—PROPAGANDA PAMPHLETS DISTRIBUTED
THROUGHOUT RABU AND VARN BY UNKNOWN
SOURCE

11

The next day, the handmaidens didn't show up to Ayla's quarters. Neither did Lady Dear. Ayla waited until the sun was middling in the morning sky before accepting that she would have to forage for her own breakfast. Stomach rumbling, she opened the bedroom door—only to come face-to-face with Queen Junn.

"Oh," Ayla said, trying not to look as startled as she felt.

"Good morning to you too, Ayla," said Junn. "May I come in?"

It was a funny question from a queen. "Sure," Ayla said magnanimously, stepping aside, and the queen swept into her room, bringing with her the faint scent of fruit and flowers, wet earth. Maybe she'd come straight from the aviary. Ayla thought Junn would sit at the little table where Ayla usually ate breakfast, but she walked right past the table to sit on the edge of the bed. For some reason, it made her look young. She wasn't much older than Ayla, but she always acted like she'd been ruling for decades instead of two years.

Ayla stood before her, waiting.

"Little spy," said Junn. "I have a job for you. It's very simple. All I want you to do is observe."

Ayla narrowed her eyes. "What exactly will I be observing?"

"The monsters. At the border between my country and yours."

"You can't be serious."

"I am always serious," said Junn. "But there's no need to worry. You will not be in danger. You don't actually have to get anywhere near the monsters. Or the Tarreenians killing them. My guards will accompany you the whole time, and you need only speak to the heartstone traders at the border, perhaps a nearby village. Really, all you have to do is stop at a local tavern, get a drink, get someone talking. See if you can glean any information about our friend the Scyre. You seem to understand him, after all."

Ayla ignored that last bit, as it felt like an insult. "And how am I getting there?"

"In a carriage, obviously." Junn's lips twitched. "I heard you're not much for horses."

Damn you, Storme.

Ayla scowled. "I suppose there's nothing I can do to get out of this."

"Not if you prefer your head attached to the rest of you," said Junn, eyes glinting, though by now Ayla knew it was a joke. Probably a joke. Almost definitely a joke.

She longed to refuse. She didn't want to leave Storme or Benjy, she didn't trust Queen Junn's assurances that she wouldn't be in any danger, and she sure as all hells didn't want to sit in a carriage with the queen's guards for the few days it would take to travel to the border and back. But . . . the blue smoke Storme had mentioned. This new weapon. If there was anything that could help her defeat Kinok, wouldn't it be something mysterious and powerful like that?

People had been using it to defend against the monsters. If Ayla could track them down, if she could get her hands on that weapon. . . .

"I want a knife," she told Junn. "A good one. Fit for a royal. Freshly sharpened."

"That can be arranged."

"One more thing." Ayla crossed her arms over her chest, studying the queen. "In case you forgot, I'm Storme's sister. If this turns out to be a trap and I die, he will despise you."

And she had the immense satisfaction of witnessing Queen Junn taken off guard, if only for a moment. The queen's expression didn't change, but something flickered in her eyes.

"Understood," she said, a bit stiff.

"Good," said Ayla. "When do I leave?"

Junn glanced at the window, at the risen sun, the sunlight falling in gleaming yellow panes across the floor. "Now."

The last time she'd been in a carriage, she'd watched Rowan die.

This time, she was haunted twofold: by memories of Rowan,

swaying, falling, and then by imprints of Crier. A palimpsest of Crier overlaying reality. Crier on the green velvet seat opposite Ayla. Crier gazing out the carriage window, chin propped in her hand, one eye gold and the other brown.

The outside of the carriage was a dull, scratched-up black, so as not to draw attention, but the inside was like a miniature version of the queen's palace: white-walled with a carved, gemstone-set ceiling, velvet seats. Ayla felt like she was riding along inside a heavily decorated skull.

Of course, she wasn't traveling alone. Aside from the driver, she was accompanied by four of the queen's personal guards—the Automa women with deep green uniforms and shaved heads—who sat in the carriage with Ayla, plus another two guards who rode along behind, *plus* two scouts who rode up ahead. It had already been three days on the road, and the Varnians had yet to display a personality. Ayla had never been so bored in her life. Not for the first time, she wished she could read better. She wished she could have brought along a pile of books to keep her occupied. But she had nothing of the sort, and all she could do was stare out the carriage window as the world slipped slowly by. In the beginning the view was gold: the miles of hills surrounding Thalen. As their party traveled farther north, toward the border of Rabu and Varn, the hills became shallower, like small creases in the earth, and the yellow grass became shrubland, with short scrubby trees sprouting up like burrs on an animal's hide. The sky became paler, the air colder. Sharper in the lungs.

They were riding parallel to the River Merra, headed in

the general direction of Lake Thea—one of the bigger points of entry into Rabu. Along the Varnian side of the border there would be plenty of small towns and villages; along the Rabunian side, villages and the southern estates. The farther away from Thalen they got, the more nervous Ayla felt. Despite the queen's insistence that this was a beginner mission, no risk. There was no such thing as no risk. And she couldn't stop thinking about the way Storme had pulled her aside right before she'd left, as the queen's servants stocked the carriage with a week's worth of food and heartstone, clothes, coin, even wine. "Be careful," he'd said, eyes grave, scar pale in the morning light.

Ayla had almost replied with something snarky—*I thought your queen said there was nothing to worry about*—but held her tongue. "I can take care of myself, brother," she said.

He shook his head. "Just . . . promise me you won't do anything reckless. Promise me you'll stay in the carriage, in the villages. Never alone." He touched her shoulder just once. "Those monsters . . . whatever you're imagining, whatever you're expecting, they're a thousand times worse. *Please* be careful, Ayla. Promise me."

"I promise, Storme," she'd told him.

Midafternoon on the second day of travel, Ayla asked one of the guards for paper and charcoal. She knew they'd brought both along, in case they needed to send missives back to the queen. The guard gave her a piercing look, as if trying to figure out what nefarious scheme Ayla could possibly pull off with a scrap of parchment and a nub of charcoal, but evidently came up with nothing, because she gave in to Ayla's request, and even handed her a thin, leather-bound notebook instead of a single piece of paper. Right—the guards were wary of her not because she was a human, but because they were dedicated to protecting their queen, and according to rumor, Ayla was a violent fugitive. It was a pleasant change, being distrusted for something reasonable.

Ayla curled up by the window with the notebook open on her lap. At first she practiced writing out her letters and symbols, writing out different combinations in concentric circles, like she'd seen on the door to the alchemy library back in the queen's palace. After a while, she found herself letting the charcoal trace across the page, forming not letters but . . . shapes, swirling lines. One line for the horizon, charcoal scraped horizontally to shade in the sky, tiny marks for the shrubs that covered the hills like spores. Black tangles of tree and brush. The final result was messy and childlike, all the lines shaky; Ayla's hand wasn't used to holding charcoal; she did not write. But it was recognizable as a drawing of her surroundings.

She turned to a new page and kept going.

She drew the Bone Tree. As best she could remember it.

She drew the sun apple orchards from the sovereign's palace, the low outbuildings where the servants lived and worked. She drew flowers: apple blossoms and salt lavender and roses. She drew, and the hours fell away like curtains to reveal the purple dusk. Outside the carriage window, darkness swallowed the shrubland, but Ayla kept drawing, the page lit only by the single lantern dangling from the carriage ceiling, a flickering yellow light. They'd be nearing the first border village by now, a small outpost a couple miles off the shores of Lake Thea. The plan was to stop there overnight; a traveler's inn was the perfect place to overhear whispers from all corners of Zulla.

As they veered back toward the River Merra, the scrubby trees became bigger, the space between them smaller, until they were bumping along a muddy road through what could generously be called a forest, a thick green lining both sides of the river. Ayla drew the river, picturing a map of Zulla in her mind and trying to get all the curves and bends right. It began in the Far North as snowmelt, cut down through the heart of Zulla, fed into by Lake Thea and continuing down into Varn, merging at last with the Steorran Sea. . . . Ayla dropped her eyes to look at her own drawing and tried to pinpoint where she was right now. How close to the river were they? She strained her ears, listening for the sound of rushing water, of the riverbank frogs that sang even in winter—

"TURN BACK!"

The nub of charcoal skittered across the page, a rough black scar. All four guards tensed, hands flying to their weapons.

"TURN BACK," the voice of their scout came again, and with the crack of a whip the carriage shuddered to a stop. "GO, GO," the scout yelled from outside, somewhere in the dark. "TURN BACK NOW—BANDITS UP AHEAD—JUST OFF THE RIVER—THEY'VE SPOTTED THE CARR—"

A whistling noise, an odd *thnk*, a wordless cry of pain.

Then, the sound a body made when it fell from a horse.

One of the guards swore and pushed Ayla to the floor of the carriage, away from the open window. Ayla could hear the carriage driver shouting and cracking the whip over and over again, trying to get the horses moving, but it was too late. Within seconds, the driver's shouting cut off abruptly, replaced by the shrieking of panicked horses. The guard who had pushed Ayla swore again, louder this time, and went for the door, one boot landing just a hair's length from Ayla's nose. "I'll fend them off," the guard barked at the other three. "Protect the queen's ward!"

And she leaped out into the darkness, slamming the carriage door behind her.

Ayla lay there on the carriage floor, frozen. Just weeks ago, she'd been in this same situation—trapped in a carriage, surrounded on all sides by an angry mob, helpless in the midst of a fight. On that day, she'd been too scared to do anything. She'd watched Rowan die from behind a pane of glass. *Never again*, she thought now, eye level with the guards' boots, heart pounding in her ears. She would not be the cornered fox tonight. She couldn't freeze up. She couldn't panic. She had to *think*.

The people attacking them were not the monsters she'd been sent here to investigate. They were just people, just—bandits, the scout had said. And they had to want something; they wouldn't just attack for no reason. All right, so, what did they want with Ayla and her party?

Of course. The answer had to be the carriage itself. Or—the horses. Unlike the sovereign, Queen Junn had no fields, no crops. No need for horses that weren't thoroughbred. The carriage might have looked old and worthless from the outside, like it belonged to any old merchant; but anyone who knew anything about horses would recognize their fine breeding. Two horses fit for a queen would fetch a pretty price. Had the bandits spotted them hours ago and waited until nightfall to strike?

The shouts from outside were growing louder, closer. It was hard to tell, but they seemed to be coming from all directions. The bandits were swarming the carriage. How many were out there? How long would a single Automa be able to hold them at bay?

The other guards seemed to be thinking along the same lines. "I'm going out there," one of them muttered, and slipped out the carriage door—a momentary rush of noise, no longer muffled, shouts and the clang of steel against steel. There was nothing Ayla hated more than just *lying* here. She pushed up onto her elbows, but one of the two remaining guards shoved her down again, boot on her spine.

"*Stay down*," the guard hissed. "Don't be a fool. If you want to make it out of this, you'll do as we say."

"What's going on out there?" Ayla demanded. "Can you see anything?" Their night vision was much better than hers.

"Just stay *down*, girl."

Not very reassuring. In her head, Ayla tried to map an escape route. If she could get out of the carriage, off the muddy road, into the thick trees . . .

That was all she came up with before one of the carriage windows exploded inward with a rain of glass and—a powder bomb? No. A sort of waterskin that burst open when it hit the opposite wall, spraying water all over the interior of the carriage, including Ayla. But the water felt strange on her skin, too thick, and that smell . . .

"Get out!" one of the guards cried. "Get out *now!*"

Through the window, a flaming arrow. It struck the wall just as the waterskin had and fell to the floor. One of the guards stamped it out immediately, but the velvet curtains had already ignited, and the first arrow was quickly followed by a second and a third. Ayla scrambled to her feet as the flames spread across the carpeted floor, the velvet benches. She understood now. They hadn't been sprayed with water. They'd been sprayed with oil. The interior of the carriage soaked with it, pure tinder. Within seconds, everything was burning. Ayla coughed, eyes watering, as one of the guards hauled her up by the back of her shirt and practically tossed her out the carriage door. She hit the ground hard, slipped in the mud and fell again, hard enough to knock the breath out of her. For a moment Ayla sat there, her entire spine lit up with pain, gasping for air, blind in the sudden darkness.

Behind her, the fire roared, and she heard the *pop* of the other windows shattering from the heat. Ayla dragged herself upright, a wall of blistering heat at her back, and tried to keep her breathing steady. She closed her eyes and saw another fire imprinted on the backs of her eyelids, as if burning inside her skull: the fire that had raged through her village, devouring whole homes and families, her *parents*. A wall of orange-gold, the ends of her hair catching like tinder just from being too close. The air wavering, smoke in her lungs, in her throat, her skin so hot she remembered being terrified it would melt right off her bones. She hadn't even witnessed the worst of it, not after Storme shoved her into the outhouse. But she'd listened. To the roar. The wood of her family's home splintering, collapsing. Distant screams.

No. She couldn't lose herself to memory. Ayla forced her eyes open and tried to make sense of the chaos laid out before her. Lit by the burning carriage, it was a riot of movement, a tangle of bodies: maybe ten bandits, human, in leather and furs, some on foot wielding short curved swords, three on horseback with crossbows. The source of the flaming arrows. All of them were converging on the queen's guards, who moved with superhuman speed, darting in and out of reach, blades catching the firelight and flashing gold like an Automa's eyes. The guards were holding their own, but Ayla could see one of them was clutching her side and another was favoring her right leg, though not slowing down. They were skilled warriors, stronger and faster than the human bandits, but still . . . it was ten against four, and the bandits on horseback, having succeeded in setting the carriage on fire, now had their crossbows trained on the guards, following their movements. Why weren't they shooting? Were they waiting for something?

Ayla tried to think. *Think.* She wrenched her gaze away from the fight only to see the carriage driver slumped sideways on his bench, two arrows sticking out of his chest. He was an Automa; he was still alive but looked half gone, eyes wide and unseeing, chest heaving, his entire front stained with blood that looked black in the darkness. The flames hadn't reached his bench yet, but they would soon. The horses were wild with panic, eyes rolling, straining at the reins. Ayla was surprised they hadn't just run off, taking the burning carriage with them, but then she saw thick, heavy chains looped around the wheel axles, leading off into the dark. The horses were trapped.

Think!

The bandits hadn't noticed her. They were preoccupied with the guards. It was only twenty paces or so to the edge of the road, the tree line. The bandits were human, they wouldn't be able to see her in the dark. She could make it.

But.

She looked back at the driver. He was still conscious. Panting like a dying animal. Watching her, sort of, if he was capable of watching anything at all. The fire had begun to lick at the bench—it wasn't soaked with oil, but it was mostly made of wood. It would burn, and he'd burn along with it. This Automa. This leech. She didn't care if he died. One less to worry about, in the end. She didn't care.

"*Dammit*," she muttered, and clambered up onto the driver's bench. She threw the driver's limp arm across her shoulders, smoke acrid on her tongue, and dragged him off the bench. He was heavier than he looked, heavier than a human would have been. The two of them landed in the mud, Ayla listing sideways under his weight. He let out a small pained noise, eyes fluttering shut. More violet blood pulsed from the arrows in his chest. Ayla wriggled out from underneath him and laid him on his back; that was all she could do. If he died tonight, it wouldn't be from fire.

And then she ran.

She half expected to be struck down before she reached the tree line, half expected the punch of an arrow to the back, but she was able to leap from the road into the woods unharmed. She paused for a second, breathless, blinking hard as her eyes adjusted to a darkness much deeper than that of the open road. Most of the trees were still bare from winter, but there were enough firs to carve the night sky into tiny pieces of deep blue glass like the mosaics in Queen Junn's palace, catching the moonlight before it had a chance to filter down and illuminate the forest floor. Even ten paces into the woods, the light of the burning carriage—which had become an inferno, bigger than the biggest harvest bonfires, a pillar of pale smoke rising up up up into the stars—was little more than a slight orange glow off the tree trunks.

Ayla took a deep breath, the cool air a balm on her scorched throat, and ran blind, losing her sense of direction almost immediately, brambles tearing at her clothes. More than once she caught a thin tree branch to the face, and it hurt like all hells, like being struck across the cheek with a riding crop, but she kept going. She ran until she could no longer hear the whooping and the war cries of the bandits, until she could no longer smell smoke in the air, and she kept going. She kept going. She kept going—

"*Oh!*"

She burst out of the tree line and caught herself, arms pin-wheeling, right at the edge of a cliff.

No—a riverbank.

Of course she'd run in the exact wrong direction. She was standing at the edge of a short drop-off, the River Merra rushing along below, the water moving quickly here. Foaming white where it tumbled over a shelf of rock. Dead end. She allowed herself five seconds to catch her breath, to reassure herself she was still on solid ground, and then she took off again, racing along the riverbank. It was easier to run here, the moonlight weak but not blocked out by the trees. Ayla leaped over knobbly tree roots, the ground slick beneath her boots, mud and wet grass. She didn't know where she was going, other than: *Away. Away, away.*

Away, until she heard voices. Cutting through the dark.

She froze, deerlike. Ears pricked.

"What about the eyes?"

Ayla crept forward. There, up ahead—a flicker of firelight. Had she stumbled across the bandits' camp? What kind of horrible luck was that? She moved silently from one tree to the next, wanting only to make sure. The trees parted before her, giving way to a natural clearing. She could see the campfire smoldering at the center, three dark shapes sitting around it.

"Eyes can fetch a pretty coin," said one, voice carrying through the trees. "Beautiful design, that is. All those vessels, each one thinner than a human hair."

"Yeah, and what of the hair?" said a second voice.

They said something else, but Ayla didn't hear it.

She was close enough to the see the whole clearing now. Three bandits. A pile of saddlebags, sleeping rolls. A roan horse tied to a thin, ghostly sapling. And.

There. Bound to a tree at the edge of the clearing.

Crier.

Somehow, Crier.

Ayla's breath hitched. Everything went still. Inside her, around her. The leaves overhead stopped rustling. The forest stopped making its forest noises. Elsewhere, the river froze over, thousands of tons of rushing water turned to solid ice. Elsewhere still, the stars stopped wheeling; the sky, like the river, crackled with frost.

Ayla stared, thinking—she was wrong, this was some other girl, some other Automa girl—but no, she knew that face. Even in the darkness, firelight offering only the faintest glow, she knew that face.

Crier.

Crier, captured by human bandits in the wilds of Varn? Crier, arms bent awkwardly behind her, thick chains around her waist, her throat, chains strong enough to restrain an Automa? Not that it looked like Crier needed much restraining. Her body was limp, held upright only by the chains, head lolling sideways. Her eyes were closed.

After about fifteen seconds, her chest rose and fell with a single breath. The fingers of her right hand twitched.

She was alive.

Like floodwater shattering a dam, the world rushed back in.

"No, no," one of the bandits said loudly, and Ayla tore her gaze from Crier. *Don't forget where you are, idiot.* "No," he said again, gesturing with a flask, metal catching the light; Ayla realized he'd been drinking. Had they all been drinking, the ones who'd remained here at camp instead of attacking Ayla's party? "I tell you, the hair never goes for much. It's the inner workings everybody's after. That's where the coin is."

Hidden in the shadows, Ayla listened.

Her eyes found Crier again. She couldn't look away.

"Slice 'em open and salvage everything you can get, that's what we do. You know what their guts are made of?" He didn't wait for a response from the others. "Maker's iron. Black magick, that. Iron that moves and breathes. The bones, too, reinforced with that alchem—alchemized iron. Don't ask me how it works. But I tell you, a single Automa knucklebone'll sell for ten silver queenscoins."

"Ten silver—?" one of the others repeated, incredulous. "For a single knucklebone?" She looked over at Crier, expression almost hungry. "Goddess, what'll we get for a whole damn skeleton?"

Well, thought Ayla. *That's that, then.*

She took a deep breath, put on a scared face, and stumbled forward, taking care to stomp loudly on the dry leaves blanketing the forest floor. The bandits leaped to their feet, spinning to face the forest, weapons drawn. Two crossbows, one nasty-looking serrated dagger.

Ayla pitched her voice high and sweet. "Help," she said. "Please, is someone there?"

"Show yourself," one of the bandits called out. The one who had been curious about the going price of Crier's skeleton.

"I'm unarmed," Ayla said, and slipped out of the shadows, into the clearing. Eyes wide. Arms wrapped around herself, shoulders hunched in. She was already small; she wanted to look smaller. "Please. I need help."

"What're you doing out here, girl?" said the skeleton bandit.

"My horse spooked," Ayla said, throwing in a sniffle. "I fell off and it ran away. I tried to find a road, but I got lost. I've been wandering for hours."

Both crossbows lowered an inch.

"Please," she said. "I'm so cold."

"Warm yourself, then," said the second bandit, sheathing his dagger. The other two lowered their crossbows completely, making a space for Ayla at the fire.

She made a show of sagging with relief. "Thank you. Goddess with you." Halfway to the fire, she stopped in her tracks and gasped, pretending to notice Crier for the first time. "Wh-who is that?"

"The most generous leech you'll ever meet," said the skeleton bandit. "She'll be buying my drinks for the next year!"

The others laughed, coarse and scratchy as a donkey's fur.

"Can I look?" Ayla asked, trying to sound nervous, morbidly curious. "I never saw a leech in chains before."

The skeleton bandit snorted. "Look all you want, but be

careful. She's a fierce little thing, that one. Stuck her with an arrow and she kept fighting. Took three blows to get her sleeping, and I don't know how long it'll take."

"Of course," said Ayla. "Sounds like you men were very brave."

"I don't know about that," said the second bandit, sounding pleased in a way that sent chills down Ayla's spine. A horrible, slimy sensation, like someone had cracked an egg over her head. "'S just the one girl."

"*Feisty,* though," said another. "Tried to bite me. I should've knocked her teeth out."

"Don't wanna lose 'em in the dark, though," said the skeleton bandit. "Worth a meal each, those teeth."

Ayla crept closer to Crier. Shadows danced on the forest floor as she left the circle of firelight. She kept her body language shivery and frightened. A scared little rabbit, a baby bird knocked from the nest. This close, she could see the bloodstains on Crier's clothes. Violet blood dried to a dark, rusty brown. Ayla's heart was kindling, her anger a burst of sparks, the flare of starving embers. "She tried to bite you? That's so scary," she said, letting her voice carry back to the bandits. "I would've cried."

The bandit said something in response, but Ayla wasn't listening. She was curling her fingers around the hilt of her bone-handled knife. Only a few paces from Crier, and Crier still hadn't opened her eyes. It looked like she really was unconscious.

"Hey," the skeleton bandit called out. "Don't get too close."

Ayla crouched down as if trying to inspect Crier's face.

Angling her body so the bandits couldn't see, she placed the knife on the fallen leaves at Crier's hip. One heartbeat, two, and she stood up and went over to join the bandits.

The fire was burning low. Near the edge there was a pile of dry wood, including the branch of a fir tree, not yet broken down. It was about the length of Ayla's arm, needles feathering out like wings.

Ayla leaned forward, warming her hands. Around her, the bandits had relaxed again. She felt their eyes on her, but not out of suspicion.

She suppressed a shiver. *Disgusting old bastards.*

She leaned forward a little farther, all casual. Then, in one movement, she snatched the fir tree branch off the ground and swept it through the fire like a broom. The dry, browning needles caught instantly, crackling into flames. Ayla didn't hesitate. Before the three bandits figured out what she was doing, she'd already brought the burning branch in a great arc around her, swiping it across their faces as hard as she could.

They *howled*, scrambling to their feet, but they'd already been drinking, and now they'd gotten a face full of fire and sharp, stinging needles. Ayla wanted to go for one of their swords— she didn't know how else to get Crier out of the chains—but she hadn't slowed them down enough. Already one of them was recovering, eyes red and cheeks wet with tears, *furious.*

"CRIER," Ayla screamed, voice raw with fear. "CRIER, WAKE UP!"

"You're dead meat," the bandit growled, and lunged.

Ayla threw herself backward, swinging the burning branch. It was enough to keep him out of arm's reach, but it was quickly burning up, now more smoke than flame. "CRIER," she tried again, but an instant later the bandit knocked the branch out of her hand. He grabbed her wrist, yanking her in. His breath smelled of wine; his skin of horsehide and old, sour sweat.

A noise at Ayla's back, a metallic wrenching.

"You're *dead*," the bandit said again, twisting his grip. The other two were straightening up, wiping their streaming eyes. "Only question is, you wanna die quick or slow?"

"Neither," said Ayla.

"Slow," said one of the other two. "Make it hurt. But don't ruin her, Han. Who knows, maybe she could fetch us some coin. Sell her hair for wigs, her bones for dogs. Her eyes for—"

But he never finished. A thick metal chain struck him across the face. He doubled over.

Crier.

Ayla dared to look back. Crier was listing to one side, favoring her right leg. She was holding her chains like twin whips. Her eyes flicked between Ayla and the bandits, lingering on the bandit with Ayla's wrist in his grip. Her features darkened with an expression Ayla had never seen on her face before. Mouth twisting, golden eyes narrowed.

"Leave now," she rasped.

Three drunk men, burly though they were, were no match for her. Crier was artless but furious, weakened but Automa-quick. She darted forward in the span of a blink and lashed out with the chains, this time catching the skeleton bandit across the fore-head. He staggered, lurching into one of the others.

Ayla used the moment of distraction to sink her teeth into her captor's arm. He cursed, rearing back, and she wriggled out of his grip. Grabbed Crier's sleeve. "Run!"

Crier tossed the chains aside and they ran. Back into the black woods, the cover of darkness, they ran until Crier gasped out, "Can't hear them anymore."

Wrist bruised, a nasty stitch in her side throbbing with every breath, Ayla slowed to a stop. She let go of Crier's sleeve . . . and Crier dropped like a stone into a well, knees hitting the forest floor. "Crier!" Ayla hissed, crouching down beside her. "Please, you have to—"

"Ayla," Crier breathed.

Ayla nodded, helpless. A thousand different responses on her tongue, none of them right.

"Ayla," Crier repeated. "Did you know you're a wanted fugi-tive?"

Then her eyes rolled back in her head, and she passed out.

How long did it take for an Automa body to heal itself?

Dawn came, the sky shifting from black to deepest blue to the soft color of salt lavender and pale pink. As the sun rose over the treetops, the surface of the river sparkled gold and then white, and Crier slept.

And curled up under the dangling tree roots, knees drawn to her chest, Ayla watched her. Crier's dark hair was fanned out around her head like a crown of seaweed. There was riverbed clay smeared on her jaw, pale against her skin. Flecks of dirt like freckles on her arms. Dried blood on her cheekbones, her temples, fingerprint-shaped, like she'd touched her wounds and then her face. Clothes stained with muck and blood. Big blooming patches of dried, purplish-brown blood. If she'd been human, she would not have survived whatever drew that much blood. Ayla thought about that for a long time.

The sky was pearly like the inside of an oyster, not quite morning blue, when Crier finally opened her eyes. She did it slowly, as carefully as she did all things. One eye cracked open, pupil dilating, then the other. She blinked once. Twice.

"Hello," said Ayla, and was rewarded by Crier's full-body twitch. Crier jolted upright and then gasped in pain, one hand flying back to touch the place where, a few hours ago, there had been a deep wound. Ayla had checked it once, just before dawn. By then, the bleeding had long since stopped. Crier's skin was already knitting itself back together, shiny like scar tissue, though Ayla knew there would be no scar. Below the surface, the damage to her inner workings—severed veins, pierced organs, nicked bone—would be repairing itself too.

Crier's hands fluttered over her own body, checking for other injuries. Finding none, she went still. Her face was hidden behind her hair, and she could have been made from stone, she was so still, all her tiny human movements—breathing, blinking, shifting—ceased. A prey animal frozen at the first hint of danger: First, you hope they don't see you. Then you run.

Don't run, some part of Ayla wanted to say. *I am not the hunter here. Not the wolf.*

Instead:

"I'm not going to stab you this time," she told Crier.

"You didn't stab me last time, either," said Crier, and unfroze. She tucked her hair behind her ear. The last time Ayla had seen her—the last time, and all the times before—Crier had been perfectly groomed. Hair clean and glossy, skin soft and smelling of rose oil, certainly no dirt or blood anywhere. Silk nightgown. Silk sheets. Only the best for the sovereign's daughter.

Now, it looked like she'd been dragged by the ankles to hell and back again. She looked like a survivor.

Ayla bit back what would have been a half-hysterical laugh. A few months ago, she would have looked at Crier and thought viciously, *You will die by my hand and my hand only*, and convinced herself that was why she hadn't abandoned Crier to the bandits. How wholly things had changed since then. Ayla hadn't been able to kill Crier that night in the palace, and she wouldn't be able to kill her now. Some things were impossible.

That begged a new question: If she wasn't going to kill Crier, what *was* she going to do?

She'd been staring at Crier for too long.

And Crier was staring back.

"Did you know all of Zulla's searching for you?" Ayla blurted out, just to fill the silence. "It's not every day the sovereign's daughter runs away from her own wedding. You've caused quite a stir."

"I don't care," Crier said hotly. "I couldn't marry Kinok. I'd rather run forever. I'd rather die." She pinned Ayla with an uncharacteristically fierce glare. "Are you going to turn me in? Finish what you started that night? Go ahead and try it. I have—" She broke off, feeling at her hip for a weapon that wasn't there. "I have—"

Ayla retrieved the bone-handled knife from where she'd stuck it in the clay behind her. "You have this?"

"I . . ." Crier's jaw worked. "I don't need that. You're human. I can overpower you easily."

Ayla felt her face grow hot. Not out of anger; she'd never heard a less convincing threat. But because, judging by Crier's expression, they were both recalling the same memory.

You're an Automa. It's your nature to overpower.

The look on Crier's face, like Ayla had struck her. Then—

Then—

"I'm not going to turn you in," said Ayla. She flipped the knife in her hand and held it out to Crier handle first.

Crier's eyes flicked to the knife. To Ayla's face. To the knife again. She took it gingerly, watching Ayla the whole time, like she thought it was a trick. But Ayla let her take it, let her sit back and slip the knife through one of the loops on her belt, secure at her hip.

Then they were just . . . staring at each other. Again.

This time, Crier broke the silence. "You didn't stab me last time," she said. "But you were going to."

A pang in Ayla's chest. "I thought I was," she whispered.

She assumed the next question would be: *Why?*

But Crier asked, "Why didn't you?"

"I . . ." Gods, how could she answer that? She didn't know herself. Or she did, but it was too messy to put into words. *Because of the tide pool. The key to the music room. Because of the night you whispered into the darkness between us:* How can I help? *Because I told you to learn more about Kinok and you did. Because you are brilliant and have never once used it to cause harm. Because you surprise me. Because I am not done being surprised by you.*

Once, in Kalla-den, at one of the stalls that sold black-market Made objects, Ayla had played with a trinket shaped like a little gold telescope. If you peered into one end, you could see grains of colored glass shifting and forming new patterns. The grains changed color, rippling blue, red, orange, rainbow, back again. Sometimes they formed images: a red flower on a field of gold, a yellow cat's eye, an emerald-green leaf. Never the same pattern or image twice. Knowing Crier felt like that. Especially toward the end, those final weeks, when Ayla had begun to realize—and refused to admit, even to herself—that she would not be able to kill her. Every time she looked at Crier, a new pattern. A new picture. A display of new and stunning light.

Crier was waiting. Her gaze was steady, but there was a tightness to her mouth, her shoulders. Like she was bracing for a blow.

"I don't think . . ." Ayla chose her words carefully. "I don't think this world would be better for your death." *No, come on, don't be a coward—if nothing else, for this, you owe her honesty.* "I don't think I would be."

"I see," said Crier.

"Do you want to know why I tried?"

Crier looked pained. "Do I?"

"That night, we were trying to steal something from Kinok's study," said Ayla. "That special compass you told me about. The compass that points not to the north but to the Iron Heart. We were trying to steal it, so we needed a distraction. It was me who came up with the idea of setting off your chime. Drawing the guards to your bedroom."

"Your idea," Crier repeated, more to herself than Ayla. "Right. Yes. Of course."

"I was angry. At Kinok. At your father. Your Kind. You. Myself." She let out a sharp breath. "Myself more than anyone. I was fucking *furious* with myself, Crier. And terrified." *Of what I felt for you. I still am.* "So I made a choice. It was the wrong one. Not—I don't mean not killing you was the wrong choice—I mean everything leading up to that. Planning it. Letting myself into your bedroom that night. If you hate me for it, I can't blame you. I'd hate me for it, if I were you." She swallowed hard. Her voice sounded harsh and miserable even to her own ears, that same anger bleeding through. That same fear. At herself, of herself. "It was stupid, okay?" she said. "It was *stupid.*"

Crier's lips parted.

It wasn't the full story. But Ayla had spent years thinking only of revenge on Sovereign Hesod. He'd killed her family; she would kill his. Blood for blood. Ayla hadn't told anyone that story. There had only ever been three people who knew the truth of her past: Benjy, Rowan, and Storme. The truth was sunk so deep inside her. She wasn't yet ready to haul it up from the ocean floor.

"I will not make that choice again," she said only. She grabbed the nearest bit of broken shell and dragged it through the clay by her foot, drawing whatever symbols came to mind—salt, iron, gold. "Anyway, I think we're on the same side now. So."

"We were always on the same side," said Crier.

Ayla shook her head. "No. Not when I was your hand-maiden."

"Oh." Crier seemed to consider that, gazing out past the tree roots to the river beyond, the quiet rush and roar of the water, smooth on the surface but surging beneath. "I see," she said. "But now that I've defected . . . ?"

"Tell me the story of how you ran away from your wedding, Lady Crier," said Ayla.

"Crier," said Crier. "It's just Crier."

"Okay, Just Crier," said Ayla, and listened as Crier told the story of Faye risking her own life to help Crier escape. The story of confronting her father about Kinok's plan to destroy the Iron Heart.

It was all Ayla could do to not visibly react.

The Revolution's goal had always been to destroy the Iron Heart. To wipe out the leeches in one go, the way the servant Nessa had sprayed poison over a swarm of locusts until their tiny iridescent bodies littered the ground in the thousands, the tens of thousands. That was what Rowan wanted. What Benjy wanted. What Ayla wanted, beneath the fire. For so long.

Sitting here on the riverbank across from Crier, Ayla forced herself to imagine it: destroying the Heart, the source of heartstone. The leeches wouldn't die out immediately. There was plenty of heartstone circulating outside the Heart—in traders' caravans, in storehouses, in cellars, in every town, village, city, estate, in Rabu and Varn and Tarreen. The humans would have to take up post in the Heart, to defend it when the leeches came, which they would. But say they lost. Say the humans held the Heart, and there was no new heartstone. It might take months, even years, for it to run out. But it would.

Ayla imagined what it would look like: Crier wasting away. Crier, starved and limp. Eyes glassy, skin cold to the touch. And she imagined Queen Junn, and Wender from the Queen's Feast. The children in the Midwiferies. Lady Dear, newbuilt. The faceless Delphi. Small bodies beneath white sheets, created and destroyed just like that. Made. Terminated.

That was what Kinok wanted for humankind, Ayla thought. That destruction, that endless crush of death, that massacre . . . He was evil for wanting it. Rotten inside, worm-eaten, putrid.

The Automae did not deserve Ayla's forgiveness. She would not give it. But she also wouldn't let them turn her into that kind of monster.

"I'm going to stop Kinok," said Crier. "I don't know how. But I will."

Ayla shook away the images of death. Refocused. "We need to make a plan."

The *we* hung between them like the bone-handled knife. Another offering.

"We do," Crier murmured. She raked a hand through her tangled hair, an oddly human movement. She seemed almost flustered. "And you? Why have you come all this way, if you were safe under the queen's protection in Thalen?"

Ayla let out a breath. "Have you heard about the monsters?"

"The Shades? The Automae poisoned by Nightshade? Yes, I know a fair bit."

"Well, the queen doesn't," said Ayla. "I was supposed to talk to heartstone traders. Gather information. It was *supposed* to be easy. I should've known better. But really, I thought if I had anything to worry about, it'd be the monsters. The Shades. I didn't expect bandits."

"People rarely do," said Crier, and Ayla was startled into laughter, and Crier's eyes went very wide.

"Plan, we need a plan," Ayla said abruptly. Her face felt hot like she'd been basking in summer sunlight, not sitting on a cold riverbank in winter. "We can figure this out."

Crier nodded. "Yes."

"We're gonna stop Kinok," said the part of Ayla that felt new, nascent, like the bud of a sun apple blossom right at the tail end of winter. "We'll find Tourmaline. Before he does. Before he destroys the Heart."

"First . . . you'll need this," said Crier. She reached beneath the neckline of her shirt, pulling out—a delicate gold chain. Ayla's necklace. Her locket, dangling from Crier's fingers, winking in the sunlight. Crier had tried to return it to her once before, in Elderell, but at the time . . . at the time, Ayla had been reeling with shock and confusion, trying to make sense of the memories they'd fallen into—and everything that came before. (Crier's hands on her face, Crier's breath on her lips.) She'd rejected the locket. *I don't want it. Keep it, I don't care anymore, just stay away from me.* Then, in Crier's bedroom, she had seen it once more. As she stood over the bed, clutching the knife, trying to convince herself she could *do this*, she could kill, she could draw blood—she'd seen the locket in Crier's hand. Crier had been sleeping with it.

Had kept it all this time, despite everything.

"Take it," Crier said now, holding it out to Ayla. "It's yours. It belongs with you."

This time, Ayla didn't fight. She took the necklace and looped it around her neck, fingers clumsy on the tiny clasp. For the first time in so long, the locket was a familiar weight on her sternum. Warm gold, red gemstone, eight-point star etched into the surface. Her locket.

"Thank you," she murmured.

"It's yours," Crier said again. "So is this one." And she pulled out a second locket. The one Ayla had seen in Kinok's study, her locket's twin. She wanted to examine it, to explore whatever memories and secrets were tucked away inside, but that would have to wait.

"You keep it for now." If something happened to Ayla, then at least one locket would be safe. "Keep it hidden."

"I will protect it with my life." Then Crier's brow furrowed. "Ayla. Your arm."

"Hm?" Ayla twisted from side to side, inspecting her arms. And she hadn't even noticed, but her upper left arm was singed, her green wool sleeve blackened and tattered, revealing scraped-up skin beneath. The wounds were shallow, but even the smallest wounds could become deadly if infected. "Damn," she said. "Okay, I need to clean this."

"One moment," said Crier, and got to her feet.

"What? Where are you going?"

"One moment." With that, she headed off down the riverbank, picking her way around slick, half-frozen patches of mud.

All right, then. Ayla scooted to the water's edge and began cleaning the wound as best she could, washing away the soot and dried blood with palmfuls of clear, icy water. It felt good. The coldness cut through the shock at seeing Crier again, the haze of confusion, awkwardness, guilt. Dread, for what was to come.

Crier returned a few minutes later with a handful of soft green moss. She crouched down beside Ayla and offered the moss, wordless. Ayla took it and pressed it to her arm, and the relief was immediate, cool wet moss on her prickling skin.

"Thank you," she said.

"Yes," said Crier, and turned her face back to the river and the forest beyond.

With darkness came a chill, heat leaching away as the shadows grew. Ayla tried halfheartedly to catch a fish for dinner. Crier offered to go hunting, to track down a rabbit or something, but neither of them were keen on being separated for more than a few minutes. For all they knew, more bandits—or worse—were still prowling the woods. So Ayla drank from the river and spent the evening pressing her hands into her belly, trying to trick it into feeling full, and Crier sat quietly, listening, always listening.

"Do you mind if I sleep?" Ayla asked, breaking the silence. For almost an hour, the only sounds had been the world-noises: singing frogs, rushing water, the rustling of the forest all around them. Sometimes, the cry of a lone owl. The sky had darkened from blue to black, the moon a ripe yellow fruit, and Ayla felt bruised with exhaustion. And half frozen. They couldn't risk a campfire, and neither of them had anything warmer than the clothes they were wearing. Ayla was trying not to shiver too violently, but she couldn't help it. Why hadn't she thought to grab one of the furs from the carriage before it burned? She had to keep consciously relaxing her jaw so her teeth would stop chattering.

"Oh—yes, sleep," said Crier. It was too dark to see her expression, but she sounded startled, even embarrassed. "I'm sorry. Sometimes I forget you need to do that every night."

"Unfortunately." Ayla lowered herself onto her side, trying to find a patch of ground without too many rocks. Again she longed for a fur, a shawl, anything to put between her and the frozen dirt. "Are you . . . sure you're all right? You can wake me in a few hours and I'll take over as watch." Gods, she felt so awkward.

"I'm fine," Crier said. "Sleep. You need it."

Ayla turned her back to Crier and curled up in a little ball, arms wrapped around her shins. Trying to preserve as much body heat as possible. And though she'd been yawning just a minute ago, the moment she lay down, her mind became a lantern she couldn't douse. How was she supposed to stop thinking about everything Crier had told her? How was she supposed to sleep when she knew Kinok was out there somewhere? Kinok, and other monsters in the dark?

"I can hear you thinking," Crier whispered.

"No you can't," Ayla whispered back. "Not even with your ears."

"How would you know?"

Ayla opened her eyes. Crier was sitting with her back to Ayla, facing out over the river. When Ayla's sight adjusted to the blue darkness, she could make out the bloodstains on the back of Crier's shirt.

"All right, then," Ayla said, just above a whisper. "What do thoughts sound like?"

"Bees," said Crier.

"You're making that up. You mean the sound of buzzing?"

"No. The sound of a bee's footsteps as it walks across a flower petal."

"That's not a real sound!"

Crier sniffed. "Maybe not to you."

"You're lying," said Ayla. "I can tell because you're terrible at it. You're using your storytelling voice."

A pause. "My . . . storytelling voice?"

Ayla shifted, pillowing her head on one of her arms. There was a tree root digging into her hip, another at her ribs. She longed for the cloudlike bed she'd left behind in the queen's palace. "Mm. Like when you told me the story of the princess and the three animals. The princess in the"—she yawned—"snowstorm. With the rabbit."

"Hare," Crier corrected her.

"Is there a difference?"

"Yes."

"Does it matter?"

". . . No."

Ayla was still far too cold, but she felt her eyes slipping shut. "You should do that again sometime," she said, not really paying attention to what she was saying.

"Do what again?" Crier asked, soft.

"I d'nno," Ayla mumbled. "Tell me a story. You know a lot of stories, don't you?"

"Yes," Crier said. "I know a lot of stories."

"Mm. Well. Don't keep 'em all to yourself." Ayla's words were slurring together. "Don't be . . . don't be selfish."

The last thing Ayla heard before the lantern of her mind finally winked out was the sound of Crier's quiet, helpless laughter.

She woke once in the night. Judging by the black sky, she'd only been asleep a couple hours. It wasn't yet her turn to take watch. Satisfied that all was well and Crier was still sitting straight-backed at the edge of the water, Ayla closed her eyes, ready to slip back under. Then a thought occurred.

Slowly, so as not to make any sound, Ayla took out her locket. She rubbed her thumb over the gemstone, then felt around until she found a bit of broken shell. Without letting herself think too much about what she was doing, she brought the jagged edge of the shell to her thumb. A prick. A drop of blood. Mimicking what Crier had shown her in Elderell, Ayla pressed her thumb to the locket, letting her blood smear against the red stone. And she was—

—she was—

Not alone.

Firelight, yellow and alive. The bundles of drying herbs hanging from the rafters cast odd shadows on the walls, like hands reaching down from above. Ayla was sitting on the lip of the hearth, fire a wall of heat at her back, and she was not alone. Leo was standing beside her, observing two figures in the middle of the room. One was Siena, with her freckles and dark curls, so similar to Ayla. The other was clad all in white. A Midwife.

They were leaning over a table, murmuring to each

221

other. Ayla got to her feet, trying to be silent even though she knew they could not see or hear her. She crept around the edge of the room, eyes adjusting to the gloom where the firelight didn't quite reach.

"Are you ready?" said the Midwife.

"Does it matter?" Siena replied.

And Ayla saw there was one more person in this room. A girl. She was lying on the table, asleep or unconscious or—gods, was she breathing? Ayla counted out ten seconds, fifteen, and the girl's chest didn't rise and fall. Even an Automa would have taken a breath in that time. Was she dead?

Ayla crept even closer, until she was standing right next to Siena. My grandmother, she thought, but it didn't feel real. Siena died before Ayla was born, and Ayla's mother had always been reluctant to talk about her. Ayla never thought of herself as a person with grandparents. With a bloodline.

But here it was: Her bloodline. Her heritage. Siena.

Her bloodline was holding a knife.

Not a knife—the blade was small and curved. It looked more like a physician's instrument than a weapon. Ayla watched, growing more and more confused, as Siena began to unbutton the dead girl's shirt. She pulled it open, careful not to bare the girl's chest entirely, and let out a shaky breath. "I'm ready," she said, more to herself than the Midwife. "Gods, I hope this works."

She brought the knife to the girl's skin, right over her heart, and pressed down. Ayla grimaced, expecting blood, but there was none. Siena hadn't made a cut. Her blade traced a path that seemed predetermined, revealing a hairline seam that hadn't been visible only moments ago. Painstakingly, using only the tip of the knife, she lifted a small section of the girl's chest. Like the tiny door of a locket, hidden away in this Made girl's skin.

Ayla leaned forward. The opening in the girl's chest was only palm-sized; she could see nothing but a sheen of red inside. The girl's heart. Unlike Automa blood, which was an oily, purplish fluid, the heart was human red. Heartstone red. Something felt very wrong, and then Ayla realized: it wasn't beating. Automa hearts beat slower than humans', and the beat sounded more like the tick of a clock than anything else, but it was still a beat. Still a pulse. This girl had none. Her heart was silent as a tomb.

"Be quick, but be careful," said the Midwife, and Ayla startled; she'd forgotten the Midwife was here. "The veins are delicate, especially without blood flow."

Siena nodded. Her dark hair was sticking to her temples with sweat, but her hands were steady.

"Now," said the Midwife.

And Ayla watched, fascinated, as Siena cut the Made girl's heart out of her body. Gently, she wrapped it in a white cloth and set it aside. Every movement was measured, purposeful. Siena knew what she was doing, Ayla realized. She knew how to navigate the inner workings of this body; she knew it like a Scyre, a Midwife, a Maker would; she knew it like breathing. Ayla found herself focusing on Siena's face more than her hands. Studying her profile, finding all the similarities between them. My nose, she thought. My chin.

The memory shifted, Ayla's surroundings blurring for a moment. When the world settled again, the Midwife was holding something out over the girl's body, offering it to Siena with both hands. A lump of deep blue stone. Smooth and polished, no bigger than a clenched fist. There were tiny etchings on it, so faint Ayla could see them only when she leaned in. Alchemical symbols. Arranged in concentric circles. She caught the four elements, then gold.

Siena took the deep blue stone and lowered it into the hollow space left behind. Ayla heard the faintest noise, like a latch clicking into place.

A pulse of blue light. The heart flared for an instant, glowing, and Siena's memory began to shift again, colors bleeding into each other, the world like wet paint smeared by a giant hand. The last thing Ayla saw was silver. Two spots of bright, starlike silver.

The girl had opened her eyes.

"Yora," Siena breathed.

12

Ayla woke when the sky began to lighten, deep blue shifting to lavender. Crier, who had played sentinel all night, now watched as wakefulness spread like the dawn over Ayla's body—first her fingers twitched, then her brow furrowed, then her lips parted, revealing a glimpse of her front teeth, then her eyelashes fluttered. Without opening her eyes, she took a long breath through her nose, a prolonged sniff that dropped into a hum at the end, a tiny throaty noise.

Ayla opened her eyes and blinked at Crier in the soft light. "We were s'posed to take turns," she said, voice scratchy with sleep. "You were s'posed to wake me up."

"You needed the rest," Crier said, and got to her feet. She brushed ineffectually at the mud on her clothes, succeeding only in smearing it further. "You can keep watch tonight, if you choose."

"Mm." Ayla tried to stand up and stumbled, one knee buck-ling. Crier grabbed her shoulder, alarmed. She was more than a little stunned when Ayla didn't shake her off.

"'M fine," Ayla said, eyes squeezed shut. "I'm fine. Just—light-headed."

"You need to eat," Crier said.

"Yeah. I'm not sure how that's going to happen, though." Ayla breathed in slowly, then stretched, body a curve. Crier let go of her shoulder. "I could try to catch a fish again."

Crier shook her head. "Our best bet is the woods. Even if we can't hunt, I can find—mushrooms, winterberries, seeds, some-thing."

"How do *you* know how to forage in the wilderness?" Ayla asked. For once she didn't sound accusatory, just curious.

"My father has a lot of books on herbology and botany," Crier said. "I read about edible mushrooms and flowers and bark and—lots of things. I know what will be growing in this region at this time of year. It's difficult, because warm days and over-night frosts kill off a lot of seeds before they get a chance to grow, but I think I'll be able to find something."

Ayla opened her mouth and then shut it again. "I see," she said. "Foraging it is."

They crept through the forest, Crier listening for bandits, hunters, any footfalls that did not belong to her or Ayla. But after an hour of nothing but birdsong and rustling leaves and the trill of river frogs, Crier let herself relax just a fraction. The ground was soft and spongy with moss, eventually giving way to a carpet of dead leaves as they wandered farther from the river. Crier breathed in and the air smelled of sap, wet soil, the earthiness of moss and the rain-smell of rotting wood. It was strange, the absence of salt. Back home—back at the *sovereign's palace*—the sea was inescapable. The air was tinged with it. The rushing tide sounded like the world itself was breathing, in and out, in and out. Filling and emptying those gargantuan lungs.

"There," said Crier, pointing to a cluster of white mushrooms at the base of a tree. "Those are safe to eat."

Ayla gave them a doubtful look. "You're sure?"

"Yes."

Crier expected an argument, but Ayla just nodded. She picked and ate the mushrooms right there, crouched over the tree roots, first in tiny hesitant bites and then in mouthfuls, hunger taking over. Crier tried not to think of her own hunger. She hadn't had any heartstone for . . . two days now? She had finally run out. Right now the hunger was a faint ache, a restlessness, an itch, but soon it would become far more serious. Already she was feeling the side effects: the wounds in her back still ached, and staying awake all night had been unexpectedly difficult. She'd nearly nodded off a couple times.

They kept going once Ayla had finished off the mushrooms. It took a while to find more sustenance, the frostbitten forest having little to offer, but there were more mushrooms and a handful of pale green winterberries. Enough to fill Ayla's belly for now. They began the long walk back to their riverbank shelter, and as the morning went on without any sign of bandits, the stretches of uncomfortable silence between them grew shorter—and less uncomfortable. Crier pointed out the gathering clouds and Ayla said, "I hope it doesn't rain, that's the last thing we need," and Crier said *yes* and Ayla said, "Maybe we could find a better shelter. These woods are surrounded by farmland, maybe we could hide in someone's barn." And Crier said, *Oh, that's a good idea*, and Ayla looked pleased. At one point Ayla started humming, absentminded, and Crier recognized the tune. Hadn't Ayla sung this for her once? *Listen for my voice across the wide, storm-dark waters. Listen for my voice, let it guide your way home.* It had sounded melancholy then as it did now, even accompanied by sunlight and birdsong and the tumbling river. A sad, lilting song. A yearning song.

Part of her wanted to press Ayla for more details about her stay in Thalen. Only a few months ago, anything to do with Queen Junn would have fascinated her. But now Junn's name filled Crier with revulsion. She couldn't forget the letter she'd received, her last correspondence with the Bone Eater. *Don't worry about the missing red hen. I took care of her.*

Councilmember Reyka—the only member of the Red Council who had ever shown kindness to Crier, who had ever taken her seriously—was dead, and Junn had killed her. Even if she hadn't raised the blade herself, she'd given the order. Why? Reyka was on their side. Reyka had been working against Kinok. Who killed their own ally?

How could you? she'd thought so many times, lying awake at night, brimming with a hot, prickling emotion she had finally identified as anger.

"You know what I feel like doing?" said Ayla, snapping Crier out of her thoughts.

The familiar gleam of the river was once again visible through the trees up ahead.

"What?" said Crier.

"Taking a *bath*."

Ayla ran for the river without looking back. By the time Crier gathered herself enough to follow after, picking her way down the slippery bank, Ayla was already at the edge of the water. She was fully clothed but barefoot, wading in slowly. It was a warm day, but the water would be freezing. Mountain runoff. Crier made her way to a little shelter and sat down, pressing her spine to the curving dirt wall, keeping her eyes firmly on her own feet. Automae were not modest about nudity, but she knew it was often different for humans.

"It's not too cold," Ayla called, and Crier glanced up automatically before forcing her eyes back down. "You coming?"

"I . . . I don't want to—intrude," Crier said, raising her voice to be heard over the rushing water.

"It's a river," Ayla called back. "It doesn't belong to anyone. Come on, don't you want to clean off all the blood?"

"I . . . ," Crier said weakly, but couldn't think of an excuse that wasn't *I can't see any part of you without wanting to see more*, so instead she just closed her mouth and got to her feet. Ayla was waist-deep in the water now, her pants discarded on the pebbly shore. She was still wearing her shirt. *Thank the gods.* Crier toed out of her own shoes and waded into the water, focusing on the bite of cold, the shock to her system. She took slow, careful steps, the river bottom slick beneath her feet. Mud and clay and smooth, flat stones, tiny black oyster shells. Each footstep stirred up a cloud of silt in the clear water. She looked up. Ayla had reached the center of the river and was pulling her shirt off over her head. Her back was arched, muscles flexing in her shoulders, and—*oh*—the tops of her shoulders were dusted with freckles just like her nose. Her spine was a curve Crier wanted to—run her fingers along, fit her palm to; she wanted to press her hand to that soft sun-warm skin, wanted to trace the faint, pockmarked scars scattered across Ayla's back like points on a map, the remnants of some human illness. Some pox. Where Crier was long and lean, Ayla was smaller, solid, compact, carved from bronze. An illustration from a faerie book, standing there in the sunlit water, tawny brown skin and dark tangled curls.

Ayla balled up her shirt and tossed it back onto the shore, then dived beneath the surface. While Ayla was underwater, Crier scrambled out of her pants and waded in up to her waist, cold punching the breath from her lungs. But it felt good, refreshing, after the days spent caked in dirt and her own dried, flaking blood. She longed for soap—not even the floral bath oils she'd grown up with—but did her best to scrub the grime off her skin and out of her clothes without it. She half walked, half swam to the center of the river, water up to her collarbone, and took off her shirt, scraping at the bloodstains with her fingernails. She was terribly aware of Ayla, only a few feet away, splashing around.

"I should make you wash my hair," Ayla said after a while. Crier glanced up to see Ayla watching her, water lapping at her chin, and was reminded of the night they'd slipped into the deep, sunken tide pools off the shores of the Steorran. The water had been freezing then, too. "And dress me."

"I would," said Crier.

Ayla's eyes widened. She ducked beneath the water again, surfacing only a moment later. "I was joking," she said, and shivered.

"Are you getting too cold?" Crier asked. Her own body had acclimated to the chill, but human bodies weren't like that. Humans fell ill so easily. "We should get out."

"I was going to wash my clothes. So they have time to dry before the sun goes down."

"Then I'll get out," said Crier. "Wash your clothes. I won't look."

"You're modest," Ayla said, as if realizing something.

"I'm not. You are." Crier frowned. "Are you not?"

Something flickered across Ayla's face, too quick for Crier to tell what it was. Ayla's wet hair was pushed back off her forehead, revealing her strong, dark eyebrows, and it made her look older. "Turn around," she said.

Crier nodded and obeyed, heading back to the shore. "Tell me when you're done," she said, sunlight sliding over her shoulders, her arms, her whole self, as she made her way out of the water, wet clothes clutched in one hand. She laid them to dry on the riverbank and straightened up, stretching her limbs, wringing the water out of her hair. Letting the sun dry her skin as it was drying her clothes. She found a flat, sunbaked rock and sat down, tipping her head back, eyes closed. All around her, the forest made its forest noises. Frogs, birds, the buzz of bees or cicadas. The *tok-tok-tok* of woodpeckers. Wind in the leaves. The forest breathed just as the sea did.

Lost in sensation, Crier didn't know how much time passed before Ayla said, "You can look now." She came back to herself in increments, limbs and body and finally mind, and turned around. Ayla was clothed in green again, squeezing the water from her curls. The sun had reached the ceiling of the sky and hung there, a white lantern. Crier had lost at least an hour. Maybe two.

Ayla coughed. "You can, um. I think your clothes are dry."

"Right," said Crier. She stood, swayed, and fell, ground lurching up to meet her. She landed hard on her side.

"Hey!" Ayla yelped, and Crier heard footsteps. A hand on her shoulder, a tight grip. "What—are you sick? Can you get sick? Is it your injuries? I thought they were healing, you said they were—"

"Heartstone," Crier mumbled, blinking hard. The world swam, refocused. "Haven't had . . . heartstone. Two days now."

She pushed herself upright. "It's fine. Still a few days before the need becomes dire."

Ayla gave her a doubtful look. "You just collapsed."

"I didn't *collapse*. I lost my balance. Like you said this morning—lightheadedness. It's fine." She took a deep, steadying breath, trying to clear away the fog behind her eyes.

"Does human food help?" Ayla asked. "You should've told me." An odd note in her voice. "I wouldn't have just eaten everything myself."

"Human food doesn't help. It would alleviate the empty feeling, but only for a few minutes. I cannot absorb energy from it."

"Oh."

Crier nodded, pressing the backs of her hands to her cheeks. "It's fine," she said again. "I just feel weaker than usual. I apologize for concerning you." No, too much. She winced, waiting for the inevitable *I wasn't concerned!*, but it didn't come.

"Okay," Ayla said instead. "Before anything else, we need to get you more heartstone." She caught Crier's expression and huffed. "Don't look so shocked! We can't do anything if you're going to fall over every time you stand up. Today we filled my belly, tomorrow we'll fill yours."

"Buying heartstone is more dangerous than foraging for mushrooms," Crier said. "We'll have to find a village or town, we'll have to disguise ourselves, we'll have to find a way to pay for it. . . ."

"Or," said Ayla.

Crier raised her eyebrows. Ayla's face was doing something

decidedly shifty. Fox-like. It felt like the kind of expression that could only preclude a terrible idea. "Or . . . ?" she prompted.

"Or . . . A lot of this farmland belongs to Varnian nobles, right? Like the southern estates up in Rabu. Lots of rich Automae around here. Lots of estates. It's better for us to stay out of the open anyway, right? I don't know if there are any Shades around here, but I don't want to risk it."

"True," Crier said slowly.

"Bet we could trick some nobleman into feeding us for a night."

She was still crouched in front of Crier, though she'd long since let go of Crier's shoulder. A tiny pathetic thought: the warmth of Ayla's touch rivaled the afternoon sun. Crier imagined her skin turning gold, a patch of gold in the shape of Ayla's hand, gold sinking beneath her skin, into her bones. How ridiculous: needing heartstone after a touch like that.

"Do you—?" Ayla started, then made a face. The concern had faded from her features; now she was looking skyward, lips pressed into a thin line. "Do you think . . . maybe . . . you want to put some clothes on?"

"Oh," said Crier, glancing down at herself. "Yes. I forgot."

"Makes one of us," said Ayla. Crier stared at her. "Come on, talk to me as you dress. It'll keep you awake. It's what my brother always made me do when I had nightmares and was afraid to sleep."

Ayla began to help her dress, eyes averted, and for a moment, Crier was brought back to the days—less than a month ago—when Ayla had been her handmaiden. Had laced her into fine dresses, poured scented oils in her bathwater, braided her hair.

"What would you like me to talk about?" Crier asked, shaky.

"Tell me one of your stories," Ayla said. "Tell me one that ends right."

"What does it mean? To end right?"

"I don't know. Just—happy. Or something close."

Crier made a soft, considering noise. "I'll see what I can do."

Once, a very long time ago, when the mountains had just begun to sprout from the earth and the whole world was white with newborn snow, there was a girl called Hana who lived in a little wooden cottage with her mama and papa. Hana was a good and clever girl. She helped her mama chop wood for the hearth fire and sow the fields with barley, and her papa make bread and sweet jam. But the nearest village sat beyond a snow-choked mountain pass, and so Hana did not have any friends to play with. She was very lonely. She tried to play with Mama and Papa, but they were grown-ups and thus did not remember how.

One day, after Hana finished her morning work, she was overcome with a rush of such loneliness that it felt like an ice-prick in her heart. She sat below a white birch and let her tears fall to the snow, and quietly she sang:

"Sister Winter, Sister Winter,
Will you let me sing for you?
Will you join me with your reed pipes?
Can we play like children do?"

Hana didn't know it, but Winter was watching from nearby. She could hear the soft little pulse at Hana's throat, taste the salt of Hana's tears. Winter was not softhearted, but something about the girl's song burrowed its way inside her snowbank chest and stayed *there. Winter closed her eyes and made the Northern Wind sing alongside Hana. A cold, howling duet.*

Hana laughed. The Northern Wind laughed with her.

And Winter, who could take any form, turned herself into a little girl, and she crept out of the woods and sat with Hana under the white birch, and that was that.

Years passed.

Winter was a monstrous friend.

Oh, sometimes she was good. Sometimes she was a girl who played and laughed and would dance all night to amuse Hana and Mama and Papa. Sometimes she kept their fields unfrozen, their garden green till solstice. But sometimes Winter stumbled through the doorway, clutching a ragged cloak in both hands, shaking fresh snow all over the floor. Sometimes she stretched gracelessly before the hearth fire, bony limbs akimbo, and sneered at the fire, and the yawning hearth, and the snow-damp firewood heaped in a corner. The chimney, cobbled together from bricks of black mud. The ax. Sometimes Winter made herself at home and stayed for months. Those were bad times for Hana's family. Winter never let the snow melt, not even in summer. There was so much ice caked onto the ground, so much permafrost, no lukewarm summer could touch it. For months, the sun was nothing but

light: pale, watery light, refracted by the frost-bowed
trees, flung in strange patterns, scattered glass-like
across the snow. Winter was beautiful and terrible,
always both at once.

Years collected like tree rings. Still Hana called
Winter her friend, and still she opened the door when
Winter showed up shrieking. Slowly, Winter began
to soften her sharp edges. How could she not? Being
cruel to Hana was like trying to stave off daybreak by
shouting at the sun. Cruelty was wasted on the kind.

Winter stirred up snowstorms, painted the sky gray
for weeks, and still Hana sang:

"Sister Winter, Sister Winter,

Let me wash your aching back.

I have watched you work from dawnbreak

Till the gloaming fell to black."

And Winter sighed her windy sigh and let Hana
wash her, and she didn't even turn the bathwater to ice.

Hana grew into a strong young woman. Her
hair was black and plaited; her eyes were rich dark
earth. Her heart was a snow-bright star behind her
ribs. But there must be a balance in all things, so as
Hana burned brighter, Mama and Papa began to fade.
Mama got very, very sick. Papa summoned healers from
a dozen villages, but no mountain teas or tisanes could
save Mama. She needed a medicine made only by the
fishing villages on the banks of the Steorran Sea, all the

way across the tundra. Papa was too old to make the
journey. Mama begged Hana not to go, but for all the
girl's kindness she was still stubborn as a goat. She left
the very next day.

Halfway through her journey, Hana was caught in
a snowstorm and became hopelessly lost. She stumbled
for days across the ice fields, starving and freezing, and
she sang:

"Sister Winter, Sister Winter,
I am lost and scared to sleep.
I have kept my lantern glowing
But the dark is very deep."

Hana was so small, and the tundra was so big.
Winter didn't hear her.

Finally, Hana was too weak to keep going. She
lay down in the snow, weeping for her mama, and she
sang:

"Sister Winter, Sister Winter,
Hear me knocking at your door.
Hear me whispering your name.
Hear my footsteps cross your floor."

She settled deeper into her snow bed. She looked
up at the night sky and tried to think of good things:
Mama and Papa and their little cottage, their hearth
fire, their mud-cobbled lives. The taste of bread and
honey. Winter's barefoot dancing, the flash of her grin.
Hana thought of all those things, and the cold sank into

her bones, and she sang:

"Dearest Winter, sweetest Winter,
I feel your kiss now at my core.
I will sleep with you till morning,
Then I'll sleep forevermore."

Hana sang until her throat was raw and her skin webbed with frost and her mouth too cold for words. Slowly, the heat left her body. The blood froze in her veins. Her heartbeat faded to a moth-wing flutter, and then silence.

Snow fell down to cover her body like pyre ash. The Northern Wind, who had sung along with Hana so many years before, swept over her and played with her black hair one last time, and then carried on westward to the mountains.

The Northern Wind told Winter what he'd seen out on the tundra.

He braced himself for her howling, earth-splitting rage.

But Winter was already gone. She could cross entire ice fields in the span of a breath, and she was leagues away.

She found Hana's body easily. The girl was dead, but a tiny spark had survived in the core of her, the last pinprick of heat in a cold hearth. You did not burn so bright for so long without such a spark. Winter didn't know much about humans—the soft golden years she'd

spent with Hana were only brief moments compared to
all the millennia that had come before—but she knew
that. She had seen that spark once or twice before in the
kindest, warmest souls.

Winter, of the snowbank breast and icy dark heart,
whose touch made green things wither with frost, knelt
down beside Hana in the snow. She cupped Hana's face
in her hands and pressed her frozen mouth to Hana's
forehead. She let her breath fan out across Hana's body.

In the purple dusk, between the snow and the rising
moon, the spark in Hana's heart flickered and flared.

Without opening her eyes, Hana sang:

"Dearest Winter, sweetest Winter,

I hear you knocking at my door.

I hear you whispering my name.

I hear your footsteps cross my floor."

Winter took her hand.

Together they crossed the tundra to the Steorran
Sea and fetched the medicine that would save Mama's
life. Together they crossed all the way back. Together
they helped Mama drink the medicine, and they helped
Papa when he broke his shinbone, and they helped sow
the fields and tend the garden and reap the summer
harvest for years to come. Winter still brought snow
down to blanket the mountains, and she still brushed
the barley and cabbages and all the wildflowers with
her killing touch, but her heart had shifted. There was

a darkness in death, but Winter knew from Hana that it wasn't emptiness or shadows or the absolute black between the stars. Death was dark soil. Death was a soft and ancient womb.

After a great many years together, it was finally time for Hana to die. She was ready for it. She lay in her bed and waited. Her starlit heart burned steady.

Winter held her as she died.

Winter carried Hana's body out of their house, past the garden and the barley fields. Past the river that had long since carried Mama's and Papa's ashes. Past the foothills and up into the mountains. She laid Hana down in a cradle of stone.

The mountains wrapped their arms around Hana. They were one.

That persistent spark, all that was left of Hana, sank deep into the stone. It was not her, but it was the old ache of her. The bright of her. The spirit of her, which would glow until even the mountains died.

And Winter sang:

"Dark-heart lover, death-part lover,
Lay you with me in the snow.
May you miss me dear each summer
May your bones be stone below."

13

They pushed on through the forest slowly. Ayla knew Crier was doing everything she could to stay strong and steady, to stay awake. At last, they saw a grand manor house in the distance, and Ayla's pulse kicked up as they got closer. What if the house belonged to one of the Automae who'd taken Nightshade? This could be a place to sleep for the night . . . or it could be a great way to lock themselves up with a monster.

But the same was true for any nearby estate, and Crier was flagging quickly. They'd just have to risk it.

The estate was small, as estates went, with only a few outbuildings. There was a grassy courtyard lined with trees, the same short twisted trees that dotted the shrubland and the hills of Varn. Beyond that, the manor house, which was vast but simple, built from sand-colored stone. Ayla could see a carriage house and what looked like a garden, fruit trees bowing their naked limbs.

Ayla and Crier paused at the edge of the courtyard. Ayla tried not to fidget under Crier's gaze. She felt strange in her own skin again, like she'd felt the first day at the queen's palace, when her trio of handmaidens scrubbed off seven years of grime. Here, on this morning, she wasn't flushed and soft and gleaming, but she had cleaned herself as best she could and braided her hair into a tight plait. Back at the river, she'd tried to tame the wispy curls at her temples, but that was a losing battle. "What else stands out?" Ayla had asked, kneeling at the water's edge, cleaning the dirt out from under her fingernails. "What else would someone remember about me?" The goal was to be as unremarkable as possible.

"Your freckles," Crier had said promptly, and blinked three times very fast.

"There's not much I can do about those." Ayla had sighed. "Maybe . . . Maybe I go alone, and you can just wait nearby—"

"No," said Crier. "If anything, it'll be the other way around."

"Have you gone mad? You're not going alone. You're a terrible liar."

Crier raised an eyebrow. "I suppose neither of us will stay behind, then. What is our cover story?"

"Uh. I don't know. I guess we could be noblewoman and handmaiden, that's probably easiest."

"No. Not my handmaiden again."

"Who says you were the noblewoman in that scenario? Maybe you were gonna be my handmaiden."

"That's acceptable," said Crier.

Ayla coughed. "I— Okay, no, nobody's a handmaiden. Different story. We're traveling alone together because we're— because we're wives."

They stared at each other. "It is more common in Varn," Crier said, her voice completely devoid of inflection. "Between the Kinds."

"It makes sense."

"Yes, that is true."

It was only later that Ayla realized two friends traveling alone together would have also made sense, but by then too much time had passed, and changing the story at the last minute would have just been awkward.

"All right," she said now, facing Crier in the cold morning sunlight. "You ready?"

Crier nodded.

They were met by a human servant as they crossed the courtyard. He bowed in deference, and it took Ayla a second to realize he wasn't just bowing to Crier. He was bowing to her, too. In Varn, she could be an elite. She, a human, could blend into the gilded spaces. She was profoundly grateful for the clothes she'd been gifted by Queen Junn. They weren't flashy— just wool pants that tapered at the ankle, a wool shirt with a subtle brocade, fur-lined boots—but they were noticeably fine, even when covered with mud stains no amount of river water could wash out.

"My wife and I were attacked by horse thieves," Ayla said to the servant, mimicking the Rabunian court accent, which clipped along like hooves on cobblestone. She didn't even stumble over the word *wife*, which she thought was very impressive of her. "They stole all our belongings—including my wife's heartstone supply."

Out of the corner of her eye, Ayla saw Crier straightening her shoulders, raising her chin. She was unmistakably Automa, and unmistakably regal. There was just something about her presence, even now, even bloodstained, barefaced, waning with hunger. "We're wives," she announced.

Ayla wanted to hide her face in her hands, but reined it in.

"Of course," the servant murmured, eyes flicking between them. "I will inform the Lady Shiza of your arrival, mistresses . . . ?"

"Clara," said Ayla. "My wife is called Wender."

That night, they dined with Lady Shiza, a Varnian noblewoman.

She was old enough that age was just beginning to show on her face, faint lines at her mouth and brow, a slight papery quality to her skin. Her hair was cropped short, her hands dripping with silver jewelry, at least three delicate rings on each finger.

"To company," Shiza said, raising her goblet once she, Ayla, and Crier were seated around the long table. The silver on her wrists and fingers glinted in the candlelight; the silver goblet reflected starry dots of yellow. "To drinking well. To iron and diamonds and the Child Queen, Phoenix of the Eastern Sea."

"To the queen," Ayla and Crier echoed, and all three of them drank. Liquid heartstone for the two Automae, dark wine for

Ayla. She'd also been given bread and a bowl of spiced pumpkin soup. She hadn't eaten since the foraged mushrooms, and it took all her self-control to eat slowly, politely, to not shove the bread into her mouth and swallow it whole. The wine was warm and bitter, with the dry, almost metallic aftertaste of a tannin-rich tea. Even one mouthful burned, warmth spreading through Ayla from head to toe, settling in her belly.

"What business brings you to my country?" Shiza asked, beckoning one of the servants over. The divide between human and Automa was not as wide in Varn as in Rabu, but the servants were still human. She motioned at him to top off her goblet. "You were attacked by horse thieves. Did it happen nearby?"

"No," Ayla said smoothly. She and Crier had come up with this story, but she didn't trust Crier to do the lying. "We were traveling along the shores of Lake Thea, just across the border on the Rabunian side, when we were attacked. It was night and they set the carriage on fire. In our panic, we ran for the forest to take shelter. We crossed the border without realizing."

Shiza cocked her head. "No trouble from the border guards?"

"We believe they were drawn to the carriage fire."

"Luck was on your side, then. What news do you bring from Rabu? What of the latest chaos—the canceled wedding, the runaway bride, the rise of Scyre Kinok?"

"The rise?" Ayla said, playing dumb. "I've heard about the wedding, but not that. What's the honorable Scyre Kinok up to, then?"

"You haven't heard?" said Shiza. "Scyre Kinok and his

followers have been marching west for days now, toward the mountains. But—come, tell me of the wedding. I love a disastrous wedding."

From the corner of her eye, Ayla saw Crier's hand twitch where it lay on the table. *Keep it together*, she thought, as if Crier would be able to hear her. She didn't know what would happen if Shiza started gossiping about the broken engagement, the runaway bride.

"Oh, I really don't know anything about that," Ayla said, waving a hand. "I don't listen to court gossip. But I've been hearing whispers of . . ." She floundered, trying to think of a way to describe the monsters, the Shades, without offending their host. The Shades had once been Automae, after all. "A . . . new threat? To the north?"

"Are you referring to the creatures with the black eyes?" Shiza asked. "Yes. I know very little. But I have seen blue smoke rising over the trees a few leagues to the west, almost every day for weeks now. I hear the smoke comes from some sort of weapon." She brought her goblet to her lips again, drinking deeply. When she lowered it, her lips were stained red. "Those woods used to be hunting grounds. All the animals have fled. First because of the creatures, and now the blue smoke keeps them away. The blue smoke—and whatever substance creates it." Her brow creased, and she stared down into her near-empty goblet as if it held answers, like the magick scrying pools in faerie stories. "I wish I knew more."

So do I, thought Ayla.

Shiza's face smoothed over again. She peered at Ayla. "You know nothing of the Scyre's wedding, and you don't listen to court gossip."

"I—" Ayla felt cold. Did Shiza suspect them? Had she recognized Crier? Shiza's face was blank as fresh parchment, only her eyes piercing. "Yes. It simply does not interest me, but perhaps I can try to remember something."

"No need," said Shiza, and Ayla's heart was a rabbit racing through the underbrush, waiting for Shiza to expose them, to call for a servant, a guard. "But I don't entertain guests as often as I would like, and I find myself deprived of vapid conversation. Please. If you can't tell me about the Scyre's wedding, tell me about your own."

Ayla might have preferred to run for her life.

"My own wedding," she said. She glanced at Crier, who had chosen this moment to become wholly focused on the plate of bread that had been set out for Ayla. "Our wedding. Of course. Well, it was very beautiful. Wender spared no expense."

At the mention of her fake name, Crier looked up. "It is true," she said helpfully.

"It was . . ." Ayla had only ever attended one wedding, when she was five years old. All she remembered was laughter, bright colors against winter snow, a banquet for the whole village, people bringing whatever they could spare. Stewed fruit and roasted fish, sweet white bread, hot buttered tea. Dancing, a lot of dancing. Snow kicked up around fur-lined boots. "It was in spring," she said. "When all the fruit trees were blooming, and there were petals everywhere, like a blanket of snow. We got married in the morning and spent the rest of the day feasting and dancing and, and drinking and receiving gifts."

"In the human tradition, then," said Shiza.

Ayla nodded. "We both agreed it would be more fun. Right, Wender? Wender dearest?"

"Right," said Crier. "We wanted to dance. Not just the waltz."

"You drank enough wine to feel it a little," said Ayla. "You tripped over my feet."

"You almost knocked over an entire table of desserts," Crier retorted, raising an eyebrow.

"But I didn't. You danced with all one hundred guests, then you tried to climb one of the fruit trees. In the dark. I had to pull you down by the ankle."

"It was a plum tree," said Crier. "I wanted a plum."

"I got one for you," said Ayla, cheeks hot.

Crier inclined her head. "You did," she said. "We shared it."

"Everyone was, um. Everyone was wondering where we went."

"You wore flowers in your hair," Crier said. Her voice was soft. Her eyes were softer.

It was quiet for a long moment. Then Shiza said, "But . . . who was in attendance? Anyone I might know?"

"You can take this one," Ayla told Crier, and went back to her soup, ignoring the drumbeat of her heart, the warmth beneath her skin.

Shiza offered them a room for the night, and it would have looked suspicious to refuse. After Shiza and Crier had finished their heartstone, and Ayla had forced down another goblet of bitter wine, Shiza bid a servant girl to lead them upstairs. Ayla and Crier waited outside the doorway as the girl made up the bed and lit a fire in the hearth. The bedchamber Shiza had given them was big and comfortable, with a canopied bed and a set of tall windows facing out over the estate grounds, lost to darkness this late at night. A writing desk sat in one corner, a wardrobe in the other. The hearth fire lit up the whole room, yellow light dancing on the walls, shadows flickering over the white plaster ceiling.

Crier sat on the lip of the hearth, warming her hands. "Thank you," she said to Ayla, eyes downcast.

For what? Ayla wanted to ask, but she was afraid of any answer that wasn't *For helping me find heartstone.* After a moment of hesitation, she joined Crier at the hearth, sitting cross-legged on the cold stone floor. Now that they were alone together, Ayla wished for another piece of bread or bowl of soup; not because she was still hungry, but because eating would give her something to do with her hands. Something to focus on that wasn't the girl in front of her. Something to think about that wasn't the last time they'd been alone in a room like this. Elderell. The Green River Inn.

Ayla climbed onto the hearth, relishing the heat after two days of sleeping on the frozen ground. She brought one leg up to her chest, wrapping her arms around it, chin resting on her knee. She could feel Crier's eyes on her. They needed to talk about what Shiza had told them, the blue smoke rising to the west, but now that they were alone Ayla could think of nothing but Elderell. Nothing but Crier's hands. Nothing but that kiss. Was Crier having the same thoughts, reliving the same memories? For the first time Ayla allowed herself to think beyond the moonlit bedroom, beyond the knife, the chime; she allowed herself to wonder: Did Crier regret the kiss? Did it mean anything to her, or had she cast it from her mind immediately and never given it a second thought? Did Automae . . . feel things like that? Could an Automa girl feel that tug in her lower belly, that fishhook pull, making her want more, want harder, want deeper, want sweeter? Want hands in her hair, on her waist, on her hips, want—? *Don't go there*, Ayla told herself, but she couldn't help it. Yesterday afternoon in the river, she had seen the whole of Crier's body, and the yearning that drummed through her wasn't anything she'd felt before, and her own reaction wasn't anything she'd felt before, the oceanic pulse between her hips, the things she wanted. Skin on skin, fingers intertwined. She'd tracked the drops of water trailing down Crier's throat, her collarbone, the curve of her back, down her bare legs when she climbed back up onto the riverbank, and looking hadn't felt like enough. Did Crier feel the same? *Could* Crier feel the same? Maybe Ayla already knew the answer. The way Crier had touched her in Elderell, hands flying from Ayla's arms to her face, fingers raking through her hair, lips parting . . .

The way Crier looked at her. Then and now.

Ayla opened her eyes—when had she closed them?—and

found Crier gazing into the hearth fire, eyes flickering gold, hands curled in her lap. Without thinking, Ayla reached out. She took Crier's hand and turned it over, palm up. Touching just to touch. A thousand excuses leaped into her mind—*you're warm and full and sleepy, you're not thinking properly, you're just glad to be alive, you just want to be close to someone*—but Ayla knew damn well there was no excuse for this. For the things she wanted. The things she didn't.

I won't pretend to understand how you could care for her, Benjy had said. *But . . . I accept it.*

Well, I don't, Ayla remembered thinking. *I don't accept it. I'll never accept it.*

"The lines are so faint," she murmured, tapping the center of Crier's palm.

Crier didn't answer for a long moment. She seemed to be holding her breath. "Lines?" she said finally.

"On your palm." Ayla held up her own hand. "See, mine are deeper. More defined. The head line, the heart line, I forget the rest. Some people think the lines on your palm predict how your life will go. How long you'll live. How happy you'll be."

"I see." Crier looked down at her palm, tilting her hand back and forth in the firelight, as if trying to reveal some hidden lines. "What does a nearly blank palm mean, then?" She smiled, but it didn't reach her eyes. "A blank future? Only the faintest happiness?"

"Nah," said Ayla. "If I believed in that kind of thing—which I don't, really—I'd say a blank palm is like a blank page. A whole book of blank pages. You're a storyteller. I bet you could fill them with something."

"Ah, so I write the lines myself," said Crier. "That's not such a bad fate."

"Not bad at all."

"What does your palm say?"

"You know," Ayla said, lips quirking, "I'm not actually sure. I think this one"—she took one of Crier's fingers and guided it to her own palm, tracing it over the topmost line, right below her calluses—"is the head line. Maybe. Mine's kind of short." She frowned. "A short head line. Does that mean I'm a fool?"

Crier smiled, small but real, nose crinkling. "You know more than I do."

"My heart line's short, too. Am I a heartless fool?"

"To be fair, everything about you is short."

Ayla's jaw dropped. "You take that back."

Crier shook her head. The smile had faded from her lips, but it glowed like candlelight in her eyes, gone dark again since she'd turned from the fire.

"Not all of us can be beanpoles," Ayla said, with a mock scowl. She went to pull her hand away, but Crier caught it. And just like that, Ayla's breath hitched in her throat, and the words left her, and she could have sworn her entire being had narrowed to that small point of contact, the place where Crier's fingers were curled loosely around her own. The *wanting* swelled inside her, blooming like peonies. In her ribs. Between her lungs. Beneath her sternum.

Crier's grin had faded. She was staring down at their joined hands, brow furrowed.

"What?" Ayla whispered.

"I want to . . ." Crier brushed her thumb almost absentmindedly across Ayla's knuckles. She shook her head. "Tell me more about your lessons with Lady Dear," Crier said in a rush. "Or your friend, the boy with the curly hair. Or your history. Your life. Those weeks in Thalen. The things you've done. The things you haven't. Whatever you want to tell me, please tell me that."

"Why?"

Crier took a breath. "I want to learn about you."

"I'm not a book," said Ayla, ignoring her own traitorous heartbeat. How it quickened. "Palms aside. You can't read me once and know everything."

"Then I will read you again and again," said Crier. She seemed to catch something in Ayla's expression, seemed to realize that wasn't the right answer. "I know," she said. It sounded like she was choosing each word very carefully. "I know you're not a book. I know I can't know everything. I know it is important to you that I do not. Or perhaps that no one does. But . . . if there is anything you want to give. One story. One solitary point on the map of yourself. One star in the constellation, one door unlocked. I will accept it, and be honored, and I will not forget."

"I don't think you'll like my stories," Ayla told her. She thought of the stories Crier had woven for her on the night of the Reaper's Moon. Not that long ago. Princesses and foxes, bears and snow-choked passes and peace treaties. In the forest: Hana and Winter, a soul sinking into the mountains, another iteration of forever.

"I'm not . . ." Crier gazed into the fire for a moment, at the black heart of it, where the flames were born and died. She took a while to answer, as she often did. During pauses like this Ayla tried to imagine what it looked like inside Crier's head. What it looked like when she gathered her thoughts, sifting through heaps of words until she found those flecks of gold. "You keep comparing yourself to a book. That is not how I see you. If I want to learn about you, it's not for . . . pleasure, or leisure, or the desired mastery of a subject. I am not trying to learn you like a language. I am trying, Ayla, to learn you like a person. Like people do, with the knowledge that I will never know everything. That it is impossible to know everything." Despite her words, she sounded a little put out about it, in a way that made Ayla want to laugh. Not unkindly. "Because you deserve to be known, in whatever capacity you wish. I am trying to become a person who deserves to know you. I want that. More than anything."

"My history is bloody," Ayla told her. "It is tied to your own."

"Mine?"

The time had come, then. For the full story. If Crier wanted to know her, she had to know this first.

"I come from a village to the north," Ayla began. It felt impossible: telling this story to this person, after so many years. "When I was nine, Sovereign Hesod's men raided my village. They burned it to the ground. Almost everyone was killed. Including my parents. I was one of the only survivors."

Crier was holding very still. She wasn't breathing.

"After that day, I managed to make my way down the coast to the village of Kalla-den. But I was starving and weak, and it was winter. I collapsed in the street. I should have died. I would have—but someone found me. Her name was Rowan." She took a shaky breath, steeling herself against the rush of memories that accompanied that name. "She took me in. She did that often—found the lost children, saved them, let them into her home. Benjy—my friend with the curly hair—grew up with me there. It was Rowan who found us work at the sovereign's palace. At my request." She caught Crier's look. "Why did I want to work for the man who killed my parents?"

Crier was silent. Her eyes never left Ayla's face.

"Because I wanted revenge," Ayla said, returning her gaze. She would look Crier in the eyes for this; she would not flinch away or hide. "I wanted to do to him what he had done to me. I wanted to find what was most important to him, and I wanted to kill it."

"That was the real reason," Crier said, voice cracking. "That was why you—that night. It wasn't just to set off my chime. Oh, gods." Then she paused, confusion breaking through the horror. "But—the first time we met, you saved my life. Why?"

"I have asked myself that question countless times," Ayla said softly. "And . . . I don't know. I hated you then, I really did. Maybe it was instinct, maybe it was . . . gods, I don't know. I couldn't let you die that night on the cliffs, and I couldn't kill you later. I thought I'd be able to. I thought—after Rowan died,

I thought the anger and grief would be enough, but they weren't. I know that now. Even if you hadn't woken up, I would've run."

"Why?" Crier whispered. "Why couldn't you do it?"

Because. Because. Because.

"A lot of reasons," said Ayla. She reached for Crier's hand again, cupping it between both of her own. "Some I'm still trying to figure out. But. In the end . . . ah, hell. Do you want to know something embarrassing?"

Crier choked out a laugh. *"Embarrassing?"*

"To me," Ayla clarified. "You've got to understand: I wanted revenge for so long. Seven years of wanting it, seven years of dreaming about it, seven years of promising myself *I'll avenge them, I'll make him sorry, I'll make him suffer* . . . and in the end . . . I just don't think I have it in me. That's the embarrassing thing. The humiliating, awful, secret thing. I never could have done it. Even if it hadn't been *you* lying in that bed, even if you were exactly like your father, even if you were cruel and monstrous and everything else I expected you to be, I don't think I could have killed you." Her eyes were burning. "I'm a coward. I'm *weak*."

"You're not," Crier said immediately. "Not a coward. Never a coward. Strength isn't measured by the ability to cause harm."

"Rowan was part of the Resistance," Ayla said, barely hearing her. "She was a leader, a *fighter*, she wanted your Kind gone, or at least, not in control of us. She wanted to liberate us. And she did things she didn't want to do. She became things she didn't want to become or—things she shouldn't have had to become.

For our sake, for the greater good, for the future of my people. And I was supposed to kill you, I was supposed to *want* to kill you, and I couldn't do it. Our mission that night failed because of me. I ruined everything."

"I still don't think that makes you weak," said Crier. "And I'm not just saying that because it was me at the other end of your knife."

Ayla shook her head, blinking back tears. "I—I can't agree with you. Maybe someday, but not yet."

"Then I will wait for someday," said Crier.

I want to know you.

The thought was clear and bright as starlight.

I want to know you, too.

That night, they slept in the same bed. Crier fell asleep almost immediately, or at least faked it well, but Ayla lay awake for hours. She listened to Crier's slow, even breathing beside her, less than an arm's length away. If Ayla were brave, she would have closed the space between them. She would have crawled over and tucked her face into the hollow of Crier's throat and breathed her in and wrapped an arm around her waist and tangled their legs together under the blankets. If she were brave, she would have done that.

But she wasn't brave. She kept to her own side of the bed, her own pillow. When she did sleep, it was fitful and plagued by wild, howling nightmares: Ayla dreamed of her mother's face, her father's, Storme's, all their faces smearing together like melting wax, devoured by green fire, then the fire was seawater, a frothing, roiling maelstrom, a series of tiny wooden huts smashed apart by the waves and sucked down, down, down to the bottom of the sea. Ayla dreamed of Queen Junn, of bloodied swords, of a war—legions of humans, starved and skeletal, up against a battalion of Automae in shining silver armor like molten moonlight, like ice. She dreamed of the Iron Heart, and in her dreams it looked like a massive cave, a mouth, a gaping maw, so dark it could have been a hole pierced into the fabric of the universe. As she watched, the darkness seemed to move. First it was shadows come to life, pouring out of the cave mouth, then it was flames again, black this time, swallowing the light. Licking at her ankles, her clothing, her flesh, too hot, *too hot*, she was burning, she wanted to scream—she tried to run and found she couldn't move. The flames were heartstone red now, more liquid than fire—the ground tilted beneath Ayla's feet and she was sliding down a slick, muddy riverbank toward the crashing river below, but the water was red, it was red and there was something else wrong, the texture was off, it didn't look like water, it looked like—

Blood.

Ayla woke with a jolt right before she fell into the river of blood. She shoved the blankets off and lay there, trying to catch her breath, worried she might be sick. The sky was still black outside the windows.

Dawn was a long way off.

14

They left Lady Shiza's estate the next morning with a pouch of heartstone dust and directions to the hunting grounds to the west, where Shiza said she'd seen blue smoke rising over the trees. Two leagues west would lead them into the foothills of the Aderos Mountains. That was where Kinok was headed, so that was where they would go. It was easy traveling at first, walking through shrubland and yellow grass. Then the hills began to rise up, wooded and rockier than Crier had experienced on her journey from the sovereign's palace down to the southern estates, to Lake Thea.

The trees weren't as tall here as they were to the east, back near the River Merra. It was mostly copses of fingerbone birches, bare with winter. Crier took the lead, listening as always for any danger, and together she and Ayla picked their way up into the foothills, navigating around boulders and thick clumps of saplings. A few hours passed with no sign of anything unusual, anything connected to the blue smoke. They had been traveling on foot since early in the morning, and judging by the sun's position it was nearing midafternoon now. Crier kept a close eye on Ayla. They'd passed a couple mountain streams, so Ayla had been able to drink her fill of water, but she hadn't eaten since last night.

Finally, just as Crier was about to suggest they stop for the day and find shelter, they found a gap in the trees, a clearing ringed with young birches—and strewn with the remnants of a human camp. By the looks of it, the camp had only recently been abandoned. The humans had tried to hide their tracks—the pale ashes of a campfire were strewn at the edge of the clearing, purposefully mixed with the dirt, and piles of dead leaves had been scuffled around to hide boot- or hoofprints. But Crier could smell those ashes, a sharp back-of-the-tongue scent mingled with the muted scents of earth and decay, and more than that, she could smell . . . something else, something stronger, like the ozone snap of a powder bomb but not.

"Crier," said Ayla. She was crouched over the roots of a tree, frowning. "Come look at this. Don't touch."

The second Crier crouched down beside Ayla, she knew this was the source of the powder bomb smell: there was a strange scar at the base of the tree, like it had been struck by lightning, the bark scorched and peeling back around a deep, piercing wound. There was a shard of stone lodged in the center of the tree's wound. Blue gemstone, a blue deeper than lapis lazuli, deeper than sapphire, like it wasn't stone at all but a piece of the midnight sky. Was this what caused the blue smoke? Was it some sort of . . . shell, for the powder bombs? Or was this the deadly substance itself?

Crier turned, scanning the rest of the clearing for more clues. She didn't see any other pieces of the blue stone, but she did see a spot of bright color on the ground, half hidden among the dead leaves and the underbrush. Caught in a bramble, like a butterfly in a spiderweb, the only reason it hadn't blown away.

One of Queen Junn's green feathers.

"Hey," said a voice.

Crier whipped around. How had she not heard someone coming? At the edge of the clearing there was a human boy. No older than Crier herself. He was carrying a loaded crossbow, the bolt pointed at Crier. She'd definitely been on the run too long, because her first thought was: *Oh, not again.*

"You wanna put that away?" Ayla said from off to the left. "We're not doing anything. We're just travelers."

The boy's eyes were fixed on Crier. "No such thing as just travelers in these woods. You're coming with me."

"To *where?*" Ayla said.

"We mean no harm," Crier managed.

He shook his head, bolt still aimed at Crier's chest. "Can't trust nobody snooping around a spot like this. You're coming with me."

Crier and Ayla exchanged a look. Crier's look was, *Let's cooperate. He might know something about the blue smoke.* Ayla's mostly involved wide eyes and dark, angry eyebrows, but Crier chose to interpret it as, *Yes, good plan.*

The boy made Crier and Ayla circle around to walk in front

of him. "Don't try anything," he said. "It'll be dark soon. You run off now, you're Shade bait for sure. You're good as dead."

"You know, I think you attract trouble," Ayla whispered to Crier, ducking under a low, thorny branch.

Do I, though? Crier almost asked.

Another half hour of tense, silent hiking, the sun sinking beneath the tree line, and they reached their destination. The boy with the crossbow had led them to a heartstone keep: a stone silo where heartstone dust was stored before traders picked it up and sold it throughout Zulla. A hundred-odd heartstone keeps dotted the foothills of the Aderos Mountains, always heavily guarded by the Watchers of the Heart. But this one had clearly been abandoned for years. The outer walls were more green than gray from soft, springy moss between the stones, tendrils of ivy snaking up the outer walls, patches of pale lichen everywhere. The roof was less of a roof and more a blanket of moss, a deep green fur speckled with tiny white stardrops.

"Inside," said the boy, gesturing at the thick wooden door.

Crier's eyes adjusted, and she saw she'd stepped into a big circular room with a low ceiling. The keep was dark and cool. Stone steps curved up one wall, leading to an upper floor. The only other notable feature was a hearth big enough to comfortably roast a boar. And, of course, the keep wasn't empty. Half a dozen humans were milling around, polishing weapons or resting on mats on the floor. They'd all looked up when the door opened, heads turning in unison like startled deer.

"Fen? What's going on?" one asked.

"Found 'em skulking around the last camp. Taking 'em to Dinara," said the boy, Fen. To Crier and Ayla, he said, "Up the stairs. Go."

They climbed the stone steps single file, Crier in the lead. At the top, another wooden door opened into a room small enough that it must have been where the Watchers used to sleep; it would have held three or four cots and not much else. The wall was lined with slit-like windows, wide enough only to aim an arrow through. Late-afternoon sunlight, warm and honey-colored, fell in narrow strips across the dusty floor. There was a doorway in one corner, a blanket acting as a curtain.

"Boss?" the boy called out. "Got something you might wanna see."

Footsteps, then the blanket lifted and another boy slipped into the room. Half his face was pockmarked with what looked like burn scars. He glanced between Crier and Ayla, taking stock of the situation, and then nodded at Fen. "Girl can stay," he said. "The leech goes."

Crier's heart plummeted, an overripe sun apple falling to the ground, bursting upon impact. Already half rotted, a pulp. She held her breath, refusing to show any emotion, waiting for Ayla to nod and say, *All right, then. The leech goes—*

"No."

Surely she'd misheard.

"You can let us go, or we can fight our way out," said Ayla. "Or, if you're who I think you are, we can stay and work together. I saw the green feather at your campsite. We're allies of Queen Junn too."

Both Fen and the scarred boy remained silent.

"Hm." Ayla took a step sideways, pressing closer to Crier. "Well, either we're going or we're staying, but either way, we're not separating. Make your decision, then. I've made mine."

"Work together?" said the scarred boy. "With the leech?"

"She's on our side," said Ayla.

Crier's heart was—

Her heart was—

The boy snorted. "You're a fool. You think you can trust anything she says? There's a reason they're such good liars: they feel no guilt. She's deceiving you. To her Kind, we're either servants or we're corpses." He addressed Crier, eyes cold. "What's your ulterior motive, huh? I assume you're gathering information on the Revolution, reporting back to someone. Who are you working for? The Scyre himself?"

"*No*," Crier said. "I'm not a spy. I would never align with Kinok. I want to *stop* him."

"She defected," Ayla said loudly. "She defied her own Kind. She risked everything to escape, to find me, to fight at my side. She is our ally. I—" She faltered, then seemed to rally, drawing herself up to her full height, squaring her shoulders and giving the boy the fiercest look Crier had ever seen. "I trust her with my life."

"Oh, do you," said the boy. "And why should I—"

"Stand down, Edrid."

Ears ringing, the words *I trust her with my life* repeating over and over in her head, Crier turned toward this new voice. It was a girl, tall and solid-looking, thickly muscled. Even though they were in the middle of the wilderness, and it looked and smelled like half these humans hadn't bathed for a week, this girl's lips were painted dark blue and her cheekbones shimmered with something like fine stardust. A sword was sheathed at her hip, a bow and quiver strapped to her back. The leader, Crier realized.

Edrid opened his mouth to protest, but the girl held up a hand and he shut it again, scowling.

"Come with me," the girl said, meeting first Crier's eyes and then Ayla's. To Fen and Edrid, she said, "Get back to your duties, will you? Show's over, go on."

Crier could feel Ayla looking at her, but she—couldn't look back. Not yet. Not while her heart was still singing like this, not while her hands were shaking like this.

I trust her with my life.

Crier and Ayla followed the girl through the blanket-covered doorway into the room beyond. It was small, barren, a sleeping mat and wool blanket in one corner and nothing else. Once inside, the girl turned to them. "It's not much," she said, gesturing at the blanket, "but it's as private as it gets around here."

"Privacy for what?" Ayla demanded. "What do you want from us?"

"Answers. But first . . ." The girl's face broke into a huge lopsided grin, and she clapped Crier on the shoulder. "It's good to finally meet you, Lady Crier!"

Crier took a step back. "I'm—I'm not—"

"Oh, don't worry, you're safe with me," said the girl, still grinning. It transformed her entire face, cheeks dimpled, eyes lighting up. "I must have seen you a dozen times over the years. Only ever from afar, and you never saw me. But I saw you!"

"Who . . . are you?" Crier asked. "How do you know who I am?"

"I'm Dinara," the girl said proudly. "Daughter of Red Hand Reyka. If I'm not mistaken, you knew my mother well."

Daughter of—

"That's impossible," said Crier. "Reyka never commissioned a child, I would have known—and—you're *human*."

Dinara snorted. "What can I say? My mother was an Automa, my ma's a human, they fell in love, they wanted a child. My ma had a good friend, a human man, and he agreed to help out." She winked. "So that's how I happened. But my mother had to keep Ma and me a secret—I'm sure you can understand why. I grew up in a village to the south, but I visited the sovereign's palace a few times, disguised as one of my mother's servants. That's when I saw you, Lady Crier."

Crier tried to think of a response, but her mind was caught on: *My mother was an Automa. My ma's a human. They fell in love.* Was it true? Did Dinara have any reason to lie? How often did this happen? Crier knew Queen Junn had some sort of . . . *relationship* with her human adviser, but Crier had assumed it was purely physical, because—because how could it be anything else?

Am I not the only one?

The thought was a revelation. Sunlight brimming over the mountaintops, spilling into the valleys and villages below. *It's not just me.* If that were true, it changed everything. If it wasn't just Crier, if she wasn't an anomaly, the only one who had ever felt like this, then—maybe this feeling in her chest wasn't wrong. Maybe it wasn't a Flaw.

After all, who had condemned her for this? Who told her it was wrong? Her father. Kinok. Who would hate her for this? The members of the Red Council, the elite, who didn't care if humans lived or died. Crier didn't believe anything *any* of them said. They didn't respect her, and she didn't respect them.

But she'd respected Councilmember Reyka.

"The village to the south," Ayla said, covering Crier's awkward silence. "It wasn't called Elderell, was it?"

"That's the one," said Dinara. Her smile faded. "Ma's still there. I tried to convince her to leave, after—after we found out what happened to Mother. After the Red Council practically paraded her body through the streets of Yanna, pretending to mourn. I don't think Ma's safe in Elderell. But she wouldn't listen."

Crier hadn't known the council had found Reyka's body. She wondered if Queen Junn had let them find it, as some sort of message. "I'm sorry," she managed. "I'm so sorry about your mother. She deserved better."

"All of us do," said Dinara. "But as long as Kinok lives, that's not what we'll get."

"Do you know who was responsible for Councilmember Reyka's death?" Crier asked carefully.

Dinara looked away, a muscle flexing in her jaw. "I have my theories," she said. "No matter who gave the order, I know

Scyre Kinok was watching my mother. Tracking her. She'd been working against him ever since he left the Heart to become a Scyre—she knew he was dangerous even then, long before he ever founded the Anti-Reliance Movement. And—I think somehow he found out about my ma and me. He started spreading rumors among the other Red Hands. About how my mother wasn't fit to be a councilmember, she was too soft, she'd choose humans over her own Kind."

A memory surfaced. Crier's first and last council meeting, when her father had given Reyka's empty seat to Kinok. *Perhaps she's finally joined the humans,* Councilmember Shen had said. *That's where she belongs.* And then, from Kinok himself: *It was odd for Councilmember Reyka to be so . . .* passionate *about humans, was it not?*

At the time, Crier had thought the statement was directed entirely at her. That Kinok was mocking her about her fifth pillar. *Passion.* But if he'd known that Reyka had fallen in love with a human, if he'd been turning the other councilmembers against her . . . He wasn't just mocking Crier. He was telling the Red Council that Reyka wasn't worth searching for.

"We have the same goal," Crier said, looking at Dinara head-on. "We both want Kinok to answer for his crimes. And . . . it can't be a coincidence you're camped here in the foothills, so close to the Iron Heart. You're trying to find it, aren't you?"

Dinara didn't answer. Her eyes flicked over Crier's face, as if searching for any sign of deception.

"Let us join you," Crier said. "Please. I—I don't have much to offer, but I am Automa. I have an Automa's senses. The Iron Heart was built for my Kind, I might be the best chance of finding it."

"That's where you're wrong, Lady Crier," said Dinara. "You and your girl can join us—any friend of my mother's is a friend of mine. But we've already got our best chance of finding the Heart."

Crier and Ayla shared a glance. "What do you mean?" Crier asked.

Instead of answering, Dinara reached under the collar of her shirt and drew out a thick iron chain. There was a battered iron pendant dangling from the end of it.

A compass.

Beside her, Ayla sucked in a breath.

"What?" Crier asked. "What is it?" But even as the words left her lips, she remembered. She had seen something like this before. In that same council meeting. Kinok had taken it out and held it up, letting it swing from his fingers like a hypnotist's pendulum, and the Red Hands had indeed seemed hypnotized. The presence of the compass had made them sit up straighter, stare at Kinok with wariness, jealousy, awe.

"This is an Iron Compass," said Dinara with a sharp, wicked grin. "We don't need an Automa's senses to help us find the Iron Heart, my lady. This thing will lead us right to it."

Do you think it's as dangerous as everyone says? The Heart?

They say it's the Heart of a great monster. A beast the size of a mountain. They say it's a living thing and that's why the leeches guard it so heavily: they don't want anyone hunting it. But that means it's vulnerable, right? They wouldn't guard it if it wasn't vulnerable. Killable. Everyone I've asked says it's in a different place—always somewhere in the Western Mountains, of course, but nobody knows which mountain, and that range stretches for hundreds of leagues. It would be like trying to find one specific blade of grass in all the golden hills of Varn. One specific gem in all the mines. Madness. But maybe I'm mad.

If they don't have heartstone, they don't have anything. We know that. How it is made? The monster? The mountains? Is it really just a gem they're mining? I think it can't be that simple. It can't be that. I don't think there's anything natural about that stone. I don't think it grows from this world. Not something as terrible as that. Is it Made, like them?

I want to know.

Maybe I'm mad.

If you get this, R, don't try to stop me. It's too late.

—FROM A CODED LETTER INTERCEPTED BY AUTOMA
SOLDIERS, CIRCA YEAR 30 AE

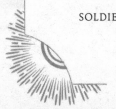

15

That night, Ayla discovered why the rebels had been camping out in the heartstone keep for three days instead of heading directly to the Iron Heart. They were making weapons. Ayla first heard the strange noises coming from beneath the floorboards as she sat in a circle with Crier, Dinara, and a few others, including Fen—who seemed to have made glaring at Crier his top priority, which meant Ayla had made glaring at Fen *her* top priority—eating an evening meal of cured fish and hard brown bread. A flask of brandy was passed around. Ayla sniffed it, took a hesitant sip, and shuddered—the only alcohols she'd ever liked were honey mead and watered-down wine, and the brandy was so much worse, somehow sour and bitter and fiery all at once. It tasted how lye smelled. She passed the flask off to the man beside her and caught Crier giving her an amused look. Ayla made a face at her, sticking her tongue out like a child, and the amusement deepened.

Then Crier cocked her head, like she always did when she was listening intently, and a moment later Ayla heard it too: a hammering sound, like metal striking stone. It seemed to be coming from below.

"Is there a cellar?" Ayla asked Dinara in a low voice. "Is someone down there?"

Dinara took a big swill of brandy. "You done eating?" she said. Ayla nodded. "Then I'll show you."

She led Ayla and Crier to a corner of the room and knelt down, and Ayla saw a small metal handle attached to one of the floorboards. Dinara tugged on it and a section of the floor lifted up, revealing an entrance to the dark cellar below. There were no stairs—just a frayed-looking rope ladder. Ayla tried not to squirm. She didn't want to climb down into the dark. She *really* didn't want to go underground. But the noises were coming louder now, and her curiosity outweighed her fear.

"C'mon," said Dinara, already lowering herself into the opening. Crier followed after, and Ayla climbed down last, gripping the sides of the ladder so tight she came away with indentations on her palms, the faint shape of braided rope.

Once she reached the bottom and her eyes adjusted to the gloom, Ayla saw it wasn't actually pitch-black down here. A couple lanterns sat on wooden shelves along the walls, casting a dim light. And there, in the center of the room, the source of the hammering noises. Three of Dinara's rebels sat on the floor hunched over . . . something.

"This is where they would've stored heartstone," Dinara said.

"Crates and crates of heartstone dust, waiting to be shipped out."

"What are they doing?" Crier asked from behind Ayla. Her eyes were fixed on the three rebels, who hadn't yet looked up from their work. One was hammering away, the other was taking each shard and carving something into the surface.

Without waiting for Dinara's answer, Ayla crept closer, to the edge of the lanternlight. Now she could see the stone wasn't black. It was a deep, deep blue.

"The blue smoke," she said, turning back to Dinara. "This is where it comes from, isn't it?"

Dinara hummed. "Got it in one, girl."

Bombs. They were making bombs.

Maybe Ayla should have been scared, but all she felt was *fascinated*. She wanted a closer look. What was this mysterious blue stone? She'd heard of saltpeter bombs, but never anything like this. Where did it come from?

She only voiced the last question aloud.

"The caves of Tarreen," said Dinara. "You ever wonder why everyone thinks Tarreen's nothing but impenetrable jungle? That hardly anybody lives there, there's only a few scattered human settlements, the whole area's strategically useless?" She grinned, dimples flashing. "Tarreen's not quite as abandoned—and not nearly as useless—as the sovereign thinks. The Tarreenians hide themselves well, but they exist. And they're sitting on miles and miles of cave systems full to the damn brim of a gemstone a thousand times more powerful, more potent, than heartstone. If you know the right magick."

Ayla heard Crier asking a question—something about the Tarreenians—but she wasn't paying attention. She was watching the boy hunched over the chunk of blue stone, holding it steady for his hammer. As she watched, he tapped away at the same spot one, two, three times, until the stone split in two, shards falling away like pieces of eggshell. She stepped closer still so she could see what the other boy was carving. Not letters. Symbols. Ayla recognized fire, saltpeter, sulfur.

A thousand times more powerful, more potent, than heartstone.

Ayla could be wrong, but she knew in her heart—in her blood—that she wasn't. She had seen this blue stone before. She'd seen it in Siena's hand, as Siena lowered it into the open chest of a lifeless Automa girl, fitting it into the hollow space where a heart should be. Ayla still remembered how the girl had twitched as if struck by lightning, eyes flying open. Irises burning silver.

Creation. Destruction. A heart and a bomb. The reason Kinok had brought her to his study and interrogated her about her family's past.

Tourmaline.

Here it was.

"How is it so much more powerful than heartstone?" Ayla asked. "Aren't they both just . . . rocks? Crystals?"

"Oh, but that doesn't mean they're the same. Crystals have different properties. Sulfur burns, phosphorus glows, chalcanthum dissolves in water. You feed coal to a hearth fire. You feed heartstone to an Automa." The nearest shelf was lined with leather pouches the size of a clenched fist. Dinara fetched one of the pouches and held it in her palm, giving Crier and Ayla a significant look. "It all depends on what you do with the crystal, with that *materia*, doesn't it?" she said. "Cinnabar is used as both poison and pigment. Inhale cinnabar dust and you'll die slow and nasty, but you can turn that same dust into the most beautiful vermilion paint. It can take your last breath; it can breathe life into art. Alchemy isn't the only way of manipulating a substance to serve one purpose or another, to create or destroy. It is not the only magick." Her lips curved up again, a natural smile. "It's the magick we're using, though."

"You're harnessing the energy," said Crier. "Generating magickal energy by carving those symbols into the stone. Like . . ."

"Flint and steel," Ayla supplied. "Is that it? The blue stone is the flint, and if you have the right combination of symbols, it's like striking flint against fire steel. Except it doesn't make fire, it makes—like Crier said. Energy. That's how the Makers create heartstone, right?"

For some reason, Dinara's smile slipped. "That's what we thought," she said. "But—"

"Boss?" the boy with the hammer piped up. He was frowning, holding a lump of Tourmaline up to the lanternlight. "Can you come look at this? I can't tell if this vein's gonna be a problem or not."

"One moment," said Dinara, then pressed the leather pouch into Ayla's hands. It was heavier than Ayla might have expected, like whatever was inside was as dense as solid lead. "Take this. Just in case."

Just in case? "Is this a bomb?" Ayla squeaked, afraid to move even an inch. Beside her, Crier made an alarmed noise. "Should I really be holding it?"

"Don't worry," said Dinara, sounding more amused than Ayla thought necessary. "It won't explode unless you throw it."

"What if I drop it?"

"That's probably fine."

"Probably?"

"Definitely. Definitely fine." Dinara's attention was already back on the boy with the hammer. "Ah, I should take care of this," she said with one last smile, and headed over to crouch beside him, examining the cracked Tourmaline.

Ayla stared down at the bomb in her cupped hands. "Probably," she said again.

"I'll carry it," Crier offered.

Ayla shook her head. "If anyone's gonna end up needing a bomb, it'll be little old human me," she said, brushing her thumb over the soft leather of the pouch. Was it a chunk of Tourmaline inside? It had to be. "No, I'll carry it."

"Be careful," said Crier.

"Aren't I always?" said Ayla, and Crier's resulting glare was the strike of flint and fire steel: first heat, then sparks, then Ayla, the tinder, was aflame.

They left the heartstone keep and started the slow, treacherous journey up into the Aderos Mountains at dawn. Dinara, compass in hand, took the lead. Fen and a few other rebels followed close behind her, then Ayla and Crier, then more rebels—the oldest ones—were bringing up the tail end.

Ayla wished Rowan were here.

Or Benjy. Or Storme. She felt so exposed, picking her way through the rocks, sun beating down from above. But she was glad to have Crier here with her, as time seemed to pull shut like a drawstring around them.

The sun hit its zenith, and their procession reached a narrow pass between two jagged peaks. A footpath barely wide enough for a horse zigzagging down the near-vertical mountainside. Dinara and the others didn't hesitate, sliding down a short shelf of rock onto the path one by one, a rain of pebbles marking each slide, but Ayla paused. There was nothing special about this pass—it was naked gray rock, dusty path, and the valley below. Dark green firs and stubborn moss clung to the rocks, the only color between stone and sky. At the other end of the valley, a thick fog was rolling in. Like white sea-foam. Nothing was obviously out of place. There were no columns of smoke; nothing to suggest they were not alone here. But something felt *wrong*.

If there was anything Ayla knew to be true, it was this: she trusted her instincts above all else. Her mind was conditioned to overthink, to doubt—*I'm being paranoid, I'm seeing things, I'm making it up*—but her body was the body of her ancestors, everyone who had lived and died before her, and their instincts were recorded in her blood, her bones, her heart. Their instincts hadn't let her down yet.

"Crier," she said, sensing Crier come up behind her. "Wait."

Crier stopped. Shoulder to shoulder, the two of them looked over the fog-obscured valley. Almost directly below them, Dinara and the others were winding along the footpath.

"Be careful," Ayla said quietly. She held up her arm so Crier could see the gooseflesh, the tiny hairs standing on end. "I don't know what's wrong. But something is. Go slowly, keep your eyes and ears open."

"I'll go in front," Crier said. "You stay behind me." She was staring straight ahead, chin raised, jaw tight. Her eyes in the overcast light were a human brown, warm and true, the color at the heart of all living things, the color of fallen leaves and forest floors and floodwater in spring, when the rivers surged up and over their banks, crashing forward, uncontainable, carving new veins into an old world. Tendrils of hair had escaped Crier's braid, curling at her temples and ears.

"Hey," Ayla said.

Crier looked at her.

". . . Never mind," Ayla mumbled. "C'mon, we're falling behind."

The two of them slid down the shelf of rock to the path below, Ayla stumbling and Crier landing with infuriating grace, and hurried to catch up with Dinara and the others. The path was even more treacherous than it looked from above, the ground slanting downward. It reminded Ayla of the tiered garden at the queen's palace, where she'd been reunited with Storme. Except these tiers were rocky and uneven, and if she took one wrong step she'd find herself tumbling halfway down the mountain slope. The path wended its way around boulders and jutting out-crops of rock, and their party walked it slowly and silently, all their concentration dedicated to not slipping. Dinara was in the lead, Crier and Ayla bringing up the rear. And the farther down into the valley they got, the louder Ayla's instincts screamed at her: *Turn back. Turn back!*

Up ahead, there were two tall column-like boulders that stood like massive gray sentinels on each side of the path. All of a sudden Ayla's mother's voice filled her head: a half-remembered story about a door to another world. *Two stones as tall as tow-ers, standing upright in the middle of a flat, barren ice field, as if a giant had plucked them from the mountains and dropped them there. From far away, the space between the stones didn't look any different. You could see the ice field through them, an expanse of white snow and white sky. You could walk right up to those stones and nothing would seem out of the ordinary. But if you kept walk-ing . . . if you passed between them . . .*

Ayla, a tiny child then, had asked: *What? Mama, what would happen?*

Nobody would ever see you again.

Dinara, at the head of the party, reached the stones, and Ayla came so close to shouting *STOP*. But of course Dinara passed between them without issue. Of course she didn't disappear; of course she wasn't whisked away to some unknown place. Ayla scowled at herself. She was almost seventeen—far too old to let herself get spooked by an old faerie story. She kept walking, forcing herself not to hesitate as she and Crier reached the two stones. Childishly, she held her breath as she walked between them, like how some people held their breath as they walked past a grave. But of course nothing happened. Ayla let out her breath. Their party had filed into a clearing of sorts, an area where the ground flattened out temporarily like the bottom of a bowl, the mountainside rising up on all sides around them. The air was colder here. Ayla saw that Dinara had paused, consulting the compass once again; the rest of them slowed to a stop, waiting.

"Those stones reminded me of a story," Crier said, coming up to stand beside Ayla. "It's about giants who turn to stone in the sunlight and only awaken at night. As soon as the sun sets, they can move around and do whatever it is giants do. But they are most vulnerable in those moments of transition from stone to flesh, and therefore it is forbidden to enter their territory during sunset."

Skin prickling, Ayla tried to focus on the story. The cadence of Crier's voice.

"Wherever they stand as stones, the giants leave big craters behind. And there's a rumor among the people of a nearby village that the giants' craters are filled with gold and precious gems. One day, a man from the village sneaks into the mountains at sunset and watches the giants awaken. Darkness falls, and he hurries down to see the craters they left behind. Sure enough, each crater is filled with the giants' treasure: piles and piles of gold and precious gems, items shimmering with magick, tapestries woven from the finest, most delicate thread . . . enough treasure to make everyone in the man's village, and the next six villages, fabulously wealthy for the rest of their lives. But the man isn't thinking about the people of his village. He is thinking only of himself. He fills his knapsack with gold, but it's not enough. He pours gold coins into his pockets, his boots, his hat. Overcome with greed, he loses track of time." Crier's storytelling voice was hushed, as if she wasn't just recounting the story, she was *there*, watching it play out before her eyes, taking care not to disturb the players.

"Go on," Ayla said. Dinara and her right hand, Fen, were bent over the compass, conferring in whispers. The others were taking the time to drink from their waterskins, shake pebbles from their shoes.

"Suddenly, the man realizes the sky is beginning to lighten. Sunrise is coming, and with it, the giants will return and settle back into their craters. Giants are creatures of habit, you see. More than that, their bodies form the topography of the mountains. If they moved to a new place each night, it would change the landscape entirely. Maps would be useless. Travelers would become hopelessly lost. So the giants always return to the same craters. The man knows he has only minutes before a giant the size of a house settles back into this crater and crushes him. Terrified, he tries to climb back up the crater wall. But, as you'll recall, his knapsack and pockets and boots and hat are filled with gold. And gold is very heavy.

"He begins to panic. He keeps trying to climb out, but he cannot lift his own weight. The obvious solution is to leave the gold behind, but the man has become blinded by his own greed.

The idea of leaving the gold behind is preposterous. He won't do it. He'd rather die. So the sun begins to rise, and he hears the giants returning. It sounds like an avalanche, their footsteps shaking the earth. And the man keeps trying to climb. He can see the giants now. He can see them finding their craters, settling in, the first rays of sunlight turning their skin to stone. And he keeps trying to save himself without sacrificing a single stolen coin."

"I hope the giant crushes him," Ayla said. "Does the giant crush him?"

"Yes," said Crier. "The giant crushes him. He dies with his pockets full of gold. And at the next sunset, when the giant awakens and steps out of her crater, she sees the man's body. She realizes what happened. And she mourns him."

"I like that story," said Ayla. "It's very—" She cut off with a yelp when Crier grabbed her wrist, yanking both of them backward. "Crier, what—?"

"*Dinara!*" Crier screamed, her voice tearing through the silence of the clearing. "*Dinara, look out!*"

The warning came just in time. Half a second later, something burst out from behind one of the rocks, a dark blur of movement so quick Ayla couldn't immediately tell what it was. But then it made contact with Dinara—or rather, her sword— and Ayla saw it was . . .

To be honest, she still wasn't quite sure. An Automa? But wrong. Its skin was grayish and bloodless, somehow leached of color, yet its veins were clearly visible even from thirty feet away, snaking black lines all over its naked body. Its head was covered in bald patches, like clumps of hair had been violently ripped out. This had to be one of the monsters Storme had seen. One of the monsters Ayla had been sent away to investigate, what seemed a million years ago, before she'd been reunited with Crier and started off on the search for the Heart. A Shade.

Dinara's sword had pierced clean through the Shade's torso, tip poking out the other side. Even an Automa should have been incapacitated by such a wound. But as Ayla watched, horrified, the monster started wriggling from side to side like a fish on a hook, hands coming up to grip the sides of the sword. Black blood ran down its wrists, down its front, and still it kept moving. Dragging itself backward off the sword.

The rebels seemed paralyzed by shock. But then Dinara, wrestling her weapon out of the monster's bleeding hands, yelled, "Ready your weapons, you fools!" and they sprang into action, just as another monster leaped down from an overhang of rock far above their heads, landing hard. If it were human, a landing like that would've shattered both its legs. But the Shade didn't even pause before surging to its feet, lunging at the nearest rebel.

"Crier!" Dinara yelled. She ran for them, circling the fight, and the second she was close enough she hurled something through the air: something small and metallic, flashing in the sunlight. The Iron Compass. It landed a few paces from Crier's feet. "Take it!" said Dinara, even as she rounded on the second Shade. "Take it and run!"

Crier didn't hesitate. She snatched the compass off the

ground and turned back to Ayla. "Come on!"

"But the others—"

"If you try to fight them, you will get yourself killed!" Crier said. "A dagger can't stop them. The only thing that can kill them is fire, a lot of it. Enough to completely destroy their bodies. We can't help, we need to run, we can't lose the compass!"

"The blue powder bombs," Ayla said. "I have one, I can—"

"Not yet. Not from here. Let's *go*, I can hear more coming."

Ayla nodded and let Crier pull her out of the clearing, back through the two stone sentinels. The mountainside rose up on one side of the path, dropped down on the other, a steep, rocky slope. Crier paused for a second, head cocked, fingernails digging into Ayla's wrist, and then veered to the left.

"This way," she hissed. "They're coming from above."

They scrambled off the path, down the slope. It was a sheer drop, no tree roots or anything to hold on to, just bare, slippery rock. The slide was painful and undignified—Ayla's palms were scraped bloody when they found footing about ten feet down, and so was her side where her shirt had ridden up a little. She flexed her fingers, wincing. "Ah, that stings."

"Sorry," said Crier, and then—BOOM. The ground shook, pebbles rattling around them, and a cloud of blue smoke billowed up into the white sky the direction they'd come. A beat, a breath, and then another explosion, so loud Ayla clapped her hands over her ears. A great punch of thunder, echoing over the entire mountain and the valley below.

"I really, really hope that was Dinara," Ayla said grimly.

"We should . . ." Crier reached up, touching the crossbow slung across her back. "Maybe we can get a good vantage point, take out the Shades from a distance."

Ayla nodded. "I don't like being useless."

"You'd be more useless if you were dead."

"Still."

They picked their way sideways across the slope, gripping onto the rocks. Crier took the lead, her footsteps falling more surely, Ayla doing her best to step in the same places. More than once, Crier tested out a foothold only for the rock to crumble beneath her weight, shale sliding down the mountainside with a puff of pale dust. It took a few slow, painstaking minutes to make their way back to the edge of the clearing, this time coming up on it from below. The air smelled like smoke and sulfur, the atmosphere thick with it, nasty on the back of Ayla's tongue. Blue smoke was still rising, and this close Ayla could hear the sounds of battle: human shouts and raw, monstrous screams, the occasional clatter of a weapon against rock.

They inched closer, climbing up a jagged rock formation that joined with one of the short walls surrounding the clearing, the side of the bowl. Once, Ayla felt herself begin to slip, but Crier grabbed the back of her shirt before she could even cry out, holding her steady until she found purchase again. They dragged themselves over the crest of the rock formation, and they crawled up to the edge, about fifteen feet off the ground. It was hard to see through the smoke; Ayla blinked back stinging tears, squinting through her lashes. There—her eyes found Dinara, sword slashing through the air. There were over a dozen humans and only three monsters, and still it seemed an even match. Two humans had already fallen. Ayla saw them, dark figures slumped on the ground, dead or unconscious, it was impossible to tell. She wanted to help turn the tide, but there was no way to throw her powder bomb without hurting the rebels too.

Beside her, Crier drew the crossbow. "They're too fast," she muttered, frustration bleeding into her voice. "They never stop moving. I don't know if I can—I don't trust myself not to hit one of the humans."

She lost her chance entirely when the world exploded into blue.

The force of the blast knocked Ayla backward. She hit the ground hard, rock digging into her spine, ears ringing so loud she couldn't hear anything else. The rebels wouldn't have thrown a powder bomb so close to the others—had one of the Shades gotten their hands on one? Everything was blue smoke. It was too thick, an impenetrable wall of blue, as if Ayla had suddenly plunged to the bottom of the ocean. *Where was Crier?* Blind, half deafened, terrified that Crier was lying unconscious somewhere, Ayla felt her way sideways and down, fingernails scrabbling at the rock. Down, down—she slipped, stomach lurching, and slid down the rock face for a few breathless moments before catching herself again, finding hand- and footholds. The air was slightly clearer now, smoke dissipating, and she could make out a large roundish boulder about twenty feet down the mountainside. A potential hiding spot. Spiderlike, clinging to the rock, Ayla made her way down toward it.

A flash of movement to her right.

Then something barreled into her, knocking her off her feet for the second time in five minutes. They separated when they hit the ground and Ayla scrambled upright, searching wildly for whatever had attacked her. A Watcher? A confused rebel?

Worse?

Her attacker appeared out of the blue smoke.

"You," Ayla breathed. "I know you. *Rosi*."

Crier's Automa friend, the one they'd visited on the mourning tour. *Rosi*. Ayla was frozen for an instant, and that was all it took. Rosi leaped for her again, and this time they didn't break apart. Ayla couldn't even scream, she and Rosi were rolling over each other down the mountainside, a wild, dizzying tumble, Ayla's head cracking against a rock so hard that black spots popped up in front of her eyes. Rosi's fingernails were ruined and sharp and she was clawing at Ayla's skin, drawing blood, and then they came to a stop and Ayla was scratching, kicking, smashing the heel of her palm into Rosi's face, mind blank with panic. Somehow, she managed to wriggle her way out from under Rosi, but only for a moment; Rosi grabbed her ankle, yanking her back. Rosi's eyes were pure black, even where the whites should have been. Twin voids. Like the other monsters, her veins were raised and black. Her blue-black tongue lolled horribly, her teeth stained and mossy, awful awful awful, a living corpse. She jerked her head sideways and Ayla couldn't help but gasp: part of Rosi's skull was caved in, rotting skin peeling back around it, black blood welling up. She must have hit her head during their fall, even worse than Ayla.

"*Shit, shit*," Ayla heard herself gasping, wrenching her ankle from Rosi's grip, trying to kick her in the face, missing. She should be dead by now, Rosi should have torn her throat out, but then Rosi tried to lunge after her and Ayla saw what was keeping her alive: Rosi's body was just . . . *broken*. Her right shin was shattered so badly the white bone had pierced through the skin, and her wrists looked broken too, the hands flapping oddly. She was moving like a puppet, like her brain was issuing commands and her body was trying to obey, but all its reactions were clumsy and delayed.

Ayla had to calm down. If she panicked, she'd make stupid mistakes and get herself killed. She had to calm down. She scrambled backward over the rocks, putting as much distance as possible between her and Rosi, even as Rosi kept lurching after her. They were barely twenty paces from a sharp drop-off. They might have tumbled right over the edge.

Weapons. Weapons. Her dagger would do nothing, Rosi probably wouldn't even feel it.

The blue powder bomb.

Ayla groped at the small pouch at her hip, head spinning. Her temple was throbbing; she could feel the hot trickle of blood running down the side of her face. Head wound, never good. She managed to stagger upright, fingers closing around the bomb, ready to throw it—

"Wait!"

Crier. She was above them, scrambling down the mountain-side after Ayla. With one hand, she was holding her shirt up over her mouth and nose. Guarding against the blue smoke.

"Crier, stay back!"

Rosi was on her feet again, eyes rolling in her head. The jut of bone from her shin made Ayla want to throw up.

"I know her!" Crier said, muffled through the shirt. "We can still save her, I know she's still in there somewhere—Rosi!"

"It's *too late*," Ayla shouted, eyes on Rosi. "Crier, I'm sorry, it's too late. We can't save her, she's too far gone. She's not Rosi any-more." She gripped the bomb tight. One throw, it'd be over. Rosi's body blown viscerally apart. Crier wasn't responding. "Crier, I'm sorry. But I'm not trading her life for mine—or yours."

Rosi lunged.

Ayla heard Crier shout her name, but there was nothing but fear in her voice; she wasn't trying to stop Ayla anymore. Ayla ran, graceless on the rocky terrain but still lighter on her feet than Rosi. More in control of her body than Rosi. She heard Rosi crawling over the rocks behind her, making this guttural, drawn-out noise, a last breath elongated, rough and broken. Rosi was speeding up. Pushing the shell of herself to the limit.

Ten more paces. Ayla was gasping, exertion and pain and ter-ror all at once. She made it to the edge of the drop-off and turned around. Rosi was coming for her, tongue lolling, skin peeling off her palms. She was coming and she wasn't slowing down.

At the very last second, Ayla threw herself sideways.

Rosi didn't.

Rosi made no sound as she fell. Shuddering, nauseated, Ayla peered over the edge of the cliff. It was a long way down.

She backed away. A hand on her shoulder. Crier.

"I'm sorry," Ayla said again. Crier was staring at the spot where Rosi had disappeared. The patch of thin air.

"No, you were right," Crier whispered. The words seemed scraped out of her. "It was too late. I was—foolish, and it could have cost you your life."

"I don't think it's foolish to believe someone could still be saved. Not at the heart of it. I don't think that's foolish at all."

Crier didn't answer.

"Rosi of House Emiele," Ayla murmured. She had no sympathy for Rosi, who worshipped Kinok and had once referred to Ayla as Crier's *pet*. But Crier had known her for years, and Crier had just watched her die. "From light you were born, and to light you shall return. Go now into the stars. They've been . . . they've been waiting for you."

She tapped two fingers to her forehead. Crier did the same, and in the sunlight her eyes burned gold, and her lashes were wet with tears.

By the time they'd dragged themselves back up the mountainside, the Watchers had come.

"Stay down," Ayla hissed. They crouched behind one of the stone sentinels, watching in horror as the rebels, alive but clearly injured, many of them slumped over as if unconscious, were bound together at the wrists by Automae in black robes, their faces hidden with silvery metal masks. The Watchers of the Heart. Ayla had never seen one, never met anyone who'd seen one; the whole point was that the Watchers never, ever left.

Until one.

Crier cocked her head, listening intently. "Someone just said Kinok's name," she whispered. "He's—he's *here*. Inside the Heart. The Watchers are saying—'Bring them to Scyre Kinok. Await his orders.'" She sucked in a breath. "One just said, 'The lady and the handmaiden aren't here. Keep searching the mountains.'"

Ayla cursed. "How in all hells does he know we're nearby?"

"Shouldn't we do something?" Crier whispered. "You still have the powder bomb, we could create a diversion. . . ."

"There are six Watchers, and Dinara's people are tied up," Ayla whispered back. "One powder bomb wouldn't give us enough time to untie them all, and anyway, there's no way we could fight off six Watchers."

"But—"

"Just Crier," Ayla said, nudging her. "I'm not saying we're not going to save them. I'm just saying we're not going to do it right now." She narrowed her eyes, trying to make out what exactly was happening. One of the Watchers was sort of . . . running their hand over a large boulder in the mountainside, where the walls of the bowl rose up. "Trust me, I'd love an explosion, I'm really looking forward to using that bomb, but we have to be smart about this."

Crier nodded. "All right, that's— Wait. *Look*."

The Watcher had stopped running their hand over the boulder. Instead, they were pressing their hand to a specific spot. They were leaning forward a little, as if putting some effort into it. At first, nothing happened—and then the stone beneath the Watcher's hand *shifted*, solid granite rippling like water, and a seam appeared in the very center of the boulder. A fracture, then an opening, the boulder itself splitting apart like an oyster shell. Revealing . . . darkness. Black rock?

No. The mouth of a tunnel.

"There it is," Ayla breathed, more to herself than Crier.

The Watchers moved quickly. It took only a couple minutes for them to herd the rebels into the tunnel, into the darkness. Then the last two Watchers were following them through, and the boulder shifted back, the two halves rejoining, completely seamless. Ayla had just witnessed it, and still it seemed impossible that the boulder could really open like that, a door hidden in plain sight.

"Well," said Ayla.

"Yes," said Crier. "I agree."

They waited for what felt like an excruciating amount of time but was probably less than an hour, judging by the sun. Then, silent with fear and adrenaline, they passed through the stone sentinels one last time. They skirted around the edge of the clearing, Crier listening for signs of anyone—Watcher, monster—approaching, until they reached the boulder.

"You remember where?" Ayla said. The first either of them had spoken for a long time.

"I remember."

Crier reached out and pressed her hand to the stone. As with the Watcher, for a moment nothing happened, and then: The shift. The ripples. Up close, it was even stranger; it felt like it should be a hallucination, a trick of the light, because stone did not move like this. Stone did not breathe like this, one moment seamless and the next cracking open. Ayla took a step back, not trusting any of it—especially when she saw tiny symbols fluttering across the surface of the stone, as if they were trapped inside and had been drawn out by sunlight, by magick. The language of the Makers. She recognized some of the symbols. Most of them, even. Two in particular were repeated over and over again: earth and transcendent, mutable quicksilver.

The door opened. They were standing at the mouth of the tunnel. Nothing but darkness stretched out before them, the sunlight illuminating only the first few paces, as if the shadows were somehow thicker here and would not let it any farther.

"Ready?" Ayla asked Crier, even though she herself was *not*. She hated darkness like this, hated how narrow the tunnel looked, how the door would close behind them and they wouldn't know how to open it from the inside and they'd have no choice but to go forward and there could very well be a squadron of Watchers waiting for them at the first bend. She hated everything about this, and she was going to do it anyway, and if she died in there it would be nobody's fault but her own.

The wound on her temple was still throbbing, though the blood at least had dried.

"No," Crier answered. "Not particularly."

"Glad we're in agreement," said Ayla, taking a deep breath. "I'd have been a bit concerned if you did feel ready. Probably would have checked you for a head wound."

"You have a head wound," Crier pointed out.

"And I'm doing a very good job of ignoring it. All right. We can't stay out in the open like this." She hopped up and down a little, but it made her head swim, so she stopped. "Hey, Just Crier. Wanna sneak into the Iron Heart with me?"

"Since we're here," said Crier, very solemn.

Shoulder to shoulder, side by side, they stepped into the darkness and were swallowed.

Ayla was blind, and even Crier could barely make out which way the needle of Dinara's compass was pointing. They moved through the tunnel as quickly as possible, Ayla clutching the back of Crier's shirt, pausing every so often so Crier could listen for footsteps. The ground was uneven and often muddy beneath their feet, the walls rough-hewn stone. It felt like they were trespassing in a rabbit's burrow, a hollowed-out, earthly realm they should never have entered.

Neither of them spoke. The air felt heavy like it did in sacred places, the hush of a cathedral or a graveyard. They followed the compass in silence for what felt like hours, making their way deeper into the belly of the mountain. Ayla couldn't help but wonder if the compass was broken; it felt like they were just walking in circles. Like they were doomed to be lost in this endless, pitch-black underground labyrinth.

Just as Ayla was about to say something, she realized: it was getting lighter.

The air changed from the dead, stale air of the deep underground to something cleaner, the faintest breeze lifting the hair at Ayla's nape. As they walked, the cave walls began to glisten with moisture; Ayla ran a finger along the wall and felt dripping water, slick fungus. Soon it was light enough to see the fungus, pale like lichen on the dark rock. And up ahead, she heard—

"Birdsong," said Crier, breaking the silence for the first time since they'd entered. "Do you hear that? *Birdsong*."

"How . . . ?" Ayla started, but didn't have to wait for an answer. They cleared a bend in the tunnel, and she found out how.

The tunnel had led them to the far end of an enormous cavern. An impossibly vast cavern, like someone had hollowed out an entire mountain, from the foot all the way to the highest peak. The sovereign's palace and all the gardens and orchards could have fit inside this space with room to spare. Ayla couldn't even see where the cavern ended, the walls disappearing into a shadowy gloom, but gods, it must have been at least half a mile long. She'd never felt so tiny. Milky sunlight filtered down from high above, and Ayla craned her neck, trying to figure out how far up this place went, but instead found the source of the birdsong: actual *birds*, turning and wheeling in the light. There must have been an opening at the top, a crack in the mountain like the mouth of a volcano, allowing fresh air and sunlight to stream down.

To illuminate the Iron Heart.

Huge and imposing, almost as tall as the cavern itself, the Heart was a castle. A fortress. A collection of spires. Clinging to the cavern wall like a massive insect, the base was formed of sheer black walls rising from the cavern floor; about halfway up, the fortress joined with the cavern wall, carved directly out of the night-black stone. Hundreds of little chambers and spiraling towers, a city in miniature. Even from here, Ayla could see huge alchemical symbols etched into the sheer walls. The four elements, plus iron and gold.

An underground river cut through the cavern. Green, slow-moving, snakelike, it curved around the base of the Heart. Pale green froth marbled the surface. Ayla and Crier were about fifty paces from the river's edge—close enough that when Ayla breathed in, she tasted the river water on the back of her tongue, briny and oddly metallic.

"Let's keep going," she said shakily.

"Yes," said Crier, and fell silent once more.

The pitch blackness of the deep underground never returned, but it did grow darker as they walked what had to be a trail parallel to the river, leading them to the fortress itself. Finally, out of the darkness: a flickering light came from up ahead, like a faraway hearth fire. Crier's pace quickened and Ayla followed, desperate to leave the dark behind. The light grew stronger and stronger, turning from deep red to orange to hearth-flame yellow, shadows scattering and reforming on the walls. The closer they got to the light, the more Ayla could hear . . . a thresher? A mill? Tumbling water, clanging metal, a whip-crack splintering noise like ice cracking on a frozen lake. She hadn't heard that sound since she was a child in Delan, at the edge of the ice fields.

"I think we're getting close," she whispered, and of course that was when they hit a dead end. Or—not. The tunnel was blocked off by an iron gate, but when they crept up to the gate, when they peered through the bars . . . It seemed they were stationed high up on a wall, overlooking a big underground chamber. And gods, it was *crawling* with Automae. Watchers. They were dressed in the thick, protective leather Ayla had seen blacksmiths wear, their faces masked. Thick white smoke billowed from the center of the cavern, where Ayla could see leaping flames and a row of huge metal vats, like the heartstone cauldrons in the kitchens of the sovereign's palace but triple the size. The smoke stung her eyes.

"This has to be the forge," she whispered. "The heart of the Heart. They're making heartstone."

Crier opened her mouth to reply, but then her eyes widened. "*Someone's coming*," she hissed.

They had no choice but to retrace their steps, racing back down the tunnel, even though the Watchers would be coming from the same direction. Ayla kept her eyes on the tunnel walls, looking for any sort of escape route, even a fissure in the stone— and then she saw it. A round, hatch-like door. She grabbed Crier's sleeve and dragged her over, praying it would be unlocked, praying there wouldn't be more Watchers on the other side—

They tumbled through the hatch into a bloodred room.

Ayla blinked, disoriented. The room was lined with wall

sconces, candles flickering behind red glass, casting a sickly, bloody light. For a moment, ridiculously, Ayla thought they'd stumbled into the Watchers' sleeping quarters. There were two rows of little white cots, exactly like the cots in the servants' quarters of the sovereign's palace. And they were occupied. Twelve sleeping bodies. Ayla tugged at Crier's sleeve—they had to get out of here, what if the Watchers woke up—

"No," Crier whispered. "Oh, no."

Then she was moving toward one of the cots. *Have you gone mad?* Ayla wanted to say. She scampered after Crier, prepared to drag her out of here by force if necessary, but . . .

Up close, this wasn't—this person didn't look like a Watcher. They didn't look like an Automa at all. Ayla frowned, something flaring up in the back of her mind, a prickle of horror she did not yet understand. She looked down at the person on the cot. The human. Their face was gaunt, sunken cheeks and eye sockets. They were dressed in plain white clothing, a shirt and pants— all of the sleeping people were, Ayla realized—but the parts she could see, the hands and feet, the wrists, the forearms—were just as skeletal.

"What . . . ?"

There was a contraption at the foot of each bed. A stone vessel with a thin metal pipe no wider than a finger sticking out of it. Ayla followed it with her eyes, from the mouth of the vessel up the edge of the cot, and then she saw the sleeping person's wrists were tied to the cot, and their ankles, so their limbs were akimbo, and the pipe ran up the edge of the cot to the person's wrist.

"Crier," Ayla said. "Crier. What is this?"

Crier was leaning over another cot, eyes huge, one hand pressed to her mouth. She shook her head once, hard.

"Crier," Ayla said.

"This one's alive," said Crier. "I think most of them are. I can hear their heartbeats. Not all of them."

"Crier, *what is this*?"

"They're being drained." She sounded oddly calm, as if she'd bypassed horror and gone straight to numbness. Her eyes flicked from the cots to the stone vessels to Ayla's face. "The Watchers are draining their blood. They're—collecting it."

Ayla staggered away from the cot. She bent over for a moment, trying not to be sick. Taking deep breaths didn't help. The air smelled so strongly of blood, thick and oily on her tongue, in her throat, in her lungs. "But they're alive," she said. "Can we . . . we have to—get them out of here."

"We'll have to wake them up. They might not be able to move, but we have to try. We can't drag ten unconscious bodies out of here."

"Twelve," said Ayla, counting the cots.

"No," said Crier. "Ten."

Oh gods. Without another word, they got to work. Ayla leaned over the first cot, this person who was not sleeping, and tried to wake them as gently as she could. Pressing at their shoulder, murmuring, "Hey, hey, wake up, please wake up." She was horribly aware they could be caught at any moment. If a Watcher walked in here they'd be done for. *Please wake up. Please wake up.*

Finally, finally, the person's eyelids fluttered. They made a small pained noise.

"I know," Ayla murmured. "I know. I'm so sorry. I want to help you. Can you open your eyes?"

Their eyebrows furrowed. They drew in a rattling breath. Across the room, Crier was speaking in a low voice to one of the others. Ayla tried to keep calm. How long had they been in here? How much time had they lost?

"That's right," she said to the person on the cot. *Focus, focus, don't panic.* "You're going to be okay. Please open your eyes."

"Hook?" they whispered.

Ayla frowned, scanning their body. She didn't see any hooks. "Please open your eyes," she said again, not sure what else to do. "Please."

"Ayla," Crier said suddenly. "The door—"

—opened.

"I've been looking for you two everywhere," said a familiar voice behind Ayla.

Ayla's heart hit the floor. She spun around, going for her knife, only to get a face full of—something, a cloud of dust, a yellowish haze obscuring her vision. Her head was swimming again, ten times worse than before. The floor was tilting, and the walls, the room balancing itself like a set of scales, tipping back and forth in a nauseating rhythm.

The last thing Ayla saw was a pair of eyes, glinting like a cat's in the flickering red light.

Kinok had found them.

It was determined, then, that the single greatest Flaw of Humankind was this "Emotion." If humans were not so ruled by emotion—ruled, in their own words, by the "heart" instead of the mind—if Emotion were removed from the equation—then Intellect could fill the void left behind; Intellect, the foundation of all scientific, political, and cultural achievement and advancement. The four Pillars of the human soul, the prima materia, are Intellect, Organics, Passion, and Emotion (or, by some accounts, Intuition) and it was decided by the Makers—after months of debate—that the latter two Pillars must, like diseased limbs, be amputated for the good of the body. Only Intellect and Organics would remain.

In the place of Passion and Intuition, the Makers chose two traits much more inclined to result in the progress of Automakind, the progress of a unified society, all minds working toward the same glorious future, unhindered by the fog of Emotion. The Four Pillars that would comprise the prima materia of the Automae would then be: Intellect, Organics, Calculation, and Reason. It was decided. And it was so.

—FROM *ON THE FORMATION OF THE FOUR PILLARS*, BY
ELIRA OF FAMILY NESTON, 782510832, YEAR 5 AE

16

Crier came to first, and spent the next hour listening to Ayla's heartbeat.

They were in some sort of cell, a small room carved directly into the mountain, stone floor and rough stone walls, a single arrow-slit window near the ceiling providing just enough low, reddish light to discern Ayla's features. Both of them were bound to the wall, wrists manacled in iron cuffs thick enough to hold an Automa. Crier on one side of the cell, Ayla on the other, a person-length between them. Enough space that Crier could not reach Ayla, even pulling the chains to their limit.

So she listened to Ayla's heartbeat.

Like the rest of the Iron Heart, the air smelled of smoke and copper. It was cloying, eye-watering; they couldn't be too far from the forge. Ayla's heartbeat was slow and even. Crier closed her eyes, concentrating on it, letting everything else fall away. She was reminded of that morning in the woods, months ago, her Hunt. Standing still beneath a high ceiling of dead, rustling leaves, a rabbit's burrow somewhere beneath her feet. Four tiny heartbeats. Back then, the world had smelled of dirt and green things, firs, oncoming winter, and Crier had been Sovereign Hesod's daughter, Kinok's fiancée. Back then, the air was cold and clear, and she'd been suffocating.

Ayla's breaths were the rush of the Steorran Sea. A push and pull. Ancient, primordial. The oldest rhythm, the first song.

Blood in Crier's mouth. Her own. The texture was different, thinner and oilier than human blood. The taste was probably different too. Ayla's heartbeat was quickening. Crier's eyes flew open and she watched as Ayla shifted, fingers twitching. She was curled up on her side, hair spilling across her face. There were long claw marks up and down her forearms from Rosi's fingernails.

Ayla made a tiny noise. Her eyes fluttered open.

"Hello," said Crier, trying not to sound hysterical.

Ayla's brows furrowed. She blinked once, twice. ". . . Crier?"

"Yes."

"'S going on?"

"Kinok found us. He used a fine powder to render us unconscious. Now we are in a cell, possibly in some sort of dungeon, though not too far removed from the heartstone forge."

"Nn." Ayla shifted again, groaning. "You talk weird when you're nervous."

"Do I?"

"Even more . . . formal. 'N like, detached. I dunno."

"Oh," said Crier, considering this. "I suppose that makes sense. It might be a defense mechanism."

"You being nervous is making me nervous."

"You probably should be," Crier told her. "We're in a very bad position."

Ayla pushed herself up on one elbow, wincing. "Panicking won't help anything."

"I am not panicking. I am quite calm, actually. My heart rate is half the speed of yours; I've been regulating it. However, I was slightly concerned you would not wake up."

"Kinda wish I hadn't," said Ayla, all the way upright now, slumping back against the stone wall. "Feels like there's one of your giants in my head. From the story with the, the craters, 'n the gold. Stomping around. Gonna break my skull."

"Well, you're wounded."

"Yeah, thanks, I headbutted a mountain. Not gonna forget that one anytime soon. *Ah*." She touched her temple, looking relieved when her fingers didn't come away red. "Horrible. All right. Do we have a plan? I'm assuming you can't muscle your way out of those manacles."

"I tried," said Crier.

"Really? Wish I'd been awake for that," Ayla said, then cleared her throat loudly. "If that's not an option . . . then what?"

Crier shook her head. "There are no viable windows, the door is almost seamless and there's no handle on the inside. Even if there was a handle I couldn't reach it without breaking the chains, which we've established is impossible."

"Damn. Maybe—"

"*Shh*," Crier hissed, heart leaping into her throat. She could hear footsteps outside. She knew those footsteps. "Pretend you're unconscious."

Scyre Kinok stepped into the cell. He took one look at Ayla and said, "I know you're awake, handmaiden."

Ayla opened her eyes and glared up at him, the picture of defiance even chained to a wall, dried blood on her temple, covered in rock dust and bloodied claw marks.

Kinok's eyes flicked to Crier, evidently dismissing Ayla. "Lady Crier," he said. "I missed you at our wedding. You made a fool of me."

"You deserve worse," Crier spat. The word *wedding* brought up all the memories of that day: sitting in silence as handmaidens flitted around her, ornamenting her. Summoning Faye, begging her to deliver a hopeless letter. Crier felt the anger inside her solidifying, molten steel shaped into a blade. "I know everything you're up to, Kinok. I know you're looking for Tourmaline. I know you've been poisoning your own followers with Nightshade—although that was a mistake, wasn't it? A failed experiment?" His face remained impassive, but Crier didn't think she imagined the flicker of annoyance in his eyes. "I know you want to destroy the Iron Heart. To make our Kind dependent on you and you alone. I won't let you do it."

Would she?

Yesterday, she would have done anything to stop him. But . . .

That room.

The bodies.

The blood siphoned slowly from their veins.

Heartstone was a red gemstone, mined from the earth and imbued with alchemical energy. Everyone knew that.

"You won't let me? Bold words from a girl in chains," Kinok said lazily. "Your naivete continues to disappoint me, Lady Crier. Such a waste of your intelligence. Such a waste of your Reason. You could have joined me, you know. You still can. I'm very forgiving." He crouched down, eye level with her, that dissecting gaze again. "I know you, Lady Crier. I have read every essay you've ever penned. You wanted so desperately to join the Red Council, didn't you? To eventually take your father's throne? We are more alike than you think. We both want power, Lady Crier. The difference is that I know how to take it."

Crier bit her tongue. She watched him steadily, refusing to show weakness; she would not give him the satisfaction.

"It is not too late for you," he continued. "Join me, and you will be so much more powerful than your father ever was. That old fool, making his nest in the bones of a dead civilization. *Traditionalism*." He spoke it like a curse, like it tasted foul. "He had no vision. No concept of innovation. Imagine what we could create together, Lady Crier. Imagine it: Beautiful Automa cities free of filth. Our Kind, ruling as we were meant to. Humans are such base creatures. Dogs rolling in their own excrement. There is no hope for them; their growth has long since stagnated; their age has ended. But for our Kind . . . there is nothing but glory in our future. Eternal glory. Immortal glory."

"You want to kill them all," she said, hollow. *And then be king. Forever.*

"No, not all. And I don't need to kill them. Banishment would be enough. Let the Mad Queen take them in; she loves them so."

"You're disgusting," she said, meeting his eyes. "You're nothing like me."

"Oh?" He feigned surprise. "Please, enlighten me."

"I don't want power," Crier said. "That's not why I wanted to join the Red Council. I don't care about being powerful. I want to make things *better*. I want to create a kinder world." Her hands were trembling, her mind clear. "Your dream is monstrous. You don't care how many die, you don't care who you crush underfoot. I will never join you. I will fight you until my last breath."

Kinok looked at her for a long moment. "Lady Crier, it is not your last breath that interests me. It is everything that comes before." And he unsheathed the sword at his hip, steel glowing dimly in the reddish light, and swung it in an arc. Crier tensed up, bracing herself.

But it was not Crier at the end of Kinok's blade.

It was Ayla.

The tip of the sword was resting at the hollow of her throat. It had not yet drawn blood.

"No," said Crier. Her own voice was foreign to her ears, flat and dead sounding. She couldn't look away from the sword tip, cold metal on the delicate skin of Ayla's throat. Ayla was breathing shallowly, holding Automa-still. "Scyre, I will bargain with you."

"Pathetic, how easy that was," said Kinok. He was looking down the blade at Ayla, eyes half lidded. So infuriatingly calm. "Truly pathetic. This is what happens when you . . . consort with humans. You have become so weak, Lady Crier. Even a fifth pillar could not make you this weak."

"I know that was a lie," Crier said. "I know you forged the blueprints. To blackmail me."

"Yet the outcome is the same. You are *weak*."

Blood in the air. He'd broken skin. Not deep. Only a few drops of blood, red and human.

"You know what?" Kinok said softly, almost to himself. "I think I will cut out her heart."

"No," said Crier, and this time she tugged at her chains. "No, take me. You can—you can use me against the sovereign. My father. You can use me as leverage against my father."

"Crier, *no*," Ayla said, barely moving her lips.

Kinok didn't even look at Crier. "Do you think your father would risk anything, anything at all, to save you? You made a fool of him."

"I—I'm still his daughter."

"Ah. No, not quite. He is already in the process of replacing you. The blueprints for one Lady Yarrow are being Designed as we speak. He didn't even wait a day. Not a single day after you ran, Lady Crier. Before he sent for the Midwives." He traced the sword tip across the wings of Ayla's clavicle, tapped it lightly on her sternum, over her shirt. No blood. He was playing with her. Relishing her fear. "Sovereign Hesod never cared about you, Lady Crier. He certainly did not *love* you. You were created to serve a purpose, and you failed to do so. What use are you to him? What leverage?"

Despite everything, that hurt. Crier thought she'd severed herself from her father, renounced him entirely, but there was a part of her that would always be the gangly newbuilt child following him around, trailing after him through the halls of white marble and gold, asking him questions, asking him for ink and parchment, asking him about the Red Council, sitting in his study with a pile of books, looking forward to their slow walks through the flower gardens and the sun apple orchards. There was a part of her that had never stopped longing for his approval, his trust, his *respect*. That part was not so easily tamped down.

"Worthless girl," Kinok said to her. "Softened, rotted, worthless girl. I am going to cut your handmaiden's heart out of her body, and you are going to watch."

"*No*," Crier said, the word wrenched out of her. She threw herself forward, her entire body weight, everything she had, straining against the chains. Kinok was raising the sword, preparing to cut. It would not happen. It could not happen; Crier would not allow it. Her mind gave way to a singular goal: pulling the chains from the stone wall. She strained against them. It felt like her arms were going to dislocate, rip clean out of the sockets. She pulled. He was smiling. He was about to cut out Ayla's heart and he was smiling.

She heard the sound of cracking stone. Tiny eggshell fissures, growing—

Then, a thousand times louder, the piercing sound of a chime.

Crier and Kinok froze in unison. The chime was so loud Crier gasped, wishing she could cover her ears; it was reverberating in her skull. It was a high, nauseating noise, like fingernails on slate, so loud it seemed to shake the walls. Then—footsteps in the corridor outside the cell. How many—a dozen? Moving panic-fast.

The door to the cell swung open with a scrape of iron on stone. A Watcher stood in the doorway.

"What in *all hells*," Kinok snarled. His expression was a rictus of cold, incredulous fury.

"There's been a breach, Scyre," said the Watcher, cowering in the face of Kinok's rage. "The prisoners are escaping. The Heart has been compromised."

17

"*What?*" Kinok snarled, and Ayla pressed her lips together so she wouldn't make noise when his hand jerked and the tip of the sword skittered sideways across her collarbone. "What do you mean there's been a breach?"

"In the western sector. The human prisoners were set free from the outside. And—provided with weapons."

"By *who?*"

Had Dinara done something? Ayla had never seen Kinok like this. His composure had shattered; he was wild-eyed, mouth like a knife slash, voice harsh and furious. Gone was the cold, calculating scientist. In its place was what could only be described as a child throwing a fit.

"We are not certain, Scyre," said the Watcher. "They overpowered the Watchers of the western sector and stole an Iron Compass. By the time we discovered what had happened, they had already made it to the labyrinth. We are attempting to track them—"

"*Shut up,*" Kinok snapped. He straightened, looking down at Ayla for a second. She could practically see him trying to decide whether he should just kill her now and get it over with or wait until later, when he could draw it out for ages like he'd wanted, when he could make Crier watch the whole thing, a sick dissection. *Efficiency . . . or control?*

She knew which he'd choose.

Sure enough, Kinok sheathed the sword. "Once again I'm forced to clean up your mess," he said to the Watcher. "Overtaken by a dozen humans. You disgrace our Kind." He swept from the room, Watcher at his heels, and the thick iron door shut behind them.

Ayla and Crier were once again alone.

"You're . . . ," Crier said. Her voice was hoarse from begging for Ayla's life. "You're bleeding."

Ayla nodded. She reached up, running two fingers along her collarbone. It wasn't too deep a cut, and it didn't even hurt that much. Just a dull, throbbing ache. She held up her fingers, tipped in dark red, almost black in the murky half-light of their cell. The rebels had escaped and were already in the labyrinth, making their way out. They didn't know Ayla and Crier were trapped in the Heart as well.

Nobody knew.

Nobody was coming for them.

The air smelled of smoke and blood, and they were trapped

in this tiny dark cell, and nobody was coming for them.

Ayla didn't realize her breathing had quickened until she heard Crier say her name, except it sounded like Crier was calling out from across a wide body of water, or through a thick fog, or through a tunnel, hollow and echoing like that.

She pressed her hands over her ears and squeezed her eyes shut, trying to calm down, but it felt like half her mind was elsewhere, a scrap of paper caught in the wind. Carried all the way back to that day.

That day. That day.

In the outhouse, the tiny pitch-black outhouse, the smell of smoke and blood and human shit. Old, sour piss. Waiting for Storme to come back. Screaming from above, screaming and the sound of a village burning, the roar of fire and the great splintering crack of roofs collapsing. Waiting for Storme to come back. Knowing she'd just seen her parents slaughtered but not quite believing it, because how could they be dead? How could they be dead for real, forever?

Waiting for Storme to come back for her. Waiting and waiting and finally accepting that he wasn't coming, nobody was.

Crawling up and out, falling once, landing hard on the foul wet ground . . .

Ayla, someone was saying. *Ayla.* Now, or then? Did it matter? Both outcomes would be the same.

Except this time she wouldn't escape. And she wasn't alone. They would both die here.

I don't want you to die, she thought hazily. *I don't—I don't want you to die. Crier, I want you to live.*

"Ayla!"

The shout startled her into opening her eyes. She felt dizzy, her head was swimming. Darkness at the edges of her vision like flames devouring paper. *Storme hadn't come.*

"Ayla, I need you to calm down," a familiar voice said. "Ayla, you have to breathe."

I can't, Ayla tried to say, but nothing came out. Her face was wet. Blood? No, salt on her lips. She was crying, which some part of her found humiliating, but mostly she just couldn't breathe, couldn't speak, her chest was too tight. Like someone had cracked open her rib cage, reached inside her, and wrapped their cold fingers around her lungs.

"Ayla. Ayla, please try to breathe. I think he's coming back, I hear footsteps. You have to calm down." Crier's voice was low and strained, like she was speaking through clenched teeth. "Ayla, I'll get us out of here, I swear to you, but I need you to calm down. Just try to breathe. Slowly, in and out."

Breathe. Ayla's brain was shivering, rattling around. She was still there, *still there,* hidden in the latrine. She had been locked inside it, in that terrible coffin, ever since.

She had never emerged. Not really.

Nobody had ever come for her.

Crier gasped, and there was a wrenching noise, the clatter of metal on stone.

A figure stepped into the cell. There was something familiar about the breadth of those shoulders, that silhouette. Ayla squinted through the darkness and the haze of her own tears.

The figure took another step forward. The light from the high, narrow window fell across his face.

For a moment, Ayla thought she was hallucinating. Or she'd passed out and this was a dream. Because there before her was *Storme*. He was a man now, but in the wavering light, she could have sworn there were two of him, one superimposed on the other, a faded imprint, a little ghost. A little boy. Barely nine years old. Ayla blinked and the child-Storme disappeared, but the older one didn't.

"You came," she breathed.

Storme let out a funny breath, almost a laugh, sad around the edges. "I came. Sorry it took this long."

Ayla took him in, her brother, her twin. He looked a little worse for the wear, hair matted with dirt or blood, a nasty scrape across one cheek. But he was whole and alive, and he was here. He'd come for her. "No, you're—you're just in time, I think," she said faintly. "But *how*?"

"I'll explain later," he said.

"You," said Crier, and Ayla finally tore her eyes off her brother. "You . . . you were Queen Junn's adviser." She sounded stunned.

"Still am, actually," said Storme, crouching down before them. "Hello again, Lady Crier. What a terrible place for a reunion. We have to get out of here before the Watchers come."

"I'm chained to a wall," Ayla said.

"Yeah, I thought you might be. Hold on." He rummaged around in a small pouch at his hip, and Crier gave Ayla a look of deep bewilderment that would have been funny under any other circumstances.

"You know each other?" she said, eyes darting between Ayla and Storme.

"You could say that," said Ayla. "He's my twin brother."

Crier's eyes widened. "Your—? And he's alive?"

"Thus far," said Storme, who was sprinkling some sort of white powder on Ayla's manacles. Then he took out a tinderbox.

"Is your brilliant escape plan to blow my hands off?" Ayla squeaked.

He rolled his eyes. "I'm not going to blow your hands off. Can you hold still for a second? The Watchers are gonna show up any minute. Our diversion in the western sector will only distract them for so long."

"Stars and skies," Ayla mumbled. "Fine. Fine. Please, for the love of all the gods and then some, *please* be careful."

"Your dead twin brother is alive and also adviser to the queen of Varn," said Crier, dazed.

"It's a long story," Ayla said. "I'll tell you later, promise."

"Shut up, both of you, stop distracting me," said Storme. "Almost . . . *ah*. Brace yourself, Ayla."

Panicked, Ayla screwed her eyes shut. There was a weird smell, like sharp bitter smoke, then a noise like a dozen snakes hissing at once. Then a flare of heat on her inner wrists, painful enough that she sucked in a breath—and the iron manacles cracked open like oyster shells, releasing another curl of smoke just as she dared open her eyes. They fell from her wrists, clanking on the stone floor.

"Oh," said Ayla. "Well, all right."

Storme snorted. Within a minute, he'd repeated the same process for Crier.

"Let's get out of here," he said.

Rubbing her aching wrists, Ayla got to her feet. Crier was still crouching; she seemed a little shell-shocked. Ayla bent down, holding out a hand. "Come on, Just Crier," she said. "Time to go."

Crier's dark eyes flicked to Ayla's hand. She took it, and Ayla pulled her upright, and—there was a moment in which Crier was standing over her, very close, and Ayla was tilting her chin up to meet Crier's gaze. Their hands were clasped between them.

"Will you *please*," Storme whisper-yelled from the doorway.

They followed him, slipping out of the cell and into the dark stone corridor beyond, and they did not let go.

Storme led them through the veins of the Heart. It was clear *something* was going on—they kept hearing what sounded like distant explosions.

"That'll be the diversion," Storme said. As they ran, he explained: "Me and Queen Junn've been keeping an eye on these mountains for ages. We've been spying on the Watchers, tracking the shipments of heartstone, trying like hell to find the Heart itself. Trying to find a way inside. But we weren't just spying on the Watchers. Junn's always known Kinok would be a greater threat than anyone believed. Since the beginning, since the first whispers of him leaving his post as Watcher of the Heart, she knew. She said, *Nobody does something like that unless they've got something else planned. Something much bigger.*"

He led them down a corridor so narrow they had to walk sideways, inching their way along the wall. "Shortcut, sorry. Anyway. That's why we went on that 'diplomacy tour,' that's why we visited the sovereign's palace. To observe Kinok. Maybe you already knew that, Lady Crier."

They emerged from the shortcut and Ayla's stomach dropped—there were people waiting for them on the other side. But they were dressed in green, the queen's emerald green, the crest of the phoenix at their throats. Three humans, two Automae, all of them grimy, the humans panting and bloodied.

"Adviser Storme," said one of the Automae. "The human prisoners have been delivered to safety. Only two of our own have fallen. We've come to retrieve you."

"Wait," Ayla blurted out. "Which human prisoners?"

The Automa gave her an odd look. "I believe they were captured earlier today. From the mountain pass."

Ayla and Crier exchanged a glance. "There's more," Ayla said. "Not all of them are alive, but—there's this room in a corridor right off the forge, round like a hatch. There are humans inside. They're being tortured, they're badly hurt, they need help. Please." She turned to Storme. "Please. I'll go alone if I have to."

"We'll go alone," said Crier.

Storme shook his head. "Find the round door," he instructed

the two Automae. "Rescue anyone still alive. We'll wait for you at the seastone."

"Yes, sir," they said in unison, and headed back down the corridor, silent as shadows.

Another explosion shook the corridor, closer now. Ayla squeezed Crier's hand, reflexive, and tried to keep her expression steady when Crier immediately squeezed back.

"Very, *very* much time to go," said Storme. "We're not too far now. I'll take lead. Bell, Rina, flank the girls. Neven, at the back."

"Yes, Adviser Storme," the humans said.

They'd only gotten a few more paces when the entire world broke apart.

The ground lurched beneath their feet, sending everyone sprawling, even as a great wave of heat billowed into them from behind. Head spinning, Ayla didn't realize what was happening until Storme gasped, "That's not us. *That's not us.*"

BOOM.

This time, the walls rattled with the force of the explosion. Bits of rock rained down on them from above, and there came a second wave of heat, so hot Ayla thought it might singe her clothes. She struggled to her feet, spitting pink where she'd bitten her tongue. Her eardrums had popped; all sound was muffled. "If it's not you, then who?" she shouted.

"Kinok," said Crier, eyes huge. "He's going through with it."

"Going through with *what?*" Storme asked, coughing.

"Destroying the Iron Heart."

BOOM. Ayla remained upright only because Crier was holding her hand. She staggered, coughing, the air thick with rock dust.

"Run!" Crier said. *"Run!"*

It was madness. Blinded by clouds of dust, skin burning with each new wave of heat, they ran. Ayla lost all sense of time and place, knew only that she had to keep chasing Storme's voice. The heat seared her throat and lungs. At one point, she heard the tunnel collapsing behind them, a rockslide, stone crushing and scraping against stone—she tried to turn around, to see how close it was, but Crier tugged her ever forward.

At last, they emerged. The entrance blended seamlessly into the lichen-spotted stone of the mountainside. Ayla didn't know exactly how much time had passed since she and Crier had found their way into the Heart, how long they'd been unconscious in that cell, but it was far past midnight now, the liminal blue-black hours just before dawn. The mountains were quiet with night, the only sounds being the singing of insects and the calls of faraway birds, farther down the mountain where green things gripped the rock. Then—BOOM. A roar of fire, a shriek of earth; Ayla saw a flock of birds take off, terrified, into the night sky.

"Look!" Crier said, pointing.

High above, at the peak of the mountain, a tower of smoke. Pale against the night, it billowed up into the stars. Endless. Ayla was struck silent, just watching. Her heartbeat was a riot; she could feel it pulsing in her dull, ringing ears. Sunlight had once streamed down onto the Iron Heart. Some crack in the mountain, a pinprick opening into that enormous cavern. Now, smoke rose up.

"He did it," Crier said. Her eyes were glassy. "Those explosions. All that smoke. I can't believe he really did it. Destroyed it. Oh gods." She looked to Ayla, searching. "Oh gods, what now?"

What now? Where the hell do we go from here?

"I don't know," Ayla whispered. "I don't know."

"Do we know which vein that was?" Storme asked the woman Rina about an hour later, as their party picked their way farther down the mountainside, away from the still-rising smoke. Rina had a map, was holding it up to catch the moonlight. A map of the Iron Heart, Ayla thought, and wanted to laugh. She and Benjy had spent so much time obsessing over such a thing back in the sovereign's palace, convinced it was the key to the Revolution. The key to everything. Well, here it was. Newly obsolete.

"Hey," Crier murmured.

They were still holding hands. They hadn't let go, not even once. Ayla's hand was sweaty; there was dirt and sweat and probably blood slicking their palms, but she didn't want to lose this point of contact. This point of warmth, solidity, in the middle of a huge and frightening thing. The machinery of war. Kinok versus Queen Junn versus—the sovereign? The human rebellion? Both?

Ayla looked up at Crier, who was already looking back. "Hey."

"I am glad we made it out alive," said Crier.

"Don't think I've forgotten what you did," Ayla said quietly. "Offering up your life in exchange for mine. I'm gonna give you hell for it later. After I've had a good sleep."

"I would expect nothing less." Her mouth twitched, a tiny crooked not-quite-smile, and Ayla felt her own heart move in her chest.

She shifted her grip, interlacing their fingers. "I could've taken him. Bastard's lucky the chime went off when it did. I was two seconds away from unveiling my incredibly advanced combat skills."

"Yes. I'm disappointed I lost a chance to witness your signature move, 'Aggressive Squirming.'"

Ayla couldn't help it. She laughed, exhausted but true. When she quieted, Crier was watching her.

Then Crier went tense, hand twitching in Ayla's grip. "Adviser Storme," she said. "Someone's coming."

Storme looked up from the map, but he didn't seem at all concerned. "I know," he said. "I'm expecting her."

Her?

No, it can't be, not out here—

But when a figure on horseback melted out of the shadows, Ayla knew exactly who it was.

Unlike the rest of their party, Queen Junn looked perfectly pristine, as if she were sitting in her own throne room instead of on the back of a shaggy mountain pony in the middle of the Aderos Mountains. She wore a cloak of silver silk; it looked like she was wrapped in moonlight. Her hair was twisted into a crown of glossy black braids. There were *pearls* in her ears.

"Handmaiden Ayla," Queen Junn said lightly, as if continuing a recent conversation.

"It's just Ayla, thanks," said Ayla. "I'm getting very tired of everyone calling me that, I haven't been a handmaiden for ages." Storme coughed pointedly, and she rolled her eyes. "Hello, *your majesty.*"

"Always well met, Ayla," said Junn. "And—Lady Crier. I did hope I'd see you again."

"Just Crier, actually," said Crier.

"Yes, of course," said Junn. "The runaway. I am pleased your loyalties did not waver. Let's get going, then. I wish to reach the seastone before dawn."

"Wait," Ayla said. "Wait, just—what's going on? Where are we going?"

Junn was already turning her horse away. "Yes, I suppose you've missed a lot over the past few days. Too much to explain right now, really, so forgive me for telling you the short version. I have taken control of the palace of the sovereign of Rabu. The sovereign himself is my prisoner. Currently, lovely Benjy is in charge. Come," she said, waving in the way of queens. "We are headed there now, and we should hurry."

The whispers become shouts.

The rumors are true, my friend.

The Iron Heart has been destroyed. Already, the heartstone stores are dwindling. Already we have turned to hoarding. Thievery. How long will it take before thievery turns to murder?

A new fear rises to the surface: Councilmember Paradem was right. Scyre Kinok is our Kind's only hope.

—FROM A LETTER INTERCEPTED BY QUEEN JUNN OF VARN, FROM RED HAND MAR TO RED HAND ILLYAN OF THE RED COUNCIL OF THE SOVEREIGN STATE OF RABU

18

Three days of riding had taken a toll on them all. It was preferable to traveling on foot, but Queen Junn's reinforcements had only two caravans, both of which were needed to transport the liberated prisoners from the Iron Heart. Most of them were so weak they could barely walk, let alone stay upright on a horse for twelve hours. They were laid out on low cots, watched over day and night by the queen's physicians. Crier had seen Ayla visiting them a couple times, in the evenings, when the rest of their party was occupied setting up camp for the night.

Crier couldn't bring herself to do the same.

Couldn't face them.

Not knowing what she knew. Or what she thought she knew. Every time she closed her eyes, she saw that room in haunting detail: the bloodred light, the black stone vessels, the thin silver tubes. The two humans who had already died. Crier had never been that close to a dead body before. It had been so jarring:

the absence of sound. She was so accustomed to hearing human heartbeats, the quiet ocean-rush of breath, that she usually tuned it out, let it fade into the background like so many other mundane noises. When she'd first approached the bodies, it had taken a few moments to figure out why everything felt *off*. It was like walking through a forest and realizing all the birds had stopped singing. Wondering how long you'd been oblivious to it, wondering what had scared them into silence. Crier had faltered, shaken her head as if to clear it. A silly instinct. But it had felt like her head was stuffed with cotton. A heavy, physical silence.

Then she'd realized what was missing.

On the first night—after they'd reconvened with Queen Junn's guard at the seastone, which turned out to be a large greenish rock; after they'd been given their own sturdy mountain ponies; after the queen's soldiers had returned with Dinara and the rest of the human rebels, who'd been locked away in one of the many chambers of the Heart, and the prisoners from the blood room; after they'd completed the long, arduous trek down the mountainside, which took the rest of the night and most of the morning; after they'd met the rest of the queen's party at the base of the mountain, switched their horses for fresh ones, and kept going, riding to a campsite a few leagues away, reaching it just as darkness fell—after all that, on the first night, Crier hadn't been able to hold it in any longer. Knowing full well she was being reckless, not finding the energy to care, she marched right up to Queen Junn's heavily guarded tent and said, loud enough that there was no way the queen wouldn't hear, "Your highness. I wish to speak with you."

She'd been expecting a dismissal. But a moment later the tent flap lifted and Junn slipped out into the night air, a small figure dressed in deep blue, blending in with the dark. Her hair was loose around her shoulders. She was careful to fasten the tent flap shut behind her, careful not to let Crier see more than a sliver of what was inside. Crier thought back to that night Junn had spent in the sovereign's palace, the night Crier had wandered the halls and heard soft, lilting noises coming from Junn's room, two voices ringing out. The queen and her adviser. Scandalous to take a human lover, Crier had thought. Now she knew that lover was Ayla's long-lost twin brother. Was that what the queen was hiding in her tent?

"Come, Crier," said Junn, motioning at the guards to stay put. "If you wish to speak, we'll speak."

They found an outcropping of rock at the edge of the camp, secluded enough that even Automa ears wouldn't be able to listen in. Junn clambered up onto the biggest rock, a moonlit boulder shaped like a tortoise shell, and beckoned. Crier, somewhat at a loss, climbed up to sit beside her. Together they looked out over the dark hills. High above, the moon was a waning crescent, a white-toothed grin.

"Speak," said Junn.

Crier's bravado faltered. She was *angry*. For Reyka, she was angry. She wanted to confront Junn, to demand answers. She'd spent weeks preparing for this moment, drafting furious speeches inside her head, thinking wildly of justice and remorse and Junn begging for forgiveness, but now the moment had come, and they were face-to-face, and all the words left Crier at once.

"I want answers," she said. "You said we were allies. You asked for my help, you said we should work together, I—I gave you names, Laone and Shasta and Foer, and you killed them, fine, I should have expected that, they were too close to Kinok, but—of all the names—I never gave you *hers*."

"Whose," said Queen Junn.

"Reyka's!" Crier snapped. "The missing red hen, Reyka, Councilmember Reyka. You killed her for no reason!"

"I did what was necessary," said Junn.

"Killing her wasn't necessary," Crier hissed. She knew she was being disrespectful, and if she wasn't careful she'd be the next Reyka. But the grief was still fresh, and, perhaps even stronger: the sense of betrayal. "She was *on our side*. She'd been working against Kinok in secret for years. She was our ally and you killed her. Why?"

"She was careless," said Junn, still so terribly *calm*. Her countenance was a lake, the surface unruffled, smooth as glass. "Kinok was onto her. He was tracking her movements, and I'm sure he had already identified a number of her contacts. Even the sovereign was catching on, and he has always been blinded by his own arrogance. Foolish man. So convinced of his own authority, he dismisses even the most obvious signs of defiance. I suppose you already know that."

Crier didn't answer.

"This is a war, Crier," Junn said. "Your only true ally is yourself. The moment Reyka started trusting the wrong people—or putting too much trust in the right people—she became a threat. Because even the right people are still people, Crier. And everyone, *everyone*, has a breaking point. Kinok is exceptionally good at finding them. Reyka's breaking point was a person, and that person was more vital than Reyka herself. That person had to be protected."

Dinara. She had to mean Dinara, but the memory that flickered behind Crier's eyes like a guttering candle wasn't of Reyka's daughter. It was of the sword at Ayla's throat. The trickle of blood. *Scyre, I will bargain with you.*

Yes. Everyone had a breaking point.

Crier felt . . . embarrassed, or ashamed. She'd broken so quickly. One threat to Ayla, and Crier would have given anything to make it stop. And she knew that if it happened again, right now, her reaction would not change.

"Reyka was a threat. I eliminated her. I took no pleasure in giving the order, but I did not hesitate to give it. This is not a game. One leak, one slip of the tongue, could result in so much more than a single death." Junn closed her eyes and tipped her head back, moonlight softening the planes of her face. With her eyes closed, she looked her age. Seventeen, maybe eighteen now. "I have always been willing to trade one life for thousands," she murmured. "I am the Mad Queen. I am Junn the Bone Eater. Funny, isn't it, considering I am not the ruler who burns villages to the ground. I am not the ruler who slaughters humans for fun. What is it they say about me? That I bathe in human blood—is that rumor still circulating? I like that one."

"How did the rumors begin?" Crier couldn't help but ask, anger bending to curiosity. She'd never given much thought to the origin of the whispers, despite always suspecting they were exaggerated at best.

"Oh, I started them," said Junn.

"What?"

"I became queen when I was sixteen years old, Crier. Mere days after my father was assassinated. The country was in chaos, my father's advisers thought me a silly little girl, the people thought me weak and naive. It didn't help that my father had always kept me hidden from the public eye, to keep his secret safe." She smiled wanly. "Of course, he didn't know I'd been sneaking out of the palace for years. But I digress."

"So . . . you started the rumors to make people respect you as a leader?"

"Not respect. Fear. I've found it far more useful in the long run."

"I see," Crier said quietly. She understood what Junn was saying. But still, sitting in the moonlight beside the Child Queen, she thought: *That's not the kind of leader I'd want to be.* Then Junn's words caught up to her. "Your father kept you hidden to . . . keep his secret safe? What secret?"

Instead of answering, Junn reached into the folds of her robes and drew out a knife.

Crier stiffened, but Junn didn't make any moves to attack her. She held up the knife, appearing to admire it, moonlight turning the blade to molten silver. Then she lowered it to her other forearm. Before Crier could react, Junn slid the blade across her own skin.

"Your majesty—" Crier gasped, though Junn herself looked calm. She wiped the blade off on her deep blue robes, pocketed it again. Tilted her arm up to the light.

Red blood oozed from the shallow cut in her forearm.

Red blood.

Crier stared, uncomprehending.

"Everyone sees only what they want to see," said Junn. "Humans, Automae; it doesn't matter. We're all the same in that respect."

"That's not possible," Crier said, even as the evidence glittered like rubies on Junn's skin. "There's no way you could hide that. From everyone. For all these years. Your whole life."

"Yet I did." Junn lifted her arm, licking at the rivulet of red, *human* blood. "Not from everyone. My personal guards know. Certain trusted advisers and elders of my father's court. My Storme."

"But . . . your heartbeat. Your eyes . . ."

Junn smiled. "When I visited your palace, did you listen to my heartbeat? Did you watch my eyes, waiting for them to flash gold?"

No, she hadn't.

Crier's hearing was strong enough to pick up any heartbeat in her immediate vicinity—and so she'd learned to tune them out. They were distracting. Unnecessary background information.

She didn't pay attention to the rhythm of the heartbeats around her unless she had a specific reason to. The rabbits in their den. Deer in the woods. Ayla, always.

Had Crier watched Junn's eyes? Only in the sense that she had, at the time, wanted them on her. She'd wanted Junn to look at her, speak to her. But had she been waiting for Junn's eyes to flash gold in the candlelight at dinner? No, why would she. Junn was an Automa—there was no reason to believe otherwise, to search for signs of deceit.

"You drank heartstone," Crier said.

"I've grown accustomed to the taste, though it gives me the strangest dreams."

"Was your father secretly a human too?"

"No. Father was an Automa. But he loved humans. Not like your father claims to love us, but like you do. Like I do. For everything we are, everything we aren't, everything we can become." She tilted her head back, baring her throat. "For our love. Our fury. For what we create: stories and cities and every last god. For our ghosts. For our drinking songs. Because . . . for every human who does a monstrous thing, a thousand others will rise against them. We have always killed and saved ourselves. Protected each other. Fought for futures we will not live to see. My father loved humans, Crier. When he was newbuilt, he met a human girl, the daughter of one of the Midwives. They remained friends for years and years, even though she was no one and he was destined to be king. When she fell pregnant by a man she wouldn't name, my father gave her coffers of gold.

When she left the newborn with the physician and disappeared overnight, he raised the child as his own." Her eyes were closed, her hair a spill of pale gold down her back. "He kept me a secret from everyone but a handful of advisers until I was older. Until I knew how to hide in plain sight."

"But you still snuck out of the palace."

"That I did. I was lonely, you see. In my room, with my books. I wanted to meet my own Kind."

"And did you?" Crier asked.

"Yes," said Queen Junn, eyes sliding open again, the light brown of fallen leaves. "Many of them. I used a fake name, stole through the city, drank my fill of wine. Early on, I met a boy. I told him I was lonely. He said he knew loneliness down to the bone. He said he'd find a way to keep me company even when I returned to the palace, and he did." Lips stained red with her own blood, smiling at the moon. "He wrote me letters."

Love letters. Crier thought of the many letters she'd drafted and never sent to Ayla. She thought of love, a creature that took infinite forms, and marveled that her Kind had ever sought to be rid of it. Had taken something hot and true and replaced it with cold, loveless bonds, same as they'd taken lifeblood from the humans in the Iron Heart and transmuted it to crystal, crushed it, drank it like nasty wine. Crier had not imbibed any heartstone since she'd learned the truth about the Iron Heart, and now, under the stars, beside a young, ruthless, human queen, she vowed to never take it again. She would find Tourmaline and survive like that, or she would not. Either way, she wasn't touching heartstone. Better for her body to wither than her soul. "Are you still lonely?" Crier asked, without really meaning to. "Even after everything? Even now that you can leave the palace?"

"I am always lonely," said Junn. "My heart, if I have one, is a house of empty rooms and empty halls. My thoughts and footsteps echo. Sometimes I feel like a guest in the house of myself. But sometimes, someone's footsteps cross my floor, and that is enough. These days, I luxuriate in my loneliness. I walk through my empty halls naked and singing." Her smile hadn't slipped. "What I really wanted was a reason to stay," she said. "And I got what I wanted."

Crier frowned. "Stay . . . in the palace?"

"Hm. Anywhere," said Junn. "Now, what is it that you want, Crier? You've escaped your gilded cage. The world is your oyster. Your pearl. What next?"

What next?

How was she supposed to answer that when she had no idea what tomorrow would bring? She'd escaped her cage once, but here she was, flying right back into it. Right back to Sovereign Hesod.

"I don't know," she said at last. To Queen Junn, to the moon, to the halls of her heart. "I don't know."

It had only been a few weeks since Crier had run away from home, and the part of her that thought she would never return had been expecting it to look completely different. To grow and change along with her. She was half right. When their party crested a hill, and Crier saw the whole of the sovereign's land spread out before her—the palace itself, the pearl on the black cliffs of the Steorran Sea, those four white marble spokes glittering in the sun; the servants' quarters, the stables and out-buildings, the orchards, the flower gardens, the yellow fields, and beyond all of it the sea—it was like looking at her own face in a mirror and not recognizing it. Crier had grown up in this place. It was the first home she had ever known, and she had known every inch of those hallways, every tapestry and sculp-ture, every flower in the garden, every book in the library. But it was a prison, too. Her gilded cage. How was it possible for something to be both? Even now, it felt like both.

Of course, it wasn't exactly the same palace she'd left. The main courtyard and half the fields were dotted with white tents: the queen's royal guard and allies. Thin pillars of smoke rose up from dozens of campfires. Crier could see the soldiers swarming like beetles all over the grounds—they numbered about a thou-sand, according to Junn.

They reached the courtyard within the hour, and riding through the makeshift army camp was even stranger than seeing it from afar. There was a big tent set up right outside the palace doors, and Crier could see physicians and Midwives scurrying around inside. The air was thick with the smells of smoke and charcoal and cooking meat, and the sound of a thousand sol-diers shouting and talking. Everywhere, people were preparing for battle.

Kinok was coming. He'd already destroyed the Heart,

positioning himself as the only chance of survival. The only one who could find Tourmaline. His next move, Crier knew, would be to take the throne of Rabu. Establish himself as king. And tell the whole world to kneel.

Varnian riders had tracked him and his army—his followers, the Anti-Reliance Movement, a sea of black armbands—as they marched from the Aderos Mountains to the east, never too far behind Queen Junn's party. Never too far behind Crier.

He was coming for her.

"Your highness," she said after they entered the palace and made their way to the great hall, after Queen Junn had called for bread and ale and heartstone. Crier stepped up beside her, feeling Ayla's questioning gaze at her back. "Your highness. I have a request."

"You and your requests," said Junn, waving away a servant boy carrying a skull-shaped teapot of liquid heartstone. "I know. You want an audience with your dear father, is that it?"

"He is not my dear anything," Crier said, not even trying to hide her annoyance. "But—yes."

"Come with me." Junn's eyes cut to Ayla. "Only you, though."

Crier nodded. She didn't want Ayla anywhere near the sovereign. "That's fine."

Flanked by guards, Crier followed Junn out of the great hall and down the long, gilded hallways to the east wing and then downstairs, to the underground quarters where Kinok had once lived. Junn led her to a nondescript door that did not seem like a door that would imprison her father—except for the presence of more guards—and stopped in front of it.

"In here," said Junn. "The guards will wait just outside the door."

Crier started to ask why—*Because you think he will try to hurt me? Because you think I will try to help him escape?*—but thought better of it. Neither answer would make her feel less ill. Instead she just nodded, slipped inside, and closed the door behind her, heard the click of the latch.

It was darker in this room than the hallway. There were no windows, of course; the only light came from two blue-green wall sconces and a single lantern. The only furnishing was a rough-hewn wooden table with a chair on each side, lantern sitting on the tabletop. A couple months ago, this had been a storage room for dry goods, extra linens. Now it held the sovereign of Rabu.

For there he was, looking as dignified as possible considering the circumstances. He was seated in the chair facing the doorway, and his posture was flawless, confident, as if the old wooden chair was his white marble throne in the Councilroom of the Old Palace. He wasn't unbathed like the prisoners they'd rescued from the Iron Heart. He clearly had not been deprived of heartstone. He looked perfectly healthy, his skin flush with color. The only difference between this Hesod and the Hesod Crier knew was his clothes: plain wool garments instead of the rich, jewel-toned brocade he favored.

She hated herself for it, but she couldn't help feeling relieved. She'd been conjuring up images of her father the prisoner for days, imagining him starved and skeletal, bloodless, half dead.

Heartstone withdrawal was terrible. She did not wish that kind of suffering on him, even if he deserved it.

"Daughter," said Hesod, and Crier realized she'd been staring, frozen just inside the door. "Come. Sit."

She started forward automatically—then stopped. "No," she said. "I will stand."

"Such a contrarian you've become." He sounded amused. "You used to be so obedient. Well, do as you wish. What is it you have come for? Am I correct in assuming you've joined forces with the girl queen?"

"No, I haven't," Crier said. "At least not entirely."

"Not entirely? This isn't a philosophical debate, child. You cannot argue one side and then the other for your own entertainment." The lantern was reflected in his eyes, twin flares of white-gold. When he tilted his head and the light caught his eyes at an angle, his irises flared gold to match. "At least come into the light, will you? I haven't seen your face for weeks."

Crier hesitated, but . . . it was only a couple steps. She took them, moving into the circle of lanternlight. "I am not on Queen Junn's side," she told him. "And I am not on your side. I am on my own side. I want to end this war before it begins. I want Kinok put on trial for his crimes. I want . . ." She steeled herself. "I want you to tell me the truth."

"That's very broad," he chided her. "Tell you the truth about what? My favorite human food? Sun apple tart."

"Tell me the truth about heartstone," she said, meeting his eyes. Her hands were shaking. They still shook every time she thought about what she'd seen in the bowels of the Iron Heart. "Tell me—tell me it really is just a red gemstone. Tell me the Watchers extract heartstone ore from deep within the earth. Tell me the Iron Heart is really a mine."

"That would not be the truth," said Hesod.

"*Gods,*" Crier choked out, one hand flying to cover her mouth. Horror flooded through her, cold and immediate, like she'd just leaped into the icy waters of the Steorran Sea. "Gods, you can't be— *Father*. Please. Please. Tell me heartstone isn't made from human blood."

"Not the truth," he said.

Her back hit the stone wall. She'd stumbled away from him. "How—how many deaths is that?" Fifty years since the War of Kinds, fifty years since the creation of the Iron Heart. Fifty years of death. "How many have died so we could live?" Not just died. She could imagine few fates worse than what she had seen in that room. Shackled to a cot, weak and delirious from a combination of blood loss and some sort of sleeping draft, knowing nothing but the darkness and the other bodies around you and the steady drip of blood into black vessels. *"How many?"*

"One drop of human blood can produce ten barrels of heartstone dust," Hesod said, dismissive. "The process is very refined. In the beginning, our Kind consumed fresh blood, and the longer we lived, the more blood we required. It was impractical. Unsustainable. The Makers found a way to transmute blood into stone, to imbibe plain ore with blood magick. They saved innumerable human lives. You're being melodramatic, Crier."

"You knew." She couldn't comprehend it. "All your years as sovereign, you knew what was happening. And you let it continue."

"Yes, I did."

"How could you?" she demanded, voice breaking. "How could you just—this, and everything else? The raids—you destroyed entire villages, entire families, like it was nothing. Like they meant nothing at all to you. Like they were just—pieces on a chessboard." She couldn't look away from him, this person who for sixteen years had been her father, this person who had walked with her through the flower gardens and let her sit in his study and taught her about politics and economics and had never taken her seriously, not once, and had replaced her with another child the moment she defied him, this person with so much red blood on his hands. "You are everything that is wrong with this world," she said. "You really are a monster."

He regarded her. His face was completely blank, no trace of shame or anger or anything. Maybe a trace of pity. "I hope you realize this outburst is yet another example of your immaturity, daughter. There is no such thing as monsters. I am Automa. I am exactly like you. The only difference between us is our beliefs. Our choices."

"You're nothing like me."

"Really? If a Scyre cut us open right at this moment, and laid bare our inner workings, we would be indistinguishable from each other. Everything you're Made of, I am Made of as well. There is nothing inside you that is not also inside me." He caught the look on her face. "Yes, I know about Scyre Kinok's little trick. Midwife sabotage, was it? Someone tampering with your blueprints, some nonsense about a fifth pillar? Tell me, daughter, did it make you happy, thinking you were *special*?"

"No," she said. "I was terrified. Because I thought my father would be ashamed of me." She blinked and a single tear fell. "I am not afraid of that anymore. I just have one more question for you, Sovereign." A question that had been burning inside of her ever since she'd learned Ayla's story. "Were you there at . . . at the raid in a village called Delan?"

The lantern sputtered. Hesod's eyes left Crier and it felt like a physical weight being stripped away, like invisible binds being severed. He opened the tiny glass door of the lantern and removed the candle in its metal bowl. It was almost entirely burned down, yellow flame drowning in the melted wax, clinging to the very last bit of wick. The trail of smoke had turned black and oily.

Hesod dipped one finger into the melted wax and held it up to catch the light of the wall sconces, watching as it cooled and hardened on his skin, turning from clear to ghostly white.

"I have been to many places," he said. "I cannot possibly remember all of them."

"You liar," Crier spat. "Our Kind remembers everything. Delan, in the north. Seven years ago it was raided and burned to the ground. Were you there?"

He sighed. Rubbed the wax between finger and thumb. "Yes, I was there. What of it? The villagers had been hoarding grain. I'd offered them a generous bargain: they were allowed to keep their land, and in exchange I collected a portion of each year's harvest. But of course they became greedy. I discovered they had been falsifying their output, calculating my portion from barely two-thirds of the real harvest. They knew it was an act of treason and they did it anyway. Was I supposed to turn my back?"

"So you destroyed the entire village."

"I believe in fairness and justice, daughter. Land in exchange for grain. If one side of the promise breaks, so too will the other."

The candlelight was dying, the darkness growing. Crier couldn't stand it. She needed to see his face for this. She needed to see the emptiness in his eyes, so she would not forget. She pushed off the wall and joined him at the wooden table, taking the seat opposite him. How many meals had they spent like this, facing each other across a table? But it had always been the table in the great hall, in the cavernous room that could have held fifty and instead held only two. Three, once Kinok came to the palace.

"I spent so long thinking I was Flawed," Crier said, leaning into the light. She knew he would be able to see the tear tracks on her face, and he would think that made her weak. "Not just when Kinok tricked me. Before, too. Because I felt things. Because I wanted to feel things. I thought I had a poisonous seed inside me, and every day it grew, and someday it would kill me from the inside out." Her voice was thick with tears, but steady. She was no longer shaking. "But I was never the one with the poisonous thing. I was never the one with the Flaw."

A sound came from the hallway outside the room. Shuffling footsteps. Junn must have sent someone to collect Crier. It was startling—she'd forgotten there was a world outside this room, that she would leave this place and Hesod would stay.

"Of course you weren't Flawed," said Hesod, soft and sweet. Almost crooning. "Of course you weren't. You are young and naive, you frustrate me, but you are still my greatest creation. My daughter. I Designed you to be my successor. To head the Red Council, to lead this nation, to take my throne. That is why I am being so harsh with you, child. It is important that you accept the reality of this world. Otherwise you will never be able to control it."

Control. That was all leadership meant to him. How had she never seen it before?

She shook her head. "You're *lying*. You were never going to let me lead. You appointed Kinok to the council over me."

"Because the world isn't ready for your ideas, Crier. I was trying to protect you." He reached across the table and she jerked away, revolted at the idea of being touched by him. If she hadn't been looking closely, she might not have seen the flicker of irritation in his eyes. "You need a few more years to grow. What kind of a father would I be if I threw you to the council unprepared? They would laugh you out of the room, you and your little essays. I couldn't let that happen to you. I know you better than anyone else, Crier, and I knew you needed more time. All I wanted was to give you more time."

As always, there was a part of her that wanted so desperately to believe him. But—

"Even if that was true, it doesn't change anything else you've done," she said. "The lives you took yourself and the lives that were taken on your orders. I have nothing left to say to you, *Hesod*. When this is over and you are tried for your crimes, I wish you all the fairness and justice you granted the villagers of Delan."

She shoved her chair back, wood screeching against the stone floor, and got to her feet. The movement jostled the table, and the candle flame finally sputtered and died, leaving nothing but the cold blue light of the wall sconces in its wake. It gave Crier the sudden impression of being plunged underwater. Of being drowned.

"You don't understand what I'm offering you, my daughter," said Hesod. He was a black shape in the watery darkness, a shadow swathed in shadows. "You have always wanted to be sovereign. I know that hasn't changed. If you ally yourself with me now, I will forgive you for running away. I will forgive you for betraying me and breaking your promise to the Scyre. I will forgive you for angering him and turning him against us. With me at your side, you could be a glorious ruler. I want to be by your side. Will you let me, daughter? I will forgive you for the choices you made. Will you forgive me for mine?"

Crier paused with one hand on the doorknob. She looked back at him, eyes adjusted to the dim light, and studied the lines of his face one last time. Then:

"I don't know if any of us can be forgiven," she said, and left the room.

Her feet took her first to her own bedroom. To her writing desk. Eons ago, in the days leading up to her wedding, her father had given her a golden key. It was the key to what he called his *trophy room*: the room where he kept all the human artifacts he'd collected over the years. Sacred objects, ancient books, relics of the War of Kinds. Sickened by the idea of it, Crier had tucked the golden key away in the drawer of her writing desk. Now, she was ready to use it.

Down one winding hall. Another. There, the door. Key in the lock. A click, and the trophy room door opened soundlessly beneath her touch. She stepped inside. The silence of this room was a physical presence. Like cotton stuffed into her ears. The door swung shut behind her, and Crier was alone.

And furious.

She had never been this angry in her life. Not when she'd realized Kinok was blackmailing her. Not when her father had given the council seat to Kinok. Not when she'd learned Queen Junn had murdered Reyka. Not when she'd run away from the palace. Not when she'd seen those bodies in the Iron Heart, seen their blood oozing slowly into the black stone vessels, realized what was happening. Not even when Kinok had pointed his sword at Ayla's throat. So many times in Crier's life, her dominant emotion had been fear. *I am Flawed*, she'd thought, and she had been afraid. *Kinok is plotting something*, she'd thought, and she had been afraid. *I will never have a say in my nation's future*, she'd thought. *Reyka is missing and nobody else seems to care. ARM is growing dangerous. I don't want to marry Kinok. Ayla wanted to hurt me. My father never cared about me. I don't know how to stop Kinok. I don't know how to save anyone. I don't know how to save myself.*

Fear and fear and fear. Frozen water in her veins, her ice-white heart. Her own body a prison. Mouth wired shut, limbs heavy with frost. The bravest thing she'd ever done was running away, and even then she'd been terrified. She'd second-guessed herself, felt guilty for leaving, wondered if perhaps she was overreacting, if she should have stayed and played the perfect, obedient child, even if it was unbearable. *Ungrateful,* her mind had whispered. *Naive. Ignorant. Helpless. You are the Lady Crier, daughter to the sovereign, and that is all you were Created to be, and you will never be anything else. How dare you defy your sole purpose?*

"No," she said aloud, staring at her reflection in a tarnished hand mirror propped on one of the shelves. Her eyes were wild and bloodshot. "No. You're wrong."

She whirled around, taking in every detail of the room, all the hundreds of objects on the shelves. Rusty old daggers and glass baubles and children's toys, a painted leather mask, fat yellowed books, a wooden jewelry box crusted with gemstones of all colors, a series of little porcelain animals, a pocket watch. A set of reed pipes, a rag doll, countless knives and arrowheads, a crown of dried flowers, a tattered white dress. This collection of stolen things. Heart hammering at her temples, breaths loud and harsh, Crier committed all of them to memory even as her vision started blurring around the edges. This collection of ghosts. Her father's crimes. She took them in, sick with fury. Grief.

Then she burst into tears.

She sank to a crouch, buried her face in her hands, and cried like she had never cried before. The loud, uncontrollable sobs of a child. A human child. Even newbuilt Automa did not cry like this; they were taught very early on what was acceptable, and this was not. Tears streamed down her face, hot and itchy, salt on her lips, as if she had an ocean inside her and it was finally brimming over.

After what felt like hours, the sobs petered out into shaky, hitching breaths. Crier sniffled hard. She lifted her head, feeling full and hollow all at once. She wiped her face, her nose, blinking away the last tears.

Then she frowned.

On one of the bottommost shelves, mostly hidden beneath the sleeve of the white dress, there was a sliver of deep midnight blue. Crier shuffled forward on her knees, skirts trailing behind her. She reached out and closed her fingers around that piece of blue. It was no bigger than a sun apple but heavier than she'd expected, heavy like a lump of iron. At first glance the surface seemed perfectly smooth. But when Crier looked closer, she saw tiny letters etched into the blue stone.

She had seen this stone before. Never in real life, only in memory. The first time she'd accidentally smeared a drop of blood onto Ayla's locket and tumbled into the memories of a man who had lived and died years before Crier was even Designed.

She was holding Yora's heart.

19

Ayla stood in a corner of the grand ballroom, which had
been turned into an armory of sorts. It was crowded with
maybe two hundred people dressing for battle. Kinok's forces
were marching on the palace. Queen Junn's guard and their
allies, Automae and humans from all corners of Zulla, had gathered. There were Rabunians and Varnians, easily recognizable,
and then a scattering of humans that had to be from Tarreen:
they had the same brown skin and dark hair as Ayla, but their
clothes were designed for hot, humid jungle, not the northern
cold. They wore loose, light fabrics in earth tones, ochres and
browns and greens and clay reds, and Ayla kept seeing a motif
of interlocking blue circles, woven or stamped onto their clothes,
painted onto their bare skin. Tiny blue stones dangled from their
ears; blue stone pendants hung at their throats and wrists. Of
course—Dinara's mysterious blue stone had been discovered
in Tarreen, after all. It seemed as sacred to the Tarreenians as

heartstone was to the Automae, or silver and gold to the humans of Rabu and Varn.

No wonder you've kept to yourselves all this time, Ayla thought, stealing another glance at a pair of Tarreenian women through the crowd. It wasn't that the sovereign had scared them all into hiding. It was that the Tarreenians were hiding something of their own. Cave systems full of blue crystals with enough destructive power to sink a nation. Hesod couldn't have known about it—he would've sent armies into Tarreen by the thousands, closed borders with Varn be damned.

The true miracle was that Kinok hadn't gotten there first.

"Hey. You're Ayla, right?"

She startled, tearing her eyes away from the Tarreenian women. Standing before her was the golden-haired prisoner from the Iron Heart. The last time she'd seen this person, they'd been lying half conscious in the caravan with the other prisoners, a physician slathering a poultice over their raw, blistered skin. They looked much better now. They were upright, for one thing, but it was more than that—it was the light in their big brown eyes, the way their face no longer looked grayish and stiff. Their hair had been washed, falling in loose curls instead of matting to their skull with sweat and grime.

She nodded. "That's me."

"I was told to bring you these," they said, holding out a pile of what looked like armor, the sort all the humans were wearing: a shirt and pants of thick, padded wool, a chest plate of hard leather.

"Oh. Thank you."

"Courtesy of the queen," they said, grimacing a little, like the word *queen* had an unpleasant taste.

Ayla raised an eyebrow. "Not her biggest supporter?"

They huffed, blowing an errant curl out of their eyes. "Well, I owe her my life and I want the Scyre of Rabu dead, so for the time being I will fight under her flag. But I don't approve of monarchs."

"What's your name again?" asked Ayla.

"Erren."

"I think you and me will get along, Erren." She took the clothes and, with nowhere else to sit, lowered herself to the floor to unlace her boots. "Mind helping me into these? I confess I've never worn a chest plate before."

"Yeah, sure." They crouched down beside her and reached for her other boot, starting on the tight laces. Now that they were regaining their strength and color, Ayla saw they were much younger than she'd thought at first. Maybe just a year or two older than she was.

"How'd you end up in there?" she asked quietly, even though it was so loud in the grand ballroom, so many voices overlapping, that even an Automa couldn't have heard them from more than three feet away. "In the Heart, in that room. What happened?" Erren's jaw tightened, and she added, "You don't have to tell me."

"No, it's all right," they said, tugging the boot off her foot. "Here, stand up and put on the pants and shirt. Over your regular clothes is fine, it doesn't matter." They held out a hand and she grasped it, yanking herself up. They passed her the heavy wool pants. "I was traveling with a group of . . . Rebels isn't the right word. Accidental rebels, maybe. Most of us were quite young, runaways and orphans and the like, just trying to survive. We took on jobs for extra coin. Delivering messages, guarding supplies, simple things like that." Their eyes were distant. "We were in the south when Nightshade first started spreading through the region. We didn't know what was happening—we thought it was a disease, some sort of virus. We didn't know if it only affected leeches or if we were in danger too—and I wanted to investigate. Our leader said it was too dangerous, so . . . I went alone. I snuck away in the middle of the night. I went to the place we'd last spotted them, I just wanted to get a closer look. It's a bit fuzzy after that. The last thing I remember is hearing footsteps and turning around to see a Watcher behind me."

Ayla sucked in a breath. "They attacked you?"

"Yeah. Hit me over the head, I think. Either way, I wound up in that . . . room. I'd sort of wake up sometimes, but it's mostly a blur." Their mouth tightened. "I'm sure the group I was traveling with thinks I'm long dead."

"I'm sorry," said Ayla. "Maybe . . . now that you're free, maybe you could find them again?"

"Maybe," said Erren. "I'm certainly going to try. If only to tell Hook he was right."

Ayla snorted. "I suppose he's the leader?" she started to ask, but the words died in her throat. Because there, weaving through the crowd, half a head taller than all the humans and even some of the Automae, was *Benjy*.

Without a second thought, Ayla ran for him. Once he caught sight of her, he began to run at her too, his funny, fawnlike run, all limbs. They met in the middle, bodies colliding, and the scent of his skin and hair and clothes was so familiar Ayla wanted to cry. He lifted her off her feet, spinning her around, and she didn't even protest. *"Benjy,"* she said the moment he put her down, looking up into his face as she'd done a thousand times over the years, ever since he hit ten years old and shot up like a weed. "You're here."

"Course I am," he said, grinning. The last time they'd seen each other they'd argued, but who cared? Who *cared*? "You know me. Can't keep me away from a good fight."

"Reckless," she said. She took a step back and noticed for the first time he was wearing the uniform of Queen Junn's guard—complete with a sheath at his hip and a shiny badge on his chest. More than that, he looked solid, stronger, older. No longer the harmless, deathless boy rebel. This was Benjy the warrior. "I see you kept up with your training."

"Turns out I'm not just scrappy. I'm pretty damn good with a sword."

"Never thought I'd see you in a queen's colors," she said, not unkindly.

"Ah." He looked away, jaw working. "I . . . That's . . . Well. It's kind of a long story. Turns out the queen's been trying to take down Kinok and the sovereign for ages. I didn't like it at first, but—she and your brother have done some damn good work.

You know I always wanted to be part of the Revolution. Well, now I am."

Once it would have bothered her, after all the grief he'd given her about Crier. It still sort of did, to be honest. But. "You can tell me everything later," Ayla said, and meant it. "Though I have to say, it's hard imagining you with a sword."

"That reminds me." He reached for his belt, where there was a smaller sheath hanging alongside the sword. He drew out a dagger and offered it to her, the blade winking in the lamplight. "This is for you. I didn't know if you'd have a weapon or not." His face turned grim. "The queen's riders have spotted Kinok and his forces. They're coming for us, and they're coming quick. They'll reach the palace before midnight."

Ayla took the dagger, hefting it in her grip. Testing out the balance, the weight. "But we won't let that happen. Right, Benj?"

Benjy nodded. "Remember," he said. "Aim for the heart."

After parting ways with Benjy, who had to go report to his captain, Ayla left the grand ballroom. She hesitated in the hallway just outside the doors, thinking. She needed to find Crier quickly; she didn't have time to wander the whole palace. If she were Crier, where would she go? Her old bedchamber, maybe? The library?

No—Ayla knew where.

She started off down the hallway. Moving in the heavy, unwieldy armor was like slogging through waist-deep mud. Ayla was out of breath by the time she reached the far end of the eastern spoke, half jogging down a dark corridor, counting off the doors as she went. There. The door covered with carvings of musical instruments. The music room. Crier's sanctuary. Ayla still remembered the moment Crier had tossed her the key to the music room, an offering, a gift and a secret and a promise all at once. Privacy, silence, a hiding place, given over with no expectation of anything in return. Was that the first time some small part of Ayla had begun to trust Crier? Was it that early on?

The door was unlocked, the knob turning easily under Ayla's touch. She pushed it open, and there was Crier. She was sitting on the low bench beside the massive golden harp, and on the surface it could have been the first time Ayla had visited this place, months ago, even the dust undisturbed. Crier must have been lost deep inside her own head—she didn't seem to notice Ayla's presence, didn't even look up until Ayla let the door fall shut behind her, latch clicking into place.

On the surface this Crier could have been the Crier of months ago, except she was wearing plain clothes, not a delicate silk gown. Her hair was loose, tumbling down her back like black water. Her throat was free of jewelry. Her eyes and lips unpainted. And Ayla knew her laugh like fishermen knew the tides. She knew the crooked pull of Crier's mouth, and the shape of her fingers, and how it felt to slide their hands together and hold on. She knew Crier was the answer to a lot of questions, and not one of them was *How can I hurt him?* She knew Crier was brave and brilliant, stubborn at the worst moments, funny in a way that wasn't obvious unless you knew to look for it. She knew

Crier wasn't a book or a map or anything else that could be read once and known in its entirety. Nothing finite like that. There was no beginning to her, no end, no parameters; her body was not the truth of her; Ayla knew that Crier herself was something as wide and endless as the ice fields or the black sea or the evening sky, just as the first stars were beginning to appear. Those first pinpricks of light.

I like knowing there's certain laws in the universe, Ayla's father had said once, a very long time ago, before everything. *You can't count on much. Can't trust most things to stay solid. But there is always some sort of force at work. Even way out there past the sky, so far away that we can't even imagine it, things work the same. Your mother would explain it better. Everything is just bodies in motion, bodies in orbit, just like here. Pushing and pulling. You know what that's called? The law of falling.*

Crier looked up. "Oh," she said, blinking at Ayla. Late-afternoon sunlight was drifting in through the windows, turning everything dusty and gold. That window—the same window Ayla had climbed through, followed by Benjy and four other servants, the night she had tried to kill Crier. The night she had failed. "Oh. I didn't even— Is something happening out there?"

"Not yet," said Ayla. She didn't move. She felt carved from wood, like she was just another one of the instruments, still and silent and formed by a gentle hand.

"I have something for you," said Crier, and Ayla realized Crier was holding something in her lap. A small bundle wrapped in cloth.

Ayla went to her, claiming the last few inches of bench. The inflexible leather chest plate made it difficult to sit down, digging into her hip bones if she hunched over even a little. She leaned into Crier's side and peered down at the cloth bundle, which Crier was cupping in both hands like it was a baby bird, something fragile and alive. "For me?" Ayla asked in a murmur. "What is it?"

Crier held it up, letting the cloth fall away, and Ayla's breath caught in her throat.

It was a deep blue stone about the size of a clenched fist, the surface smooth and polished. Ayla had seen this stone before. Not in real life, but in memory, Siena's memory, this blue stone like a cut of night sky in Siena's hand. Ayla stared down at it, speechless. Tourmaline. True Tourmaline, not in its rawest form like the stone that formed the blue powder bombs, but alchemized Tourmaline. Maker's Tourmaline. Yora's heart.

There were tiny symbols etched into the surface. Concentric circles: the four elements, then gold. It was repeated all over the stone, except in one place.

"How . . . ?" she rasped.

"It was in my father's trophy room," said Crier. "With all his other artifacts of war. It was mixed in with a collection of human jewelry, covered in dust. It must have been there for years. Perhaps ever since the raid on your village. I'm sure he thought it was just another gemstone. Another little trinket."

Ayla couldn't speak. She couldn't look away from the stone. Was that a flicker of movement in the very center, the heart of the heart? A tiny pulse, the faintest bluish glow, even after all these years without a body, all these years spent just gathering dust? Was Yora's heart still beating?

"It belonged to your grandmother," Crier whispered. "And now it belongs to you. It is your heritage, Ayla. Take it, and do with it what you will."

This is a bomb, Ayla thought, staring down at it. *This could be a bomb.* If she wanted, she could turn it into the deadliest powder bomb yet and take out an entire battalion, take a hundred leeches in an instant, turn the tides of this war, *that's for my village, that's for my parents.* She could destroy half the palace if she wanted to, with Hesod inside.

Crier winced, lifting a hand to her forehead. When she noticed Ayla's questioning look, she explained, "I . . . haven't had heartstone. Since the Iron Heart. I'm . . . I'm beginning to feel the effects."

No heartstone since—Ayla swallowed. Not good, not good. Kinok was coming, and Crier was his number one target. If there was any fighting, if she was in harm's way for even a moment, and she hadn't had heartstone in days . . . She wouldn't heal. She'd be as shaky and vulnerable as a starving human. She'd be in danger.

Ayla could use Yora's heart to destroy half the palace.

Or.

"Crier," she said. "Do you trust me?"

"Yes," said Crier.

"Do you want this war to end?"

Crier's brow furrowed. "Yes. Of course."

"All right." Ayla let out a shaky breath. She looked up at Crier, their faces so close together she could see the flecks of gold in Crier's eyes, the inhuman smoothness of her skin. This person Ayla had come to know so well. This person she trusted with her life, with everything in her. This person she would follow into a black labyrinth, a battlefield. *How did I not know?* she wondered, searching Crier's face. *If anger is a powder bomb, this is a hearth fire. This is—*

"I have an idea," said Ayla, voice sounding faraway to her own ears. Was she leaning closer? Was Crier? Their noses were almost brushing, she could feel Crier's breath on her lips, she was breathing in the scent of her, salt lavender and sea. "It's dangerous. It might not work."

"I'm in," said Crier.

"Oh, hell," said Ayla, and kissed her.

The first time they'd kissed, it had been: Wild. Hot and messy and desperate, hands clutching at clothes and tangling in hair, gripping so tight it hurt, mouths working furiously, bodies crashing into each other, Ayla's back hitting the wall, Crier's fingernails digging into the soft skin behind her ears, both of them gasping from shock or pain or anger or a combination of all three and then a hundred other white-hot, electric feelings flaring between them and disappearing just as quick when reality flooded back in. The first time they'd kissed, Ayla had wrenched away from it and hated herself for days, weeks; she'd replayed it over and over in her head and hated herself for that, too. She'd tried so hard to forget how it felt: Crier's fingers in her hair, Crier's taste like a drop of honey on her tongue, the hollow sound of their teeth knocking together, how it only made her want to press in deeper. She had tried so hard to forget, only to find that forgetting was impossible.

This, though.

This, right here, right now.

If their first kiss had been unforgettable, the words for this one hadn't been invented yet.

Ayla kissed Crier, and this time she focused on memorizing everything she hadn't cared about last time. The shape of Crier's mouth. The fullness of it beneath her own. The way Crier drew in a slow breath through her nose as if trying to calm herself. The way she went Automa-still, as if afraid any sudden move-ment would bring Ayla to her senses, as if this wasn't the best choice Ayla had made in her whole damn life, as if this didn't make more sense than anything. For a moment, neither of them moved. The kiss was soft, close-mouthed, a brushing of lips, a flicker of breath. Then Ayla just—broke. She pulled away just far enough to take a breath and then pushed in again, pressing a second kiss to Crier's mouth, firmer this time, a question or an answer or a reaffirmation or everything at once, it didn't even matter, because Crier's lips parted in a wordless *yes*, and the kiss bloomed into something hot and bright, something Ayla felt in every inch of her body, toes curling in her boots. Now Ayla was reaching up, sliding her shaking hands into Crier's hair. Now she was shifting to straddle the bench so she could face Crier head-on, get the angle just right. One of Crier's arms curled around Ayla's back, drawing her somehow closer. They melted into a series of deep, lush kisses, hot and dizzying and endless, lips moving together, Crier's mouth opening beneath Ayla's, the taste of her like summer rain. Ayla pushed into her over and over again, taking her mouth, already addicted to this, to *her*, to Crier, everything about her, taste and scent and the warmth of her skin under Ayla's hands. In the end it was Crier who drew back, shuddering. Overwhelmed. Her mouth was swollen, the shine of Ayla's kiss on her lower lip. She swallowed hard; Ayla's eyes tracked the movement of her throat.

"Oh," said Crier.

Ayla cracked up. There was a war on their doorstep and she was *laughing*, doubling over, forehead thunking onto Crier's shoulder. *"Oh,"* she echoed, still laughing, and nuzzled her face into the crook of Crier's neck. Crier's hand was still resting on her back, warm even through the thick wool armor. "Oh indeed."

"Shut up," Crier said, sounding flustered. "I don't think I'll be able to form full sentences for a week."

"That was a sentence."

"Shut up!"

"I don't know if I'll be good at this," Ayla whispered. She straightened up, gesturing between them, so there was no confusion. *This. This this this.* "But," she continued shakily. "If we survive today. If we make it out alive. I want to—try. With you." She cleared her throat. "If you—if you want that, I mean. With me."

"I want that," said Crier, and leaned in, pressing their

foreheads together. Her eyes were closed, brows furrowed as if in concentration. Her mouth was still wet, kiss-bruised, and something about that made Ayla want to—*have* her, just have her. "Ayla. I've wanted that for a long time."

"Okay," Ayla breathed. "Then—"

Somewhere outside the palace walls, a war horn sounded.

They pulled away from each other, equally wide-eyed. "Damn," said Ayla, twisting around to look out the windows of the music room, though of course she couldn't see anything but sky and orchard. "I thought they wouldn't be arriving till nightfall."

"Kinok lives to defy expectation," Crier said tightly. "The idea you mentioned. What was it?"

Ayla ran a hand through her hair, trying to clear her head. Focus, she had to focus. "Kinok's followers," she started. "They're with him because he convinced them he can find an alternative to heartstone, right? They don't know heartstone is harvested from human blood, but they always knew the Iron Heart was vulnerable. They knew it was your Kind's biggest weak spot, and if it were ever overrun by humans, or the caravans sabotaged, anything like that, you'd all starve. That's how he's been selling them on Tourmaline, that's how he tricked them into poisoning themselves with Nightshade. And now Kinok has destroyed the Heart. His followers *have* to stay with him, because he's the only one who can save them. The only one who can save your entire Kind. The only one who has the answers, who's searching for Tourmaline. Or so they think. Right?"

"Right," Crier said.

"So . . . so what do you think would happen if someone showed them Kinok doesn't have the answers?" Ayla said. "If someone showed them we already found Tourmaline, and *we're* the only ones who know how to use it?"

Crier frowned. "But we don't know how to use it."

"This is the part where it gets dangerous," Ayla told her. She reached out for Crier's hand, interlacing their fingers. "I do know how to use it. How to activate it. I can *prove* it works, that your Kind can use it as a new life source. I know I can. It's dangerous, but if you go out there right now you won't heal. You're already weak; you could die, Crier. Please, if you won't take heartstone, let me save you with this. I swear to you I will not hurt you. I swear you'll be okay. Do you trust me?"

"Yes," said Crier without hesitation.

"Okay. The only thing is I can't do it alone. We're going to need someone with experience."

"What kind of someone?"

Ayla met her eyes. "We're going to need a Midwife."

It was like a reenactment of the memory she'd seen in the locket.

Firelight, yellow and alive. The bundles of drying herbs hanging from the rafters cast odd shadows on the walls, like hands reaching down from above. Ayla was sitting on the lip of the hearth, fire a wall of heat at her back, and she was not alone. There were two figures in the middle of the room. She couldn't see their faces, but she knew one of them had to be Siena. The other was clad all in white. A Midwife.

But this time, Ayla stood in Siena's place.

They didn't have a physician's table, so Crier was lying on the floor of the music room, Ayla and the Midwife she'd fetched from the physicians' tents—who had introduced herself as Jezen to Ayla, and to Crier had said, "Good to see you again, lady, even in times like this"—kneeling on either side of her. When Ayla had explained what they were about to do, Jezen had shook her head hard.

"No," she'd said. "That's—that's unprecedented. We have no idea how that would affect her vessel. She could die."

"It's not unprecedented," said Ayla, even as the words *she could die* rang through her head. "It has happened once before. I saw it."

"How—?"

"We don't have time," Ayla said. "I'll explain everything later, but for now, we don't have time."

And Jezen, grim, had nodded.

Now, kneeling over a wide-eyed, silent Crier, Ayla willed her hands to stop shaking. They had to stop shaking, she had to be steady for this. One slip-up, one moment of clumsiness, and—

Don't think about that.

They had cut open the front of Crier's shirt, just enough to expose her collarbone and the top of her chest. It was terrible that Crier would be awake for this, but Jezen had assured them opening the seam in her chest wouldn't be painful—it was Designed without nerve endings. The dangerous part would be the few moments in which Crier didn't have a heart at all.

"Are you ready?" Jezen asked Crier.

"Yes," Crier whispered.

Jezen looked at Ayla. "Are you?"

"Does it matter?" said Ayla.

"Fair enough."

Like the other Midwife had, all those years ago, Jezen lowered her blade to Crier's chest. She didn't have the delicate little physician's instrument Ayla had seen in the memory; she had only a small dagger. But it was well sharpened, and it would have to be enough. Jezen ran the knife along Crier's skin, finding that same near-invisible seam, the skin splitting apart easily. No blood. Using only the tip of the knife, she pried open that small section of Crier's chest. The door to her heart. Crier had squeezed her eyes shut the moment the blade touched her skin; she kept them shut now. Ayla brushed her fingers over Crier's forehead. "It's okay," she murmured. "It'll be over soon."

"I trust you," Crier breathed.

And I will trust myself, Ayla thought. *I have to.*

Crier's heart, unlike the Automa girl's heart from the memory of Siena, was beating. Ayla could hear it ticking like a clock, could *see* the faint vibration of each pulse. She saw where the tiny gold and copper veins fed into it. This was the challenge: fitting the new heart into Crier's chest at exactly the right angle, reattaching the veins and vessels. Ayla remembered the sound she'd heard in the memory, like a latch clicking into place.

The blue heart rested on the flagstones beside her, nestled in a scrap of cloth. Ayla raised her head to look at Jezen. The Midwife's eyes were an unusual green, like chips of emerald.

It was time.

So carefully, shifting her knife only the tiniest fraction of an inch each time, Jezen began to cut Crier's heart out of her body. Ayla watched, unblinking, as Jezen severed the veins one by one, detaching them cleanly from the surface of the heart. The veins seemed alive, moving independently of each other, like wiry, hair-width blades of grass swaying in a nonexistent wind.

Jezen severed the last vein. Crier's face smoothed over instantly, her whole body going lax. Ayla swallowed hard, trying not to panic. This was what it looked like when Crier died.

But it was temporary. Ayla picked up the Tourmaline heart and held it in both hands, waiting, as Jezen lifted Crier's old heart out of her chest. There was the familiar hollow space, the pocket left behind. Ayla shoved aside her panic, took a deep breath, and let instinct and memory take over. She turned the blue heart in her hands, matching the angle to what she had seen in Siena's mind. She remembered the positioning of the alchemical symbols: fire, water, earth, air, gold. *Here, just like that.* Then, without hesitating, she lowered the Tourmaline heart into the hollow in Crier's chest. She pressed it into place, feeling Crier's inner workings flutter beneath the pressure, flexing and shifting to accept this new object. *Maker's iron*, as the bandits in the woods by the River Merra had said. *Black magick, that. Iron that moves and breathes.* She held out a hand and Jezen passed her the knife, and Ayla slid the tip of the blade under Crier's veins, guiding them into place. The etchings on the surface of the heart weren't just letters. They were a map. The tips of the severed veins matched perfectly with the points of each letter, latching on. Stilling once more.

Ayla pulled the knife away. There was a faint, almost inaudible sound. Like a latch.

Nothing happened.

Ayla sat back on her heels, waiting. For Crier's eyes to open, for her chest to rise and fall again.

Nothing.

"Ayla," Jezen said.

"No," Ayla said, louder. *Think, think.* Why hadn't it worked? What was different? What would it take to breathe life into this heart?

The only other time she'd seen Tourmaline come to life, it had been in the hands of a boy with a hammer. He'd been making a bomb. Ayla remembered the symbols he'd etched into the surface of the bomb, ready to be activated with a drop of blood. Fire, saltpeter, sulfur. Mortar. Salt. And she remembered what Lady Dear had said, on that sunlit afternoon in the palace at Thalen.

Have you heard of the language of flowers?

White roses for secrecy. Oleander for caution. Combine different types of flowers, and you can construct entire messages. So it goes with the language of the Makers.

"Ayla," Jezen said again, but Ayla wasn't listening. She grabbed the knife again and bent over Crier's lifeless, lightless body, biting her lip so hard she tasted blood.

Fire, saltpeter, sulfur made a bomb. That was where she'd start. She needed energy, but not too much all at once; a slow burn, not an explosion. Ayla held the blue stone in place with one hand, careful not to touch the veins, and with the other, she lowered the knife. Using the very tip of the blade, she began to scratch the first symbol into the surface of Yora's—Crier's—heart.

Moon and water for transformation. Fire for energy, tempered by earth, to keep it from raging out of control. Phosphorus to invoke light; magnesium to keep it burning. Salt and copper for life, for blood. Ayla carved the eight symbols in the shape of a circle. Then, in the center, she connected them with an eight-point star. She could feel Jezen's eyes on her, but she didn't look up. She just ran the knife over the pad of her thumb, waited for a bead of red blood to well up, and pressed her thumb to the eight-point star.

Nothing happened. *Oh gods, oh gods*—Ayla was about to pull away, panic rising in her throat, when—

The Tourmaline began to glow.

Pale blue light emanated from it, as if the stone was a lantern and Ayla had just lit the candle, reflecting on the underside of Crier's chin, lighting up Jezen's face from below. But—

"*Oh*," Ayla breathed.

The heart wasn't the only thing glowing. All over Crier's body, all over her arms and legs and the exposed part of her chest, tiny cracks were forming. No—not cracks. *Symbols*. They must have existed all this time, invisible to the eye: alchemical symbols etched into this Made girl's skin. Now, as the power of Tourmaline spread throughout her body, the symbols were *glowing*, emitting a pure white light, flickering even brighter with each pulse of Crier's heart.

"It worked," said Jezen, reverent. "I can't believe it worked. A *new heart*."

One of the music room windows exploded.

Ayla and Jezen didn't even have time to react before a figure leaped through the broken window, glass crunching beneath their boots when they dropped down onto the stone floor. They were dressed all in black, their face covered with a silvery metallic mask. A *Watcher?*

"I'm here for the sovereign's daughter," the Watcher said, their low, rough voice muffled behind the mask. "Hand her over and live. Resist, and you will die."

"I choose resist," said Ayla.

"Then die."

The Watcher closed the space between them in less than a second. Ayla threw herself over Crier's body, slashing blindly with the knife. She was shocked when it actually made contact, violet blood spattering the floor, but it was barely a scratch. The Watcher, eerily silent, Automa silent, fisted a hand in her hair and yanked her upright. Ayla caught a glimpse of their eyes through the slits in the mask. Then she was fighting hard against their grip, jabbing the knife at anything she could reach, hoping only to buy Jezen and Crier some time.

"You're the handmaiden," said the Watcher. They were holding Ayla at arm's length. She couldn't reach them, the knife useless in her hand.

"So what if I am," she snarled.

"Bad luck for you," said the Watcher. "Scyre Kinok wants only the sovereign's daughter alive. Everyone else dies. But the handmaiden dies painfully."

They threw her sideways. She hit the wall hard, skull cracking against stone, and crumpled to the floor. Dizzy and gasping, bile in her throat, Ayla saw only a pair of shiny black boots advancing on her before she was pulled to her feet again. The Watcher wrenched her head back, baring her throat, and Ayla clawed at their wrist, their arm—she'd lost the knife when she fell, heard it skitter across the flagstones—but it wasn't enough, it wasn't anything, even the strongest human couldn't compete with an Automa's strength, and Ayla, though quick and clever, was not the strongest.

The Watcher let her struggle hopelessly for another few seconds, then threw her to the floor again. Ayla cried out and curled up into a ball, lifting her arms up to protect her head, waiting for the blow, the knife strike, but it didn't come. The Watcher had told her they'd make it painful, draw it out, and they meant it. Instead of going for her skull, they drew a leg back and kicked her in the shin.

The pain was indescribable. Like someone had set off a powder bomb on her leg, but instead of blowing it to pieces, the explosion just kept going. She *heard* her bone shatter under the

Watcher's boot, felt her leg burning, surely it had burst open, surely it was bloody and mangled, surely this level of pain could not be contained by her skin. Ayla felt herself scream, the sound ripped from her throat, animal and raw, a sound she wouldn't have thought herself capable of making. The pain was radiating up through her body now, coming in waves, her mind was flashing white, she was screaming again, if she felt this for a moment longer, even a moment, she'd go mad. Where was the Watcher? Why didn't they just finish her off?

Panting, trying not to vomit, Ayla cracked one eye open. The Watcher was—gone?

No.

Crier had woken up. She was on her feet, and she was glorious, even through the haze of pain. The runes were still glowing on her arms, her collarbone, even her cheeks and forehead. Jezen had closed up her chest again, but Ayla could *see* the blue heart pulsing, the blue glow swirling just beneath her skin. And her eyes—her eyes were glowing silver white. Just like Yora's. This was the power of Tourmaline. Energy derived not from blood—from suffering, from death—but from the elements, magick, the belly of the earth.

She was weaponless, but it didn't matter. She stepped forward and the Watcher stepped back. They were brandishing their dagger, but their hand was shaking so hard the blade was trembling in the air.

They were afraid of Crier.

They were *terrified*.

Crier lunged. The Watcher scrambled backward and escaped through the broken window, and then it was just Crier, Ayla, and Jezen again, the room silent save for Ayla's harsh, racking breaths.

"*Ayla,*" said Crier, and flew across the room, falling to her knees beside Ayla. Her hands fluttered uselessly over Ayla's body, her leg. Ayla couldn't see her own shin—she couldn't move, could barely keep her eyes open—but whatever Crier saw made her features twist with horror. "Midwife Jezen," she said, sharp and controlled. Oh, that was bad. The only other time Ayla had heard Crier's voice like this was when Kinok had a sword at Ayla's throat. "Midwife Jezen, she needs a physician. Now."

Outside the window, outside the music room, the sound of war horns. Like braying animals. Time slipped and Crier was saying, "Ayla, wake up, Ayla, open your eyes, come on," and there was a second figure hovering over Ayla, all white, ghost white, like Luna's dress in the marketplace a thousand years ago, before everything. Jezen was speaking. Her voice was higher in pitch than Crier's, high like bells. Ayla could only make out every third word. *Shards of bone. Bloodstream. Kill her.*

It will kill her.

"Fetch a physician," Crier was saying. "Please, go fetch a physician, there's no time, I'll stay here with her—"

No.

No, that wasn't the plan.

"Crier," Ayla gasped, black spots popping up behind her eyes. "Crier, you—go, you have to go. I'll be okay, I promise. Just go."

"No," Crier said. She sounded close to tears. "No, I'm not leaving you. We just need a physician. This is so bad, Ayla, this is so—"

"I can save her," Midwife Jezen cut in. Crier's head snapped up, those starry, glowing eyes darting in the direction of Jezen's voice, but Ayla wasn't about to take her own eyes off Crier. Her head was so heavy, vision turning dark and blurry at the edges, and she'd be damned if she looked at anything else.

"If I move quickly, I can save her life," said Jezen. "But if Kinok's assassins already found you here, we're all in danger. You are the target. He wants *you.* The best thing you can do for Ayla right now is to get far away from her. Go, Lady Crier. Whatever it is you're going to do, do it now. Go and *stop him.*"

"But—"

"Go!"

Pressure on Ayla's forehead, hot against her icy skin. Then the shape of Crier, little more than a shadow now, was gone. With nothing left to look at, Ayla closed her eyes and let herself sink into the numbness, the dark water, feeling only relief when it closed over her head.

20

The heart inside her chest was not her own.

Crier could feel it beating. She could feel it throughout her entire body, stronger than a normal heartbeat; with each pulse, the Makers' symbols on her skin glowed brighter, winking like stars. She held up one arm in front of her face, examining the previously invisible markings. The symbols etched into her skin. All her life, she had been carrying these threads of magick. Only now were they revealed to her, as Yora's heart filled her with a new kind of power. Words floated through her mind, the opening lines of the first book she had ever read. *The Maker's Handbook.*

All things possessed a certain prima materia, a pure, intangible substance older than the Universe Itself.

If humankind is formed from such material, from organ to bone to flesh to even the intangible Soul, then surely the Maker can transmute human life.

She had always been strong.

But for the first time, Crier felt truly alive.

Her mind kept trying to analyze and categorize each new sensation, to take this huge nebulous feeling and wrangle it into a shape that made sense. But how? Consuming heartstone paled in comparison. It had always felt like stepping from cool shadow into a patch of sunlight. A comforting warmth, a small replenishing of strength. This was—drinking moonlight. This was her whole body weightless and airy. Crier thought if she went to the sea cliffs right now, the tide would rise to meet her. If she pricked her fingertip, she'd bleed molten silver.

She let her body guide her through the familiar halls of the palace. As she neared the main entrance, she could hear a clamor of voices from the grand ballroom. Human and Automa, so many voices, a hundred at least. Queen Junn's army. The Tarreenians. The other humans, servant and rebel alike. Was there a difference between the two? Maybe not. Ayla probably didn't think so. Ayla would probably say: *To exist in this world at all is an act of rebellion for us, Just Crier.*

Ayla.

Just keep moving, Crier told herself. She trusted Midwife Jezen. More than that, she trusted Ayla. If Ayla said she'd be okay, then she would be. It was simple as that. Ayla would hold up her end of the bargain—it was time for Crier to do the same.

She didn't see anyone else until she reached the main entrance. Eight members of the Green Guard were stationed inside the huge wooden doors, faces impassive, weapons in hand. When

Crier approached, she got the distinct pleasure of watching their eyes widen in shock, if only for a split second. She smiled to herself. Silver eyes, skin covered with glowing runes; she probably looked like a creature from the old stories. One of the deep-sea fish-women who lived in the crevices of underwater rock formations, mouths open, using their long, luminous tongues to lure in prey. Or a candle-witch from the western mountains: a monster who took the form of a beautiful girl, who led her admirers deep into the mountains, lantern bobbing happily for miles and miles while the poor souls in love with her stumbled ever forward through the blinding snow, until they froze to death and the candle-witch devoured them whole.

I am coming for you, Kinok, Crier thought.

To the guards, she said, "Let me pass."

"It is not safe outside the palace walls, Lady Crier," one of them replied. "The Scyre's battalion has arrived."

"I understand that," said Crier. "Let me pass."

Whatever their orders, Crier was not their charge. Moving as one, the Green Guard bowed their heads and stepped aside, clearing the way. Crier pulled one of the heavy wooden doors open just enough to slip through the crack, and then she was free. Outside, late afternoon was shifting quickly into early evening, the sky deepening from clear blue to the color of a new bruise. The air was cool on Crier's skin. She took a deep breath, filling her lungs, and kept going. There were more guards stationed outside the doors, but they made no move to stop her; they would have been able to hear the conversation from within.

She left them and the palace behind.

The main courtyard, like the servants' quarters and the orchards and the fields, had been repurposed for battle. There were a dozen cloth tents dotting the grass, horses tied around the perimeter, Automae and humans hurrying around between the tents. All of them were suited for battle. Some, like Ayla, were in padded wool or what looked like riding leathers. Some were more heavily armored, in shimmering chain mail or chest plates of solid metal, swords at their hips. Many of the Automae wore the white masks of Varn, and it was eerie, all those blank, empty faces, featureless except for eye slits, like statues come to life.

As Crier made her way across the courtyard, everyone who saw her stopped and stared. Some of the humans shrank away from her, frightened. She wanted to tell them there was nothing to be afraid of, but that could come later. For now, she had one mission. She would not stray.

Only two people didn't shrink away. Ayla's brother, Storme, was standing by one of the campfires, conferring with Ayla's curly-haired friend. Benjy. Their heads were bent together, Storme's hand on Benjy's shoulder. They both looked up when she approached, and their eyes widened.

"What . . . ?" Benjy started.

"You," Crier said to him. "Go to the music room. Ayla needs you."

"What? What's wrong with Ayla? Is she hurt?" Storme demanded, even as Benjy gave Crier a nod, clapped a hand on Storme's shoulder in farewell, and took off back toward the palace in a long-legged sprint.

"You," Crier said to Storme. "Go to the queen. Tell her to give me half an hour with Scyre Kinok. Just half an hour."

"You've gone mad," said Storme. "No, no way. Ayla will have my head on a pike if I let you get yourself killed."

"Adviser Storme. Please."

She looked at him steadily, waiting out his deliberation. "Fine," he said at last. "Fine. I'll tell her."

"Thank you," said Crier. "After that, go to the music room. Ayla needs you, too."

Kinok's army was easy to spot. Even from the courtyard she could see them. The sovereign's palace was seated where gentle, grassy hills flattened out to meet the cliffs of the Steorran, and Crier could see it: a fuzzy yellow light on the western horizon, at the crest of a hill, close and coming closer. The slow burn of torches. And there, floating above the light, she could make out the tallest war flags. Most of them were black, like the robes of a Scyre, like the armbands so many people had worn to Crier and Kinok's engagement ball. Like Nightshade. But some of Kinok's followers were marching under their own colors. Crier saw more than one family crest belonging to a member of the Red Council. Shen, Yaanik, Paradem. It was one more pang of betrayal. They hadn't just turned against the sovereign—they had turned against Rabu itself.

She squinted. They were definitely still moving. At this rate, they'd reach the edge of the sovereign's estate by nightfall.

Hopefully, they wouldn't make it any farther.

Crier paused in the middle of the courtyard, ignoring the stares and whispers all around her, weighing her options. Should she wait for them at the edge of the estate? Should she attempt to meet them halfway?

"Crier!"

Something prickled at the back of her mind. Why did she know that voice? She turned, scanning the crowd that had gathered, a circle of humans and Automae watching her with mixed fear and wariness and curiosity and, on a few faces, something she could have sworn was awe.

"Crier!" the voice repeated, and this time she saw him, wriggling his way through the crowd and breaking free, stumbling into the ground zero of empty space around her.

Hook. The boy who'd saved her from the Shades on the river, the rebel leader with his group of lost children. She felt her mouth drop open. The last time they'd seen each other, on the white shell banks of the Queen's Cove . . . Crier had thought surely that was it, their paths would never cross again. But here he was, a little worse for the wear—there was a bandage plastered over his left ear, and his left eye was badly swollen—but very much alive, grinning even, just as wide and toothy as she remembered.

"All of you quit your gawking, give her some space," he said loudly, making a shooing gesture at the crowd. Then he strode right up to Crier, looking totally unconcerned about the silver-white light pulsing from her skin. "Hello again," he said, giving her a jaunty salute. "I'd hoped to find you here, but I'll admit I didn't expect you to be glowing."

"You—" she started, not knowing how to finish the sentence. *You made it? I'm glad you're alive? I'm glad to see you again? I thought you wanted nothing to do with me?* "You— hoped to find me?"

"Yeah." His smile faded. "I . . . regret it. Leaving you there, I mean. I'm sorry."

Crier nodded. "I forgive you," she said. She didn't have the time—or the desire—for anything else. "You were looking out for your own. I understood then and I understand now." It was the most human thing in the world. "We both got here in the end, didn't we?"

"That we did," he said. "By the way, I think it bears repeating: you're, uh, glowing?"

She leaned in, hyperaware of all the eyes on them, all the ears pricked to catch their every word. "I found Tourmaline," she told him, lower even than a whisper. "I found it, Hook."

His eyes widened. He opened his mouth to respond, but no words came.

Crier waited a few seconds, but he still didn't speak. "Hook?" she said, tempted to wave a hand in front of his face. Was he really that shocked about Tourmaline?

Then she realized: He wasn't looking at *her.* His eyes were fixed on something just past her shoulder, and he was still frozen. He was barely even breathing.

Crier turned, following his gaze. At the edge of the crowd

was a human with golden hair. They were tall and fine-boned, elegant. The last time Crier saw this person, they'd been laid out in the physician's caravan, looking for all the world like a corpse. Like a skeleton, gaunt and terrible, eyes sunken deep into their skull. She remembered their arms, bandaged from wrist to elbow.

Their face was a mirror of Hook's. That same breathless, helpless shock.

Then—

"I am going to *fucking kill you,*" Hook gasped, and lunged for them. Crier didn't even have time to be alarmed before Hook practically threw himself at the golden-haired human, both hands twisting in the front of their shirt, dragging them down till they were nose to nose. "I'm going to *kill you,*" he said again, almost incoherent, words blurring together, giving the human a hard shake and then falling into them, pressing his forehead to their chest. "I'm going to kill you, Erren, you *ass,* you utter fucking bastard, I swear on all ten thousand gods I'm going to *kill you,* I hate you, do you have any idea—do you have *any idea—*"

Erren.

Erren was one of thousands, Hook had told Crier. *To find them—to save them—I'd risk walking into a trap. I'd risk just about anything.*

I know what you mean, Crier had said.

"I'm sorry," Erren said, sounding dazed. They hadn't made any moves to defend themselves. "I'm sorry. I know, I'm sorry."

"You *don't* know," Hook snapped.

"You're right. I don't know. I'm sorry."

"That's probably the first time you've ever admitted someone else is right," Hook said, and then, "I hate you," and then, "I will *never* forgive you, in this life or the next," and then he pushed up on his tiptoes and took Erren's face in his hands and pressed their foreheads together, then their mouths.

Crier turned away, quite certain she shouldn't be watching this, only to be confronted by another familiar face.

"Hello, Lady Crier," said Faye.

"You're alive," Crier said, stunned. The last time she'd seen Faye, the scullery maid had been surrounded by the sovereign's guards after helping Crier escape. She'd hoped Faye hadn't been punished with death, but the sovereign wasn't known for his mercy. Crier had feared the worst. But Faye was alive, standing in front of her, clothed not in a scullery maid's uniform but in a yellow dress Crier recognized from her own wardrobe.

And, moths to a lanternlight, they kept coming. Bree fought her way out of the crowd a moment later, took one look at Hook and Erren—who had stopped kissing and were now holding each other so tight Crier couldn't tell where one ended and the other began—and rattled off a long string of curses, some in languages even Crier didn't know. Then Bree was dragging Erren out of Hook's arms and into her own, and Faye said, "*You*," and Crier turned to see Dinara. Crier knew Dinara and the other rebels had been rescued from the Iron Heart, but hadn't gotten a chance to exchange more than a handful of words with her during the journey east.

Crier glanced between Faye and Dinara, taken aback. "You know each other?"

Dinara shook her head, but Faye nodded. "In ink and thread," she said, and offered no further explanation.

"Crier," said Dinara, stepping up to her side. "What are you doing?"

"I had the same question," came Hook's voice, and he joined her, hand-in-hand with Erren. Bree followed, though she still watched Crier with open distrust. And just like that, Crier was facing the five of them—Hook, Faye, Dinara, Bree, Erren—and they were looking back at her, expectant.

"I'm going to find Kinok," she said, willing her voice not to shake. She wished Ayla were here. Things were easier with Ayla. "I'm going to stop him."

"What, by yourself?" said Hook. "You'll be killed."

"Kinok won't kill me," said Crier. "At least not yet." She looked around their small circle, meeting the eyes of each person one by one. "I'm ending this," she said, trying to sound braver and more confident than she was. "I'm the only one who can do it. The only one with any chance of getting his followers to turn."

"Are you insane?" Bree demanded. Still the same Bree, then. "What, you're just going to march right up to his army and say *Please bring me to Kinok*?"

Crier thought for a second. "Yes."

"To be fair, she is glowing," Hook muttered.

"This is a fool's errand," said Dinara. "Even if they don't kill you on sight, who's to say they won't just knock you out and deliver you to Kinok in shackles?"

"I know how to make them listen to me," Crier assured them, silently praying it was true. "Please trust me. I have to do this, and I have to do it alone."

"You don't," said Erren, speaking for the first time.

Hook rounded on them. "Erren, don't even think about it."

"You don't have to do it alone," they said. "I won't try to talk you out of it. I'd do the same thing in your position; I'd do whatever it took. But you're wrong. You don't have to go alone." Erren caught the look on her face and huffed. "Look, I don't know you, and I sure as all hells don't like your father, but you saved my life. I know you and Ayla told Junn's guard to go back for me and the others. If it weren't for you, I'd be dead right now. Or worse, I'd still be alive. In there. In that room. So—I'm coming with you."

Crier shook her head. "I can't let you—"

"I'm coming with you," Erren repeated. Their expression darkened. "If nothing else, give me the pleasure of watching Kinok's downfall firsthand. He owes me some blood."

"But—"

"I'm coming too," said Hook. "No, don't even try to talk me out of it. First of all, I'm never letting this idiot"—he gestured at Erren, who scowled—"out of my sight again as long as I live. Second of all, I've always liked an adventure."

"This isn't an adventure, it's a suicide mission," Bree snapped, and then, "Gods be damned. I guess I'm going."

"As am I," said Dinara. "I'll go just for the look on the Scyre's face."

"I . . . ," Crier said weakly. "I can't ask you all to . . ."

"My lady," said Faye. "Don't you know? You're not the only one who wants to end this. Before the death toll grows."

The heart that did not belong to Crier throbbed inside her chest. Part of her wanted to cry. Part of her wanted to keep arguing with them. Part of her wanted to say *thank you, thank you, I didn't want to be alone for this, I have never wanted to be alone.* But she'd already dawdled long enough. The yellow flicker of Kinok's army was drawing ever closer, so close now she could see the details of the family crests on the war flags. An owl, a serpent, a sword and shield, a red crystal shaped like a teardrop. She knew them all.

She closed her eyes for a moment.

In the palace, in the music room, there was something worth dying for. Worth living for.

Crier opened her eyes.

"Stay close," she said, looking at all five of them in turn. "Kinok wants me alive. But only me."

"Don't worry," said Hook, giving her a tiny smile. Crier remembered: golden hills, Lake Thea swallowing the horizon, yellow grass rippling in the wind. *Are you my friend?* she'd wondered then. Perhaps this was the answer. "We'll stay right by your side."

There was a story Crier had read and reread about a thousand times. She had memorized every word of it, could picture each illuminated page, could flip through them in her mind.

As she walked to meet Kinok's army head-on, Crier told herself the story of Hana and Winter. She let the story unspool inside her. She thought of Hana and Winter and old bones, ice fields, starlit hearts. And the heart that did not belong to her continued to beat steadily, and the symbols on her skin held their strange silver-white glow.

They walked, and around them the gloaming fell into place. That was all right. Crier could see in the dark. She could see Kinok's army, maybe two hundred strong—so much smaller than she'd expected. She could see the war flags and the torches and lanterns and illuminated faces. She could see thirteen members of the Red Council right up front, and behind them a sea of familiar faces: nobles and landowners and other elites, Automae she had seen at balls and weddings and political gatherings, Automae who had visited the palace each year as a gesture of good faith to the sovereign. The sovereign. Truth be told, Crier couldn't blame them for defecting, for rebelling against him. She'd done the same thing.

But she could blame them for the black flags.

For the man they'd chosen as their new king.

And there he was.

Kinok, the war hero, the Watcher of the Heart, the Scyre, the hunter, the scientist, the angry boy playing at war. There he was, emerging from the front lines, his customary black robes switched for red. His army was a silent mass behind him. They had stopped marching. The space between Kinok and Crier had shrunk to the length of a courtyard. Here they were, at the place where the sovereign's fields met the low, grassy hills. Crier drew a map inside her head: half a mile north, the road that led to Yanna. The River Daedus. She and Kinok were facing each other across an expanse of grass that looked black in the gathering darkness. Everywhere, there were patches of tiny white flowers. Stardrops.

"Brace yourselves," Bree muttered. "Any second now, they'll start firing arrows."

"They won't," said Crier. "Not if you stay behind me. I told you. He wants me alive."

She started forward again, and the five of them followed. Compared to the army before them, they were nothing. Six against two hundred. Not the best odds.

Though—in the end, wasn't it six against one?

Crier only stopped when she could see the whites of Kinok's eyes. Barely fifty paces between them now. And the strangest thing was happening: as Crier drew closer, Kinok's army drew back. Not on Kinok's orders, not on anyone's orders. The councilmembers holding the front lines were breaking formation, backing into each other, exhibiting a kind of mass gracelessness Crier had never witnessed from her own Kind. At first, she didn't understand why they were backing away. Why they were *looking* at her like that.

"They're scared," said Hook, as if listening to her thoughts. "Crier. They're scared of you."

Oh.

A voice rang out across the space between them. "Hold your ground!" Kinok ordered, and Crier's attention was on him again, and, *oh, oh*, he looked *furious.* "I said *hold your ground!*"

His army went still. But the fear on their faces—cold fear, Automa fear, a slight widening of the eyes, a tightening of the jaw—remained. Kinok couldn't order that away.

He couldn't control it.

He couldn't even keep it off his own face.

Crier squared her shoulders like Ayla did, holding her chin high. "Kinok," she said, not bothering to raise her voice too much. They were Automae. They would hear her. She held out her arms, palms up, the glowing runes on full display. "Guess what I found."

"You didn't," he said. "You didn't."

"Oh, I did. Yora's heart. Tourmaline. I have it; I know how to create and activate it. I know how to turn Tourmaline into a life source. Our next life source." Then, to his followers: "I am living proof that Kinok cannot give you what you seek," she said. "He can't even keep you alive. He's the one who destroyed the Iron Heart!"

That got their attention. More than one head turned to look at Kinok, a ripple of movement.

"The days of heartstone are over," Crier continued. "What can the Scyre offer you? Nightshade? The black dust that drives you mad, eats away at your body and mind without ever letting you die? The black dust he's been using to poison his most loyal followers?" She took a shaky breath, thinking of Rosi, of the countless others who had died in one of the worst ways imaginable, Nightshade eating away at their minds. "Scyre Kinok is a traitor and a murderer. He is *tricking you*. He doesn't care about Anti-Reliance—he doesn't care about anything but power. He wants to kill my father and take the throne and you were just pawns in his game. He would kill all of you in a heartbeat."

"I implore you, do not listen to this foolish little girl," Kinok said lazily, all traces of fear replaced by arrogance. "You remember Lady Crier: a naive child with nothing better to do than spin stories. Every word from her mouth is a lie, same as her father. Look at her, look what she's become!" He flung out an arm, gesturing at her, as if everyone wasn't already looking. "She is a spineless, Reasonless human sympathizer! She is a traitor to her Kind!"

"And the only one who can keep our Kind alive," Crier said, and reached up to undo the pin at her throat. Her shirt fell open where Ayla had made the cut, exposing Crier's collarbone, the tip of her sternum—and the place where Yora's heart beat within her chest. The epicenter, her new core. You could practically *see* the heart through her skin, like looking at the sun through a piece of parchment; the entire left side of Crier's chest was pulsing with a pale blue glow. "See for yourselves," she said, addressing the army, the Automae. "The power of Tourmaline."

The murmurs were growing louder. More and more heads were turning in Kinok's direction, but not because they were awaiting his orders. Crier saw the outrage on their faces, the suspicion, the mistrust, the burgeoning signs of dissent. It spurred her on.

"It's over, Kinok," she said. "Queen Junn's army is waiting for you at the palace. They outnumber you by a thousand. It's *over*. You failed to create a new life source. You failed to find Yora's heart. You failed to transmute Tourmaline. This is your last chance to do something right. Will you march to certain death? Or will you surrender now and live?" She raised her voice. "Every single one of you has a choice. Death, or surrender?"

"And what happens if I surrender?" Kinok said, and his voice was high and raw. "Imprisonment? Public execution? That's not a *choice*, you stupid girl." He whirled around to face his followers. "With time, I can transmute Tourmaline. I can promise you eternal life. Eternal power. Cities free of human filth. Remember why you're fighting with me, remember why you chose me. Because Traditionalism—*her father's doctrine*—is holding you back. We can do away with it, we can create a new society. We can all be kings."

"You would never share the throne," said Crier.

"*Shut up*, you *wretch*—"

"Scyre." It was Councilmember Paradem who had spoken. "If even half of what she says is true, you have already broken your promises."

"It's not true!" Kinok said. "Oh, you're just as much a fool as she is. You're all so weak, so easily swayed, I should have known you'd turn on me. You're supposed to be the superior Kind, but you're no better than humans. Made of nothing but filth and fear." He turned his back on them—and started for Crier. He moved fluidly, first in a walk and then a run, closing the space between them in mere seconds. He stopped barely ten paces from her and drew his sword, moonlight catching the blade. The same sword, some part of Crier registered, that had only three days ago bitten into Ayla's skin.

"Kinok," Crier said, heartbeat quickening. "You can still surrender."

"Shut up," he sneered. "Shut your mouth, you've said enough. You won't give me a Tourmaline heart? Fine. I'll cut it out of your chest myself. Right after I cut out your lying tongue."

Behind her, Crier heard Hook and the others shifting positions, readying their own weapons. Preparing to defend her. She tensed up, terrified that Kinok would attack them first just to get them out of the way, but his eyes never left Crier's face. Oddly, he didn't even seem to notice her companions. They were *right there*, all five of them right at her back, and it was like their presence didn't even register in his mind. *Because they're humans*, Crier realized.

"Kinok, just surrender," she tried. One last time, one more chance. "It's not too late."

"It is for you," he said, and raised his sword.

He leaped forward and Crier stumbled back, arms flying up in a futile attempt to shield herself, because she couldn't dodge him, the others were right behind her, she couldn't risk one of them catching the blow—but it didn't come. The blow, the cold bite of steel, didn't come. Crier opened her eyes—when had she closed them?—and went still.

The blow hadn't come because Kinok was—*he was*—Crier couldn't make sense of it. Her mind was caught up in all the separate details: the shock in his eyes. His sword on the ground. The dark spot on his bloodred shirt. Pieces of information. Just pieces of information. Then he made a low, wordless noise and lifted one hand to his chest, brushing his fingers over the spot. The dark spot right over his heart. It was growing, spreading across his shirt, a blooming black rose. A spill of ink.

Faye, who was standing before him, raised her dagger a second time. She stabbed him in the heart again. And again, metal sinking into flesh.

She took a step back. Her arm moved in an arc. For one wild moment, Crier thought she was slapping Kinok across the face. But when Faye lowered her arm and the dagger slipped from her fingers, landing soundlessly in the soft grass, Crier saw the truth of what she'd done. The black line she had drawn across Kinok's throat.

He fell to his knees. Crier wanted to look away but couldn't. Or maybe it was that she felt like she shouldn't, like this was a price she had to pay: bearing witness. Kinok made another noise. It was wet and rasping and awful, and Crier thought numbly: *That noise will haunt me for the rest of my life.*

Faye took a few steps back. Her face was shiny in the moonlight, wet with tears.

"That's for my sister," she said to Kinok. "That's for Luna."

Then she turned around and walked away.

For a long time, Crier could not follow her. She stood there in the meadow, in the sea of stardrops, in the dark. When she was newbuilt and still fragile, Crier had walked this meadow on the shaky legs of a newborn fawn, brushed her fresh-woven hands over the tiny white flowers, marveled that anything could be that small, that delicate, that easily crushed. Now this meadow cradled the body of her enemy, once her betrothed, his violet blood seeping back into the earth. *From light you were born and to light you shall return.* Was it true, even for him? Did she want it to be?

Was it terrible that she didn't?

So much of her life had been a dream life, she saw now, a veneer of gold over decay. She'd been foolish, naive, accepting her father's teachings without question, held aloft from the suffering of those around her. Those like Faye and Luna. Like Ayla.

And yet. That dream she'd had. Of changing the world, making it kinder, increment by increment, seed by seed, fighting for those who would come after her, for futures she would not live to see—that dream thrummed within her still, in her new and powerful heart.

This part of the fight had ended, quick and bloody, but there was still much work ahead. She turned, at last, ignoring the Red Hands in their confusion and shock, and began to walk side by side with Hook and the others toward home, toward Ayla, the beacon, the true wash of starlight.

Ayla, she had written once. *I could stand anywhere in this world and I swear my line of sight would end on you. I swear I'd find you in the dark.*

Much work to do. Good thing, then, that she wasn't alone.

*PEACE AND OPEN BORDERS BETWEEN
RABU, VARN, TARREEN!*

The Scyre Defeated!
The Mad Queen Victorious!
The People Have Spoken!

CONCERNING THE FORMATION OF THE
HUMAN-AUTOMA COUNCIL FOR THE THREE
NATIONS

*Founded by Her Majesty Queen Junn of Varn;
Lady Crier of Rabu; Storme, Head Adviser to Her
Majesty Queen Junn of Varn; Benjy of Rabu; Ayla of
Rabu, Apprentice to Midwife Jezen of Rabu; Brielle,
Alchemist of Tarreen; Elan, People's Leader of Tarreen*

*In keeping with the spirit of the peace, and the
newly opened borders between the Sovereign State
of Rabu, the Queendom of Varn, and the Collected
Territories of Tarreen, certain players of politic and
science from each of the three major nations of Zulla
have formed an Alliance, to advocate for the Rights of
all Humankind within Zulla . . .*

THE TREATY OF THALEN

between

THE SOVEREIGN STATE OF RABU, THE QUEENDOM OF VARN, AND THE COLLECTED TERRITORIES OF TARREEN

The Protocol annexed thereto, the Agreement respecting the operation of Tourmaline mines in the collected territories of Tarreen, which will allocate certain amounts of raw Tourmaline, specified within, to the Sovereign State of Rabu and the Queendom of Varn, for the purpose of alchemical transmutation into the objects known as Tourmaline Hearts; for FIVE YEARS, beginning on the dawn of the Spring Equinox of Year Forty-Eight Automa Era and extending to the dawn of the Spring Equinox of Year Fifty-Three Automa Era, or until an Artificial Life Source is successfully synthesized,

respecting

THE CONTINUED EXISTENCE OF AUTOMAKIND

IN PEACE AND HARMONY WITH HUMANKIND.

*Signed at the Queen's Palace at Thalen, Spring
Equinox, Year Forty-Eight Automa Era*

—PAMPHLETS DISTRIBUTED THROUGHOUT ALL ZULLA,
BY THE HUMAN-AUTOMA COUNCIL FOR THE THREE
NATIONS, YEAR 48 AE

*Traditionalism tells us we can learn from the humans
of one hundred, five hundred, one thousand years ago.
Can we not learn from the humans of today?*

—FROM *NEOTRADITIONALISM AND THE LIBERATION
OF HUMANKIND,* BY CRIER OF FAMILY HESOD,
9648880130, YEAR 46 AE

SUMMER,

YEAR 48 AE

EPILOGUE

I t was summer, and the air in Yanna smelled of salt.

As she half walked, half ran up the white marble steps of the Peoples' Library, Ayla found herself biting back a smile. The sky was delphinium blue, the sun a high white coin, she'd just come from visiting Storme—bidding him a quick goodbye before he left for Thalen—and the streets of Rabu's capital city were lined with paper lanterns. Tomorrow night Yanna would celebrate the summer solstice, and the city was already alive and buzzing with anticipation, music rising through the air like steam, or like wheeling seabirds.

Ayla pushed through the heavy wooden doors of the library. As always, the silence felt physical: the heavy, musty quiet of this place, as if the books themselves swallowed all sound. And as always, she headed straight for the spiral staircase. Half the second floor was dedicated to rows of reading chairs and study tables, and that was where Ayla knew she'd find—

Crier.

The smile became impossible to bite back.

Crier was hunched over a table in the far back, dark head bent over a massive book. She didn't look up as Ayla approached, and didn't react at all when Ayla hopped onto the table, swinging her legs. In this position, the hems of Ayla's loose cotton pants rode up, and you could see that one of her legs was human, and the other was Made.

That was how it went if an Automa struck you hard enough to shatter bone and a Midwife was your medic.

That night in the music room, once Crier had left and Ayla was alone with Midwife Jezen, she had been given a choice. "You have to decide," Jezen had said, touch cool and light on Ayla's shin. Ayla didn't remember what happened after this, but she did remember this. "You have to decide. I can save you but you have to tell me yes."

"What happens if I say no," Ayla had mumbled, eyes closing. She'd already passed out once, and she could feel the water rising up again.

"You will die. The bone is shattered, it's broken the skin, there is bone marrow in your bloodstream and it will clot in your veins and kill you. If I take you to the Midwives' tent right now, *right now, Ayla*, I can save your life, but you might not like how I do it. You have to decide."

"Save my damn life," said Ayla, and passed out.

Jezen had.

So Ayla's right leg was Made from the knee down.

The first version had been grisly, the result of panic and desperation—a simple apparatus to knit Ayla's veins together so she didn't bleed out on the table. But in the weeks after, as Ayla began very slowly to heal, Jezen had dedicated herself to improving the Design of Ayla's leg. She had worked until it was as complex and seamless as an Automa's leg, perfectly balanced to hold Ayla's weight, perfectly connected to her body, as if she had been born like this. When the leg was newbuilt, Jezen had offered to complete the transformation: to cover everything up with freshly woven skin, so it truly would be indiscernible from the rest of Ayla's body. Ayla had said no. Covering it up felt too much like hiding a battle scar, like pretending nothing had ever happened. She didn't want to pretend. So her right leg was Made from the knee down, and it looked like what lived just beneath an Automa's skin. It was a limb of Maker's iron, gleaming and metallic, nearly unbreakable.

Now, it reflected the sunlight streaming in through the high windows, flashing gold. Over the last month or so, Ayla's visits to Jezen had changed from visits to a sort of . . . apprenticeship, almost. Like Siena before her, Ayla found herself wanting to learn more and more about Making. As she grew steadier on her new leg, she began to wonder: What else could Automa technology, the science and magick of the Makers, do for her Kind? And Jezen had said: *Let's find out.*

With Crier's help, they'd been trying to learn more about the mysterious H. Thomas Wren had stolen her work and buried her name; history had forgotten her. She'd been lost. But Crier believed she could be found.

"Hey," Ayla said. "Hey, Just Crier."

Crier made a small noise of acknowledgment and did not look up from her book.

Ayla sighed wistfully. "Remember the old days, when I'd walk into a room and you'd just *stare?*" she asked. "You couldn't take your eyes off me, and I tried so hard to keep mine off you. If only I'd known your attention would be so fleeting." She flung an arm across her face, the picture of melodrama. "I can't believe I lost you to *books*. Well—maybe I can."

The corner of Crier's mouth twitched. She still didn't look up.

"I told you once I'm not a book to be read," Ayla continued. "I take it back. I'm a book. Read me."

Crier looked up. "We are in the *library*," she hissed.

"Then read me a story."

Crier's eyes narrowed. It was lovely, the expression on her face. It made Ayla want to do and say a lot of things, most of them soft. Mostly she was grateful all over again that Crier's eyes had shifted back to brown. It had taken ages for the sheen of silver to go away entirely, mist dissolving in the morning sun. Yora's heart had been even more powerful, more potent, than any of them could have predicted; Siena had Designed it for a creature who required much more energy than the average Automae, and besides, magick that did not rely on human sacrifice was purer, undiluted by evil. As Kinok thought, it could have powered a physical vessel for much longer than heartstone—but that kind of energy took its toll. The glow, the burn, the silver eyes. The Midwives predicted the vessel would remain alive, but at a cost: the pain of a soul on fire. Scyres and Midwives from Rabu and Varn alike plus human alchemists from Tarreen had worked together to create a more functional Tourmaline: deep blue hearts that powered Automae like heartstone, but without the use of blood. Without the weight of human suffering. Without the lightning strike of too much power all at once. Right now, the Tourmaline was mined from the caves of Tarreen as per the treaty, but the Makers aimed to create an artificial version. An infinite source.

Eventually, like the rest of her Kind, Crier had been given a new heart.

"Your third," Ayla had said.

"Fourth," Crier had replied, giving her a soft, significant look, and Ayla had yelled and fled the room and then come back to take Crier's face in her hands and kiss her hard and then fled again, cheeks burning.

Anyway. It was summer and the air in Yanna smelled of salt and Crier's eyes were brown again, and it was good.

"C'mon," Ayla wheedled. "One story."

"Why don't you just find one and read it yourself?" Crier said.

"Just because I *can* read now doesn't mean I want to do it all the time," Ayla said. "Besides, haven't I mentioned? I like your storytelling voice."

Crier hummed. "You've mentioned."

"This is me mentioning it again."

"Careful," said Crier. "I might get the impression you're fond of me."

Ayla made a face at her. "Wouldn't want that."

"No, never." She smiled up at Ayla, everything about it warm and gentle in a way that still felt impossible sometimes. Still made Ayla nervous, sometimes, because in her experience the warm and gentle things didn't last; they just burned. But she was trying. Always, she was trying. "What if instead of reading you an old story, I tell you a new one?"

Ayla raised her eyebrows, intrigued. "You'll make it up?"

"I could." Oh, she was being *shy*. "I've been . . . trying it out. In my head."

"Tell me your story," said Ayla, then sat up a little. "Wait—I almost forgot. Hook 'n' Erren want to say goodbye before we leave the city again. We're to meet them at the Dancing Fox. Hook said to bring weapons, just in case Bree insists on swindling innocent patrons out of their coin."

"All right. Story, Dancing Fox, then home?"

"Then home." They were set to depart the city at dusk, to reach the palace by midnight. The palace. *Home.* It wasn't home, not forever, but there was still so much to be done—after Hesod's trial and subsequent imprisonment, and the confirmation that there would not be another sovereign, Crier had taken it upon herself to turn the palace into a sort of patchwork house of science. The east wing was a hospital, the west wing a series of laboratories Ayla frequented, as they were researching ways in which certain properties of the Automae—faster healing, sharper eyesight—could benefit human lives. Ayla's leg had been a starting point. Midwife Jezen worked in that wing, and some days Ayla found herself visiting just to say hello.

The members of the new council often gathered in the north wing, which meant Ayla could see Storme and Benjy, both of whom had positions in Queen Junn's court, Storme as the ever-loyal adviser and Benjy as a representative of Rabu. Ayla and Storme were still relearning each other, making up for the lost years, growing steadily closer. It was different with Benjy. There was a distance between them, small but noticeable, that had not existed before. There were things they had to relearn about each other as well. But they, too, were growing more together than apart. Ayla refused to lose him, and Benjy refused to let her, and they were both stubborn enough to make it work.

"Home," Crier murmured.

Ayla felt something swelling inside her. A green thing, taking root. It was not an unfamiliar sensation. She tilted her head back, gazing up at the domed ceiling of the library far above their heads. It was covered in paintings that had survived the War of Kinds and all the fifty years since, the colors dusty and sunfaded but still visible, deep twilight blues and sea greens and the red of late sunset, of wine, of vermilion, of Ayla's soft and human heart. She didn't recognize any of the gods in these paintings, but Crier did. Crier probably knew every last one of them, their stories and symbols and the things you were meant to sacrifice in their name. Ayla thought to herself: *Someday I'll ask.* Someday.

In the coming weeks or months or years, whenever there was time, she'd ask. And Crier would look at her and smile.

"Now," Ayla said, reaching out to take Crier's hand. "Will you tell me your story?"

Crier looked at her, and smiled. Wide and bright as the whole damn sky.

ACKNOWLEDGMENTS

Well! Here we are! We made it, folks!

Let's get down to it. Sorry, Kieryn—this time it's family first. Don't kill me.

Mama and Papa, thank you thank you thank you for supporting me and loving me and believing in me from afar. I miss you, I love you, I really hope by the time you're reading this the damn pandemic is over and I've already hopped on a plane home. I know how lucky I am to have parents like you; I do not take it for granted. I am immeasurably grateful for you, today and every day.

Piera, thank you for having my favorite brain. Thank you again for loving ugly things without trying to turn them beautiful. Tony, you're the coolest, always. I miss you, I love you. Fiona, you're one of the strongest people I know; I take inspiration from you. Paul, thank you for having more confidence in my abilities than I do.

Kieryn, you were the star of the book one acknowledgments, I'm not going to repeat all that. You know who you are and what you mean. Thanks for consistently saving my ass.

Thank you to Yes Homo for the laughter, for the unconditional love and support, for being there, for being yourselves, for being up for anything: a venting sesh, a Zoom night, a protest, any kind of adventure. Thank you to Amy for the playlists, the enthusiasm, the hand holding, the beach sunsets. You're a stahh, I love you.

Thank you to the LP: C, E, I, J, K, P, R, W. Y'all are golden all the way to the core. You made a dark time a hell of a lot lighter. Thank you to Ivy for the witching hours, for your galaxy brain, for feeling close even though you're far. I can't put emojis in here but you know which ones I'm thinking of.

Thank you to Patrice, lifesaver and ass-kicker extraordinaire, for being brilliant and unstoppable and the all-around best. I feel like I could ask you the meaning of life and where we go after we die and you would not only have the answers, but they would already be written down and annotated. Possibly in a spreadsheet of some sort. I would die on a battlefield for you.

Thank you as always to Lexa and the Glasstown team, present and past, for believing in this story and making it come to life in my head and on the page. Lexa, you've been here since before "Once upon a time," and here we are at "The End." It's been a wild ride, and I am so glad to have taken it. I am honored to have been trusted with this story, with these girls. I think we did it justice. Thank you.

Thank you to Brandie Coonis for your help and encouragement, to Maha Hussain for your hard work and creativity, and to Megan Gendell for making this book readable. Once again, I am sorry about all the commas. Thank you to the Inkwell folks for your thoughtfulness and input from the beginning to the end.

Thank you to Karen Chaplin for your eagle eye, to Rosemary Brosnan and everyone at Harper for caring as much about this story as I do, for taking my draft and nudging it into something that makes sense. Thank you to David Curtis—I can't believe how beautiful this cover is. I don't know how you managed to top *Crier's*, but you did. Thank you to the marketing and publicity team for putting your weight behind this book about queer girls, I truly appreciate it.

And of course, thank you to the readers. I think the best part of the story is whatever the reader creates once they've closed the book—if someone cares enough about the story to start telling their own stories about it, in any form, that's the best. A great many people did that with *Crier's War*, and I am forever grateful. Yes, I am talking about your memes. And your incredible art, and fanfiction (I can't read it, but I know it's out there), and very cute "Currently Reading" threads, and headcanons and Iron Heart theories and all of it. I wrote Crier and Ayla's story, but now it belongs to you, and you're doing such wonderful things with it. Thank you for reading, thank you for caring. I hope this ending fits with whatever you needed it to be. I hope it made you feel hopeful. To the queer readers: I hope you feel loved. In this world, in every world, you are loved. By me and Crier and Ayla and the whole damn universe.

I love y'all. Thank you for supporting Crier, Ayla, and the rest from beginning to . . . well, not ending. Beginning to second beginning, I'd say. The happiest of beginnings.

Thank you, thank you, thank you for loving these girls like I do and beyond. I'll wrap this up with what I said last time because it's more important now than ever: I told you my story. Thank you so much for reading it. If you've been waiting for a sign to tell yours, this is it. Pretend we're at a campfire—I'm scooting over to make room for you. I'm passing you a s'more and saying, "Welcome! We've been waiting for you! Whatever you have to say, whatever's been collecting in your heart and the corners of your mind, the world is ready to listen. Let's hear it!"